After working on local newspapers in Devon and the East End of London, Diana Norman became, at twenty years of age, the youngest reporter on what used to be Fleet Street. After marriage (to film critic Barry Norman) and motherhood (they have two daughters), she settled down in Hertfordshire. She is now a freelance journalist, and a writer of biographies and historical novels.

Her first book of fiction, *Fitzempress' Law*, was chosen by Frank Delaney of BBC Radio 4's *Bookshelf* as the best example of a historical novel of its year. Her other books include *King of the Last Days*, *The Morning Gift*, *Daughter of Lir*, *The Pirate Queen*, *The Vizard Mask* and *The Shores of Darkness*. The last two of these titles are also published in Penguin.

BLOOD ROYAL

DIANA NORMAN

PENGUIN BOOKS

PENGUIN BOOKS

Published by the Penguin Group
Penguin Books Ltd, 27 Wrights Lane, London W8 5TZ, England
Penguin Putnam Inc., 375 Hudson Street, New York, New York 10014, USA
Penguin Books Australia Ltd, Ringwood, Victoria, Australia
Penguin Books Canada Ltd, 10 Alcorn Avenue, Toronto, Ontario, Canada M4V 3B2
Penguin Books (NZ) Ltd, Private Bag 102902, NSMC, Auckland, New Zealand

Penguin Books Ltd, Registered Offices: Harmondsworth, Middlesex, England

First published by Michael Joseph 1998
Published in Penguin Books 1999
1 3 5 7 9 10 8 6 4 2

Printed in England by Clays Ltd, St Ives plc

To Charlie Clifford

CHAPTER ONE

THERE ARE TWO portraits of Lady Cecily Fitzhenry, both in private collections. The first is by van der Myn and was done in 1733, the same year in which she altered the course of history.

The painter, of course, was unaware that his subject belonged in the category of Helen of Troy and Joan of Arc, women who, for a moment, held the destiny of their country in their hands – or, in the case of Helen of Troy, somewhat lower down. Unlike Helen and Joan, Lady Cecily kept her nation *out* of war. She also kept the fact that she'd done so under her hat.

Had he known Lady Cecily's national significance, van der Myn would have disposed of the hat and asked her to sit for him with a helmet on her head and a trident in her fist against a background of *putti*, victory swags and grapes. He was that sort of artist, one of those who came to England in the first quarter of the eighteenth century and flourished by painting the rich as they wanted posterity to see them.

As it is, the portrait's in his usual blandly flattering style, showing a pretty woman in pretty clothes. What's rare in it is the black child included in the picture: it has no slave collar and, instead of standing behind her chair, sits on her knee . . .

The other portrait of Lady Cecily is by Hogarth and was executed seventeen years earlier without her knowledge, while Hogarth himself was in his apprenticeship as an engraver. A stolen, rapid and charming charcoal sketch, perhaps a cartoon for an intended engraving, it shows a slim young woman running through a wintry St James's Park – the Palace is in the background – with a pair of skates in her hand.

Had she known that she was being sketched by a common or garden apprentice, the Lady Cecily of those days would have

1

bewailed the laxity of Charles II, under whose reign commoners like Hogarth had been, and still were, allowed to walk the Park and gape at the sport of their betters.

The sketch shows that Lady Cecily is setting the fashion with a skirt that scandalously displays her ankles. It is naughtily entitled 'Maid of Honour?' – this at a time when it was generally assumed that female courtiers *had* no honour – probably an early example of the cynicism that caused Hogarth to be ignored by the aristocracy.

The date on the sketch is fortuitous and poignant: 23 February, 1716. That afternoon Lady Cecily was kindly to accede to her cousin Anne's request to accompany her to Scotland – and thereby begin the process that was to lead to her downfall. We now know that the young woman in Hogarth's drawing was running towards a future containing an unwelcoming marriage, highway robbery, espionage, dark inns and, eventually, the country's salvation. Her own, too.

We also know, from the discovery of her scanty and intermittent diary for 1716, that as she ran through St James's Park that morning, Lady Cecily's thoughts were occupied by nothing more weighty than the Countess of Crakanthorpe's claim that her (the Countess's) waist was so small it could span a space occupied by only an orange and a half.

'Tiny,' the diary says. 'If lumpy. And if true.'

Hogarth's sketch is in monochrome, like the Park where white trees were crystallized against a military grey sky. In life, the young Lady Cecily was in sapphire, skates dangling from one hand, the other tucked in her swansdown muff, which matched the edging of her hood.

Hurrying towards the lake with her nonsense, Lady Cecily was as old as the century, prettier than the average, richer than most and bluer-blooded than practically anybody, certainly more so than Caroline, Princess of Wales, whom she served as Maid of Honour and who was German, poor thing.

On the lake kingfisher colours dipped and swooped around the majestic scarlet of Princess Caroline, but not too closely – out of respect and a *soupçon* of doubt as to whether the ice would hold Her Highness's weight. The freezing air was shot with aromatic currents, the steam of fresh horse manure, the smell of coffee, chocolate and charcoal from the lake edge where lesser-hued servants prepared hot beverages, tending braziers and warming-pans for the comfort of the courtiers.

Before she could reach it, snow was sliced from the nearest tree by the notes of a trumpet and Cecily had to stand still. The King was returning from his morning ride.

Lady Cecily dropped into a curtsy. His Majesty was dismounting. Now for those embarrassing pauses while he searched for English sentences.

'You are Fitzhenry.' Pause. 'Zezily.' A thick forefinger under her chin raised her.

'I am, Your Majesty.'

'Bretty.'

'Thank you, Majesty.'

'Vere are you going? Vat are you doing?'

'To the lake, Majesty. Her Royal Highness is skating this morning. The ground's too hard to hunt. Lady Mary Wortley Montagu's there and Lord Hervey, and Mr Pope . . .' She chattered inanely to ward off the inevitable; he hadn't caught her alone before.

'Bope? The boet? I hate boets. And bainters.'

And his skating daughter-in-law *and* his son. Not too fond of England either. Should have stayed in Hanover and made everybody happy. But Cecily smiled at him; for all his brocade and velvet, he looked like one's friendly local butcher.

The beefy face stared glumly down at hers. 'Veux-toi monter à cheval avec moi, ma chérie?'

It was his regular euphemism: they'd told her he'd use it – and she had her answer ready. 'Such an honour, Sire, but you have been too occupied perhaps to remember that I am a royal ward. My devotion to you is as to a father by law.' She gave him time to catch up and grinned at him. 'It would be incest.'

(As Hervey said later on, when she told him about it, 'Such subtlety, my love,' and Cecily said, 'He doesn't understand subtlety,' and Hervey said, 'And you, my dear, are no Machiavelli.')

3

The King became glummer. 'Farder.'

'Yes.'

'Incest.'

'Yes, Sire.'

He grunted and crunched off like a depressed farmer whose yield is down, his horse and entourage plodding after him.

Tsk, tsk, the Hanoverians. Uniformly vulgar. Amiable peasants. There'd be no percentage in broadcasting the fact that she'd been asked to be a royal mistress when the two trollops he'd brought with him from Germany had all the beauty of ale vats without the charm.

The old chap was lonely more than anything: Mary Lepel had once entered von der Schulenburg's apartment to discover him and the Hop-pole occupied in nothing more lascivious than cutting out paper dolls.

Cecily joined the company on the lake, apologizing to Princess Caroline, '. . . but I was delayed by Sir Hubert who has had a letter from the Countess of Crakanthorpe which mentions that . . .' she rolled her eyes for maximum effect as the skaters teetered round her '. . . her waist encompasses no more space than that occupied by an orange and a half.'

At once it was the rage, the men as caught as the women whose hands fluttered a projection of the size. Lord Hervey cried for a tape measure, a tape measure, his kingdom for a tape measure. Poor Pope began to compose 'The Waste of a Waist'. Princess Caroline beamed upon the to-do with the patronage of one whose figure had been expanded by German sausage and four babies in eight years.

Eventually she said, 'I am gold,' so they rugged her and tugged her back to the Palace. Footmen divested them of their cloaks in the Great Hall and they danced into what were once Anne Boleyn's lodgings where a fire burned in the two enormous grates of the Gallery. Oranges were sent for, and a sempstress with tape measure.

It's a pity the early Hogarth didn't catch them on canvas then. Living, pastel architecture. We should see nothing loose about them, except their morals. The boned, skirted brocade of the men's coats stiff. The women's heads mere pin-tops in round-

4

eared caps, their upper bodies from the breasts down flattened by boards in order that no wrinkle interrupt the line of satin until it reaches the giant skirt, which itself is smoothed over hoops so strong that if their owner should fall over she becomes an upended bell, her kicking legs double-clappers.

They are a generation despaired of by the one that fought Queen Anne's wars and which now sees its sons such as Lord Hervey fondle lap-dogs, step like pee-wits as if the floor is slippery, parget their face with rouge and powder their wigs blue. In the absence of war, they expend their courage in duels or the hunting field or at the card table, stoically languid as they are pinked, break a leg so that the bone sticks through the boot, or lose a fortune.

The young women are rebellious, prepared, like Lady Mary Wortley Montagu, to run away from an arranged marriage and take the man of their choice.

Male and female, they chatter through church services because their religion is unbelief, political, merely a design to keep the lower classes – 'the mob' – in order.

Lord Douglas slices an orange with his sword. Should the half be laid face down next to the whole one, or on its side? Cecily bets one hundred guineas that her waist will prove equal to the comparison. Thin Lord Hervey lays two hundred on his. The Hon. Sophie Breffny, Cecily's plumper cousin, takes them on.

The tape measure defeats them both: Lord Hervey loses by another whole orange, Cecily by only a few segments.

Looking back on that, the last of her careless days at court, Cecily was to see herself and the others as spun in glass; fragile, comic figurines lit against the advancing dark of a winter's afternoon, the afternoon when Anne asked for her company to Scotland.

For a long time Cecily relived those few hours over and over, as if by doing so she could alter her reply to Anne's request, say, 'No, cousin, I am otherwise engaged.' It was difficult to believe that an invitation so lightly accepted would result in what it had. One butterfly action could not, surely, have set off an avalanche of such proportions. By concentrating hard, she might change it, force her past self to remain in King George I's court and live out the future her upbringing had led her to expect.

Later still, of course, she understood that her country had needed her and by a tortuous route had led her to the saving of it.

It had been Meant.

In any case, her ties of kinship and affection to Anne had been too strong to countenance refusal. If the past were to be changed it would entail Anne not asking in the first place, which would necessitate going further backwards in time and preventing the Jacobite Rising of the previous year which, in turn, would involve . . .

It may be that the spark fizzing along the trail of powder leading to the Jacobite rebellion of 1715 had been touched off in 1642 when Charles I, still believing he had a divine right to rule as he pleased, clashed with those who didn't and civil war broke out between the two.

Or in 1688, the Glorious Revolution, when Charles's stubborn and Catholic son, King James II, showing every sign that he held his father's beliefs, was dismissed from his throne and country by his Protestant people, afraid he would force them back into popery.

Or in 1708 when *his* son, another James, made a bungled attempt to land in Scotland from France and raise an army.

Or in 1714 when Queen Anne, last of the Stuart monarchs, died. Strictly speaking, she should have been succeeded by James III, her half-brother, but as the exiled lad appeared to be as stubborn as his father in matters of religion, the British invited his nearest Protestant relative, George of Hanover, to rule them instead. At least, the Whigs did, being the natural descendants of the civil war's Parliamentarians. The Tories, sitting lethargically in their shires, were reluctantly prepared to put up with the German as long as he protected the Church of England. The Jacobites, James's supporters, even the few who were Protestant, were not.

But the explosion point, the moment when spark touched barrel, came on 1 August 1715, as the Earl of Mar, a Tory and

6

known associate of James Stuart – now merely Pretender to the throne – appeared at a royal levée in London and approached the new king in order to inform His Majesty of his loyalty and his hope of being confirmed in the post of Secretary of State for Scotland, which he had held under Queen Anne.

The King turned his back on him.

The gesture was a mistake if George hoped for a quiet period in which to settle into his reign. At once, the Earl of Mar left the levée and galloped to his home in the eastern Highlands of Scotland where he raised in rebellion the clans favourable to the Stuart cause.

That also, as it turned out, was a mistake. The Earl had been too hasty. Nobody was ready. The Pretender himself was still in France. Jacobites in England were taken by surprise and failed to cohere.

Nevertheless, Britain was alarmed as rebel forces won Sheriffmuir, forced a crossing of the Firth of Forth to spread terror among the Lowlands and the Presbyterian Scots loyal to King George, and penetrated the Border into Lancashire before being defeated at the Battle of Preston.

The Pretender, having only just arrived, had to turn round and go back to France.

The Earl of Mar was able to join him, but most rebels were not. Some were taken to London where two of their leaders, the Earl of Derwentwater and Viscount Kenmuir, were tried and executed along with four others.

Some 1,500 were tried in Lancashire, where they'd been captured, a large proportion being transported to the colonies. Other rebels were awaiting trial at Edinburgh Castle, among them Viscount Strathallan, Lord Rollo and Viscount Stormont.

But the main concern of the women gathered in Cecily's apartments at St James's Palace in London that February afternoon was for another of the Edinburgh prisoners, Lord Keltie of Portsoy, the father of Anne Insh, first cousin to Lady Cecily Fitzhenry . . .

'Apartments' was a generous term for two small rooms in St James's Tudor gatehouse but they indicated Cecily's standing with the royal family that she had them at all. Nearly all the other Maids of Honour shared bedrooms and used a communal drawing room.

Exertion on the ice had given the Princess of Wales a cold and she remained in her apartments with only Lepel and Bellenden in attendance. The Prince of Wales was in his, undoubtedly with Mrs Howard – he kept to such an orderly rotation in servicing his wife and mistresses you could set your clock by it. The Palace was quiet. Outside, snow muffled footsteps and carriage wheels and bowed the branches of the Park's trees.

It was Mary Astell's fifty-eighth birthday and Lady Mary Wortley Montagu had fetched her from Chelsea to take tea with the three Maids of Honour who were her former pupils: Cecily, the Hon. Sophia Breffny and Miss Anne Insh, who had not yet put in an appearance.

On their way the two older women had called in to see Lady Cowper, the Lord Chancellor's wife, and it was her account of the execution of Lords Derwentwater and Kenmuir in the Tower of London that dominated the conversation. They needed to tell the tale quickly, before Anne arrived, as it would be tasteless to recount it to someone whose father was facing the same fate in Edinburgh. They were all worried about Anne: since her plea to go to her father in his prison had been refused by the King, the girl had kept withdrawn into herself. Cecily hoped that the occasion of Mrs Astell's birthday party would tempt her into attending it.

'Did Lady Cowper actually see it?' asked Sophie.

'Of course not,' said Lady Mary. 'She had it from her husband. Poor man, he *must* be there, having passed sentence. So dreary for him, his wife being Lord Widdrington's cousin and all.'

Lord Widdrington had lent his troop to the rebel forces.

'Will they chop Widdrington too?' Sophie was still young enough to be ghoulish.

'Sophie. *Please*,' warned Mary Astell.

'Possibly not,' Lady Mary said. 'It would be expedient to show clemency now. The mob that bayed for every Scotsman's blood last week is turned sentimental. We passed it, did we not, Mrs Astell?'

8

'Near a thousand, I swear,' said Mary Astell. 'All in sympathy for the rebels. Shouts up for King James, shouts down for German George, white cockades everywhere.'

Lady Mary nodded. 'One nearly stuck one's handkerchief in one's own hat for very fear.'

Everyone dutifully smiled: Lady Mary Wortley Montagu had never been afraid in her life. Her very dress fearless, drapery flowing, crowned by a jewelled turban she'd brought back from Turkey, her curled, mirror-work slippers reflecting the fire, she lounged on Cecily's settle, a brilliant parrot against the dark panel. The day she turned Jacobite would be the day King George must tremble. So far he was safe: Lady Mary was a staunch Whig, something Cecily found incongruous in her – she was so . . . Jacobean.

Yet all in the room were touched by the executions: Mrs Astell because she was a High Tory who, though she did not condone rebellion, believed the succession should rightfully have been James's, the other women because so many of the rebel leaders were men to whom, through the maze of aristocratic marriages, they were related.

'Anyway,' Mrs Astell finished the account like the good teacher she was, 'dear Lord Derwentwater made a noble end. Perhaps that swayed the crowd. Poor boy, so young and his dear wife pregnant, he was dismayed at first but recovered and made a speech. He said he died for King James and was sorry he'd pleaded guilty because by that he had credited with the title of king a person who had no right to it.'

'Oh, the romance,' said Sophie, clasping her hands and swaying. 'Go on. Did the axe chop clean?'

Mary Astell turned to Cecily. 'Lord Kenmuir was even more composed. The Sheriff asked him if he had anything to say and he declared he came to die and not to make speeches.'

Cecily poured more tea for her guests. She had stayed with the Kenmuirs more than once and felt distress that made her irritable.

'If they were going to rebel,' she said, 'they might have done it properly. How could my uncle be seduced into such an enterprise? A rebellion in James's name when the man hadn't even

9

arrived . . . Hamlet without the Prince of Denmark, damned if it wasn't.'

'Do you tell me, my dear Fitzhenry, that you would have approved it had it been more efficient?' Lady Mary pretended shock she did not feel. Cecily's unfashionable inability to dissemble her views enabled those who were jealous of her riches, her looks and her descent from one of England's oldest families to misrepresent her in a court where bitches of both sexes fought for advantage. Those who were assured of their own standing, and Lady Mary and Princess Caroline were among them, valued her.

The question was one to which Cecily, like many of her class, had yet to formulate an answer. She did not believe in the divine right of a king to interfere with her church, law and liberty but she was convinced of the sanctity of blood and succession. The Pretender, so young and alone in France, so good-*looking*, had God on his side, while the fat Hanoverian occupying the throne had only Mammon on his.

Though Maid of Honour through right of birth and chosen by Princess Caroline because of it, Cecily often asked herself uneasily whether one *should* be serving the daughter-in-law of a German who could decapitate so many of one's relatives with a stroke of his pen.

Besides, young Sophie was right: there was romance in a lost cause when it was accompanied by speeches from the scaffold and the whiff of heather and the distant skirl of pipes . . .

'Another meringue?' she asked. 'Louis says they are *épatantes*.' She'd had them made especially for Mary Astell, who could afford few luxuries. Herself, she had no interest in food, regarding it merely as fuel; Society's four-hour dinners bored her – another advantage to her enemies.

Outside mist blurred the shadowy trees and put a sheen on chimneys, arguing a thaw.

Then Anne Insh came in and slammed the door behind her. 'My father is taken ill. They sent word. I'm for Scotland this minute. I have permission. For you also. It is arranged. The King says we may go if the Princess says we can. She just has. He is so ill. It is gaol fever. I beg you to come with me.'

10

She was shaking with anxiety and resolve. Her blue eyes, which had a deep line below them that slanted from their corners, were directed at Cecily.

And the older Cecily, reliving that moment, hears the younger Cecily's immediate response: 'Of course.'

Less formidable women would have blanched at the journey but to these the weather was another servant to command. Cold, the lateness of the hour, distance, the menace of highwaymen, were inconveniences that wealth and spirit must overcome. When Cecily asked, 'But how shall we go? There'll be no stages and my rattler's at Cook's for repair,' she was only concerned at the delay that finding another coach might cause.

Sophie said: 'We'll take mine. I'm going to come. He's my uncle too.' The relationship was more distant than Cecily's, Lord Keltie was merely her second cousin once removed, but since she'd provided the solution to the problem, it was accepted that, yes, Sophie must go.

Mary Astell thought of their reputations. 'Lady Cecily, it is not fitting you should travel without a chaperone. I shall come with you.'

Cecily paused in the act of taking money from her box. It would be a hard enough journey for three young women; for someone of Astell's age . . . but Mrs Astell's compact little body quivered with anticipation, her jet-button eyes shone. 'Bless you,' Cecily said.

Should they take a maid? No, it was decided: with four of them in the coach it would be comfortable; with five, over-crowded. They would be staying at inns overnight and could just manage to pack, unpack, dress and undress themselves, and their hair must stay unmanaged until they arrived in Scotland where they were to stay with friends of Anne's who would provide the appropriate servants.

Should they take a male companion? No, again. They'd have outriders for protection who, with the coachmen, would be armed.

Only Lady Mary Wortley Montagu stayed silent.

Sophie was sent off to instruct the coachmen, Anne to find fur rugs, the maids to pack, footmen for food and wine.

11

It was Cecily who managed the enterprise. Capability was not a trait admired in women – it was the *ton* to be absent-minded – but, when a friend was in need, Cecily could bustle, and she bustled now.

A voice came out of the shadows of the corridor. 'Where are you going, lady?' He scuttled after her, spider-like.

'A-visiting, Your Holiness.' Anne would not want her business confided to a notorious gossip like Pope.

'I'll come.'

'There won't be room.'

'I'll be your foot-warmer.'

'No, my dear, I thank you.'

She was his adored of the moment, perhaps she genuinely liked him. He laid poems of worship on her altar, wordy incense to her nostrils. He was the most charming companion in the world but he was wearing. Even if she could have taken him, she wasn't going to spend the journey to Scotland with those lustrous, vulnerable eyes continually watching her face for rejection.

Pope writhed. 'You shall be taking Lord Fanny, of course.'

'Indeed, I shall not,' she said, guiltily. She had considered it. Lord Hervey might act the hermaphrodite but his wooing of the night before had shown distinct, and masculine, possibilities.

The poet's voice belled like a siren's down the corridor after her:

'Where'er you walk, cool gales shall fan the glade,
Trees, where you sit, shall crowd into a shade:
Where'er you tread, the blushing flowers shall rise,
And all things flourish where you turn your eyes.'

She grinned. He'd offered that one to Lepel last week. 'No good, Alexander,' she called over her shoulder, 'I'm busy.'

Behind her, the delicate face twisted to become as ugly as the poor body beneath it in which passion could flame too high and burn too easily into hatred.

Princess Caroline was red-nosed and kind when Cecily went to bid her goodbye. The Prince of Wales was with her: he usually returned to her apartments when he'd been disporting himself with a lover in order to tell her about it. He took mistresses because it was expected; his wife was the real romance of his life. He would make an upside-down king, Cecily thought.

Kissing Cecily, Caroline said: 'If he is ill, poor, foolish man, for his daughter and nieces to see him before he die is good. Yet such climate it is. I fear for the coach to turn over. You haf outriders?'

'Yes, dear madam.'

'Lady Cecily, you haf ever seen *Busen* like so?' The Prince of Wales was fondly indicating his wife's undoubtedly magnificent chest.

'*Herrlich*, Your Highness.'

'I sink so.'

'Return to me soon, *liebchen*,' said Caroline.

As she waited for Sophie to curtsy her farewell, Cecily thought that fear of a further, nationwide rebellion must be receding or the Hanovers would not be so complacent in allowing three of their Maids of Honour to go and minister to a rebel. Or else Lady Mary was right and it was wise to begin to show clemency in case the mob's fickle sympathy turned Jacobite. In fact, she thought, George had already shown surprising forbearance in ordering only two deaths.

(Lady Cecily was choosing to ignore the sentence of drawing and quartering, which was being imposed on four other rebels at Tyburn, and the thirty-four still to hang in Lancashire, and the number who would die in prison. These were lesser beings, commoners, and probably deserved it.)

Backing out, her last sight of the future George II and his wife was one of connubial contentment. *Very pretty*, she thought, and then, dutiful to fashion, *but bovine*.

The travellers gathering round Sophie's coach, or running back into the palace for something forgotten, were infected with excitement, even Anne. Here was adventure.

The coachmen were less enchanted.

'Has Hobson fixed frost nails to the horses?' asked Cecily.

'Have you, Hobson?' Sophie called.

'No, I ain't. But I fixed 'em to their shoes.'

'Oh, stop scowling, Hobson. It'll be exciting.'

13

Lady Mary was grave. 'I should come with you.' She took Cecily's arm and led her behind the coach. 'I wish you were not going.'

'Madam, it's not like you to be cautious.' This was the woman who had eloped with Edward Wortley. Who had accompanied him on a diplomatic mission to Turkey. Among foreigners. *Black* foreigners.

'I am concerned. Cecily, I want you to promise me you will remind the others whose servants you all are. Keltie is your relative and it is right to nurse him, but remember he is also a traitor.'

'Forgive me a moment, Lady Mary.'

Cecily stepped away to address herself to the second coachman who was cramming their wrapped skirt hoops – it would be impossible to get into the coach while wearing them – into the back pannier without consideration.

She turned back. 'I beg your pardon. Yes?'

'Guard yourself, I beg.' Cold took beauty from Lady Mary's face, leaving it bony. Her eyelashes had gone in a bout of smallpox, which had left her otherwise unmarked, and the loss emphasized her fierce eyes. 'Anne is rash in her anxiety and her nature leads her to extremes. You must guard yourself and her. And little Sophie. I wish you were not going.'

Cecily kissed her. 'I am Roland at Roncesvalles. The Saracens shall not pass. Tell Pope he may write an epic on it.'

'Roland died at Roncesvalles.'

An older, wiser Cecily remembered the words. Looking back, the scene was vivid to her: the piles of dirty snow in the courtyard illuminated by footmen's flares, the horses stamping, guards staring. She could even recall the particular blue of the horizontal stripes on her stockings as her younger self lifted her skirt and put one foot on the coach step. *Don't go, you clodpoll. Turn back.*

Cecily climbed in and settled herself next to Mary Astell, putting her arm through the holding strap and wiggling her fingers in farewell to Lady Mary. There came the crack of Hobson's whip and the lurch as the coach wheels unstuck themselves from the snow and began to turn.

14

The light from St James's lamps, glowing fuzzily through the mist, was blotted out as Anne pulled down the blinds to keep out the draught from the windows.

The wheels were almost soundless as they turned towards the Great North Road, making for Scotland . . .

CHAPTER TWO

THE BREFFNYS' FAMILY coach was ancient and enormous. 'Like travelling in the Step Pyramid,' reads the last entry in Cecily's diary, 'only colder.'

Slush permeated its floorboards and made the straw at their feet damp. The bouncing of its springless carriage began the chafing on the occupants' backsides that would end in sores. Every lurch into a foot-deep rut jarred their spines. The coach lamps outside cast little light inside so that they were in darkness.

Nobody complained: Mrs Astell was a Stoic, the girls aristocrats.

Indeed, inside that over-large, icy black shaker flinging them about like dice was an air of holiday. Though she was the kindest of employers, attendance on Princess Caroline included hours of standing through civic functions and loyal addresses, kneeling for daily services in the Chapel Royal and spending endless evenings at cards.

'Frizelation and dangleation', their terms for flirting and getting themselves pursued by young men at court, were fun but involved energetic concentration on their looks and wit, not to mention guarding themselves from the barbs of other Maids of Honour.

Here, now, among loved and trusted women, they could loosen their stays and let their tongues run as they pleased while Mrs Astell's pedagogy took them comfortably back to the years when the three of them had formed what she called her 'female academy'.

'When Sir Robert Carey rode from London to carry the news of Queen Elizabeth's death to James VI of Scotland, he reached Doncaster that same night,' she said. 'What date was that, Sophia?'

'Don't know,' said Sophie.

'Sixteen three,' said Cecily.

Mrs Astell nodded. 'He galloped into James's palace court-yard in Edinburgh two nights later. Four hundred and ten miles in under sixty hours. Therefore we may average his speed at . . . Sophia?'

'Nearly seven miles an hour,' said Cecily, 'but I'll lay guineas he had better weather than we shall.'

In fact, the journey took them almost a fortnight, Hobson declaring at the first stop: 'You can't ask me to do more than thirty mile in this weather, Miss Sophie, you can't.'

'I could,' said Sophie, though she didn't.

'Thirty miles,' said Mrs Astell, not passing up the opportunity, 'the distance a Roman soldier marched in a day.'

But, as they ate a good supper at that night's inn, her didacti-cism overstepped itself and alarmed them: 'A doctor friend of mine has taken an inventory of patients in Bedlam and do you know which profession forms the largest group? Apart from abandoned women, of course?'

'Which?'

'Coachmen and hackney-carriage drivers.'

'Why?' asked Cecily, intrigued.

'Doctor Forbes thinks the continual motion has a deleterious effect on their . . .' Mrs Astell lowered her voice '. . . *glands*.'

Their eyes went to the door where Hobson, his fellow-driver and the outriders were stiffly carrying in the ladies' overnight luggage, rime glistening on their cloaks and hats.

'How are your glands, Hobson?' Cecily called.

'Cold,' Hobson told her, massaging blood back into his fingers.

'Oh dear,' said Sophie. 'D'ye think he'll run amok and kill us all?'

'Not Hobson,' Cecily assured her, but she kept a wary eye on the man as the weather turned worse after Grantham.

Not often did she question society's status quo but every now and then a happening or chance remark, such as Mrs Astell's, would awake the fear tucked away in the mind of all England's élite – that its élitism rested on the consent of that quiescent monster, the common people, which, should it become restive, could overwhelm its masters. And mistresses. In England, the servile hand rarely held an assassin's dagger, as happened in lesser countries, but one couldn't be too careful . . .

Anne, chafing at having to stop at all, would have driven harder but Cecily, unconsciously pursuing the policy that had protected England from revolution for twenty-eight years, argued restraint and thus kept Hobson's glands from turning nasty.

In any case, thirty miles a day was enough for all of them. True, highwaymen had retired into hibernation and would have had poor pickings even if they hadn't; often, the women's coach was the only one on the road. But the roads were dangerous in themselves.

They became weary at having to make frequent descents in order to lighten the coach when the horses refused the steeper hills and must be led up them and down. Frost misted the windows, so that they either opened them to see the countryside and froze, or kept them shut and saw only each other.

Accommodation worsened among the steep hills of the north, where landlords were not expecting passing trade. Indeed, Lady Cecily was to say in her mature years that it was by experiencing poor inns that she became aware of what a good one should be.

Their last, the first they'd stayed at in Scotland, was a mere croft with beaten earth for a floor and a naked child sitting in the dripping destined to fry their eggs – the only meal on offer. They had hoped by now to be at Lord Petrock's, the house outside Edinburgh of one of Anne's father's friends, but were still too distant.

'Usually we Scots'll not use an inn,' said Anne, defending her national honour. 'Our hospitality is given and received in each other's homes.'

The landlord overheard her. 'So it is, mistress, mair's the pity. We're petitioning the Parliament on it.'

'If you cleaned your kitchen,' Cecily felt she had to tell him, 'you wouldn't need to.'

Next day, as they drove in through the arched passageway of Fetlaw Place into a courtyard, accumulated exhaustion overtook them. Lord Petrock had been hunting. He strode through a hubbub of horses, hounds and jockey-capped men. 'Anne. Ladies. Here you are the long last and it's a blithe day that brings you to my door.'

Too tired to curtsy, Cecily listened to an introductory roll-call of Mac-this and Mac-that. Lady Petrock rescued them: 'You long-tongued chiel, Donal, will ye let the weary lassies stand till Doomsday? Come away to your rooms, my dears. There's a log to your fire and a bedside posset.'

After a change of clothes, the travellers descended to an enormous and draughty hall, in which numerous huntsmen and guests were preparing to do justice to a dinner of turkey pie mashed with ruby jelly, salmon pasties, painted hams and Château Margaux 1713. Only the chairs of Anne and Lord Petrock were empty.

'They'll be in soon,' said Lady Petrock, when Cecily inquired for them. 'Take of some duck, now, Mistress Astell. We hang it in our fig tree for flavour. And when were ye last in Scotland, Lady Cecily?'

'Not since seventeen eight for my misfortune,' Cecily told her. 'They were afraid the Pretender would whisk me off and marry me.'

It was true. A spy in the French Jacobite camp had reported to Robert Harley, then Queen Anne's most trusted minister, that there existed a list of aristocratic young women whose pedigree and Anglican faith might make one of them an eligible bride for James, rendering him more acceptable to his people. Eight-year-old Cecily's name was on it. Accordingly, after James's attempted invasion in 1708, Cecily had been forbidden to accept Lord Keltie's invitations to spend the summers with Anne at his castle of Cairnvreckan as, until then, she always had, in case she was abducted to become a pawn in the Jacobite game.

'And a bonny bride King James would have found ye,' said Lady Petrock, heartily.

King James? Had Lady Petrock intended a compliment? That the marriage would have qualified James to be king? Or did the woman always refer to the Pretender in such a manner? Cecily sat up straighter and began to look around for signs of Jacobitism.

Her study was inconclusive. The priest next to her, whom she'd first suspected to be a papist, turned out to be Episcopalian, Scotland's equivalent of the Anglican Church. On the other hand, many of the '15 rebels, like Lord Keltie himself, had been Episcopalian.

This was the Scottish Lowlands, territory loyal to King George, and it had suffered as badly as anywhere when the Highland army came rampaging down from the hills on its way to the Border. Lady Petrock had already apologized to the company for the quality of the cheese, 'for didn't the damned caterans burn down my dairy when I refused them comfort. "Friends or unfriendlies I can neither help the one nor frustrate the other," I told them.'

Yet, the next minute, tears were in her eyes as Cecily and Sophie told her what they knew of the executions of Lords Derwentwater and Kenmuir. 'God save their faithful souls.'

Cecily thought: I wonder, am I in a nest of Jacobites? (Jacobites, like vipers, always had nests.)

Lord Petrock came in and, to her relief, gave the loyal toast.

Nevertheless, she watched carefully to see which hands passed their glass over the finger-bowls as a sign that their owners were pledging not George but the King over the water. She sighted so many that she failed to see whether Lady Petrock's had done the same.

Anne had not appeared by the time the ladies left the gentlemen to their port and tobacco.

Because of the short winter daylight, dinner had been early. It was only six o'clock when the two girls and their teacher, pleading fatigue, retired.

By then, Cecily had reached the conclusion that the Petrocks were as politically ambivalent as so many of their class, as she was. Possibly the execution and imprisonment of their friends had rekindled a waning admiration for the Jacobite cause while convincing them at the same time of its hopelessness.

After they'd helped a tipsy and ecstatic Mary Astell to her room – 'Did you taste of that potailzie pie, Sophie? Cecily, what *is* potailzie pie?' – Cecily told Sophie her conclusions as they readied themselves for bed, a four-poster known as 'The Forfar', presumably because it could have accommodated most of Forfar in it.

'These people are sound enough,' said Sophie, yawning. 'They congratulated me on my earl.'

'Proving them incapable of treason,' Cecily said. 'Sophie, don't you *ever* think of national matters?'

'No.'

Sophie was the only one of the three cousins with a settled future. She was contracted in marriage to the Earl of Cullen, even younger than herself but whose charm of appearance and disposition had won her heart at their first and, so far, only meeting.

'Where can Anne be?'

She woke them up. 'You must dress, Cecily. I've told Hobson to have the coach ready but he's balking. Sophie, wake up. Tell Hobson we're for Edinburgh at once.'

'Now?' Cecily looked at the candle: four of its divisions had burned down. 'It's ten o'clock, for Lord's sake. It's still night-time. Why must we go now?'

'Now. We must go now. Lord Petrock saw him yesterday and says he's so ill. Cecily, *please*.'

Still objecting, Cecily began to dress. 'They'll never admit you at night-time. It's a skidding prison, not a skidding inn.'

'Our pass from the King is for myself and a companion and doesn't specify hours. They'll let us in.'

Our pass. *Us*. Anne was expecting her to go into the prison as well. She had not envisaged that. 'But isn't it too dark to journey?'

'There's a moon. Hobson can do it if Sophie tells him he must.'

Cecily's every instinct was telling her to leave Sophie behind: Anne's wildness was disturbing and she wanted time to ask more questions and consider the answers – why, for instance, could they not go in the Petrocks' coach? – but Anne was allowing her none. Anyway, Sophie, with her usual enthusiasm for adventure, was already dressing.

The brightness of a large moon reflected back a frost which turned the road into a broad, white path on which they were the only travellers. Now was the time to question but, after a few attempts had been brushed aside, Cecily held her tongue.

An orphan with no memory of either parent, Cecily had been raised by dutiful, kindly but aloof adults without any fervour of affection. In return she'd felt none for them, reserving it for her cousins, her old nurse, Edie, and, later, for Mary Astell.

Nevertheless, unable to understand it, she admired daughterly love in others. Anne's consuming, scalding fear for her father awoke pity in her and an almost religious respect: here was agony at the foot of the cross. Not to assist her would be near impiety.

In any case, she owed her cousin what childish happiness she'd known. During her early years her regular visits to Lord Keltie's Highland castle were windswept, pony-riding, alien, peat-smoked freedoms that had become invested in her memory with magic. After 1708, when they'd had to stop, Anne had sacrificed a part of each year to spend it away from her beloved father and stay in England with Cecily, occasionally at court, more often on Cecily's fenland estate of Hempens where, thanks to the lax interpretation of her duties by Lady Black, Cecily's duenna, the two of them, sometimes accompanied by Sophie, had been able to slip off with Edie's gamekeeper husband into the watery joys of punting and wild-fowling among the reeds.

It was a debt. If Anne was calling it in now, Cecily was prepared to pay it.

Within half an hour they were at Edinburgh's west gate where a guard of soldiers was sufficiently impressed by the royal pass to let them through with no more than a quick inspection through the coach window.

As they rattled up the hill towards the Castle, the stone frontages of the city's astoundingly tall tenements had the sheen of black marble. Ice, however, had not diminished the smell from the contents of a thousand chamber-pots which the citizens

21

emptied from their windows and now crunched beneath the coach's wheels. Sophie held her nose.

'Auld Reekie,' Cecily said.

'Sophie,' said Anne, 'please stay with the coach while we go in.'

'I want to come in with you.'

'Please. Hobson might go off in search of refreshment, you know what he's like. We must have you ready to drive off the moment we come out.'

They'd reached the cliff-face of the Castle. Anne descended, pulling up her hood, pulling up Cecily's, telling Hobson he must stay here, he *must*. Cecily followed her, cricking her neck to look up, and saw a body hanging from a wall, its face blurred where the cold had halted its decomposition. A breeze had come up and was swaying it.

The royal pass was scrutinized by ill-tempered guards, suspicious of a Jacobite plot to arm the prisoners. When they found that the basket Anne carried contained nothing more than a jug of beef tea, a flask of whisky, some food and medicines, they relaxed. On Anne's offering them the whisky, they took it. They wouldn't allow the coach in, even though they'd searched it, but Anne said not at all: she and Cecily would enter by the picket and walk the rest, if one of the good gentlemen would be so kind as to light their way.

Steep, winding roadways, shadows, moon glinting on flint-locks, on the buckles of soldiers' bandoliers, on faces pinched and mean from cold, the sudden stench of faeces from a grating, tunnels streaked with algae and smelling of urine and flaking whitewash, the echo of a man crying, the rasp of keys . . . These brought the fact of the rebels' defeat closer to Cecily than any account of executions and how massive was the authority that they had flouted. This was subjugation.

'Best room in the house,' said their guide, unlocking a small door. 'You got an hour and I'll be back. I'll even leave the glim, can't ask more than that.' He left and the key turned on them.

Without his lantern there'd have been no light in the room which, if it was the best in the house, spoke badly for the others. It was roughly ten foot square with a sloping ceiling, contained a table, two stools, Lord Keltie lying, coughing, on a box bed, and another man at that moment scrambling up from a pallet on the floor.

Anne went straight to her father, leaving Cecily and the other man facing each other. He was tall and young, in his twenties, and embarrassed, slyly manoeuvring a lidded chamber-pot further under the bed with his foot. A grating high up in the far wall allowed cold air into the room but not enough to dissipate its stink.

'Do be seated,' he said.

Cecily hovered, wanting to assist Anne who had raised her father's head and was spooning cough medicine into him, releasing into the cell the refreshment of balsam and horehound.

'He's best left to her,' the young man said. 'Be seated, I beg.'

As she sat down on the stool at one side of the table, he introduced himself – 'Guillaume Fraser, madam, at your service' – and took the other opposite. 'This is most good of you.'

'Not at all,' she said, amused at the drawing-room exchange. 'Cecily Fitzhenry.'

He smiled back and she became aware of a response in herself. He was not conventionally good-looking. Had he been a woman, the French would have called her *jolie-laide*. The face was a shade too long, its skin too sallow and, at the moment, badly shaven, his lips too full. But the smile took these components and turned them into something to catch the breath.

'I was with others in the dungeons but I begged leave to attend on him,' Fraser said, nodding towards the bed. 'He is very ill, I think.'

Lord Keltie's cough had the dry insistence of consumption. Anne was weeping as she fed him her beef tea.

Cecily's hands twitched at her own inadequacy: she should have brought more food – both men were gaunt. And rugs. Fraser was shivering: his jacket was laid over Lord Keltie, leaving him in his shirt.

She took off her cloak, unwound the silk shawl she wore underneath and handed it to him without comment. For a moment he wanted to refuse, then wrapped it round himself, smelling it and closing his eyes. She was moved, knowing that the first femininity he had encountered for months was hers.

'Guillaume?' she inquired; she liked to know to whom she spoke. His speech was cultured enough but there was emphasis on the last syllable of some words and the placing of others was foreign.

'A French mother. My father was the Fraser of Carslaw but followed King James into exile after 'eighty-eight. I was raised at St-Germain-en-Laye at the court of Her Majesty.' Otherwise known to Whigs as 'that papist harlot', though everything Cecily had heard about Mary Modena had argued unvarying fidelity to James II and, since his death, to his cause.

This young man was the Carslaw, was he? Cecily mentally scanned her exhaustive genealogical lists. The French mother, then, was the daughter of the Marquis de St Jacut. She could excuse herself for the attraction she felt: he was nobly born. Unfortunately, he was also a Roman Catholic. Cecily avoided looking at the crucifix he wore on a chain, not only out of revulsion at its realism but so that she should not stare at his neck, a pleasure to the eye.

The warders had deprived the prisoners of their wigs to humiliate them, revealing that Lord Keltie was bald and that Fraser's dark hair, though lank from the battlefield, was fine with a slight wave that Cecily would have liked instead of her own strong blonde curls. He'd tied it back with a piece of string.

He was still embarrassed. 'Mistress Cecily . . .'

'*Lady* Cecily,' she said automatically.

'. . . Lady Cecily, I would not have you associate me with Simon Fraser. My kinsman, yes, but a turncoat. When he saw how things go – went, he ordered us to leave the field. I spat in his eye and marched to join Lord Keltie's banner.'

Under the circumstances, she thought, Simon Fraser's move seemed sensible; she asked whether this Fraser regretted his own.

He winced as if she'd been rude, then smiled. '"If it be a sin to covet honour, I am the most offending soul alive."'

Her favourite play.

He seemed to think it important she should know he'd not

laid down his sword at the end but had been physically dis-armed. Telling her about the battle, he was a small boy explain-ing a black eye; he couldn't help it. The shame of capture made him grimace.

'Cecily,' said Anne.

Cecily went to the bed and saw her uncle's almost luminous, and fatal, pallor. She'd known nothing but kindness from him. She curtsied. 'I regret to find you in these circumstances, my lord.'

With effort he said, 'My dear niece, my dear girl.'

'Cecily,' said Anne, 'I am sorry, but in a minute I am going to dress Father in my cloak. I want you to walk with him down to the coach and drive away. The hood will hide his face. They will think he is me, overcome with grief. When you're outside the city, make for Leith. There's a boat in harbour there awaiting the tide, the *Good Hope*. A coaler. It will take him to France.' She met Cecily's eyes: 'I'm sorry.'

'I . . . Give me a minute, if you please, Anne.' She walked to the wall with the grating in it and lifted her hands to grasp its bars, pressing her head against stone.

It had been obvious if she'd only . . . The duplicity of it. Anger came, then went. Fear came and stayed. The skidding Petrocks had arranged it but shrunk from further involvement. Little wonder they wouldn't lend Anne their identifiable, skidding coach. Fraser would have known other women in France, prettier and more sophisticated. *Why has that entered my head?* Anne had no right to ask this. She's lunatic. Doubtless, one of his Frenchwomen would have done it but I am English and it is treachery.

'Cecily.'

Which do I betray? My king? My friend? She felt Anne's hand on her shoulder. It had been there a hundred times, when she'd needed it. 'You should have told me.'

'Cecily, they'll never know it was you. You and Sophie shall be in bed at Fetlaw Place by the time it's discovered. It could be any woman. They don't know your name – or your face, you had your hood up. They'll never prove it was you.'

They'd have a skidding good idea. And if it didn't work,

25

which was likely, they'd know then. But at the same time as she thought this, she was projecting her imagination to the moment when she refused to do what Anne asked, walked out of this place, an upright and loyal subject of German George, leaving these hopeless, loving lunatics behind her . . . She could not.

'Very well.' She turned and saw respect on his face. He'll pay more than Anne or I. Assisting an escape. If he wasn't facing death before, he is now. He's as grateful as if he were going himself.

Oddly, the conviction that she could do nothing else came when they were helping Lord Keltie to rise and her hand touched his bedclothes to find them cold and mildewed with damp. Such slovenliness. The man was a peer of the realm, whatever he'd done. If they couldn't treat noble prisoners better they *deserved* to lose them.

She was filled with a relief greater than she'd known; she found herself giggling as they draped the cloak over Lord Keltie's bald head. Anne glanced at her, then had to sit down on the bed to laugh. A guffaw came from Fraser. They were bonded in amusement at themselves, three minuscule Davids against the giant of Gath.

But oh dear, oh dear, it wouldn't do. It was inefficient. Reluctantly, Cecily said: 'It won't do, Anne.'

Anne turned, frozen in the act of laughing.

Cecily said: 'It won't do, my dear. It must be you who goes.' As Anne began to protest, she went on: 'Consider. I don't know where Leith is. Neither does Hobson. Nor Sophie. You must be the one. We look enough alike. Go with him to France; it is the sensible course. I shall stay here.'

Later, over and over, she was to ask herself whether she would have made the offer if Fraser hadn't been present. And was ashamed of the answer: she might not have. She condemned her younger self for a child on a high wall, 'Look at me, how brave I am,' or, worse, a strumpet strutting before a potential client. Prepared to trade ruin, possibly her life, for one glance of admiration from a desirable man.

Nor could that foolish young Cecily resist adding the one argument that Anne would never refute: 'Your father needs

26

you.' And was immediately terrified at what she had done.

Her cousin flung herself on her, sobbing.

Anne was tall, like Cecily – their height came from their mothers who'd been sisters – her father short, so the cloak trailed the ground; good in one way since it covered his boots but bad in that an observant eye might notice it hadn't trailed before. They put Anne's muff over his hands. They used the tiny scissors from the hussife in Cecily's pocket to cut off some of Anne's hair and Cecily stitched it to the edge of the hood so that a piece curled down his shoulder. They spooned more linctus down him in order that he should not cough, begging him, if he must, to make it high, like weeping.

Insanity, Cecily kept thinking even as she worked: her uncle wasn't the right shape, he moved like an old man; in any case, he was too weak, he wouldn't manage the walk down the hill.

Lord Keltie took a little food. Fraser ate the rest.

Anne and Cecily said their goodbyes, knowing they might be saying them for the last time. 'They'll not be too hard on you, are you sure?' begged Anne. 'Tell them I bombazed you into it.'

'I most certainly shall.'

'You'll come to France, my dear, my dear?'

'Indeed. And soon.'

The insouciance was a pretence: she'd never been so afraid in her life. When they heard the rattle of keys and the gaoler's step approaching along the passageway outside, she wanted to fall on her knees and beg everybody's pardon because she could not continue with the charade. It can't work.

Instead she scrambled into Lord Keltie's bed, pulled the covers over her head and attempted a masculine cough. It sounded like a fox in rut. This couldn't work. She heard the cell door unlocked, the 'Time, ladies, please' of the gaoler, knew it couldn't work, heard the cell door close behind shuffled foot-steps, knowing it couldn't work. They'd gone.

After a while she raised her head, into silence – and darkness: the gaoler had taken the lantern. She got up and felt her way to the table, taking the stool opposite Fraser; she couldn't see him but she knew he sat three feet away from her, listening.

They listened together. They could hear the normal sounds of the Castle, or whatever passed for normal in that place. An exchange of shouts echoing up from a courtyard made her start, but Fraser's hand pressed down on hers. 'No. They change the guard only.'

She strained her hearing to catch the sound of a coach driving down the setts outside the gateway, but it wasn't possible over the wind which had got up and now moaned through the grating. He stood up – she could just see the paleness of her shawl against the wall. 'Nor'west. Fair stood the wind for France. Shakespeare's wind.'

He came back and sat down again. 'And Scotland's. It whistles "The Pipers of Strathdearn", did you know that?' He crooned the song, in a shaky, ridiculous baritone, to calm her.

'They must be away by now,' she said.

'Yes.' Her hand was raised and she felt his face against it. 'You are a most gallant lady.'

'Thank you.' She didn't take her hand away. 'When do they come?'

'At dawn, if we have luck. Though there's a particular sergeant, if he's on duty we are turned out to shiver at any time, day or night. He says he looks for arms. We say he's a Presbyterian bastard.'

'It's a pity we have no light or cards. I'm a good card player.'

'As well we haven't, then. I'm not. Let us discuss Shakespeare.'

They discussed Shakespeare. It made him seem very English: she'd somehow thought St-Germain Jacobites would prefer Molière.

'Shakespeare was a Roman Catholic, you know that?'

'Nonsense,' she said, enjoying the intimacy of arguing with him.

'But yes.'

The extraordinary thing was that even had he not been so personable, she would have liked him; she was almost giddy with recognition, with the sense that they'd held this conversation before. She had never come across a mind so attuned to her own. Even when they disagreed they understood each other.

28

He said his favourite was *Romeo and Juliet*. 'I staged it for Her Majesty at St-Germain. I was Romeo.'

It was a ruse. They both knew it. So that he could quote the balcony speech. There was nothing else to do but fall in love. Under sentence of death it was necessary to affirm youth and life. There was no time for flirtatious exchanges with an abyss about to claim them; at least they could fall into it in each other's attractive arms.

She listened to him making verbal love to her, absorbing every word through the darkness, every inflexion of his voice, hoarding them against the years to come, silently begging what light beyond the window breaks to stay unbroken for ever and leave them in this noisome, lovely darkness, wishing he'd make the move they both knew he was going to.

She'd had no use for her virginity the moment she'd set eyes on him. Bewigged, posturing, rouged courtiers, how could they compare with this raw man? What time had been wasted on the artificiality of puppets now that her future had contracted into what minutes were left with flesh and blood, this gladiator in the ring of life and death?

In the circle in which Lady Cecily moved, chastity was not the ball and chain it had been to previous generations of girls. As Lady Mary Wortley Montagu had once pointed out: 'No one is shocked nowadays to hear that "Miss So and So, Maid of Honour, has got nicely over her confinement."' But the convention of allowing the man to make the first move still held firm, and so Cecily, dying for him to make it, waited until he did. And waited too long . . .

They weren't lucky. From the world outside came the stamp of boots, orders, protests from prisoners rousted from other cells. The Presbyterian bastard was on duty.

Immediately, he moved. The table was shoved aside. His arms were round her, she had her cheek against his neck. 'My heart's darling.' He held her away from him for a moment. He said: 'They can hang me but I'll return for you, Lady Cecily, Lady Cecily.'

'And I'll be waiting.'

She was taken to the governor of the Castle, who didn't know

29

what to do with her and kept her in his own house while he sent to England and King George to find out.

Eventually she and Sophie and Mary Astell were driven back to London under guard and in the charge of a Scots Presbyterian, Archibald Cameron, a lawyer from the Procurator's office who was going to England on his own business. He was a penny-pinching young man, who made them stay at the cheaper inns and accounted for every expenditure in a notebook, a Lowlander in a fox-coloured wig. Sophie taunted him, singing 'Over the Hills and Far Away' out of the coach window to where he rode beside them on his inferior horse. Cecily didn't speak to him at all.

The King refused to see her. She was taken instead to his minister, Sir Robert Walpole. They'd already met at court where she'd watched with surprise his success at worming his way into the Princess of Wales's favour – and thought less of Caroline for allowing him to do so: the man was of no blood whatever, a jumped-up squire, a Whig nakedly out for power. His own advance on her – 'We must be close friends, Lady Cecily, as we've been close neighbours. I'm a Norfolk man with acres not far from Hempens' – she'd treated with the contempt it warranted: 'Indeed?'

Now he was her inquisitor.

She faced him out over the matter of Sophie's involvement, stating the truth that Sophie, like Mary Astell, had known noth-ing of the plot. 'Nor did I, until we were in the cell. I'm no Jacobite, but my uncle was dying. Anne is my cousin and my friend. He was *dying* – ask the warders at the Castle. The only one betrayed is the executioner.'

Again, she was unlucky. Rebels were escaping their prisons like bubbles blown in the air. Old Borlum Mackintosh, the sixty-year-old defender of Preston, had broken out of Newgate with thirteen other Jacobites, one of them his son.

The Earl of Wintoun used a watch-spring to saw through the bars of a window in the Tower and got away safely into exile. In Lancashire, four slipped out of prison. Thirty more took over the ship transporting them to the colonies and sailed it to France.

The English public, ever admiring of slippery coves, had begun to jeer as it counted.

One escape in particular that caught its fancy was yet another from the Tower of London, this time the Earl of Nithsdale's, which had been procured by Lady Nithsdale – he'd walked out in her cloak – as Anne had procured Lord Keltie's. And exactly two days before.

'They're laughing at us, maid,' Walpole told her, mildly. 'And this little exploit by Miss Insh'll have 'em laughing the more. That's iffen they find out about it. But p'rhap they woon't, p'rhap they woon't.'

Cecily shrugged as if she had no care either way. In fact, she was more afraid than she had been in the Edinburgh cell. Walpole stood in front of her chair, with his back to the Whitehall window, legs apart, arms behind his back under his coat, his thick belly extended until it almost touched her, cutting her off from light and, it seemed to her, from air.

' 'Tis you I'm thinking of,' he said. 'Your reputation.' He pronounced it 'repootation', acting the Norfolk bucolic, not to put her at her ease, but to emphasize that he, a simple country squire, wielded power over lineage. 'Cavorting in a cell, *with* a bed in it, *with* a young Jacobite? What'd your ancestors think? What'll the *world* think?'

She kept her face expressionless.

'Nice little tidbit that'd be for the presses, wouldn't it?' He put up his hand and stroked one of his chins. 'No, no, I think – and His Majesty do agree with me – we'd better get thee safely married. And I know just the man as'll make ee a fine husband.'

She refused and he broke her. There was no outright coercion: she was merely allowed to read a paper, a letter from an agent in the pay of Lord Stair, British ambassador in Paris. It reported the recent arrival in France 'of the traitor Keltie and his so-called daughter'.

It added: 'The old man is near defunct but we may have the lady spirited away back to England, if so your Ldship wishes, to face what punishment for her treachery yr Ldship thinks fit.'

She knew Stair to be the most efficient spy-master her government had possessed since Elizabeth's Walsingham: he could lay his hand on Anne whenever he wanted. And would.

'And what do *thee* think fit for a wench like Miss Insh as betrays king and country, Lady Cecily, eh? Perhaps we do need an example as'll stop the mob's laugh, eh, Lady Cecily?'

The memory that she'd pleaded, wiped her face on Walpole's boots, was a scar she carried for the rest of her life, being aware, even as she did it, even as she couldn't help doing it, that it was futile.

She was married to an old man called Sir Lemuel Potts two months afterwards.

'Thee'll learn to love 'un as I do,' Walpole said. 'He's a fine man, fine, he'll be a proper husband to you, and as good a neighbour to me.'

CHAPTER THREE

AT HER LONDON house in Spring Gardens, Lady Cecily Potts awoke with a headache: she'd drunk a bottle of claret before retiring. Come to that, she drank a bottle of claret before retiring every night: four years of marriage to Lemuel had taught her the value of going to bed insensible.

Her sister-in-law's voice rasped from the doorway: 'Ain't you dressed yet? There's the carriage downstairs.'

'Go away, Dolly.'

'Shan't then. 'S Lemmy's big speech today. We got to be in the gallery for it. You promised him.'

Oh, God, another day. 'Send Jane up.'

'What we wearing today, your ladyship?'

'I don't care.'

Be-stayed and be-skirted she descended to find her sister-in-law handsome in a hat and next-to-best summer dress.

'You are not coming,' Cecily informed her.

'I am, then.'

They jostled in the hall until Cecily stood back. 'You are not coming, Dolly.'

'And who's to stop me?'

'It pains me to tell you,' Cecily said, gloating, 'that the Strangers' tipstaff informed me you wouldn't be welcome. Not after the last time.'

Dolly Baker wagged her head in derision. 'Pains-me-to-tell-you, pains-me-to-tell-you. I can't help if me bladder's weak. They should've let me out when I asked.'

'A lady holds her water,' said Cecily, who, on days like these, carried a small portable *pot-de-chambre* attached to the right-hand underside of her hoop; a skirt the size of a tent might be hell in a crowd but it had its advantages.

Dolly bared her teeth. 'And I wouldn't know about that, I suppose?'

'Indeed.' Dolly was not the least of the crosses Cecily had been forced to carry these last four years. She was a well-favoured female, Cecily's senior by ten years, with a natural taste for dress, but she was so far down the scale of civilization that, as far as Cecily was concerned, she was off it.

Sharing a house with the woman was like being caged with one of the less mannerly animals. Dolly was no more capable of considering her effect on others than a wild pig rampaging through a forest.

Even to be irked by the creature was demeaning, still more to glory in putting it in its place. In any case, overall victory in humiliation belonged to Dolly whose piss had overflowed between the balusters of the Strangers' Gallery and dripped on two honourable members seated below, one of whom had been leaning backwards and received a direct hit in the eye.

The only comfort to be gleaned from the occasion, as far as Cecily was concerned, was that the afflicted members were Whigs.

She, Cecily, had been sitting next to her at the time, might even have been taken for the culprit had not Dolly sung out her apologies and gone on to give the amazed House a dissertation on urinary problems in general and hers in particular until the tipstaff ushered her out.

Whether, at that moment, Lemuel, who'd been seated not far away from his unfortunate colleagues, prayed for death as she had, she didn't know. With his usual pretence that all was perfect in a perfect world, he'd made no mention of the incident.

Neither, thank God, had Pope: she'd feared he would hear of it and write one of his lampoons. But that gentleman was waiting for a greater degradation, she realized: some act of her own, taking to opium, procuring a lover, as did other despairing wives. And, God knows, she'd been tempted, if only to break the boredom.

Then he'd place her. Then would come the squibs, the ballads, the sniggers, her reputation shrivelling under his acidly disappointed satisfaction. He'd done it to others.

Not yet, Mr Pope. Not ever. I am Lady Cecily Fitzhenry, whoever my husband may be.

When she'd known the marriage that was to be forced on her, she had gone to him, unsuspecting, at Twickenham, expecting for herself the compassion she'd always shown to him. He could be kind: he supported with a pension some sick woman he'd befriended and had been known to weep at man's cruelty to animals. Also, as a Roman Catholic, he would have some sympathy with what she had done in Edinburgh.

Instead of the friend, she'd encountered the wit: 'My dear, the degradation. *Potts*. A cataclysm. Such a *clanking* name. You might cook with it, or piss in it, but never, *never* marry it.'

She'd turned on her heel then and hadn't spoken to him since.

As she left the house in Spring Gardens that June morning of 1720, Cecily stepped into a heat in which stock and share prices were soaring along with the temperature. So was insanity. London, like other financial centres, was infected by a new plague – speculation. High and low had contracted it. Away in the City, emblazoned coaches blocked the narrow lanes as their owners fought with commoners in the doorways of 'Change Alley to put their money into companies that had risen like buns in the heat of somebody's imagination.

The noise from Drummonds, the Scottish bank, where it stood on the corner of Spring Gardens and Charing Cross, attracted her attention so that she paused on the steps. It appeared from the crowd at Drummonds' doors that Jacobites were struggling to buy South Sea shares as loudly and patriotically as anyone else. *How vulgar*.

Cecily, having never wanted for money, had no care for it. In any case, her interest in national affairs had dwindled now that she had to view them as Lemuel Potts's wife. The rage which had overtaken an entire society, even its élite, left her uninterested and dull.

She'd forgotten that Drummonds was Pope's bank. He was in the crowd milling in the street, distinguishable in his black, shorter by a head than anybody else, even the women, his body like a hunched bat's topped by the head of a cherub. She wondered why his defection should have hurt her almost more than the others.

It was to be expected that Lady Cecily would be shunned by the royal family she had offended. Her expulsion was immediate. No explanation was given – Walpole had advised King George that it would render him ridiculous were it known that two of his own daughter-in-law's women had assisted the escape of an enemy. Word of it got about at court, though it was kept from the general public.

However, Cecily had not expected that her contemporaries among the courtiers would shun her too. Couldn't they admit her action as an impulse of family loyalty and not a Jacobite plot? They could not: she was invited nowhere, no cards were left for her, no congratulations sent on her marriage – they'd have been a mockery, in any case.

A proud head had fallen into the basket, hurrah. It shouldn't have been held so high. Mary Lepel had flung herself on Hervey like a wolf and married him; at a chance meeting in Hyde Park, they tiptoed, arm in arm, past her as if avoiding a turd, seeming triumphant.

What Cecily missed in interpreting the attitude of her former friends was the influence of fear. The 'Fifteen had been a closer-run thing than the Government liked to admit: the number and quality of those who'd joined the rebellion indicated that George of Hanover's throne was not on firm foundations and it was in the interest of Sir Robert Walpole, struggling for top place in the cabinet, to keep telling him how shaky it was.

Look to me, Your Majesty, I'm the man to save you from your danger. If Jacobites had not existed, Sir Robert would have had to invent them. To a certain extent he did: the court had begun to see them under every bush. To proclaim oneself a Tory, even, was becoming grounds for suspicion as Sir Robert spread his gospel: who opposes the Whigs must, *ergo*, be Jacobite. If even Maids of Honour proved faithless, who could be trusted? Why did this minister not say 'Amen' to the final 'God Save the King' when a brief was read in church? Why was there a white rose among the embroidery on that lady's petticoat?

Lady Mary Wortley Montagu, who remained Cecily's friend, would have pointed out to her that her former colleagues were not necessarily triumphing over her. That the shadow, perhaps of plotters or assassins, certainly of suspicion, loomed across palace corridors and nobody who wanted to keep their place dare allow it to fall on them by associating with Lady Cecily and her darkened name.

But Lady Mary had gone on her travels again. Among the loyal, only Mrs Astell remained in England. Anne was exiled. Sophie had been taken by her young husband on an extended Grand Tour. Which left Cecily in a desert of middle-class Whiggery. With Dolly.

Pope, emerging from Drummonds, glimpsed Cecily where she stood on the steps of her house. She saw his look. Immediately, her chin and her parasol went up. 'Westminster, John.'

It gave her satisfaction that her carriage wheels sent dust over poet and crowd as it passed. Though the poet noticed, the crowd did not: it was too intent on getting rich. You can transmute fluid mercury into silver and give me 200 per cent return? I'll buy in. Intend to trade in hair, 400 per cent return? Take my pension. Settle the Tortugas? Mine copper from the Welsh mountains? Make butter from beechnuts? Turn salt-water into fresh? Revolutionize the art of war with Puckle's Machine Gun? Yes, yes, I believe in square cannon balls: 800 per cent return? Here's cash for which I've mortgaged my cottage/house/castle. Make me rich. A new nostrum for the clap? Only let me buy in.

The largest bubble of all soars and shimmers in the national hothouse, its translucent, rainbowed, insubstantial circumference reflecting not only the greed of those who leap after it but a nation's romance: the South Sea Company, at present offering 1,050 per cent.

The very name is irresistible, conjuring up doubloons, pearls, Spanish galleons with sails of silk, black ivory and gold moidores.

It's patriotism to buy. To help the National Debt and in doing so remember Drake, remember Hawkins, Ralegh, and make my fortune. Buy. Buy. The King's in. And the Prince of Wales. *And* Walpole, old Brazen-face himself. Buy, buy. Thomas Guy has just made a profit of £180,428 and will found a hospital with it. And him the meanest man in England. Buy quick, *quick*, before they close the subscription.

It was a relief to turn by Charing Cross and hear the tuneful hectoring of the street traders offering a more honest return of flounders, of oranges, delicate cucumbers, twelve-pence-a-peck oysters and lily-white vinegar threepence a quart.

Oh, God. From down an alley came the echoing tenor of someone singing, quite beautifully, 'The Pipers of Strathdearn'. *My heart's darling.* 'Stop the carriage. Stop.' Careless of her doeskin slippers, her skirt ballooning behind her, Cecily ran to the mouth of the alley, fending off higglers.

It wasn't him. How could it be? A drunk cradling a filthy blackjack looked up at her out of his only good eye. Irish, probably.

'Damn you,' she said. She fumbled in her pocket for coins and threw them at him.

'God bless your ladyship. May the road rise up to meet ye.'

'You be damned,' she said again, quietly. He probably would be – sooner rather than later if he persisted in singing Jacobite songs. She went back to the carriage. 'Drive on.'

The sot had transported her back four years and four hundred miles away to an Edinburgh prison cell. Damn him, damn him. She'd accommodated the pain but then some reference, a line of Shakespeare, that wastrel's song, refreshed the old, beloved agony.

She'd known it couldn't be him and still she'd responded.

The awful little Scotsman in the fox-coloured wig, the one who'd been their gaoler on the journey back from Edinburgh, he'd told her what they'd done with Guillaume, privately, soon after her marriage.

'It is concerning the prisoner Fraser, Lady Cecily. I thought ye'd wish to be acquainted with his circumstance.'

'Indeed?' She'd kill to know, but damned if she showed desperation to this Presbyterian pen-pusher. That he'd had the temerity to come to her with it at all argued an insight he shouldn't have – but if he didn't acquaint her with 'the circumstance' in one second she'd tear his heart out. She'd struggled to find out on her own, without success.

'Representations were made and his sentence was mitigated to one of transportation to the colonies,' the Scotsman had said.

That was mitigation, was it? But it wasn't death. He was alive. Somewhere. She'd allowed herself to ask idly: 'Which colony?'

'It'll be the West Indies, but which one I do not know.'

She nodded a thank-you. Horrible little man: he was becoming familiar; he'd set up his shingle somewhere in Town and managed to worm his way into doing business for both Lemuel and Walpole so that his wig for ever bobbed up somewhere at gatherings she must attend.

She suspected him of at once gloating over her and pitying; he spoke of the 'representations' made on Guillaume's behalf as if he had made them. One of those who wanted a finger in every pie. But not mine, you mannikin; not mine.

At Westminster, the tipstaff regarded her with caution. 'No Mrs Baker with you today then, Lady Cecily? Only, see, Mr Dodington's white duffel coat was ruined. And the Scotch member, he's still complaining his eye smarts.'

A tap of her shoe on the marble floor of the lobby reminded the man of his duty, but as he led the way to the gallery, she saw his shoulders heaving: 'Right in the eye.'

He thought it *funny*.

Cecily was constantly amazed at how people mistook Dolly. Not only minions like this, aristocrats, too, forgave her behaviour as an example of rough but good-hearted, low-class, outspoken Englishness, the spirit that won their wars for them.

'*Un phénomène.* A *one*, is she not?' Lady Mary Wortley Montagu had said, after watching Dolly unblinkingly drink tea from her saucer.

'And thank God for only one.' But Cecily did not say so: a lady did not run down relations, however gross. She found no good heart in Dolly, merely an inability to recognize any imperative but self-indulgence. It blinded the woman to class so that she used Lady Mary's drawing room as below stairs. Below stairs she welcomed new servants with camaraderie, demanding their dismissal when they took advantage.

She was untameable, trusting nobody but herself and her brother – and only him, thought Cecily, because clinging to his coat-tails had dragged her from an early and impecunious widowhood to her present comfortable place in her sister-in-law's house.

The day's debate in the House, concerned with curbing the rash of small bubble companies floated to exploit the present madness for speculation, had attracted a large attendance for June. As Cecily took her seat fifteen feet above their heads the smell of the members' oranges, boot oil, hair powder and perspiration rose to meet her. What the air would be like if all 508 members of Parliament were crammed into this space of sixty feet by thirty ... but they never were nor would be. Below Cecily was a social range that spanned a half per cent of the population, voted into their seats by an electorate of 4 per cent. For the most part they were landed gentry who hunted in the autumn, entertained at Christmas and had better things to do during spring and summer than swelter in the Commons. In January and February perhaps ...

But today the Whigs' muster-masters had whipped in their hounds. There were some two hundred members present, most of them on the Whig benches, lolling to consider their spurred boots, some cracking nuts or sucking oranges, others whistling or talking. It was made difficult to hear the lonely speaker on his feet on the Tory side of the House, deliberately so. Sir William Shippen MP was a Jacobite, a declared opponent of the Hanoverian monarchy and Walpole.

He sat down. A Whig member stood up. Cecily composed her face into an attentive mask and prepared to doze with her eyes open. This was Lemuel's moment: she'd heard his speech rehearsed twice already and had been bored out of her wits both times.

The House wasn't waiting to be bored. The Speaker shouted, 'To order, to order,' at a stampede caused by members recalling an urgent appointment in the coffee room and hurrying to keep it.

An attack on him in the Tory press had once said of Sir Lemuel Potts: 'The honourable gentleman invariably acts as a Dinner Bell so quickly does the House empty when he starts to speak.' Dinner Bell he had been ever since, even to his own Whigs.

The top of his head, to which Cecily's sightless gaze was directed, was an embarrassment in itself. He persisted in a black frontless wig, combing his own, thinning, grey front hair, of which he was proud since he had none on his crown, back over it and blending the two with bear's grease, giving him the appearance of an ageing, foppish badger.

His tailor had persuaded him that his figure, which was tall but stooping, suited the martial style, and dressed him in a red coat braced so stiffly in its skirt that, when he walked, his arms swung at an unreasonable distance from his sides. His behaviour with his cane – he was brandishing it with one hand now, his notes in the other – had been invented by himself and included such a variety of actions that it was unsafe to sit within several feet of him.

Cecily's attempts to send him to Weatherfield for his coats and Mazzini for his wigs had resulted in a kindly: 'Permit me to know what is suitable for a man in my position, my dear.'

It was difficult to argue: such stubbornness and refusal to recognize how ludicrous he was had, indeed, taken him from Cheapside clerk to the status of MP and landed baronet.

That and his marriage to herself, of course. And an inexhaustible capacity for doing what Walpole told him. Walpole, the coming man.

The same Tory paper that labelled him Dinner Bell had published a cartoon depicting an arched and tiny Lemuel Potts being used as a boot-scraper by a giant Walpole. The balloon issuing from its mouth read: 'Anything to oblige, Sir Robert.'

Whether Lemuel had seen it, Cecily didn't know. Probably he'd not have been displeased if he had: to be Walpole's slave was not only his means of advancement but his joy.

He'd served the man first as a minor clerk in the Treasury, then as chief clerk, then in the House itself, fetching and carrying, bringing messages and whispers to and from members, telling his master whose vote could be relied on for which particular question.

By giving this useful dog a bone, Walpole had provided the House with another loyal Whig MP and increased the dog's usefulness.

And Lemuel's bone had been colossal – a baronetcy, Cecily's fortune and land, which carried with it the parliamentary seat of Hempens, and Cecily herself, forty years younger than he was.

In return, he thought and spoke and voted as Walpole wanted.

There was silence in the Chamber. Cecily blinked. Was it over? No, her husband was merely glancing for approval from his master on the front bench to one side of him. Walpole was still there. The man's huge frame was stretched out, his hat over his eyes, his fat red cheeks displaying the country-bred health so disappointing to Cecily who daily prayed that he would die.

My life is passing.

She was having one of her panics. Nausea suffused her stomach and throat. How have I offended Thee? Put the clock back, O God. Stop the coach. Another chance, Lord.

Lemuel droned on. He'd reached the bit about the Riot Act. What it had to do with anything, she didn't know.

Neither, it seemed, did Walpole. He stretched out a hand to catch Lemuel's cane as it swung. 'The Riot Act? My dear friend, the Riot Act? No need to read it. The mob is already dispersed.'

Smiling weakly, Lemuel looked about the near-empty chamber, gave a bow and sat down.

She followed him out to the coffee room. He was protesting to Shippen: 'You should not rub Sir Robert so hard, Sir William.'

'But I should, Sir Lemuel. It is for his benefit. The more ministers are rubbed, the brighter they be.'

'In that case,' said Walpole, coming up, 'I am the brightest minister that ever was.' He bowed to Cecily, snatching her hand and kissing it. 'And how does my freshest primrose?'

His primrose gave a barely perceptible nod.

As usual, he radiated fresh-air heartiness, as if he'd just come from ploughing a furrow because his ploughman could not do it as well. His accent was still Norfolk's; he was everyman's countryman, the essence of rural England. But the hand that enveloped hers was as soft as her own.

He turned to his acolyte. 'And no bud on our primrose yet?'

'Any moment, Sir Robert.' Lemuel's voice rose to a tremolo of gratification. 'We try hard, we try hard.'

'Plant deeper, Lemuel, that's the way of it. Plant deeper.' His eyes were on Cecily's, to involve her in his own sexuality. She stared back at him. *You overgrown hog.* She had abased herself to this man, pleaded, clung to his ankles.

Given his master's permission to be coarse, Lemuel expanded on the theme of his and Cecily's marital doings, his cane going in all directions, as if the two of them romped the nights away in physical bliss. William Shippen moved off, embarrassed.

Lemuel knew no better, an ironmonger's son. He was being manipulated so that Walpole could encompass her in some perverse liaison; that lustful man. He was the supreme manipulator. With Parliament, the source of the King's money supply, eating out of his hand he'd not only purchased George's dependence, he'd made him enjoy the sale. Despite the King's lack of English and Walpole's ignorance of German or French, they'd become two bluff fellows together, calling their mutual greed 'being practical', sharing lavatory jokes, winking at each other when they talked women – all in dog Latin.

Finding the Princess of Wales cleverer than her husband and father-in-law put together, Walpole had conquered her too, and through her the Prince of Wales, playing the honest countryman still, but cultured this time, interested in art, children. Caroline had adored him.

How does he do it? Studying the humorous, beefy face, Cecily could see no sign of the artifice that lay behind it. His gift lay in giving any utterance the ring of common sense. He could suggest the House paint itself with woad and make it seem the practical thing to do.

His platform was peace; keep England out of war. Admirable, of course, and popular, though Cecily suspected his concern to be less for the lives of English soldiers, or even the country's good, than for maintaining a stability by which its landed squire-achy and City men and, naturally, Walpole himself could line their pockets.

Marvellously, the general perception of him was of his own invention: if it was favourable to Walpole, it was favourable to England. Bridge between King and Parliament, amiable, watch-ful giant from a Golden Age where sun-browned peasants paused their harvesting to salute the carriages of their kindly, wealthy masters.

When he'd blackmailed her into marrying Lemuel he'd exuded patriotic, fatherly concern. 'For your own sake, maid. And your cousin's, and the country's. Thee'll see it in time. He's a good man is Lemuel Potts.'

She supposed he was. There was no evil in Lemuel, just mind-withering silliness. Look at him now. Still bleating his is-she-not-beautifuls, such-a-lucky-man-as-I-ams and expect-good-news-any-days.

The risk he took. He depended on her not to give away the truth, not to cut through the male babble of this coffee-stained, tobacco-smoked room with the shout: 'The old fool's impotent.'

She wouldn't *because* he trusted her, because for better for worse she was now Lady Cecily Potts and the old fool's dignity, such as it was, had become her own. She wouldn't because of Walpole. Because of Pope and all the rest who found pleasure in her downfall. They'd trussed the calf on their altar, but she'd be damned if she'd give them the satisfaction of hearing it bawl.

Walpole was becoming restive at her aloofness. He put his huge face close to Cecily's under the pretence of studying it. She smelt wine. 'Where's our lady's patch?'

'My lady refuses paint, powder or patch, Sir Robert,' Lemuel apologized with a touch of pride. 'She leaves her skin as God intended.'

Another example of his silliness: if God had intended women's complexions to be shiny He wouldn't have invented French talcum mines. For Lemuel's sake she couldn't proclaim her Tory sympathies by wearing a patch on the left cheek, but damned if she'd be tricked out as a Whiggamore by wearing one on the right.

Just before the members returned for the division, Sir Lemuel said uncertainly: 'They wavered a little today, Sir Robert.'

South Sea shares again, she supposed. Lemuel was obsessed with their price and employed runners to bring him hourly accounts of it.

Walpole's hand crashed into his back. 'Where's your faith, my lad? I've subscribed to more stock myself this very day.' He grinned at Lemuel. 'And tomorrow I'm for Houghton. Will ye dine Wednesday?'

It was Cecily's misfortune that her estate of Hempens was a bit west of King's Lynn, Walpole's borough seat in the Commons, and less than a day's ride from Houghton, the Walpoles' Norfolk home.

In giving Lemuel Cecily, and therefore Hempens, Walpole had strengthened the Whigs' control of the area and at the same time made Lemuel his neighbour.

For Sir Robert to put the invitation in the form of a question was rhetorical. They had, in fact, planned to go to Cecily's manor in Surrey. Now, at Walpole's intervention, there was an instant change of direction. Lemuel said: 'Of course, of course, Sir Robert. Thank ee.'

'*You* may dine at Houghton, Lemuel,' said Cecily. 'I shall not.' It was her sticking point. She'd been forced into a marriage, she'd been defrauded and dishonoured. What she would not do was grace the author of these humiliations.

'Eh? What's this?'

'I am otherwise engaged,' she said.

'Are you, my dear?' Lemuel dithered. 'How?'

She met Walpole's eye. 'Otherwise.'

As it turned out, the next morning Cecily was given a legitimate excuse not to go into the country at all, though it was one she would rather not have had, in a note from Lady Catherine Jones.

She took it into the dining room where Lemuel was urging the household into a frenzy of packing. 'I shall not be accompanying you, Sir Lemuel. Mrs Astell is ill.'

'That old foolospher.' Dolly was filling a box with plate.

'But, my dear, my dear . . .' Lemuel saw the tilt of his wife's jaw and stopped protesting. 'You will join us later, I hope?'

'When she's better.'

Appallingly, Dolly wondered whether she, too, should not stay behind: she was a townswoman through and through. 'I hate Hempens. All birds and quiet and them stinking bogs.'

'Fens, Dolly,' Cecily said. 'They are tidal fens. Surely you will not pass up dinner with Sir Robert?'

'There's that,' her sister-in-law admitted. 'Lays on good vittles, does Sir Rob. An' he's a lad.' She winked. Dolly flirted outrageously with Walpole, convinced he fancied her person.

And he probably does, thought Cecily. She stood on the steps to see them off. It was months since she'd seen Hempens and she ached for it, but to visit it in company with her husband and sister-in-law was like watching children in hob-nail boots caper on rare, ancient mosaic.

Of all her estates, Hempens was the smallest and most impoverished and held most of Cecily's heart and history. Her nickname among the Maids of Honour had been 'The Wake' from her family's claim of descent from the great Hereward, he who'd carried on England's fight against William the Conqueror after all other Saxons had surrendered. Whenever circumstances became too hot for them in the outside world, generations of Fitzhenrys had taken to their island on the fen-edge to lie low, unpursuable and unbetrayed, until things cooled down and their enemies went away.

One quarter on Cecily's coat of arms gratefully featured a bittern, that hider in the reeds.

Fitzhenry tradition had it that an admiring Conqueror had married the Wake's daughter to one of his own men, Rollo the Dapifer, and it was a descendant of that union who had married

Geoffrey Fitzhenry, Henry II's only faithful, but bastard, son. The same tradition existed among the long-memoried fenlanders: kings came and went unheeded; it was the Fitzhenrys who ruled that secret area of England and even now, because Saxon custom allowed women right of ownership, in the fenlanders' mind Cecily was more their lord than the unknown George who sat on the throne in unknown London.

For her part, she was more at ease among those ill-favoured, web-footed men and women than with all the fashionable of Town. They were her people and she was embarrassed when they had to bear with Dolly's insults, keep their faces straight at Lemuel's attempt to play the squire, bring down birds with their ancient fowling-pieces and pretend it had been his shot.

The few with a vote had been bewildered by Lemuel's demand to cast it for him, a Whig. They had returned a Tory since voting began but, because he was Cecily's husband, they'd sent him to Parliament and Lemuel had said: 'See, my dear, what a few casks of free ale can do.'

As a girl she'd spent hours at the top of the Lantern, Hempens' little lighthouse, watching the sea, weaving a beleaguering dragon around the base of the tower and concocting the hero who would one day come-a-sailing to the island to rescue her from it; brave, of course, tall, handsome ... but she'd never been able to limn his face.

It certainly hadn't been Lemuel's.

Time and again since her marriage, she'd remembered that pubescent dream with bitterness. *What fools ye young girls be.*

Well, Cecily thought, as she watched the coach wobble round the corner of Spring Gardens and out of sight, with luck, Dolly will drown in the mere. 'Free,' she said. Upstairs in her bedroom, she shut the door and twirled towards the powder room. 'Free,' she shouted at Lemuel's empty wig-stand, 'free,' as she dragged a pillow off their bed and kicked it.

Of such transitory, petty liberties was her life made up; they enabled her to keep going, like a drunk making from chair to chair to cross a room.

On her wedding night she'd made a prepared and dignified

speech to her husband: 'You know I come to this marriage unwilling, Sir Lemuel. You possess my lands and my fortune, I do not expect you also to possess my person. I shall be a loyal wife in all matters but this.'

Even if he'd been a sensible man his blue-veined legs would have been too much for her. As for the tasselled Turkish night-cap . . .

He took her declaration for the timidity of a virgin. She hadn't yet learned his greatest strength: he saw things as he wanted them to be.

'I understand your nervousness, my dear lady, but I shall be tender. I have experience in the arts of love.' He'd been married before, to a shopkeeper's daughter who'd given him four children, none of whom had survived the age of twelve.

'Your arts will not be needed here. Not tonight, nor any night,' and she'd retired to bed in her dressing room. But another of her husband's strengths, she discovered, was perseverance. He insisted with a persistence and ardour that could almost have been rape. However, with what she regarded as the grace of God, his firm stand on his marital rights did not extend to anywhere else. There were protests on her part, much puffing and blasphemy on his, but in the end he penetrated her body no more than her mind.

He didn't apologize either for insistence or impotence. Instead, in the morning, he was smug, as if they'd achieved perfect union.

She came to think he believed they had, that by every morning some alchemy had altered his perception of the night before and gilded it. Adding to horror, he winked and beamed at every acquaintance, especially Walpole, as if he were invested with the prowess of a bull.

It was lesser inflictions such as that, such as Dolly, slapped on her like mortar, cementing the greater awfulness of the marriage itself more closely, that had very nearly crushed her.

She couldn't eat and became ill, missing Sophie's wedding – though, in many ways, it was a relief that she didn't have to encounter her former friends.

Lemuel for once listened to good advice and called in the

only physician who could have saved her. Dr John Arbuthnot, formerly a royal doctor, had treated Cecily's childhood ailments. Like all Queen Anne's courtiers, he blamed Walpole and the Whigs for the loss of his position under George.

He sent everybody from her room. He didn't take her pulse or look at the pot of her urine which Dolly had put out for him to sniff, but sat on the bed and told her straight out that she was dying ... 'from an affliction known as Walpole poisoning. How and why did the Whiggamore bastard marry ye to this gawk?'

Cecily shook her head. Arbuthnot still kept in contact with Society; if he didn't know her connection with Lord Keltie's escape, she wasn't going to tell him.

'Walpole poisoning,' continued the doctor, 'is fatal to those without courage or spirit. As in this case.'

'I'm too tired.'

'Ye're too proud. You always were. For whatever his reason, and for his own betterment if I know the man, Walpole's rolled you in the midden and you'd rather sink than stand. That's my diagnosis. Good God, girl, the world still spins. And, though maybe I shouldn't say it, ye've more years in which to watch it do so than has Lemuel Potts.'

'I know what you're doing, old leech,' she said, 'but I can't.' She turned her head away from him.

He sat on by the bed, watching her. He knew his Cecily.

I can't rally, she thought, there's nothing to rally for. Walpole has murdered me, he might as well put me in my coffin.

She could hear the mourners. Poor Lady Cecily, so young, once so promising. And Dolly standing, smirking, by the grave-side. *Wearing my clothes.*

At that Cecily had sat up in bed. Was it for this that Hereward had held out against the Normans?

If, somewhere, her beloved was enduring the humiliation of slavery, then so could she. *Give me my Romeo: and, when he shall die, take him and cut him out in little stars.*

The doctor was right: Lemuel was an old man. Her sentence was lighter than Guillaume's: his was for life, whereas hers had a term.

She was Lady Cecily Fitzhenry: she would live on – if only to spite Dolly.

So she did. It was a more remote, sterner Lady Cecily who arose from that bed. On the nights when Lemuel shared it with her – they became fewer – she tried to blank her mind and anaesthetize her body, not only to combat revulsion but in order to empty both of the memory of Guillaume Fraser's touch.

Remembrance of that was kept for the luxury of when she was alone, for when Lemuel went from home, which, thank God, thank God, was today.

Her bags packed, she left the house in Spring Gardens and was driven to Mary Astell's cottage in Chelsea. Which was where she became a Jacobite spy.

CHAPTER FOUR

CECILY WAS MET at the door of Mary Astell's Tudor cottage by Lady Catherine Jones. 'Thank the Lord you've come. Can you stay?'

'Of course. How is she?'

Lady Catherine put a finger to her lips, tiptoed Cecily past the stairs into the book-crammed parlour and shut the door. 'She's had the breast removed. The surgeon said he'd never seen such endurance. *Quelle femme*. She refused to let us hold her down nor made a sound.'

'Will that cure it?'

'We must pray that it will.' She was only a few years younger than Mrs Astell, but whereas Mary looked her age, Lady Catherine retained the fine-boned delicacy that asceticism and breeding had given her. Today, however, her face was gaunt. Having been instructed in which remedies must be applied, Cecily packed her off to get some sleep; she owned a large Stuart mansion further along the road.

The Astell cottage was the smallest of the residences that lined this part of the Thames; Chelsea had become fashionable and, although it was still a village bound by the river on one side and pasture on the others, Society was beginning to buy up such land as was available. Mary Astell had been offered a large price for hers but had refused, saying she could not lose the view.

Cecily stood for a few moments at the window to look out on it, sniffing the memories the parlour held in its store of books and the acrid bunches of elder and wormwood which Mrs Astell hung from the beams to repel flies, watching the river through the railings which bounded the other side of the cow-patted road. The railings were new: no longer could a stag, escaping from the Battersea Hunt, swim the river and leap up the bank from the beach to find sanctuary in the woods behind Mary's garden, as one had, disrupting the lesson of the small Cecily, Anne and Sophie who had sat in this room.

It had been a history lesson, if she remembered right . . .

'Now then, young ladies, do we believe that Richard III killed his nephews in the Tower?'

'No,' said Cecily, defending her Plantagenet blood.

'And why not, Lady Cecily?'

'Because he didn't.'

It wasn't good enough. She, Anne and Sophie had to study Holinshed's Chronicles and compare those with Buck's vindication. They acted Shakespeare's *Richard the Third* with a cast of four before setting it in context both with Richard's time and with the age in which it was written. They'd come to no definite conclusion on Richard's guilt, nor did Mary Astell give them any, but this and other examples had taught them that a saint could be depicted as a villain, a bloody conquest as liberation – or vice versa – depending on the political leaning of the historian.

Pope had once remarked to her of the pupils in Mrs Astell's tiny academy: 'An Englishwoman, you, a Scotswoman, Miss Insh, and an Irishwoman, the Hon. Sophie – you were the makings of a joke.'

But only we three know just how great a joke it was.

When Queen Anne had seen fit to entrust her ward's education to Mary Astell, Lords Breffny and Keltie had followed suit, thinking themselves daring in boarding their daughters to school instead of educating them at home but considering it would advantage their girls to know something of the classics, as well as music and needlework, like the daughters of damned nonconformists did. Wasn't Mrs Mary Astell an acknowledged scholar, for a woman? And a good Tory? Wouldn't it help the girls to an even greater marriage? They'd thought no further.

Smiling, Cecily left the window and climbed the angled staircase to tend to the greatest revolutionary of the age.

Mary Astell was asleep, her hair in neat plaits, her plump face yellow-grey against the pillow. With its narrow bed, a *prie-dieu* and a linen press, the room was as sparse and clean as a nun's.

Cecily settled herself on a stool by the bed. *Compared to you, little woman, Cromwell was a stick-in-the-mud and Guy Fawkes a pillar of convention.* Levellers, Diggers had only tried to turn the world upside down; Mary Astell cored it like an apple. The centre on which it had spun so far, she said, was rotten. There was no divine rule that men should govern women, it was merely an arrangement that suited them. Women and men should be partners, not ruled and ruler.

At first her teaching had been unexceptionable. They learned no Latin or Greek for Mary Astell had none, so they read Homer, Xenophon, Virgil, Cato, and Caesar's commentaries in translation, without the weariness of labouring through the originals as boys had to.

Botany studies were conducted on walks along the hedgerows and water-meadows of Chelsea, herbal lore in Mrs Astell's Elizabethan garden, deportment from graceful tea-times at the house of Lady Catherine Jones or that of Lady Mary Wortley Montagu.

Only gradually, as they grew older, did they realize that they were being taught to question the status quo.

Men, said Mary Astell, gave themselves a superior education and women little or none. And then blamed women for ignorance. 'Too often we appear silly,' she told them, 'but even while men castigate us for being foolish, they cajole us into more foolishness that they may seem more masterful. Have not their vast minds laid kingdoms waste?'

She looked at Sophie when she said: 'Men who try to woo

you by praising your incompetence are false lovers. Their words are but deceitful flatteries to keep you from obtaining those very qualities that could make you admirable and strong.'

They recognized the circumstance. The muffed throw in Dutch pins, the arrow flying wide of the target, being outrun and therefore caught by a boy in May Day games, these instances were chaffed at by Anne's brother and his friends at house parties.

But where was the harm? Chaffing was better than exclusion. And as for being outrun – one *wanted* to be caught. Often, one pretended vapidity for the sake of that warm, male laugh.

You didn't secure a boy's attention by a dissertation on the Beatitudes: Cecily had tried it and knew. Better to pretend: 'Are those the Surrey Beatitudes? Related to the Copelands?' Thus gaining the epithet 'delightful' and being drawn into the dance.

'I don't wish to be strong. I don't want to carry *my* husband over the threshold,' said Sophie. 'And I'm too pretty to be a virgin, everybody says so.' She may have missed the point, but in one sense she spoke for the three, who all dreamed that the outcome of the marriage to be arranged for them would be tall, handsome and enveloping, though they were realistic enough to know it might not be.

'Yes, and your intended husband will say the same,' Mrs Astell told her. 'You will be flattered into becoming one he can entirely govern. You will be under his will, you will be his for life, and cannot quit his service, let him treat you how he will.'

She said something bewildering. She said: 'Do not accept the male version of the universe. I want for you the freedom and the power to decide for yourselves what is important.'

And the Cecily sitting now beside her teacher's bed thought: I'm beginning to. I didn't then.

Privately, the cousins had agreed that on the subject of the sexes they could learn nothing from Mary Astell who, like all ladies past nubility, assumed the title of Mrs but was a spinster, poor thing.

Nevertheless, they never betrayed her subversion, knowing that they would instantly have been taken away: they feared she might be burned for a witch. Though she had lunatic ideas, they were invigorating. The girls found themselves secretly light: they had the sense that Newton's Gravity went up instead of down, a nonsense law that nevertheless pulled them out towards new stars.

Nor did they betray the dawning realization that Mrs Astell adored Lady Catherine Jones in a way no woman should adore another.

'She's a Sappho, I'm sure that's what she is,' Sophie whispered, wide-eyed, as she reported to the others in their bedroom one night after sneaking a look at Mrs Astell's diary. 'You know, belongs to the isle of Lesban. *That*'s why she ain't married.'

'Lesbos,' said Cecily. 'You're right. Of course.'

They discussed but discarded the idea that she and Lady Catherine were physical lovers. Cecily's bed was nearest to Mrs Astell's bedroom and she never heard anyone else in it, though sometimes, through the intervening wall, had come the hiss of a scourge and the flap as it hit flesh, and the sound of weeping.

They were less shocked than the daughters of chapel-going dissenters would have been. They were from the class that didn't consider itself bound by the petty morality of the *bourgeois*; they knew that 'goings-on' were not restricted to couples of opposing sex. Had not dear Queen Anne's friendship with the Duchess of Marlborough been *extremely* close before it degenerated into animosity?

Cecily would have liked to talk to her guardian about Mrs Astell, convinced that the Queen would not have been surprised by her teaching, had even procured her as tutor to Cecily because of it. But by then Anne had begun her slow decline and was too harassed by her ministers to see her ward more than once a year.

According to Lady Mary Wortley Montagu, the Queen, when a Princess, had wanted to endow with £10,000 an academy for girls which her friend, Mrs Astell, intended to set up. The project had been stopped on the grounds that it smacked of popery and convents.

With all this, there was not a hint of impropriety in their teacher's dealings with them, no breath of unnatural affection.

Her only passion was for the expansion of their minds and that passion so selfless, so ferocious, they had sense enough to be grateful. 'You are fortunate young women,' Lady Mary told them, 'but I beg you to guard your learning with as much care as you would hide a crooked leg. Learning in a woman is a deformity.'

Sophie was too young, too flighty, and Anne too dependent on her father's love for either of them to accept Mary Astell's strictures against Society as anything more than eccentricity. For Cecily alone the tuition went deeper, although it wasn't for many years that she realized that the unconventionality of her response to disaster, her ability to survive it, was grounded in Mary Astell's questioning of the world according to men.

Even now, in the marital desert in which Cecily found herself, she was able to draw sustenance from the secret well of philosophy and poetry which Mrs Astell had created for her. Without it and without her pride she would have become sourer than she was, would have bickered like a fishwife with Dolly, would have treated Lemuel with open contempt instead of polite reserve, and generally deteriorated into spite.

What it did not do was slake her hatred of Walpole ...

'Don't, oh, my dear, don't,' said a voice from the bed. Mrs Astell was weeping.

'What is it? Are you hurting?'

'"O for a falconer's voice",' cried Mary Astell, "to lure this tassel-gentle back again." And you were. So gentle, so gay. I beg you not to ruin your life.'

Cecily stretched her lips to a smile. 'I am resigned, I assure you.'

'Are you? At that moment you had the look of an assassin.'

'Nonsense,' Cecily said again. 'It is you who are the patient. We must dress that wound, Lady Catherine says, and then it will be time for supper. I have buttered shrimps and some of Louis's best meringues.'

The wound was appalling but Dr Arbuthnot, another neighbour, said that if Mrs Astell had survived its infliction she could survive its healing. They kept her in bed by allowing her books and by promising that, if she took her medicines and ate her meals, she could resume worship at St Luke's in three Sundays' time.

The difficulty was the visits of her anxious friends. Half Chelsea came to inquire after Mrs Astell's health and, in order that she should keep it, Lady Catherine and Cecily had firmly to curtail the visits of neighbours such as Dean Swift, Bishop Atterbury, Lord and Lady Cheyne, the naughty Duchess of Mazarin and Sir Hans Sloane.

So it was that the two men calling themselves Sir Spender Dick and Mr Arthur Maskelyne, arriving on the doorstep late one evening, found themselves bustled upstairs by a brusque and weary Cecily and told they had a quarter of an hour with Mrs Astell, no more.

To judge by the laughter when she went to fetch them, Mary Astell had enjoyed the fifteen minutes, but as her visitors descended the stairs, she called Cecily back from the door: 'Who were those delightful gentlemen?'

'You don't know them?' She hurried downstairs to count the spoons. The men were waiting for her. 'Who are you?' Cecily demanded. In the dark hall their figures were intimidating; she subdued an impulse to call the watch. 'Mrs Astell tells me she is not acquainted with you.'

'An omission it has been charming to rectify,' said the larger shadow, 'but, indeed, had we been given time to explain – the fault, of course, was ours, the lateness of the hour, your most natural mistake – we should have presented our business as lying with Lady Cecily Potts, if you are she, which, to judge by a beauty that is become legendary . . .'

'It's about Guillaume Fraser,' said the smaller shadow.

She seemed to be standing dumb before them yet she could not have been because, next moment, they were facing her in the parlour.

They were no more extraordinary than other visitors to the cottage. Sir Spender was large and florid, like his sentences, Maskelyne medium-sized and unexceptional. But she could not type them. Such adventurers as Lady Cecily knew were part of the establishment, already at ease in it and intent on flying higher. These two came from another place entirely. Gentlemen, perhaps: Sir Spender's accent was cultured, his clothes opulent, while Maskelyne dressed to pass in the crowd. Adventurers, certainly – there was a slant to their eye – but in what she could not guess. Grub Street possibly. Their linen was not laundered but it was the fashion among high Tories to distinguish themselves from Puritan rabble by wearing their neckcloths grubby; she could forgive them that.

She would forgive them anything if they would give her news of Guillaume. 'Fraser?' she inquired, attempting calm.

Maskelyne took up a position by the window and produced a pair of dice which he kept flipping in the air and catching on the back of his hand. It was Sir Spender who answered her. 'I cry you mercy for my friend's abruptness, Lady Cecily. He has been immured four years in Edinburgh Castle for his beliefs and has not yet reaccustomed himself to gentle converse . . .'

Cecily's foot began to tap. Sir Spender bowed to it.

'The person he has just mentioned *and need not mention again* . . .' here Sir Spender narrowed his eyes at his companion '. . . is a young gentleman we believe you once encountered in a place it is again unnecessary to name. A brave young lord who suffered in a cause to which – do I go too far? – all in this room are sympathetic.'

What was in the room was silence. Maskelyne's hand closed on his dice and stayed still. It was the moment when the archer's knuckles go white as he pulls back bowstring and arrow. *Caution*, screamed Cecily at herself. She said nothing.

Sir Spender smiled and nodded as if she had. 'Our young lord, true to his brave nature, assisted in the escape of his commanding officer, an escape which – you will understand me, Lady Cecily – reflected the nobility and courage of all concerned in it and . . .'

Blackmail, she decided. 'I am too weary to go round the mulberry bush, Sir Spender, or whatever you call yourself,' she said. 'If you cannot state your business you must go.'

'Wait, will you.' It came from Maskelyne at the window. She was taken aback by its sharpness.

Sir Spender struck his forehead with the heel of his hand. 'What fools we mortals be. Maskelyne, we are bumpkins. We have approached Lady Cecily backtofore and small wonder she suspects us.' He delved into the breast of his coat and produced a letter which he waved in circles several times before handing it over. 'My bona fides, madam.'

The seal was Viscount Bolingbroke's, instant reassurance. Her godfather, her father's dearest friend who, even though exiled, had written to her every year on her birthday. The address was La Source, Orléans, France.

'My dearest young Wake,' it read. 'May I introduce Sir Spender Dick? Between you and me the man is a rascal but one who has ever been faithful to me and those I love. If you can help him, do so, for my sake. If he can help you, use him, for your own.

'Could I but send an enchanted boat to England, you should cross the water and sail up the Loire in a trice, to land in my park where you would find the tenderest welcome, dear god-daughter. Yet our next meeting may necessitate fewer miles for you and take place sooner than you anticipate.'

His image streaked across her memory and was gone, leaving a brilliant comet's tail. A flickering man: Queen Anne's Secretary of State one day, loyal adherent of the Pretender the next, defector from the Jacobite cause the day after. Who knew what he was now? *I don't care.* Henry St John, Viscount Bolingbroke, had a pedigree nearly as long as her own. She trusted blood not politics. He was one of Us.

Sir Spender Dick was watching her. '*C'est mieux, Madame?*'

She nodded. 'But what has it to do with Mr Fraser?'

'You shall hear the story.'

She sat them down. As much for herself as the men, she fetched the claret she had brought with her for medicinal purposes; she was on edge and stories told by Sir Spender seemed likely to be extended.

What it boiled down to was that after her uncle's departure from Edinburgh Castle, Guillaume had been returned to the common prison where the less noble Jacobite rebels were confined. There, he had encountered Maskelyne to whom he'd confided how and with whose assistance the escape had been managed.

'I don't believe that to begin with,' Cecily said. 'The person to whom we refer would not bandy a lady's name in such a place.' She'd been given no bona fides for Maskelyne; she didn't like him.

His voice came from the window. 'I know it, though, don't I?'

The Castle governor knew it, she thought. So did some of the warders. Guillaume, Guillaume, you would not have gossiped of me.

'However it was,' said Sir Spender, hastily, 'Maskelyne shares your concern for this person and has instituted a search for him.'

'Has he found him?' asked Cecily casually. She was a married woman: she must not show eagerness. Every instinct was urging her to caution. But she had released a lock of hair from her cap and was twirling it round a finger – a nervousness not lost on the men.

'We are on his trail, ma'am, on his trail,' Sir Spender said, 'though it lead us to the teeth of hell.'

'But where is he?'

'We hope to have news shortly. Information, Lady Cecily. Information is what turns the wheels of this sad world. You, for instance, may have information which will return England to the dignity she has lost. Information is what will bring us to wherever the brave young man has been taken.'

She was confused. 'How?'

Sir Spender leaned back, head turning as if he were regarding a painting. 'You see, Masky? Such directness. Did I not tell you Lady Cecily would be our friend? She can have as little love for our present masters as we, did I not say so?'

'Female coming up the path,' said Maskelyne.

In a second Sir Spender was out of his chair. 'We must pursue our conversation at a better time and in a more convenient place, ma'am,' he said. 'Shall we say tomorrow night? Across the river?' He indicated the letter in her hand. 'Sir Henry St John kindly rents us his hunting lodge but we are careful not to, er . . . overly burden the old gentleman's hospitality. May I suggest you come masked?'

He was urging her into the hall and she noticed that he and Maskelyne stood back so that the lantern in the porch did not shine on them when she opened the door.

Maskelyne was nearest her. 'And come alone,' said his voice in her ear. Then they had bowed to Lady Catherine and were gone.

'More friends?' asked Lady Catherine. 'I hope they have not tired her.' She went upstairs.

They tired me, and I'm not sure whose friends they are.

But the hook had been dangled, and taken, and the next night it pulled a masked Lady Cecily across the river towards Battersea to the ancient manor that was Viscount Bolingbroke's family home.

The waterman was confused: whores on their way to an assignation did not usually have so haughty an address, nor pay so well. He tried badinage but was told to keep his breath and pull, damn him.

His confusion was as nothing to Cecily's. Why am I going?

She had studied the memory of the conversation in the parlour like a lawyer perusing a witness's statement for every inference.

Her godfather was attempting to be received back into the country, so much was obvious from his letter.

When she was twelve Cecily had been allowed into the Visitors' Gallery at the House of Lords to hear Bolingbroke speak. What the speech had been about neither then nor now did she have any idea, but she'd been on her feet at the end of it, cheering, along with most of the noble lords. If he'd blown the trumpet call, she'd have enlisted.

She supposed he was calling now; she supposed she was enlisting.

Although in exile, attainted for high treason, he was the Whigs' terror; she'd once heard Walpole admit it. 'Iffen he can persuade the Pretender to turn Protestant, he'll be back in quicker'n hell will scorch my arse.'

But Bolingbroke hadn't persuaded the Pretender to turn Protestant, and he'd left him, as he'd left his own wife and his people and everybody else over the years. Walpole had wiped his fat face with relief. '*Now* the bastard's dead.'

But if any mortal can resurrect himself, you can, Cecily thought. And if I can help you to scorch Walpole's arse, I'll do it. And if it will release Guillaume I'll do anything.

Through four bitter years she had prayed to put the clock back so that she had never gone to Edinburgh, never met him. Loving him was the extra turn of the screw on the rack of her marriage. But if he, at least, can be released from *his* bondage . . . anything, I swear it.

Will you turn Jacobite spy? That, reflection had convinced her, was the sum of what the two rogues in Mrs Astell's parlour were asking. 'Information,' the large one had said. 'Information will lead us to him. You, for instance, may have information which will return England to the dignity she has lost.'

And what other information did she have than that which she learned as the wife of Sir Lemuel Potts, Whig MP and confidant of Sir Robert Walpole?

The realization had come to her in the early hours and she'd cried out. They had sought her out for this. For this terrible thing. For the most intimate and blackest of betrayals.

For the rest of the night she struggled in the sticking web. Whom would she betray? A husband who'd been forced on her?

A husband nevertheless. Fidelity is expected.

But by what right? Did they buy my soul as well as my body?

You'll betray England.

But James Stuart is England and a skidding sight more English than George of Hanover.

He's a Roman Catholic.

Who keeps Protestants in his employ, who has promised to preserve the Church of England.

No Fitzhenry ever betrayed his anointed king.

Who is my king? And, in any case, I can give you Sir Alfwege Fitzhenry in the Wars of the Roses and Long John Fitzhenry who went over to Cromwell and . . .

But can you demean yourself by associating with the likes of Sir Spender and Maskelyne?

Can I be more demeaned than I am as wife to Lemuel Potts? Sister-in-law to Dolly?

On and on it went until Mary's walking stick tapped the bedroom wall between them. 'Are you unwell, Cecily? I hear you moaning.'

'A bad dream, my dear. Go back to sleep.'

By the morning she'd been in no firmer mind.

Yet here she was ... and her eyes were gleaming through the holes of her mask. And the clunk of the oars as they moved against the rowlocks was like the slow beat of a drum. And the smell of the sea coming up the Thames on the breeze mixed with the scent of the apple blossom she could see in pale clouds on the Battersea bank. And light from the lantern on the prow of the boat wobbled on water that had carried a thousand escapers and even more adventurers to new shores.

For the truth was that Lady Cecily was not crossing her Rubicon solely for love of one man and hatred of another. She was twenty years old and the four of those years that she had spent as Lady Cecily Potts had not only been bitter and lonely but very, very, *very* dull.

She was highly nervous: she was about to mingle in a company that, if discovered, the authorities could, and would, delight in obliterating as a gardener pouring boiling water on an ants' nest. She expected passwords and cloaked figures huddled round a dark lantern. What she found was a house in the woods, the light and conversation within unconcealed, resembling in its activity a meeting house of one of the friendly societies beloved by the bourgeoisie.

It was an old hunting lodge. Cecily remembered hunting the surrounding Battersea forest with her godfather, wonderful chases, flecks of sweat on Blonde's neck, returns to the lodge and its awaiting tables set with food under the high and beautiful roof. Sir Henry, Bolingbroke's father, too old to hunt any more, had lent it to his exiled son's adherents.

A lounging and, in her view, far-too-lenient sentry let her pass at the mention of Sir Spender Dick. Inside, flambeaux burned in the holders providing light for men working at a printing press at one end of the room and women grouped together in the straw at another, needles and tongues busy over a large piece

61

of material. The buttonless black coat of a man who sat at a table making lists reminded her that a surprising number of Quakers were Jacobites.

A boy carrying a pile of flyers from the press dumped them on a bench. Cecily cricked her neck to look. At the top of the page was James Stuart's depiction as a sun-god, the handsome profile casting rays of light beneath which was the caption 'Advenit Ille Dies' (That day is coming). Underneath, a crude cartoon showed George I and von der Schulenberg romping on a bed bowing under their combined weight. There was a verse of the ballad:

> *He* does not make his Country poor
> Nor spend his Substance on a Whore,
> His loving Wife he does adore,
> For he is brisk and Lordly.

Definitely Jacobite. The contrast between the virtuous young Pretender's home life and George's was one exploited by James's followers.

Nobody questioned her. There was no sign of Sir Spender Dick nor of Maskelyne. The heat and noise in the hall drove her through the door opposite the one she'd entered to a lawn scattered with rustic chairs and beset with lanterns hung in the trees.

''Lo, Cessy,' said an arbour. 'What are you doing here?'

Cecily sighed. So much for disguise. She sat herself by Toby Ince, happy to find one of her own class. 'How did you know it was me?'

'The head, old soul. Nobody carries it like you. I've wondered if you'd be joining us Jacks one day.'

'What are *you* doing here?' Toby came from a long line of Lancastrian recusants but she'd not known him for an active Jacobite. He'd been a friend of Anne's brother at Oxford and had squired her to the occasional ball.

'Oh, must keep up with what's being plotted, ye know. And the pater sent me with some funds for the Cause, though he says if the Whigs keep on taxing Catholics like they do there won't be any more.'

'Are they plotting? This looks more like an apprentices' outing.'

'Plotting, all right. Big plot. Better you don't know.'

She was relieved. 'I'm glad one of you shows caution. Suppose a gamekeeper comes by? Won't he wonder what's going on?'

'Probably think it's an orgy. Wouldn't be the first in St John's grounds. Jacks have got to meet somewhere, Cessy. We're so scattered and our communication's hopeless. I never even knew the 'Fifteen was a starter until it was over.'

'Good job you didn't.'

There was a silence. She knew what he was going to ask her and tensed herself.

'Heard anything from Anne?' The question sounded idle.

'No,' she said, gently. 'But I heard from Sophie when she and her husband were in Paris. They met somebody who'd seen her at St-Germain.' She took his hand. 'Toby, she's become a nun.' After she'd read Sophie's letter, she'd laid Anne in the mental compartment where she kept things to hate Walpole for. Anne, who would have, should have, married – perhaps to this most suitable Toby who'd loved her. Anne, who'd wanted children.

After a while he said: 'I see.'

'I don't. How could she do such a thing? It was after her father died. I wrote to her brother asking for news but he didn't reply.'

It had been bitter to learn of her uncle's death soon after his escape to France. Unworthily, but frequently, the question had recurred: 'Why didn't he die sooner?' Anne would not then have been forced into exile, a traitor, nor she, Cecily, into marriage with Lemuel Potts.

Toby roused himself. 'I wrote too. He wrote back saying he'd cast her off. He's wriggling himself back into German George's favour, d'ye see, trying to regain the estate. Denounced his father's part in the 'Fifteen, his escape, everything. Won't have anything to do with a rebel sister.'

Damn the 'Fifteen, thought Cecily. So many people made barren. Anne, Guillaume, Toby here. Me.

She sat on, holding Toby's hand, watching moths hitting themselves against the glass of the lanterns.

The Quaker bustled up to them. He had a portable writing desk held by a leather strap round his neck, giving him the appearance of a pedlar. 'Art thee Cecily Fitzhenry, also called Potts?' he asked.

'I don't think they heard you in Chelsea,' she said. 'Perhaps you should say it louder.'

'She is,' said Toby.

The Quaker ticked a list. 'Thy title in the Cause shall hence-forth be Mrs Butcher.'

'It won't,' said Cecily with energy. '*Butcher*, indeed.'

'Put her down as Mrs Shakespeare,' Toby said. To Cecily he said: 'We've all got code names. Mine's Rowbotham, God help me.'

She spent much of the evening aimlessly following Toby around, listening to conversations that did nothing to reassure her about the Jacobites' efficiency as plotters.

'I say we march on the Bank of England first. Then the Tower, then the Exchange.'

'No, no. Tower first. Then the Bank of England. *Then* the Exchange. Er, where *is* the Exchange?'

She nudged Toby. 'Are they really planning to rise?'

'One day. When the time's ripe.'

She shook her head. If it was left to these incompetents the time would never ripen: they'd be rounded up by Walpole's agents long before. She felt nervous just to be in their company. And the way they bandied names around . . .

'Sir William Wyndham will lead it in the West Country, of course.'

'Of course. But he says it'll have to be after the harvest's in.'

Hopeless. And yet also innocent, so English in their amateur-ishness. (Cecily was typical of her countrymen in believing that stealth and deception were attributes that flourished more happily among foreigners.)

But if the *naïveté* was endearing, it was also dangerous, and she would have left the lodge then and there had it not been vital to her to learn how much progress Sir Spender had made along the trail that led to Guillaume Fraser.

*

64

He didn't put in an appearance until after midnight, and she was only alerted to it then because a disturbance broke out by the stairs and she saw him – brawling. Swords were out. Sir Spender was duelling with a thin man in grey and displaying an excellent command of oaths if not swordsmanship. Maskelyne defended his friend's back, swinging his rapier in a semi-circle, daring anyone to take him on. Nobody was.

It was Toby who, with ease, put up the two men's swords with his own. They seemed grateful for his intervention. He took Sir Spender off to a corner to cool down while others did the same for the man in grey.

'What was all that about?' Cecily asked, when Toby came back.

'Oh, Sir Spender wants Viscount Bolingbroke to take command of the Cause on his return. Mr Chalmers thinks Bolingbroke's a traitor who deserted once and might again.'

'Does this sort of thing happen often?'

'I'm afraid it does, rather. We're leaderless, you see.'

'It's hopeless, Toby.'

'No, it isn't.' His tone caused her to look up, to see he was nearly crying. 'We've got to keep the flame burning, Cessy. There'll be no good times until King James comes again.'

'You really believe that?'

'Give my life for it.' He swallowed. 'Sorry for the Enthusiasm.' Enthusiasm was the dirtiest word in upper-class vocabulary, applied to the rantings of Puritans and similar riff-raff, to hellfire sermons, sectarianism, praising-the-Lords, and other embarrassments.

They were summoned up the stairs to a gallery room where, to Cecily's relief, Sir Spender, Maskelyne and a few others were plotting nothing more seditious than their next news sheet which, as it turned out, was seditious enough.

'We must belabour the German rat,' a man in a bag wig was saying, 'tell the public how he murders his wife by keeping her in a Hanoverian dungeon that he may disport with his whores.'

At her place on a bench at the back of the room, Cecily's foot began to tap. She was curiously affronted. Sophia Dorothea *had* committed adultery, after all. And the 'dungeon' was the castle at Ahlden where, admittedly confined, she still managed to spend 18,000 *taler* a year. The King might be a usurper but he was no wife-murderer; indeed, it was in his interest to keep Sophia Dorothea alive since there was a widely believed prediction that her death would be closely followed by his own.

'Nominally, the poor female is Queen of Great Britain,' persisted the bag wig.

'They're divorced,' Cecily pointed out.

Maskelyne gave her a look that said: Who asked you?

'We are grateful for any contribution Mrs Um-shakespeare can make to our knowledge of court matters,' Sir Spender said, firmly.

Under cover of other conversation, Cecily whispered to Toby: 'Why does Maskelyne treat me as if I'd murdered his father?'

'Didn't have one,' Toby murmured back. 'I'm given to understand the man's a bastard, actual or figurative.'

The other purpose of the meeting, it transpired, was to gather news which could be of use to the Pretender, who now had no access to the larger, international scene since the death of his supporter Louis XIV and was wandering, homeless, in Italy. France, beaten to her knees, had perforce become an ally of England, and one of the conditions of the alliance was that she turned James off her soil.

Cecily's foot jittered faster as she listened to gossip considerably more ill-informed than the man whom it was meant to inform. One of the gathering presented an item that was supposed to throw light on the Government's policy towards Sweden and which, it seemed, had been garnered from Lord Townsend's footman. Another had been to the Channel Islands, where it was common knowledge that the young Louis XV was to be affianced to the Prince of Wales's daughter, Anne.

This caused excitement. A Protestant princess of England married to a Catholic.

Cecily's voice cut through the babble. 'I know for a fact,' she said, 'that young Louis will marry the Infanta of Spain.'

Walpole had entertained a dinner table at which she'd been present with this gobbet from his agents and had waxed coarse on the projected wedding of a boy aged ten to a two-year-old bride.

She was getting on the meeting's nerves, but Sir Spender Dick's eyes lit up like an angler who'd hooked a fish. 'She knows,' he said.

Downstairs, after the meeting, he said: 'It would be interesting, dear madam, to learn the details of the Quadruple Alliance, should you learn of them.'

'It would be more interesting to learn what has happened to Mr Fraser,' she said back.

He nodded. '*Touché*. But a thousand men were transported after the 'Fifteen and if records were kept they are sparse.'

She was suddenly weary. This large, overshadowing man was embroiling her in his game and returning nothing.

He saw her droop. 'No, no, no, no,' he reassured her. 'Maskelyne has already talked to a ship's captain who believes there was a Fraser on one of the boats headed for Barbados. The name is common among Scots, we know, but we have a sympathizer in Barbados and have sent inquiry. We must be patient. In the meantime, our hope lies in the restoration of King James which, in turn, will bring our lads home to us.'

It was said without his usual forced gallantry. It caught her off guard and brought tears to her eyes. She felt his hand pat hers. 'Despair not, madam. He is alive. You have it on the word of Spender Dick.'

A priest had entered the hall and the Jacobites were gathering round him on their knees. Cecily and Toby joined them.

The service was carefully œcumenical in view of the disparate religions represented by the hall's Jacobites, and the more touching for that. The priest prayed for King James III and those who had lost home, love and life through duty to him.

The concentrated silence in the lodge allowed in the sound of nightingales singing in the forest. A woman near Cecily was weeping. For the first time, Cecily had a sense of inclusion with the group. Others here had suffered loss. Guillaume, I'm so lonely for you. So lonely.

The material the women had embroidered hung on a wall behind the priest's head like a reredos, displaying the profile of

James Stuart and a caption echoing the Jacobite ballad, 'The Lost Lover'. If the needlework was crude, the words spoke to Cecily as if only now were she being given sympathy. These people grieved not only for their king but for Guillaume, for those who'd gone into captivity with him, for her. She was caressed by mutual understanding.

Instead of communion bread, a newly minted medal was put into the cupped hands of each of the congregation. Again, it showed the head of the Pretender.

'Cuius Est' asked the lettering around the obverse; at once 'Whose is it?' and 'He whose it is.' On the reverse was a map of Great Britain and Ireland and the word 'Reddite'. Restore.

Look at him to whom I belong, said the medal. Therefore give me back to him and unite the images on my sides. The King cannot regain his kingdoms alone. Help him. Awake, you brave, the barbarian invades us. Defend your mystical, Christ-like, anointed master.

Like a horn calling the fyrd from sleeping farmsteads, the legend of the medal summoned Britain to its ancient duty. It was Arthur's banner streaming from the hilltop of Baden, it was the moon of the Grail shining through dark ages.

And it spoke to Cecily and, through her, to a thousand Fitzhenrys. Are you to bend under the yoke of Walpoles? Be trodden under the boots of German kings? Become a Potts among Pottses? Enlist with me and this pathetic army around you and march out against the host of Whiggery. Better death than dishonour.

Above her head, somewhere in the gallery, a flute began to play. The tune was 'The Pipers of Strathdearn'.

Cecily heard it with little surprise. Here was confirmation. Her lover was lending his voice to a song which, however faint, was the sweet antiphon to the paeans of her humiliators. We Jacobites cannot be defeated; we have all the best tunes. The Whigs appeal to head and pocket, they cannot prevail against this oldest and deepest of mysteries.

One by one, the kneeling men and women around her kissed their medal as an oath of fealty to their absent king.

Cecily didn't. Against the unseen hands that dragged at her

emotions, she found herself holding back: they were demanding her total allegiance and a Fitzhenry didn't give it just for the asking. True, the night was filled with portents and luring, siren voices. But it was also full of bloody fools and she wasn't one of them.

Common sense insisted on knowing why she should risk her life for a Cause which was very pretty in its way but for which she'd felt no previous strong allegiance. Turn back, it said, romance is dangerous. You'll be betraying your country.

But romance had its own logic and questions. Betraying which country? The market-place that Walpole has made of England? Which sold you to the highest bidder? The country of Lemuel and Dolly Potts? Shall I walk away from here to that?

Oh, God, don't magic me. Give me a sign that has reason.

She stared down at the medal in her open palm, swaying her hand from left to right in the tension of decision. Light from a flambeau caught the lines of the long-featured face at an angle so that it more closely resembled that of a man she'd only seen by the flickering flame of a candle in a prison cell. *Guillaume.*

After all, there was no decision, dammit. You could only choose love. Cecily bent and kissed the profile of her lost lover and her king. She would go to war for them both.

Watching her from the shadows, Sir Spender Dick uttered a Nunc Dimittis. Landed.

CHAPTER FIVE

ENGLAND WAS SO peaceful that summer of 1720 that at the end of June King George felt safe in indulging himself with a visit to Hanover.

Walpole stayed on at Houghton, where his daughter Catherine was in a decline, and occupied himself by buying every available estate in the vicinity in order to strengthen his hold on the Norfolk vote.

Lemuel kept to Hempens, despite Dolly's protests, in order to be near Walpole.

Sir John Blount, the man behind the South Sea Company's flotation, went to Tunbridge Wells to take the waters. (Nobody was quite sure what the Company *did*. Blount talked impressively of a plan that involved exchanging Gibraltar for a rich section of Peru, but it didn't really matter: something wonderful would come from the South Seas. People still jostled to have a part of it, though, strangely, the Company's stock price was suddenly refusing to rise.)

Cecily returned to her house in Spring Gardens. She wrote to Lemuel, telling him that her absence from Hempens would continue: 'My patient is not yet recovered. Therefore, I am accompanying her to Lady Catherine Jones's castle in the Welsh mountains as a retreat from the summer's discomforts and infections.'

It was almost true. Mrs Astell's health was not making the progress her friends wished to see: mountain air was called for. But it was Lady Catherine Jones who accompanied Mary to Wales. Cecily delayed joining them for two weeks.

As if to gladden her husband's heart, she began issuing invitations to tea to such Whig ladies as still stayed in Town, among them pretty Maria Skerrett, Sir Robert Walpole's latest mistress. The ladies accepted with alacrity – the high-nosed bitch was paying them attention at last – to find their hostess flattering in her assumption that their knowledge of world affairs was as great as their husbands', or in Maria Skerrett's case, her lover's. Mostly it was.

After some of these gatherings, not all, Cecily wrapped herself in a cloak, tiptoed from Spring Gardens with stealth and at Charing Cross hired a sedan chair to take her to her destination – usually some dire alley off the City where the chair excited as much comment as a gold coach with trumpets – gave her name as 'Shakespeare' to the lounger at the door, climbed a rickety staircase and passed on her information to Spender Dick, large and florid, in the dingy room at its top.

The role of spy was invigorating. It gave her purpose and a delicious naughtiness. They think they've tamed Cecily Fitz-

70

henry? They can think again. She liked the risk entailed in these outings; even more did she enjoy the sense that she was fighting back. If her snippets of information advanced the Cause, good; if they brought forward the release of Guillaume Fraser, wonderful. But it has to be said that these were peripheral advantages: what she was basically doing was making rude gestures in the direction of Sir Robert Walpole's arse.

She had her own code of honour. Nothing Lemuel had mentioned to her in private was given to the Jacobite news-gatherers, however useful it might be to them. What the wives told her, or what could be elicited from other sources, was fair game. It was a fine and perhaps ridiculous distinction but it made her feel less of a Clytemnestra.

She didn't separate her new Jacobite conviction from her desire for personal revenge: the two were inextricably mixed in her mind. When she looked at her medal she saw Guillaume's face on it. When she pictured that poor, landless nomad, James Stuart, she saw her cousin Anne and her forced celibacy, her own lover slaving under a tropical sun, her blighted present and future.

By July the heat had driven everybody who was anybody out of London to the country. As Cecily prepared to leave for Wales – she was actually putting on her dust veil in her bedroom, ready for the journey – she received another visitor, this one uninvited.

'Mr Archibald Cameron, my lady.'

Damn, damn. 'What's *he* doing here?'

She loathed the man. Through being in charge of her during her journey in disgrace from Edinburgh to London it was as if he'd seen her naked. It was humiliating to keep encountering him now that he'd inveigled himself into Walpole's and Lemuel's business.

It disadvantaged her, too, that it was he who'd brought her the news that Guillaume had been sentenced to transportation rather than death. He'd paraded it as kindness, but it was gall and wormwood to her that he was aware she'd cherish the information. He *knew*.

Of all things, the most terrible to Cecily as Lemuel Potts's wife was pity. Not compassion, not the understanding she received from true friends like Mary Astell and Lady Mary Wortley Montagu, but pity mixed with satisfaction, the what-a-shame, the sighed: 'Poor soul, what does her breeding avail her now?', the shake of the head that said: 'Ah, looks and wealth are no defence against disaster.'

The thought that fashion, that Whigs especially, might use her condition as an Awful Warning while revelling in their own was intolerable. She almost literally had not been able to bear the glimpse in the faces of acquaintances, who'd once envied her, of how-the-mighty-are-fallen. It was why she allowed no trace of hurt on her own and took her gruel with apparent composure. They'd get no extra enjoyment from her pain to take back to their coffee houses.

It was into this category that she docketed Archibald Cameron: the jumped-up clerk sneered at her. She adjusted the veil over a face that had stiffened into impassivity and stared through it into the Florentine looking-glass. I look old. My youth is passing.

She swept down to the hall. 'Sir Lemuel is not here, Mr Cameron. And I am just leaving.'

The lawyer was staring, puzzled, at one of the busts. Cecily gnashed her teeth in chagrin. Lemuel had begun to buy art the moment he'd learned that Walpole was collecting paintings and statuary. She'd suggested he use William Kent as his buyer – Lemuel had the judgement of a lemming. But, with his usual permit-me-to-know-my-dear, he'd instead employed a trickster he'd met in a coffee house. Spizzini declared himself Italian and a painter. 'Newgate and inn-signs,' was Cecily's opinion.

'Now 'ere is a *magnifico*. Roman bust. I dig it up my own self at Pompeii.'

'Got it's head missing,' Dolly pointed out. 'My brother ain't buying *that*.'

Spizzini had hardly blinked. He found a Greek head in his pannier and cemented it on the bust. The result had pride of place in the hall. Dolly said it gave the place 'grander'.

'Sir Lemuel is not home,' repeated Cecily.

'Will he return this night?'

72

'No.' She was surprised, not for the first time, at how her memory shortened him: he was probably three or four inches taller than herself but his neatness and pedantry appropriated the epithet 'little man'. He'd learned to ape his betters in the matter of dress – on the journey to London he'd worn the outrageous best of some Lowland back-street tailor – and the ee-aw Glasgow accent had softened into something approaching English. The wig, however, was still fox-coloured. He said: 'Is he gone far, may I ask?'

'He is at our Norfolk home.'

'Oh, aye.' He seemed agitated. 'Could ye take him a letter frae me, Lady Potts?'

'Lady *Cecily*. I fear not. I shall not be seeing him yet.'

'Oh, aye.' Still he hesitated. At last he burst out: 'Lady Cecily, have ye no influence over your husband? I'm afflicted with concern that he's maybe too rash with his investment in the South Sea Company. It's a chancy business, looking e'en more chancy as the days pass, and I've told him so but he'll no heed me. I spiered, as it's your fortune too . . .' His fervour dwindled as he caught her eye.

'Mr Cameron,' Cecily said, 'Sir Lemuel's business is his own. As for my fortune, it is handled by three gentlemen, Colonel Brandling, Mr Phipps and Mr Tate, whose expertise in these matters I trust as, I am sure, does Sir Lemuel. I bid you good day.'

'Colonel Brandling . . .' he began, but Cecily was tinkling the bell for the footman to show him out.

The *vulgarity*. Had nobody told him one did not mention money to a lady?

Queen Anne had appointed the solidly impeccable Colonel Brandling, Mr Phipps and Mr Tate to handle Cecily's estate; they had seen to it that her yearly allowance was appropriate for her style. Occasionally they had asked her to sign documents concerned with rents, tenures, etc., all in such order that it didn't occur to her to question them.

When the lawyer had gone, Cecily set off for Wales. On the Great West Road her carriage passed that of Sir John Blount of the South Sea Company, returning unexpectedly from Bath.

Cecily waved. Sir John did not wave back: he appeared too preoccupied to see her.

In the veiled sunlight of coal-smoked London, the South Sea bubble that had floated so entrancingly, and so long, blurred and wobbled from the slightest of tremors, as if an earthquake in China had sent a vibration along a fault to disturb England's air. Sir John, somebody said, was selling. Selling his own shares. It was enough. The breath on which people told each other the rumour spread the contagion of panic.

By September, South Sea price had dropped to 135. King George was summoned back to reassure the stock-market but reports of the directors' dishonesty were too widespread. There was no El Dorado in the South Seas or, if there were, the Company hadn't found it.

The news was slow to climb the sheep-cropped slopes of the Brecon Beacons and Cecily remained untroubled by anything more than Lemuel's letters asking for her return before Parliament met for a new session. She arranged to meet him and Dolly on 1 October at Cambridge, where Lemuel hoped to address the students, before travelling on to London together.

At the inn she found Dolly packing. 'Where's Lemuel?'

'London. He had a message this morning. We're to follow him immediate.' Dolly looked accusingly at her sister-in-law. 'He's been very worried.'

'Indeed? His letters said nothing of it.'

'Mustn't upset Lady High-nose,' said Dolly.

'What has he been worrying about?'

'Don't know.' He hadn't confided in Dolly either.

They arrived in a London that looked much as usual, perhaps better, in the amber euphoria of an autumn evening, the low sun touching everything with slow, unreal contentment – the immigrant women still harvesting the fields along the Edgware Road, the murderess hanging from Tyburn's gallows, yoked maids returning with empty buckets to the milk-walks.

Crossing Hyde Park, a far-off roar coming from Whitehall told them a mob was rioting in the manner of mobs.

As the coachman helped her out to the steps of Spring

Gardens, Cecily saw Lemuel at an upstairs window, watching her. She waved to him while the second driver unloaded the boxes. He didn't move.

'He's rum,' said Dolly, joining her. 'What's a matter with him?'

Very slowly, still looking at Cecily, Lemuel raised his arm as if in valediction, then turned away.

The coachman was knocking on the front door for a footman to come and let them in. Dolly pushed him aside and began slamming the knocker. Cecily had packed her key: she scrabbled for it in her travelling case, scattering smallclothes over the steps, found it, and rammed it into the lock.

They heard the shot as the door opened.

Lemuel was in his powdering room. He'd left a note pinned to a wig stand but he'd fallen against it and blood mingled with its ink, rendering it unreadable. He was still alive.

'The ball will be lodged in the cerebrum's cortex,' said Dr Arbuthnot, interestedly, an hour later. 'He'll have put the pistol to his left temple but angled it too far upwards. If he'd pointed it straight, he'd be dead this minute. D'ye see the paralysis to the right side? The facial palsy? The cortex of the cerebrum, sure enough.'

'Why don't you *do* something? For God's sake, Dolly, stop screaming. Why don't you do something, damn you?'

'There's little enough to do.' Dr Arbuthnot crossed the room, hit Dolly across the face and helped her to a chair. Returning, he said: 'There's little enough *to* do. Keep him still. Keep the bandage dry. Reassure the poor fellow. If he lasts the night, he'll maybe see out his allotted span, God help him.'

As the doctor turned to leave, Cecily asked: 'What could have possessed him to do it?' He'd given the servants the day off. His face at the window had been a child's, lonely and afraid, waiting for the mother who would never come home.

'What's possessing men all over the city to do the same.'

She still didn't understand.

If there was a time for the Pretender to retrieve his crown it was now, while the Hanoverian throne rocked from the biggest explosion ever produced by the pricking of a bubble.

Revolution seemed likely: people raged against a government which had acquiesced in a plan that ruined them. And against a royal family – mistresses and all – which, as it turned out, had accepted bribes from the South Sea Company, as had ministers and MPs.

Editorials called for the directors to be hanged and said, if they weren't, the defrauded might do it themselves. Mobs attacked culprits' coaches. Lord Lonsdale, who'd speculated disastrously, tried to stab the arch-villain, Sir John Blount. Not only the high but the low had paid heavily for now worthless bits of paper; some too heavily. Suicides took place in garrets and in mansions, overcrowded lunatic asylums had to shut their doors against the lines of broken, staring men and women who were guided to them.

Eight days after Lemuel's attempt at suicide, in a counting house just off Threadneedle Street, Lady Cecily Fitzhenry put her fingertips carefully on the documents she'd been examining and raised her head: 'I don't understand. Everything?'

'Everything,' said Colonel Brandling. Mr Tate began his long explanation all over again, but she kept her eyes on Brandling. He'd been stout in all senses; the essential country-gentleman-in-the-City Tory. She remembered him galloping beside Queen Anne's hunting carriage as it jolted through Windsor Park, waving the stump of an arm he'd lost at Ramillies, hallooing. Now, he seemed to have shrunk inside his clothes. His eyes stared back at her from under fronded eyebrows with the tranquillity of despair.

She leaned forward and shook him by the stock round his neck. 'How can it be everything? It can't be everything. Surrey? What of the Cheapside tenements? The farms? Dorset. What about Dorset?'

'Lady Cecily. I beg you.' Mr Tate disentangled her hand. 'We were powerless. Sir Lemuel ignored our advice. He seemed influenced by Sir Robert's example and frantic to outdo it. We sent letters to Hempens in August when the fall reached 900 but the mail's delay . . .'

Walpole. 'Has Walpole lost too?' It would be some satisfaction. Mr Tate ran his finger round his collar. 'Gibson, Jacob and

Jacombe are no ordinary bankers. Jacombe acted on his own initiative and managed to extricate at least some of Sir Robert's investment . . .'

She said flatly: 'But you didn't manage to extricate mine.'

'We're not bankers, Lady Cecily, merely advisers. Sir Lemuel . . .'

Around her, the darkly respectable linenfold panelling, the portrait of Queen Anne when she was still sixteen stone, the chased red-leather cases on their shelves, were unwavering, substantial. A thrush sang on the cherry tree in the tiny backyard. 'Where's Mr Phipps?' She'd get sense out of Phipps.

'Phipps cut his throat yesterday,' Colonel Brandling said.

After a while she asked: 'Why didn't you tell me?' She wasn't referring to Phipps. It hadn't occurred to them to tell her, she could see that. At the moment of her marriage she'd become a woman *couverte*, her legal existence obliterated by the body of her husband, no matter that the husband had less financial acumen than a carrot, nor that he'd gambled – and now lost – an estate worth £70,000. *Her* estate.

She said: 'And what do you intend to do about it?'

Tate burbled something about a meeting of creditors. She watched Brandling watching her, seeing no more pity for her in his eyes than hers had for him; he'd gone beyond pity, even for himself. Presumably his losses were as great as hers. She hoped they were.

'Hempens too?' she asked.

He nodded.

She got up and walked to the door, collecting her parasol from the hat-rack, turning to look at them for the last time. 'Well, gentlemen,' she said, 'since you have no advice for me, may I suggest that you follow the most excellent example set by the late Mr Phipps.' But still she hadn't taken it in.

The City was abnormally quiet. The only disturbance came from a mob at Ludgate applauding a preacher who was advocating a return to the ways of ancient Rome where parricides were stitched up in sacks and cast, alive, into the Tiber . . . 'for are not these South Sea rogues the parricides of their country?'

Part of the crowd rushed her carriage – a coat-of-arms

suggested royalty – but John stood up from the driving seat and called: 'She's lost everything, an' all,' so they left her alone, some of the men taking off their hats, as if a funeral was passing.

Still Cecily couldn't take in the magnitude of what had happened. The city that had rebuilt itself so magnificently after the Plague and the Fire stood around her like a monument to survival, assuring her that she, too, could not be permanently ruined. Like the last Roman matron, fleeing her home as the Vandals broke down the gates, Cecily was unable to understand that she wouldn't be back.

Disbelief and her carriage took her to Spring Gardens – to lose both. As she went in, the footman holding the door for her asked for his wages. She stared at him.

'I want my wages, my lady,' he said again. The rest of the staff crowded up from below stairs, emboldened by his example. Icily, she gave them what money was in her purse. She paid the rest with a diamond ring off her finger, throwing it on the floor.

Dolly was in Lemuel's bedroom feeding him his supper, scooping up the residue of each mouthful as it fell from the slack side of his mouth and spooning it in again. 'He said "Dolly," today,' she said. 'How'd you get on?'

Cecily told her. She snatched Dolly's spoon away so that she could lean down and put her face on a level with her husband's. 'Bravo, Sir Lemuel,' she said, clearly. 'You have achieved what six hundred years failed to do. You have brought down the house of Fitzhenry.'

'Don't talk to him like that. Look at him,' Dolly said. 'What d'you mean, "everything"?'

'Your brother mortgaged every property I own to buy South Sea stock. He borrowed to buy more by using my name and jewellery as security. The servants did not receive their wages this year and the beef which made that soup, so the cook has just informed me, was obtained on credit.' She cocked her head. 'Yes, I think that constitutes "everything".'

'Gawd.' Dolly venerated money, even if she didn't venerate people. She regarded her sister-in-law with something like respect, seeing her for the first time as a person wronged. Then came the realization that Cecily wasn't the only wronged soul in the room. 'I gave him my savings,' she said. 'Hundred and forty-two pound what Daniel left me. Lemmy said he'd triple it. That ain't gone too, has it?'

'Probably.'

'Oh, my lord.' Dolly covered her mouth and rocked. 'What'm I going to do?' Weeping, she shook her brother, making his head loll. 'How'd you do such a thing? You was always so clever.'

'If he'd been clever,' said Cecily, going to the door, 'he'd have shot straighter.'

Walpole didn't return to London until November. It was wise of him to stay away and keep his boots clean while everybody else stumbled crotch-deep in revelation and recrimination: it fostered the illusion that he'd been uninvolved in the speculation hysteria, a sober man who'd evaded the disaster that had overcome others.

He didn't see fit to mention that he'd shown no more foresight than anyone else. He hadn't bought as extensively as some, but he'd done it at the wrong time and had only been saved by the skill of his banker.

No matter. Other ministers had been exposed so deep in bribery and corruption that they'd lost the country's trust. Floundering Britain needs leadership. The throne, the City, trade, business are drowning. Here comes Walpole, consummate politician and, seemingly, wise with money. Save us, Sir Robert.

He did. At least, he saved the throne, City, trade and business. He did it by stifling inquiry. He protected King George and the bribe-accepting royal mistresses – if the house of Hanover fell, the house of Stuart would be back.

He fought off the country's demand for the heads of the South Sea directors, even saving most of them from loss of wealth. They numbered thirty-three and between them commanded perhaps £2 million in capital as well as international interests; ruining them would be a disaster to commerce. (Also, there was to be an election within the year and the directors had powerful connections.)

79

Robert Knight, cashier of the South Sea Company, escaped to France and took incriminating evidence with him. Relieved, Walpole and the King opposed any attempt to extradite him.

Suspected of deep involvement, James Craggs, the Postmaster-General, and his son, the Secretary of State, hastily and obligingly died; the father by an overdose of opium, young Craggs through smallpox.

As Chancellor of the Exchequer, John Aislabie bore much of the country's blame and was condemned to the Tower, crowds dancing in the streets as he went. His estates were sequestered but, thanks to Walpole, he got them back later. (Aislabie had political influence in a large area of Yorkshire.)

Sir John Blount, who'd amassed £183,334, was stripped of all but £1,000. (He'd offended Walpole by providing the House with details of the Company's and ministers' peculation.)

The only person in the affair to be hanged was a South Sea clerk who'd absconded with £4,000. (Nobody bothered to save him.)

It seemed well, therefore it *was* well. It was a matter of perception: with no revolution and no witch hunts, trade began again and the economy mended itself.

The triumph was deservedly Walpole's. He had two great allies: the rioters – the establishment had been frightened when it saw common people getting out of hand – and the Jacobites, who informed the Pretender that the country was in such turmoil he could take over successfully without any foreign aid. A bungled invasion plot was quickly discovered and suppressed, and again the establishment closed ranks. Better the devil you knew . . .

Walpole received the gratitude of his king and power of such supremacy that he began to be known as 'Prime' Minister.

A vitriolic press drew parallels between highwaymen who were hanged for a few shillings and well-connected robbers of millions, who weren't. The South Sea investors and annuity-holders yelled even ruder names as they gathered in large numbers at the door of the Commons, demanding their money back.

But Walpole was unmoved: Tory scribblers weren't his constituency, nor were the poor, nor those whose ruin had left them useless – such as his former henchman Sir Lemuel Potts. Perhaps he was unaware of Lemuel's condition: he had high matters and a thousand petitioners competing for his attention.

Cecily refused to approach him for help but Dolly did, running after his coach with other angry, pleading men and women.

She left notes at his house but suspected the footman of tearing them up the moment she turned away. 'Robert wouldn't do this to me, not if he knew,' she said. 'We used to have great laughs together.'

'He's still laughing,' said Cecily.

The creditors' meeting had not gone well. Mr Tate had advised her not to attend. Legally, he explained, all Lemuel's creditors had to settle for the percentage that he was offering them, on Lemuel's behalf, of the amount owed. 'If even one demurs there can be no agreement to save the debtor. Sir Lemuel will have to pay in full.'

Two demurred. There was no agreement to save Lemuel.

'So what happens now?' she asked, when a worn Mr Tate returned from the meeting.

He shook his head. For the first time since she'd known him, he sat down in her presence without permission. 'You could fly the country,' he said, wearily.

It was because of Dolly that they didn't. The thought of 'abroad' frightened her and brought her wits back. As the bailiff's men knocked on the door of Spring Gardens, she became active, throwing Cecily's court clothes into a travelling case. 'Give me your rings,' she said. 'Don't stand there. Give me your fucking rings.'

Cecily caught on. She tore off her rings. In a cupboard was the case containing the valuable ivory-chased duelling pistols the Doge of Venice had given her father. She tossed it to Dolly.

'They'll go round the back,' said Dolly. 'Tell 'em you're coming.'

Cecily leaned out of the window, heeling a pair of shoes with jewelled buckles in Dolly's direction as she did it. 'Just a moment, gentlemen. Allow me to dress and I'll open the door.'

Together they sat on the travelling case and locked it. They carried it downstairs to the parlour where Dolly clambered out of the back window into the brick-walled shrubbery. Cecily handed her the case. 'Don't let 'em turn you out,' Dolly said. 'I'll be back.'

Cecily watched her through the back gate, then, very slowly, walked along the passage to open the door.

The bailiff's men were professional and jolly. They hefted the furniture out onto the road and wrapped it in sacking, complimenting Cecily on its quality. 'Nice spinet, mistress. We took Lord Pitland's last week but it weren't a patch on this. Look at that bloody inlay, Josh.'

Queen Anne had given it to her. Her father had bought the gold épergne and cutlery in Venice. The gold-chased glasses had been a gift from Princess Caroline. The carpets had come from Persia. The men rolled them up, took down the damask curtains, tassels and rails, unscrewed the chandeliers from the ceiling and the delicate wrought-iron flambeaux holders from the walls. They debated whether the Chinese wallpaper in the drawing-room should be stripped off and decided against it. They emptied the kitchen of everything but a kettle and a pot. A Louis Quatorze ormolu clock chimed 'Walpole, Walpole' as it was carried off. Cecily heard it.

She spoke only once. 'That is my mother.'

Josh agonized for a moment, then ripped off the back of a filigree frame and doubtfully handed her the miniature portrait from inside: 'Shouldn't do this, you know.' It had been painted just before the Countess died in giving birth to Cecily.

Josh had to be firm about the Italian bed with the velvet tester in which Lemuel was lying. 'More than my job's worth. Ain't you got somewhere else for him, poor old soul?' Cecily indicated the divan and with great care they lifted Lemuel on to it.

Dolly returned to give them the rough of her tongue. 'Take the bloody roof off next, I suppose.' Josh told her no, the house itself was claimed by another creditor using other bailiffs.

They were left in an empty house in which the only light was a tallow candle from the kitchen. Cecily's head pulsed with pain and the mantra: 'Walpole. Walpole.'

Two days later Lemuel was arrested for debt and put into the Fleet.

The Fleet river had once run – and in Cecily's time oozed – into the Thames just west of the City walls. Over its six hundred years the prison on the east bank had burned down on several occasions, the last during the Great Fire of Charles II's reign. Cecily had many times driven past the rebuilt Fleet, considering its long, exterior brick wall and entrance too elegant for the rogues who famously chose to stay behind it rather than come out and pay what they owed. On principle, she'd always ignored the hands gesturing from a grille in the wall, their owners begging for charity and crying: 'Pray remember poor debtors.'

There were indeed 'politic debtors' in the Fleet: wily and comparatively wealthy men who'd run up debts they had no intention of paying, preferring to live well in prison than face poverty outside. But most of the Fleet's inhabitants were insolvent and, unlike criminals serving a defined sentence, they were in for life. Unless some angel paid their debts. And angels were few.

Supporting Lemuel, Cecily and Dolly had to attend a well-furnished office in a house just outside the prison while a man she vaguely recognized was threatened by the Fleet's Warden, Bambridge: 'It's back to Corbett's for you, sir.'

'Not Corbett's. I can't go back to Corbett's.' The prisoner's voice was high with terror. Aimlessly, not really interested in somebody else's plight, Cecily wondered where she'd heard it before.

Bambridge clapped his hands soundlessly together. His nails were manicured, he was well dressed and would have been handsome except for a protuberant upper lip, like an owl's beak. Mice and voles wouldn't have liked Thomas Bambridge. 'We need more garnish, Mr Castell. This prison don't run on good intentions.'

Castell. John Castell, yes. An architect. Lady Mary Wortley Montagu had introduced them once, praising his book *The Villas of the Ancients Illustrated*.

'There is smallpox at Corbett's, Bambridge.' The architect

spoke reasonably, trying for control. 'I haven't had smallpox. Any other house, I beg you.'

The Warden stood up: 'Do *you* tell *me* that my sponging houses are diseased? I won't have it. Do you garnish or not?'

'I *can't*. I haven't got any money.'

'Gaolers, take this man to Corbett's.'

The Fleet was a royal prison; until then Cecily didn't know, having never considered the matter, that it was also a business.

The telling thing was not merely John Castell's horror as he was dragged away past her but the knowledge that she and Lemuel had been meant to witness it.

'Sir Lemuel Potts, is it not?' said Bambridge. 'Welcome, sir, welcome. We hope to make you comfortable. And this must be Lady Cecily. Honoured, ma'am.' He nibbled on the title as if it had a tail and squeaked. 'I think we may offer you accommodation suitable to your condition. The Master's Side is comfortably spacious, not too high-priced, near the coffee- and taprooms and in easy reach of our chapel . . .'

Like the ogre-ish landlord of some inn, he handed them over to one of his gaolers: 'Carver, conduct Sir Lemuel and these ladies over the road to the John Donne Room.'

The gatekeeper charged five shillings to unlock the prison door for them. In the reception area the book-keeper who took down their details demanded 3s. 6d for doing so. Carver's price for carrying Lemuel's case up to the third floor was a shilling. The John Donne Room was certainly spacious but had no furniture: Carver, apparently, would rent them a bed, chairs, etc. at 6s. 2d. a week while the kitchens hired out eating irons and would provide what meals Sir Lemuel liked – at a price. 'He can eat free once a day in the Dining Hall,' Carver said, 'but it ain't recommended for delicate stomachs.'

'Twelve shilling a week?' shrieked Dolly, on learning the rent of the Donne Room. 'I could hire Blenheim Palace for that, you grasper.'

'Ah, but do it lodge debtors?' Carver had taken to her.

'Ain't you got nowhere cheaper? We wouldn't be in this spew-hole if we was flush.'

'We'll stay here for now,' Cecily said. They were all exhausted and Lemuel's head was beginning to shake as it did when he was confused, while the smell and sounds from the Commons Side across the court outside the window, where the poorest debtors were incarcerated, were uninviting. Nevertheless, her purse had been emptied by the unexpected charges. Dolly had left the travelling case in the safe-keeping of a friend in Cheapside.

While they waited for the furniture to arrive, Dolly said: 'You got to write them letters now.'

Cecily gritted her teeth. 'I'll see.' Soon it would be necessary to beg for help but to do so would be the end of the person she had been. After that she'd be *poor* Lady Cecily; she and Lemuel condemned to some tied cottage or living out their lives in the least-used room of a great house, batteners on the charity of those whose politeness would eventually become impatience. She'd seen it before.

True friends would have sought her out already. Mary Astell had written to her immediately, while she was still at Spring Gardens, offering her and Lemuel her home. Cecily had written back, gratefully declining; neither Mrs Astell's means nor her health could tolerate indigent guests for long.

With Sophie and Lady Mary Wortley Montagu still abroad, Anne in exile, it turned out that there *were* no true friends. Most of those who'd brought her up had been elderly and were now dead. Her other acquaintances, the fashionable, had themselves suffered losses in the crash – and not just of money. Many, like the Prince and Princess of Wales, were suspected of accepting South Sea Company bribes and were keeping as far as possible out of the public gaze while they tried to mend their shattered finances and esteem.

In any case, few could have afforded to settle Lemuel's debt: they were in nearly as bad a case as herself. Dolly, trudging the streets to sell or pawn Cecily's chattels, reported that emblazoned snuff- and patch-boxes, silver and jewellery were a glut at the pawnshops.

Cecily didn't even consider turning to her Jacobite acquaintances for help: in the best of times they could barely help themselves.

It was for Lemuel's political friends that Cecily saved her contempt. The Whig party was facing a general election with the South Sea scandal still hanging around its neck; it had little time for a supporter who'd shown himself incapable of managing his own economy, let alone the country's, especially since, incapacitated as he was, he no longer qualified for a seat in the House. Following its leader's example, the party was trying to forget he existed.

And he won't for much longer in these conditions. Lemuel was pulling her sleeve, uttering the inarticulate sounds he made when he was bewildered, looking round the cold, empty room and beginning to cry.

At least there was one decision she could make. 'I'll have to stay with him,' she said brusquely.

Their original idea had been that she and Dolly should rent somewhere near the prison and visit Lemuel by day. Dolly had already found them a room in Red Lion Court and herself a job, which involved working at night in a Fleet Street baker's.

Dolly nodded. 'That'll be best.'

Best? *Best?* How easily these commoners adapted to hell. She was in its flames and she still didn't believe it.

It was night by the time the room was furnished and they'd settled Lemuel. Dolly turned back at the door: 'Let me sell them bloody pistols at least.'

'No.'

'Look, I know what you're keeping 'em for and you can't. They'll chop you quick as liver.'

'No.' One of these days she'd meet Walpole again.

The decision to share Lemuel's imprisonment had been taken for the main part because Cecily could not, *noblesse oblige*, leave so helpless a creature alone in its system. Anyway, better to be hidden behind walls than to be seen coming out of a cheap dwelling by some acquaintance in a passing carriage. And, in fact, there were many worse places than this expensive part of the Fleet where money could purchase privacy, good food and service.

Also, it buoyed her up during that first cold night, lying on a pallet, to think: '*He* once went through this. *He* lay on the floor next to a sick old man's bed as I am lying now.'

But it was a difficult analogy to sustain as, one by one, the items in the travelling case were sold. After two months, penury forced them to move to a cheaper room, still private, but on the Commons Side and next to what Bambridge termed 'one of our houses of easement', a stinking lay-stall. Guillaume's fellow prisoners had been soldiers, not male scum who drank the taproom dry and vomited outside her door, nor female scum like the one in the next room who screamed as she went into labour. Nor, she was sure, had Lord Keltie wet his bed as Lemuel did and continued to do every night, costing 4s. 4d. a week for laundry.

She put the memory of Guillaume away, like a woman folding old love letters into lavender. She didn't want to cheapen it; she would keep it for later. And then she would think: *What* later?

But it is difficult for someone of twenty years to envisage that there will be no 'later'. Still she didn't write the begging letters and still she refused to let Dolly sell the duelling pistols. A persistent optimism at the back of her consciousness insisted that a *deus ex machina* would eventually appear to put everything right. All around her was the living and, often, actual death of those to whom the god in the machine failed to appear. But she was Lady Cecily Fitzhenry . . .

Nevertheless, the days went by and her expectation deteriorated into dreary plans: Dolly must smuggle more bread from the baker's. If I wash Lemuel's sheets myself . . . but where can I dry them?

Despair made her lazy. She tried to dig in metaphorical fingernails to stop herself slipping towards what she knew was disintegration of body and soul, to pull herself together, but matters had slid out of her grip too quickly. Her old life was now somewhere above; she was being tipped down a slope into a pit she couldn't climb out of.

Dolly, who visited them each day, became exasperated at Cecily's inertia. She resented that it was she who now maintained them, even though she found the power it gave her enjoyable. 'All you got to do is look after poor Lemmy when I'm at work and you can't do that proper.'

It was true. Or, rather, it was true for the first few weeks. She cared for Lemuel's immediate needs but she watched his struggles to speak with detachment, wouldn't assist his attempts to walk. Walpole was the cause of her fall but this dribbling, inarticulate old fool had been his instrument. She could hardly bear to touch him.

'He done it for you, you know,' Dolly shouted at her.

'Oh, what?' asked Cecily wearily. '*What* did he do for me?'

'Tried to double his money. He wanted it for you. Poor bugger, he was always trying to make you notice him.'

After a while she came to think that, in this, her sister-in-law had more insight than she had. Perhaps Lemuel's conscience had seen his wife's contempt for him, seen herself and her estates as a gift he hadn't earned. Perhaps his speculation had been an attempt to lay booty of his own at her feet. Certainly, she could remember a hundred occasions when he'd vied for her attention without knowing how to get it. And, apart from his sexual insistence, he had always been kind – repellent, but kind.

All this didn't make his speculations less blameworthy but it gave some inkling that they'd been motivated other than by idiocy and greed.

One afternoon after Dolly had brought their food and Cecily had placed Lemuel's bowl on a table by his side, leaving him to feed himself – she couldn't be bothered and in any case it was time he used his right hand more – she heard him shout and looked round to see that he'd put the full bowl on his head. Egg pudding dripped over his forehead.

His anger – the first he'd ever shown in her presence – evaporated under her eyes and he cowered. He was frightened of her.

'Oh dear,' she said, 'this won't do, will it?' She cleaned him up, fed him, called for Carver to sit with him while she went out to the street market and paid a penny to dip in a wig-bag on an old-clothes stall. She found a full-bottom that had led an exhausting life in the legal profession, took it back and asked Carver to fumigate it.

When she put it on Lemuel's head she smiled at him for the first time in their acquaintance. It made him cry again.

88

Carver approved: he had a soft spot for Lemuel. ''Andsome as Solomon, you look, Sir Lemmy.' He didn't: his lop-sided face was like an anxious child's peeping through curtains, but it was as an anxious child that Cecily could tolerate him and began to treat him.

Nobody could live in the Commons of the Fleet without being dirtied, physically and mentally. As far as possible, Cecily kept herself and Lemuel aloof from what went on outside their cell and managed to live on what Dolly provided without selling her body for more as many of the Commons women – and men – were obliged to do.

Even so, it was during this time that she lost a bloom which even the four last years hadn't quite scoured away and her eyes gained the knowing look that comes from seeing human beings at their most brutal and degraded. She also acquired a vocabulary so expressive and foul that it gave her release to use it, then and later.

Thomas Bambridge had bought the office of Chief Warden of the Fleet for five thousand pounds. Within a year he had recouped that sum and from that time on made a regular annual income of another five thousand from what he called 'presents' and 'fees'. Those who couldn't, or wouldn't, give them were made an example to the rest and were kept, crouching in irons, in a section of the prison known as Bartholomew Fair.

Female prisoners who took his fancy were allowed to make another sort of 'present', while anybody who had a title attracted his particular attention – a debtor on Cecily's floor, ironically called Sir William Rich, had been dragged off to Bartholomew Fair and loaded with irons for no other reason than Bambridge's dislike of baronets.

Cecily, both titled and female, being only the wife of a debtor, was not strictly speaking his prisoner but he kept an eye on her with the interest of a man watching his plum tree for the moment when the fruit was ready.

In March she was summoned across the road to Bambridge's office. He had an account book open on the table in front of him. 'This won't do, Lady Cecily. We were informed that our rent had to be paid in advance, were we not? Yet we are behind, yes, behind. What are we to do about it?'

Cecily said nothing.

He came from behind the table and advanced protectively on her, his eyes on her bodice, beak nibbling. 'You know, don't you, Lady Cecily, that any financial embarrassment you suffer may be settled most amicably between us? Most amicably. My door is open to you, tonight if you wish, any night, Lady Cecily.' He kept repeating the title: the subjugation of her rank was as important to him as her body.

'Get away from me, you fucking bastard,' she said.

His nails scratched her arm as he led her to the door. 'We'll see, Lady Cecily. Any night.'

Outside, a cold winter's rain had emptied the street and its traders had cleared their stalls and gone, leaving flapping tarpaulins and a detritus of orange peel and squashed cabbage leaves.

Cecily stood in it, her shoes to the uppers in mud, calm at having reached the lowest floor of hell. Here it is and I shall sink no further. Lemuel must fend for himself. Were he in his wits, he'd insist on it.

Lemuel was the debtor, not she. Pity had kept her by his side. She had done what she could for him but marital loyalty did not, could not, extend to whoring in order to protect a husband she had not wanted to marry in the first place. She must leave him to his fate.

It is desertion.

'No, I am not abandoning Lemuel. It shall be for his advantage. I shall go to Mary Astell. Yes, yes, that's what to do. From Mrs Astell's I can write letters, pester, conduct a campaign for his release. It is not abandonment. Were he in his wits, he would urge me to go.'

It is desertion. A Fitzhenry does not flee the battlefield.

'What of Maurice Fitzhenry in the Civil War? Sir Thomas Fitzhenry at Bosworth? They lived to fight another day. It is not desertion, it is . . . strategic withdrawal.'

Chattering, mad, she picked her way across the street to go and tell her wounded she was leaving him on the battlefield.

On the Fleet Bridge, a horseman cantering towards the prison saw her and called her name but his voice was lost in the hiss of rain.

Lemuel wasn't in his room. She ran along the corridor to find Carver, who said: 'Bambridge's orders.'

'Where is he?'

'Bartholomew Fair.'

'Christ God.'

She ran down flights, struggled through the drunks outside the Commons taproom who grasped at her, across the court where, in daytime, prisoners were confined in the cemetery of the 'Fair' and shared the air with the corpses who'd died in the night, down another flight to a keepers' area which was separated from the Fair itself by a large grilled gate beyond which was darkness.

She snatched a flambeau from its sconce and went to the gate, ignoring the protest of the night keeper. 'Lemuel.'

Figures squirmed into the pool of light cast by the torch, some blaspheming, others pleading.

'*Lemuel.*'

To the right someone was mewing. She angled the torch so that she could see him. They'd put his legs in irons, his wrists were manacled to his neck.

She wasn't aware of telling the keeper to open the gate, but he did it. She crouched beside Lemuel. 'There, there. Cecily's here. Don't be frightened.' To the keeper she screamed: 'Get these fucking irons off.'

'Them's a Bambridge special,' he told her, 'seven and six garnish to get them off.'

'I'll kill you. Get them *off*.'

Behind the keeper a voice said: 'I should get them off, laddie, or I'll kill you mysel'.' It was the Scots lawyer, Archibald Cameron.

He had some sort of release with him. Grumbling, he paid all the garnishes necessary to get Lemuel past the main gates and out into a waiting hackney, which took them to his rooms in Lincoln's Inn. Lemuel was put into his bed and a message sent to Dolly where to find them.

Because Cecily seemed incapable of doing it for herself, he took off her shoes and lodged them to dry on the fender of his not-too-generous fire. He brought her bread and cheese and a hot toddy. He kept explaining.

After a while, she said: 'You'll have to forgive me. I seem unable to stop crying. What is it that you are trying to tell me?'

It was something about another meeting of creditors. She grasped only the fact that Lemuel was free and would remain so. She cuddled it like a pillow and fell asleep on it, while the lawyer's voice went regularly on, less like a god's in a machine than a creaking pump.

The next morning she woke up, stiff but warm, on the fireside settle, covered by a blanket.

A bustling, stout woman told her Master Archie had gone out, but his compliments to Lady Cecily and there was breakfast on the fire, Sir Lemuel'd had a peaceful night and she, Mrs Tothill, would sit with him if Lady Cecily wished to avail herself of Master Archie's purse and go out to purchase herself any garments she might require.

There was one guinea in the lawyer's purse. 'I see he's not expecting high fashion,' she said. She was aware it was a shameful comment but she had been mentally denuded, stripped of the person she had thought herself to be – and once again in front of the Scotsman. She had imagined her world to be structured and found that, instead, it consisted of a thin crust over a morass of shit. Blood, breeding availed you nothing if you fell through. Because she had nothing else to do it with, Cecily tried to cover her nakedness with the tatters of dignity and sounded shrewish.

When Dolly arrived, she and Cecily went out together, Dolly full of questions Cecily couldn't answer. 'I don't know. He seems to have arranged everything, though how ... He's probably acting for somebody.'

'He's a bloody gift horse, that's what he is. Don't you go spitting in his teeth, now. I know you.'

'I have no intention of spitting in his teeth.' But it persisted in rankling her that she was indebted to him. She comforted herself that he must be the agent for someone greater than himself. He'd taken his bloody time. A day earlier, and she wouldn't have had to contend for the rest of her life with the knowledge that she'd lost courage.

The rain had stopped, though it was still a grey day. A wind scurried gowned lawyers and white specks that looked like snow around Lincoln's Inn Fields. Not snow, but early may blossom from the hawthorn trees.

'Oh, Dolly, it's spring.' She, who hadn't once cried in the Fleet, now couldn't rid herself of a tendency to weep.

It was calming to cross the great square of the Fields and let their eyes travel the long, uniform lines of Inigo Jones's terraces.

'I'd better buy a dress, I suppose.' The two women strolled on into Clare Market, without discussing their mutual irritation over the last few months, not so much forgiving each other as forgiving themselves.

Cecily bought herself a serviceable bodice and petticoat, a pair of pumps – and a rabbit-skin muff for Dolly.

Returning, they climbed a stone staircase to the top floor, past progressively smaller doors bearing the name of a legal firm. The smallest read: Archibald Cameron, Attorney-at-Law, D.LL. (E'burgh). Inside, it was both his home and office, cheaply and sparsely furnished, but neat. He'd saved on his furniture, which was of deal, presumably to buy the books that were piled on all available surfaces.

The bed's cupboard doors were closed and Lemuel sat on the settle, apparently listening to the lawyer who was repeating the explanations he'd made to Cecily the night before.

'He don't understand,' Dolly said. 'You tell us instead.'

Archibald Cameron began again. They gathered, picking it out from the Habeas Corpuses, statutes, chattels, equities and the Debtors Act 1678, that he had called another meeting of creditors which, this time, had agreed to a settlement. 'Done this all by yourself, did you?' admired Dolly. 'What about Brandling, Whatsit and Howsyourfather?'

'It was necessary to act without consultation and I'd be grateful if, now, Sir Lemuel or, in view of his weakness, Lady Cecily could regularize my position by a signature on this wee document. Desperate situations demand desperate measures. I'm only sorry it took sae long.'

As she signed the wee document – a straightforward enough authorization – Cecily couldn't rid herself of the idea that the man was laughing at them. He had small, bright eyes, which avoided hers, and a mouth so thin and wide it turned pedantry into a joke; the face of a comedian. What were they to him, or him to them, that he should have gone to such trouble on their behalf? A suspicion began to form.

'What now?' asked Dolly. 'Are we still in the sirreverence or ain't we?'

'Would that be a euphemism for excrement, may I ask?'

'It is.' They nodded solemnly at each other.

'I can safely say that the, er, midden has been avoided,' Cameron told her. 'I am even in a position to offer a property for your consideration as a refuge. For now, at least.'

'We'll take it.'

'What is it?' demanded Cecily. She wasn't keeping up, and her distrust was growing by the second. 'Is it one of my properties?'

'I fear not. Your entire estate has mitigated the debt. I'm rare sorry. This is an inn.'

'An *inn*?'

It *had* been an inn. The Bell at Woolmer Green. Relinquished by the former landlord, who'd fallen prey to the disease common to landlords . . .

'What disease?'

'The drink, ma'am, demon drink. I've nae seen the property yet mysel' but the agent impressed me with its qualities and, since it was going cheap, I ventured the capital given me on your behalf by an anonymous well-wisher . . .'

'I have no well-wishers,' said Cecily.

For the first time that day the man in the fox-coloured wig looked her straight in the eye. 'Ye have, ma'am, ye have indeed.'

'It's Walpole, isn't it?'

'*Walpole?* D'ye mean Sir Robert?'

She was not taken in by his flummox. 'You may tell your master, sir, that I am not accepting the gift of some mildewed ale-house as his conscience's price, not a spar, not a twig, not a penny. D'ye hear me?' She reached for her cloak, urging Lemuel to his feet. 'Come, Dolly.'

'For Chrissake, Cessy . . .'

'IT'S NOT WALPOLE, WUMMUN.' A fire-iron clattered into the hearth, the fire blinked.

Cameron himself seemed surprised and said quietly: 'Your pardon, mistress. For certain Sir Robert would assist your plight did he know of it, but will ye not accept my word that he has no hand in the matter. Nor is he my master, though I'll not deny that much of my work just now is on his behalf . . .'

'Who is it, then?'

'Anonymous,' said the lawyer, thinning his thin lips. 'Ye'll know the meaning of the word, mebbe?'

Cecily was unimpressed by people whose lack of breeding led them to show anger. However, it seemed the fellow was telling the truth. Satisfied it wasn't Walpole, she lost interest in the anonymous donor; no doubt some acquaintance was trying to help her while sparing her pride. She didn't want to know. She had to accept the offer: they were financially and physically exhausted; the 'refuge' could harbour them until she had the strength to consider what to do.

She ached for her lost Hempens. However low the Fitzhenry fluctuating fortunes had sunk in the past, the family had managed to retain possession of their fenland home as a den in which to lick their wounds; had it been still hers she would even now be heading for it to lick hers, to lay her head on her old nurse's lap and be comforted. While in the Fleet she had written to Hempens' new owner, a Peterborough builder, begging him to allow Edie to stay on in the gatehouse as caretaker.

'Where is this Woolmer Green?'

It was in Hertfordshire, thirty miles north of London; she envisaged something secret, thatched and small, hidden and bowery, where Dolly could dispense ale to the local bumpkinry while she sat under a tree and an assumed name to breathe in hay-scented, throstle-songed air. She could think no further. 'Please order the carriage at once.'

'Ye canna go yet. I've had nae chance to examine its condition, nor will have for a while – I've an important court case. The whiles Dame Tothill here will provide ye lodging . . .'

But in this Cecily wouldn't be overborne. She could examine the property as well as he. 'We must go now.' Privately, she couldn't bear to stay in London: it had contaminated her, she wanted to burrow into wholesome country earth until the sickness passed. Also, she wanted to be away from this lawyer who'd seen her total debasement and, if he'd acted quicker, could have saved her from it.

They left for Hertfordshire that afternoon. Not in a carriage, but a carrier's cart that had transported chickens enjoying the best digestive health to Clare Market from a poultry farm near Stevenage and was now returning.

'Aye, well,' had said Cameron, braving Cecily's eye, 'we'll clean it up for ye, but there's no siller left for carriages and such.' To Dolly he doled out enough for their midway overnight stop at Potter's Bar. 'And there's twopence to send me word by the post ye've arrived.'

Cecily said stiffly: 'In the Fleet there was a man called John Cassels, an architect I think he was. I'd be grateful if you would find out for me what happened to him.'

'Cassels, is it? I can tell ye what happened to him. He was a friend of a friend of mine by the name of Oglethorpe. He died in a sponging house of the smallpox.'

Something caught up with Cecily on that windy, plodded journey north. It chased after her, sometimes blending with the shadowed road. Until then it had been kept at bay by the necessity for movement, Lemuel, avoidance, all the activity that had enabled her to argue with the lawyer, buy a dress. She, who had been too sophisticated to credit the supernatural before, had been presented with it, subjected to emotions at their extremes that had made her aware of a presence outside herself.

The Devil? Then the forked and horned picture they painted of him was a cartoon; what was following her was vast and dark, the true ruler of the world. More wonderful than God, that powerless force for goodness. There was no goodness. But there was Something and it was following her.

Dolly attempted conversation but gave up and addressed herself only to Lemuel, since the driver was as taciturn as Cecily.

Late next day, the cart lurched to a halt on a dark section of road at the bottom of a steep hill. 'Here y'are, then.'

Dolly gave an anticipatory: 'Ooh-er.' To their left, almost hidden by trees, were the gables of a considerable, if ancient, building, a carved stone arch providing an entrance to one side. It was difficult to see its condition by a moon that came and went between fast-moving clouds. No candles or lamps burned behind the mullions of its windows.

Dolly was asking the driver to light them in.

He shook his head. ''Aunted, my missus says.' Released from the concern that they might have cancelled the journey and, thus, his carrier's fee, the carter quoted his wife at length: 'Ol' Rosy, he conjured up the Devil while he was 'live an' left un in possession now he's dead. Nobody don't come near the place but that ol' bell do ring for corpses.' He pointed to a small white bell tower perched among the black angles of the roof. 'Ol' Nick rings that, my missus reckons. Nobody else, only wickedness. So my missus do say.'

Yes. Old Nick. He would be here.

The driver wouldn't help them in. Out of compassion for Lemuel he allowed Dolly to borrow the cart's lantern, saying his horses could see their way home and that he'd call for it when he again came south. Then the iron-bound wheels rumbled him away into the night.

They crossed the weedy forecourt to the arch and found themselves in a long, rubble-strewn yard. The balusters of the narrow flight of steps, which led to an upper storey, had gone.

Dolly was cursing all Scottish lawyers and their antecedents. Cameron had given them a key, an enormous thing, but it wasn't needed. They turned left into the inn through a doorless doorway.

Inside there had been a taproom once: ale-soaked wood mingled with mildew and the sour smell of torn lath and plaster. The space was huge, perhaps it had been divided into other rooms – here and there broken wainscoting, which had once held panelling, ran across the floor.

There was even a suggestion of beauty in its dimensions but, like Cecily, its substance had been stolen from it: needy, greedy hands had torn up most of the elm floorboards, rolled away the great barrels, ripped out wood and moulding and unputtied the glass to fit into less lovely windows.

'Where can we go now? We're finished, oh, Lord, oh, Lord.' Dolly sank to her haunches, Lemuel worriedly plucking at her.

There was nowhere to go. This ragged, beaten floor was the undercroft of the levels through which they had fallen.

But this is where I stop.

Cecily was amazed at the energy of the thought, the first activation in her lassitude in two days, as if from some remnant of gut overlooked by the depression that had disembowelled her.

The March wind outside howled like a dog through the gaps of the room and shifted the bell in its high cupola so that it swung against its clapper, emitting a light clang. Dolly screamed.

In the centre of the rubble there was a splay of moonlight that came from a hole in the roof. Cecily stepped into it and looked up through bare rafters to the moon. Then, as her first Fitzhenry ancestor had done when he watched his enemies and sons burn his birthplace, she took her soul away from God.

Clearly, almost conversationally, she said: 'Since God had no use for what I was, I offer what I am now to you, Prince of Darkness.'

She waited; she didn't know what for. She heard Dolly gasping, heard the wind and another ring from the bell. She said: 'I shall break all laws but yours, follow you all my days, if you will help me prosper so that I can take revenge on him who has brought me to this. This I swear.'

It didn't sound absurd; the night was ready for such a profession and she felt it stream upwards towards the moon, that ultimate warlock. And anyway, the Devil answered her.

He said, 'That's handy.'

98

CHAPTER SIX

THE DEVIL'S NAME was Tyler. As he and his companion clambered down from the rafters where they'd been hiding, silver coins fell out of a handkerchief into which he'd been counting them. He made no bones about it: 'Ill-gotten gains.'

They were at the mercy of two armed men who, satanic or not, were demonstrably criminal and using the inn as a hiding place. Yet from the first Cecily experienced little sense of threat. Even Dolly, once she'd stopped screaming, chided them for the fright they'd given her.

'*You* was frit?' Tyler told her. 'What about us? Thought you was the bloody beagles.'

Whether the two women's peril would have been greater if they'd been less obviously poor, Cecily didn't know. There was no sexual danger: Tyler, the leader, was intrigued by her, but not as prey. He expressed amazed admiration at her profession to the Prince of Darkness. 'Never heard the like,' he kept saying. 'Chilled me to the crackers as the saying is.'

The three were treated as benighted travellers. Tyler and his brother, Ned – 'Nebuchadnezzar for short' – built a fire, toasted bread and cheese on it for all of them, brought straw for their beds and produced a firkin of ale. Ned did most of the work. Self-contained, seemingly less intelligent than his brother, though older, he whistled tunelessly and limped bandily, like an ostler.

Cecily's attention was on Tyler, as his was on her. Excepting her nurse, she had not before felt affinity with one of the lower orders, but with Tyler there was at once rapport. It was a sign of her dislodgement from her old self that she felt it now, but it was more than that: deep called to deep with a disregard of boundaries which was new to Cecily and with Tyler was a way of life. Medium height, thirty, perhaps forty, years of age, plainish, brownish, his appearance was so unexceptional most people forgot what he looked like when he was out of sight. He traded on it. Even his speech, while it belonged below the salt, had gained so many accents in his travels that none was identifiable.

When she spoke to him Cecily found herself cutting through niceties, as if using a *langue de guerre* known only to them.

'Me?' he said, when she asked what he did. 'I work the roads. Gentleman of the high pad, like.'

It was to be moe than fifty years before the Newgate Calendar, protesting that it was an Awful Warning of the Progress and Consequence of Vice, gave details of the lives and cant of rogues to an eager public, but they were already common knowledge in prisons. And Cecily had been in prison. 'A highwayman,' she said.

He nodded; he knew she wasn't shocked. 'And you, Duchess? Hunting lady are you, if I may ask?'

'I have hunted.'

'Kept your own horses, I dare say? Servants too, I'll wager.'

He nodded again as she nodded. It was enough for now.

They ate supper in a limbo, Dolly too despairing to wonder what would happen next, Lemuel content with food and warmth, Cecily appalled but stirred by the promptness with which the Devil had answered her call, and watching his hoofs.

'What's the matter with Ned?' she asked. The man was wincing.

'Needs rest,' Tyler said.

'He needs a bandage,' Cecily said. There was blood seeping through a tear in Ned's breeches. 'Dress it for him, Dolly.'

'What, him? I ain't –'

'Dress it.' They kept a supply for Lemuel, who often stumbled.

It seemed in the order of things to watch Dolly treat a wound on a man's leg that had been clearly scored by a bullet.

After the others had gone to sleep, it fitted into the same alien recognizability of the night that she should stay awake to listen to Tyler on the art of the highway pad.

'See, Ned's heart ain't in it. He's horsy, our Ned. Horses, horses with him. At bottom he's honest. Ain't had my education, ain't been where I been. Don't pay attention. And, see, on the pad, you don't pay attention you get shot. Or the judge hands you a hemp collar.'

Tonight, Ned had not paid attention.

Highwaymen who worked alone, Tyler told her, made a fatal mistake – 'Three months an' they're dancing the gallows' waltz' – because there were crucial moments during a hold-up which demanded the presence of an accomplice, in Tyler's parlance a 'cove'.

He enumerated them on his fingers. 'One, when you orders 'em to throw down their guns. Coachmen – we call 'em "companions" – first. Then "bleeders", that's the passengers. You'd be surprised how many of them innocent-lookin' prickers go armed. Two, tipping the cole. Taking the valuables. Three, cutting the leaders' traces so they can't follow. All them times your peepers is off 'em, and when your cove's peepers needs to be *on* 'em. See?'

She saw. 'How long have you been on the pad?'

'Year.' He expected her to be impressed. 'Six months more an' Ned and I buy an ale-house. You don't want to pad longer'n that. Too chancy.'

'How much do you make in a night?' It was his manner that was impressive: it had the conviction of a skilled artisan discussing his craft.

'Depends. There's some just got fluff in their pockets. Most's got a reasonable tattler. Occasional, one of your coolers's wearing ear-bobs, rings and such.' He glanced sideways at Cecily. 'It's the fencing, see. I got a safe fencing-master but he's making cheese out of me along of I can't tell when jewels is jewels or when they're glass. And Ned don't know a sapphire from a snaffle, as the saying is.'

He fell silent and for a while they listened and watched the moonlight come and go through the open rafters as the wind softly dinged the bell on the roof and curved the smoke of their fire. Cecily sensed that Tyler, like a good horse-master, was letting her graze.

She supposed she should be shocked. Here was a man who took innocent people's possessions away from them – and discussed it as if he were a cooper explaining the making of barrels. Was it a sign of how quickly the Devil had possessed her soul that she *wasn't* shocked? Perhaps. Or perhaps she had joined

the ranks of those so dispossessed that robbery was an alternative, and necessary, form of survival.

Moon men. Shakespeare used the term somewhere for
night villains like these. One of the histories, she thought it
was.

'See,' said Tyler, pulling his ear, 'gentleman on the pad, he
needs a reliable cove, educated, like, clever.'

*The fortune of us that are but Moon's men doth ebb and flow like
the sea.* That was it.

'Or a covess.'

He'd said it at last.

She turned to look at him, searching for what it was that had
cut off this most ordinary-looking man from the very root of
convention that he could discern in her, a woman, a suitable
partner in crime. The same knife that had so cut *her* from everything that held her to the normal, she must suppose.

He met her eyes. 'See, there I was, perched in them rafters
like a pricking seagull, wondering if you was the hue and cry,
wondering what the Devil I'd do while Ned rested. And then
you said what you said. Gawd. Fair froze me fetlocks, as the
saying is. But Meant, that's what it was. Meant.'

She had answered his need as he seemed to be answering
hers.

'*Are* you the Devil?' she asked him.

He sighed. 'Reckon I must be.'

Cecily woke up the next morning to find that she'd bedded
down among rubble near the skeleton of a cat. There was no
sign of Tyler or Ned. Or, for that matter, of Dolly and Lemuel,
but there were sounds of activity somewhere.

Aching, cold, she went to the front windows to see what could
be seen in the dawn. Everything was quiet. A wagtail drank
from a puddle formed in a rut. Yet that wide track beyond her
forecourt was the Great North Road. With Watling Street, some
miles to the west, it was the artery that pumped life back and
forth between London and the north.

Opposite, leading off to the east, was a smaller track, which
wandered between fields and copses. On a hilltop a mile beyond,
perhaps where the track led to, she could just see the stump of

a church tower. There was no traffic. If there were villages around – and the only sign of one was the distant tower – they kept their activity to themselves. Her inn was nobody's destination. She wasn't surprised. Cameron, the fool, had bought her a ruin.

The grey March morning breeze scuttered brief showers across the yard outside. She found Dolly at its end in what had been a sizeable kitchen. The mantel above a fireplace that could have accommodated a cart was still in place, but the doors to the brick bread-ovens had gone, like the spits and jacks. Dolly had got a fire going in the great hearth and improvised a tripod out of iron spars from which hung a pail of simmering porridge. She was busy with another pail, some roots and pieces of raw pork. Lemuel huddled by the flames, watching her.

'Them blaggers left it us,' she said, when Cecily inquired.

'I thought I'd dreamed them.'

Having something to do had returned Dolly her poise and therefore her aggression. 'They're villains, you know that, don't you? Don't you? Robbers.' She turned back to her cooking, grumbling. 'Bargaining with Old Scratch. What got into you? Talk of the Devil and see his horns, and so we bloody did. Well, don't come whining to me when he collects his dues. An' he will. You don't cheat the Devil.'

'Something had to be done.' Cecily squatted down to peer into Lemuel's face. It was the colour of putty except for the shiny red crescent beneath his eye where the skin dragged down. The good side of his mouth turned up as he tried to smile at her.

She tucked his shawl more closely about him and stood up. 'Don't make too much smoke. We don't want anybody to know we're here. What *is* that, anyway?'

'Workman's pail. Ma used to make one for Pa.' She'd cut up vegetables, interleaving them with pork, and sealed it with a huff of pastry. 'Good job one of us got enough nous to feed that poor brother of mine.'

'Tyler gave you all that?'

'Not him. The other bugger.' Dolly tied a cloth over the top of the pail and hung it over her fire. She was more animated than she'd been for weeks. 'Pump still works, thank Christ.' She dusted her hands on her skirt. 'You could make something of this place.'

As she explored, Cecily realized you probably could – with sufficient money. Reduced to its bones, multi-roofed and short-walled, the building remembered medieval entertainment. Generations had been kind to it, adding on pieces to extend comfort, not begrudging the cost of masons and carpenters who'd known what they were about. Monkish stone gargoyles spouted rain-water at clogged drains, Jacobean finials adorned gable-ends, barge-boards were pierced with Tudor tracery. A once–espaliered pear tree and an apricot struggled for life against ivy. The horse-trough was a lead Roman cistern, too heavy to be stolen.

Hugging the wall for safety, she climbed the outside stone staircase to a long balcony. Here, upstairs, were unexpected passages and levels, hidden rooms, stairways and attics.

Two chambers, the largest, contained privies from the Middle Ages which had been built out into the wall – this part was stone – over corbelled pipes leading to a cesspit.

Dolly found a cellar under a trap in the kitchen. At the far end of the yard was another arch leading to stables. It was topped by a loft reached by ever more lethal steps. Over the other side of the stable wall was what had been a kitchen garden.

Cecily, venturing beyond the stables to an orchard, discovered an odd bridge crossing a stream and puzzled over the smoothly rounded holes in it until Dolly enlightened her: 'Shit-house. Some bastard's taken the hut down.' The stream would have carried its burden into the woods, which covered the hill beyond the meadows lying at the back of the inn. Cecily followed it.

In between showers the sun came out, warming a faint, elus-ive scent from clusters of primroses, yellowing catkins that wagged in the breeze. At the edge of the trees, she stopped and listened. Not woods, these. Forest. It had an echo, birdsong, of course, but also a thousand rustling, creeping creatures going about their business. Herne the Hunter's land still. She turned back to the inn.

Outside the taproom mullions, the Great North Road had come to life. Carters raised their whips in salute as their teams lumbered past each other. One was watering his horses at a pond in the inn's forecourt and she experienced a second's exasperation of ownership. 'Who told him he could?'

A hunt passed. A parson jog-trotted south. Nobody looked towards the building shielded in its trees: its decrepitude was part of the landscape. Old Rosy, whoever he'd been, had given it the *coup de grâce* of a diabolic reputation that averted decent eyes. The wind-blown bell hurried people by. She owned an invisible inn.

Sad, though. The Roman cistern in the yard put the Bell among the ages. History made visible had marched back and forth before these windows. A centurion might have halted his men here and downed his Falernian before heading off to guard Hadrian's Wall; from here monks could have tended pilgrims on their way to our Lady of Walsingham; even Henry II, that ceaseless voyager . . .

There was a vibration in the stone sill beneath her fingers and in a spatter of mud and noise a team of four horses and their vehicle went by, weighted by the gradient of the hill and taking at speed the slow bend past her inn. It was there, it was gone. A coach.

'Leaves St Albans at dawn,' Tyler had said. 'Next stop Buckhill.'

If she wasn't mistaken she'd promised to assist him, whose face she couldn't remember, to rob such a conveyance tonight.

This cold March morning there was none of the inevitability that had attended last night. But she knew she hadn't been insane. What else could she do? Starve? Go on the parish? More preferably, hang herself? She'd be damned if she did. Well, she was.

To Cecily, then, that she should commit highway robbery was less shameful than the indignities she had suffered since Edinburgh. It was aggression where everything else had been infliction. Her choice. Her spit in the face of society. Better to be shocking than pitied.

If she were caught, she'd make a speech from the gallows

that would echo down the Great North Road to Whitehall. You, Walpole. I robbed you.

Even as she rehearsed the scene, she was comfortable in the knowledge that it was unlikely: Tyler had disappeared into the night like the goblin he was . . .

He came back with Ned that afternoon, trotting into the stable-yard by the woodland approach. Both were on horseback and Ned led a mare. They'd brought sacking for the windows so that light from the inn shouldn't excite inquiry, brooms, shovels, bedding, food and drink, male clothing for Cecily, a pistol and a mask.

When she showed him her father's excellent pistols, he shook his head. 'Boastful,' he said. 'Somebody'd remember 'em. You don't want to be remembered no more than a tree in a copse.' The attire, the horse, everything he'd brought for her was unre-markable. And she must wear gloves: 'Them hands is too lady-like, as the saying is.'

'Boasting', as Tyler called it, was the downfall of most of his fellow highwaymen. They made a tavern their headquarters, buying drinks and women, living the short life of glory until some pricker betrayed them for the price on their head. 'Ned and me, we don't want the glory, we wants the cash.' Cecily could have acquired no more cautious accomplices with whom to begin her life of crime.

Ned insisted she make practice gallops on the plain bay mare he'd chosen for her, and himself adjusted the stirrups. (She took 'chosen' to be a euphemism for stealing but Tyler said, no, they'd bought the mare at Hertford market – 'Nappin's too chancy.') She paraded in the 'kicks' to get used to the feel of breeches, learning to slouch and let her hands hang down. Tyler declared her hair boastful and produced a lank wig to cover its curls, an addition that altered her appearance amazingly.

Nor were the preparations over when she and Tyler set out, which they did through the forest to the rear. 'Know your retreat,' Tyler said, 'old army ruffle.'

Their destination was Harpenden Heath, ten miles away to the west. Crossing the country by forest tracks and bridle paths that evening, the two highwaymen saw and were remarked by few people. Tyler pointed out landmarks by which Cecily could find her way back if they got separated, where it was safe to gallop once the moon was up, where it was better to pick their way.

He made her jump a tree that had fallen across a narrow track so that the mare was used to it.

'*Were* you in the army?'

For the first time he was curt with her. 'P'raps I was. P'raps I wasn't.' He'd shown little curiosity about her past, except to ask her on whom she had sworn revenge in her speech to the Devil. 'Ain't a local cove, is he? Only we don't want no tantoblin on our own patch.'

'Robert Walpole,' she told him.

He puffed with relief. 'That's all right, then.' Prime Ministers were everybody's game.

At Watling Street they took up position in a hangar of elms at the top of a rise. 'Always pull your jacks on a rise, see, when they're going slow. I known padders as was run over by the jack they was going to pull speeding down a hill.'

Above them rooks circled and cawed against a greying sky, their beaks full of twigs. From deep in the trees they watched empty ox-carts plod towards the village, men and women sitting on the tailboards too tired from their day's planting in the beanfields to look about them.

Beside her the figure of Tyler darkened into a seedy statue.

Lord God, if they were caught it would be assumed she was his moll. She could face the gallows but not the assumption that she'd sunk to bellying a common rogue. The mare tossed her head at a vibration of her reins. Cecily regarded her trembling gloves. 'Hubris,' she said. 'I'm not a person for this. I'm going home.'

He kept his eyes on the road. 'Where's home?'

It was a hit. 'Home' was a mouldering inn and Lemuel sat in it, shivering and hungry. *There must be other ways.* But this was the one the Devil had put into her hand.

She stayed on. The road emptied, rooks settled down on their untidy nests, the horses chewed on their bits, the moon came up.

Don't think. Her knees had turned fluid: she wouldn't be able to control the mare. I am Lady Cecily Fitzhenry and I am about to rob a coach. How am I here? Walpole, that's why I'm here. Walpole.

Above all, she shared this moment with Guillaume. I'm fighting your enemy in my own way, my dear, my dear. Be with me now.

There was a tremor in the tilth of the forest floor. Then she heard it. Away in the darkness, a dragon of hoofs, leather and wood was flapping its way south to its St Albans lair.

Beside her, Tyler pulled up his mask. She did the same. The two highwaymen took their pistols from their holsters and cocked them.

They could hear the huff of tired horses labouring up the rise, see the waggling beam of the coach lanterns. She was bereft of time and feeling. She followed Tyler out into the open.

The coach dragged to the breast of the hill. It was enormous, pulled by giants. She and Tyler were puny.

'Rein in.' Tyler's voice rasped over the rattle of wheels.

Why should it? Why doesn't it mow us down?

She was yet to learn how dreadful masked figures in the road looked to two weary men on a coach-box, how flimsy the coach company's uniform greatcoats became at the sight of pistols, how little the pay of ten shillings a week compared to braving a bullet, what value – now they might not see them again – bestowed on wife and children at home.

The driver reined in.

'Throw down your arms.'

She saw the white flash of the guard's eyes as, slowly, watching Tyler, he bent down to the shotgun at his feet, then let it drop.

'Down.' The two men clambered down. Cecily moved to the left of the team, to guard the offside door in case one of the passengers made a break for it. She heard Tyler's command, 'Out,' listened to the grumbling and shrieks as the bleeders descended, waited for his all-clear in backslang. 'Secart.'

She moved to the onside to saw at the team's traces with Tyler's knife. Thick, encrusted leather resisted its sharpness. The horses' necks were foamed, steam rising from their coats in the fermented smell of sweat; they were glad to stand while she fumbled and cut. One piece of harness fell to the ground, she began on another strap, making a better job. She was through. If anybody drove the team now, it would merely circle. She nodded to Tyler and nudged the mare to stand alongside him in front of the line of passengers with their hands in the air.

By God, they were obeying. They were afraid. *Afraid.* Underneath her mask her teeth bared. Here's for you, Walpole.

'This'll not hurt, ladies and gentles,' Tyler sang out, cheerfully, 'not iffen you do as you're told. My apprentice here will come behind you for your offerings. Hand 'em to him backwards and we'll all be neat as ninepence, as the saying is.'

Cecily dismounted and walked behind the line of passengers – 'Never get between a bleeder and my gun' – taking the proffered valuables.

There were six bleeders. She had no compunction. In the tension beforehand her nerves had formed the image of Walpole, and six Walpoles was what she saw. Those who glanced behind them and looked into the eyes above her mask recounted the experience ever after, taking their similes from the animal world.

She snatched a heavy purse from a fat Walpole in velvet and tapped her pistol into his neck when he wasn't quick enough with his timepiece. A thin, elegant Walpole yielded two rings as well as a purse and a timepiece. A grumbling Walpole had a snuff box. She was only prevented from half strangling a short, stout Walpole in shawl and bonnet, who produced merely coppers, by Tyler's intervention: 'Leave the soul her basket, lad.'

Cramming the gains into her saddlebags, she got back on the mare. Together, pistols pointing, she and Tyler backed their mounts until they were in the shadows of the hangar. A volley of blasphemy blasted after them.

'Ride.'

They turned and rode. Through moonlit tracks, cantering between trees, taking meadows at the gallop, they rode.

'Easy. Easy.' Cecily's howls of triumph woke the ghosts of long-dead wolves and flapped owls out of their branches while

Tyler came after, smiling the smile of an indulgent mother.

Back at the inn she demanded that they pull up another jack the next night. 'You hold your horses,' Tyler said. 'We don't do nothing without we reconnoitre. Army term that is, means know your ground. S'pose we run into other padders? Can get nasty, that can.' As an extra caution he made her look at Ned's leg. 'Know what that is?'

'A bullet wound.'

'No, it ain't. It's luck. Could have been higher. Could be you next time. You pay attention. You're gettin' boastful.'

Ned's leg wasn't healing, mainly because Dolly, of whom he was afraid, hadn't let him rest it, instead insisting he clear the rubble from the taproom and one of the bedrooms.

'Lemuel and me ain't rats,' she said, when Cecily scolded her. 'We can't live in shit while you're away doing whatever you're doing.'

'You know what I'm doing.'

'No, I don't.' Dolly had withdrawn the hem of her garments; her own dishonesty allowed petty cheating, doing people down and bilking bailiffs' men but not highway robbery. Neither then nor later would she allow the subject to be discussed in her presence.

She was right, though: they couldn't squat in rubble. On the other hand, making the inn fit to live in would require help which, in turn, would reveal their presence in it.

Cecily took the problem to Tyler, who said: 'We'll ask the fencing-master when we see him.'

A fence wasn't the sort of help Cecily had in mind. 'Is he local, then?'

'Ain't he, though.' His wink said she'd get no more out of him.

They robbed the Peterborough coach just north of Baldock three days later, another from Anglesey at Markyate two days afterwards and another south of Hatfield the following week.

On each of those nights, before she went to sleep, Cecily's body shook with terror as, re-creating the scene, she made a mistake, a bleeder produced a gun, a knife; she had to shoot.

The routine simplicity of the reality was horrifying. Her

victims' obedience haunted her, not out of pity but at their potential for harm. Something could have gone wrong. That it hadn't was nearly as dreadful as if it had.

This was reaction: while the robbery was in progress she was suffused with the ferocious glee of a bully.

The hoard in the rafters of the inn became sufficiently large for Tyler to declare it ready to take to the fencing-master.

That night, following Tyler on his horse with bulging saddle-bags, Cecily on her mare crossed the Great North Road and for the first time took the track opposite her inn, breathing air sweet with blossom and cow-pats. The track led through a ford and past a pond, wandering uphill all the time towards the crest in can't-be-bothered aimlessness.

At the top they rode north along one of Hertfordshire's heights. To their right the ground dropped away in the moonlit stripes of a common field before undulating away to the flatness of East Anglia.

'Datchworth,' said Tyler.

Cecily wore highwayman kicks as a precaution but had to resist the impulse to take off hat and wig and give her hair the freedom of the night breeze.

There was no light to the east except the moon's but on her left, beyond a small, plank bridge crossing the gleam of a moat, a rushlight shone in a churchyard where a figure was sharpening a scythe on a tombstone. It called out, 'Who's 'at?'

'Tyler. Is he home?'

'Yep.'

They circled the moat through trees to where a lantern hung from above a gate which had specifically ornamental pillars. 'Tyler,' said Cecily, alarmed, 'this is a magistrate's house.'

'Ain't it, though.' His voice was amused.

Across the moat by another bridge into a cluster of barns towards a porch and light beaming through leaded windows. They dismounted and tied the horses to a hitching post. A thin woman clicked her tongue at them but led the way by a flagged passage into a room musty with books where a small man sat reading by a fire, a glass at his elbow.

'Sergeant. Delightful to see you.'

'Evening, Colonel.'

'Rum, I think, my dear. Do you think rum, Sergeant? Does your lad think rum? Yes, definitely rum.'

They drank rum with sugar and lemon, Tyler seated opposite their host, Cecily keeping to a stool in the shadows, endeavouring to believe what she heard and saw.

The Colonel was dressed like a pasha with a Turkish turban on his bald head and curved slippers on his tiny feet. The only suggestion of the military was a patch he wore over one eye. Like his house, he was elderly and glowing. 'Juvenal,' he said, laying aside his book, 'such a joker. You must read him, Tyler. What would we do without his *quis custodiet ipsos custodes*, eh?'

'We'd be lost, Colonel.'

'We would, we would. Now then. Don't tell me you've been finding things again?' He wagged a miniature finger.

'Funny enough I have, Colonel.' Tyler tipped the contents of the saddlebags on the mat before the hearth.

'*What* a lot of things, what a lot. Lying beside the road, were they?'

Tyler nodded.

'You know, Sergeant,' said the Colonel, blinking at the heap, 'one can't help wondering if this isn't stolen property. *Filch* is the word, I believe. Some robber's hoard that he dropped in his escape.'

'I wondered that myself, Colonel.'

'*Cantabit vacuus coram latrone viator*. Do *you* think the traveller with empty pockets sings even in the robber's face, Sergeant?'

'Get on with it, Colonel.' Tyler was beginning to tire.

The little man wasn't. 'Small hope, I think, of finding the owners now. One could advertise, of course, but in the meantime the finder must be rewarded. I shall take them off your hands. Ask my wife if she'd bring the scales, will you? Two shillings an ounce for silver, three for gold is fair, I think. Don't you think that's fair, Sergeant?'

The woman who'd let them in brought disapproval and a pair of scales to the fireside, then left them to the weighing of the filch. Cecily watched it with rising anger. The little pricker was *robbing* them. Timepieces with jewels were worth considerably more than their weight at two shillings an ounce, so was the silver-crested snuff box she'd taken off a lordly Walpole at Markyate. When it came to the ring from Peterborough, she intervened. 'Oh, no, you don't. That's a diamond.'

'Glass, I think. Don't you think it's glass?'

'Diamond.' She picked it up and scored his wineglass with it. Then she remembered she wasn't wearing gloves.

The Colonel sat still for a moment, peering at her from his one eye. He reached for her fingers and pressed them to his lips. *'Non Angli sed Angeli,'* he said. 'Tyler, Tyler, you let me give rum to a lady? Champagne, we must toast this moment in champagne.'

'We'll have a fair price instead,' Cecily told him.

He was a true fence: there were the difficulty of disposal, the glut since the South Sea crash, his expenses, the risk, etc. But he was facing a woman who'd sold her soul for those trinkets and knew the value of it – and them. Eventually he handed over a hundred pounds, a quarter of what the heap was worth but more than Tyler had expected.

'And you're a magistrate?' Cecily was still incredulous.

'I have the honour to have been appointed by Her late Majesty to keep the peace in this area which, I am happy to say, I do.'

Mainly because their bargain was that Tyler operated out of it.

His name was Grandison. He was also a Mason, a member of the Hertford Society of Poetic Appreciation and Philosophy, toxophilist, master of the Stevenage Hunt, lord of this manor of Datchworth, a hundred acres and forty-nine villagers, the second son of a knight, who'd despised him, a disappointing husband.

It was impossible not to like him: he expounded his provenance and failures with devastating frankness and good humour, sometimes standing up and spinning on his small feet in *joie de vivre*.

A grasping fence, but a generous host: they drank champagne from French crystal and they drank it to 'Confusion to that arch-villain, Robert Walpole, and all Whigs'.

He was one on his own but if there was a type under the

eccentricity it belonged to that of the passed-over second son, the misfit who never won the approval of his parents, a spirit larger than its body, possessing a taste for literature and beautiful things beyond his income. Hence, Cecily supposed, his complacency in fencing stolen goods.

Unselfconscious, he sprawled at her feet murmuring: 'I adore you, my Penthesilea, my beauty in male attire. No, no, not Amazon. A moon goddess. Great is Diana of the Ephesians.'

Cecily shifted him off her boots. 'Get up, sir.' She wasn't discomfited: he reminded her of Lord Hervey miniaturized.

He was also kind. When Tyler told him that Cecily was in residence at the Bell, his concern was for her comfort. 'You shall have the Packer brothers. Good lads, though troublesome when unoccupied, as they are until harvest. The Packers, don't you think, Sergeant?'

As she and Tyler wandered back down the hill, Cecily asked: 'What do Grandison's villagers make of him?'

'They're used to him. He's a good squire. Sees 'em right, cares for the young 'uns – which is only fair seeing as he's fathered quite a few of 'em.' Tyler was anxious to dispel any doubts about his fence's masculinity. 'Very susceptible to a pretty pair of saucers, is the Colonel. There's more than one maid gets talked into the hay by his flummery.'

'How did he lose his eye?'

'French cavalryman's lance. Blenheim. Saving my life, mad little bugger.'

Next morning the Packers, four of them, reported for duty, standing before Cecily in a line of descending age and height which still counted in the youngest and shortest at six foot tall. *What do they feed them on in Datchworth?* They stared over her head with the animation of oxen. 'Ah,' she said. She didn't know what to do with them.

Dolly did, putting them at ease and to work by shouting at them like a galley-master. Their usefulness was as great as their size: Cecily watched the eldest and largest, Cole, lift an errant oak beam from the taproom floor as easily as if it was a dandelion. Warty (who wasn't) mended ceilings, Tinker retiled the roof. Like all Datchworth men, their nicknames related to incidents in their past, which set Cecily wondering about the youngest, Stabber, an excellent plasterer.

Basically, they were forest men who were able to survive when Grandison had no work for them by their customary right to collect its wood and turf, take any of its deer that wandered into their gardens – it was astonishing how many did – graze their cattle and geese on its grasses and fish its streams.

Dinner at the Bell was improved by the addition of venison and trout to its table, by rooks plucked for the pie, mushrooms and plover eggs – all gifts left in the kitchen by a surly Packer who refused thanks.

It was Tinker who made the discovery in the roof. He brought it down to the yard, unwrapping it from the cloth in which it had been tied.

Everybody gathered to look at a faded inn sign, still attached to the chains which had once suspended it. Some primitive artist had painted on it the semi-naked figure of a woman wearing feathers and a ferocious smile, holding a spear aloft.

'What's them words say?' asked Stabber.

Cecily rubbed the dust off the letters with her apron. 'The Belle Sauvage.'

'What's that mean when it's at home?'

'The Savage Beauty.'

'Never knew that. We allus called that the Bell.'

'No wonder that lost bloody custom,' said Tinker. 'Wouldn't like to meet her of a dark night.'

It was too worm-eaten to keep. That night they put it on the fire in the taproom and watched it burn. Goose-pimples of superstition raised themselves on Cecily's skin as the painted face gave her a last grin through the contortion of flames, like a message of approval from the Devil.

On market-day she borrowed a cart and horse from Colonel Grandison and took Lemuel and Dolly the seven miles into Hertford to buy provisions and rudimentary furniture out of her robbery gains. With the house being resurrected from death, it was impossible to conceal its occupation and, Cecily thought, unnecessary; to be *persona grata* with a magistrate and the Packers reduced the feeling that she had taken up occupation in enemy territory. Those who required her name were told she was Mrs Henry who'd brought her disabled husband from London for country air.

Two nights later Cecily and Tyler were holding up a coach outside Hatfield on the Great North Road; the usual procedure, frightened Walpoles standing in a row next to sullen coachmen. She no longer looked at them.

It wasn't until she'd remounted and was backing the mare into the shadows preparatory to riding off that one staring face in the line of staring faces, white in the light of the coach lamp, lost its Walpoleness.

On the way home Tyler said: 'What's the matter, Duchess?'

'Back there. There was a man . . . I know him.'

'Shite. Did he recognize you?'

'I don't know. No, I don't think so.'

'Who is he?'

'His name's Cameron. He could have been coming to see me – and Lemuel. He's a lawyer.'

'Shite.'

Next morning, just in case, to emphasize the absurdity of connecting Lady Cecily Fitzhenry with robbery, she dressed in her only remaining good gown. Peering into the flecked shard that was her looking-glass, she thought: Not a padder. But not Lady Cecily either. Her skin, eyes and teeth were still good but their character was altered by a battered spirit. She was twenty-one years old and looked thirty. She brushed her hair for the first time in days and covered it with a clean cap.

Dolly said: 'What's got you up like a Christmas beef?'

It was a long day. Tyler had made himself scarce. Cecily told Ned, who was now living in one of the bedrooms, to hide the mare, then took Lemuel for a walk. They picked celandines and primroses to make unhighwayman-like posies for the taproom.

The lawyer arrived on a horse in late afternoon. He was his normal self, as far as she knew what was normal with him. 'Who were yon gentlemen I've just seen leaving?'

Relieved, Cecily said: 'Men from the village up the hill. They're helping us get in order.'

'Lord bless us for that. I thought they were bears.'

Dolly was delighted to see him: 'You didn't half buy us a pig in a poke, you. Look at the place.' She took him on a tour of inspection.

They ate in the taproom on a plank over trestles, the four stools and the settle from Hertford market looking lonely in the enormous space around them, its only comfort provided by the fire – there was an abundance of rotten wood to burn.

Over dinner Archibald Cameron complimented Lemuel on his improved health. Dolly said: 'He can talk a bit now. If you give him time.' Which she never did.

'I've passed the day with the Hatfield magistrate,' Cameron said. 'Did ye hear my coach was robbed on the way here?'

'Never.'

He nodded. 'Two villainous rogues as ever swung from a gibbet.' He described the hold-up, dwelling with hyperbole on the ugliness and ferocity of the robbers and bewailing the loss of his timepiece and money. 'One pound, four shilling and eightpence halfpenny.'

Dolly joined in with easy condemnation. 'I don't know what the world's coming to. You can't sleep safe in your bed.' In rejecting any involvement with Cecily's profession, she had put it from her mind. She so ignored her sister-in-law's night-time comings and goings that, Cecily realized, she was truly unaware that the lawyer's timepiece and cash were stored with other filch in one of the many secret cupboards upstairs. 'Shocking, ain't it, Cessy?'

'Indeed.'

After dinner, the lawyer offered her his arm. 'Will ye take the air with me, Lady Cecily?'

Coolly, she took it, confident now, and they walked together through the yard and the stables to watch the sun set behind the trees of the forest.

There was no alteration in his tone as he said: 'And now, if ye will, I'll have back my timepiece and one pound four shilling and eightpence halfpenny.'

She was dismayed, then angry. 'Damn you. How did you know it was me?'

'I know ye.'

117

'You didn't tell the magistrate?'

'I did not.'

'Why not?'

'I'd have your explanation first.' All at once his anger outdid hers. He held her by the arms and shook her. 'Woman, what possessed ye? Have ye no shame? Cavorting in sin and male clothing?'

She shouted back at him: 'No, I haven't any shame, they took it away in the Fleet. As for this shit-hole, it only looks bare now. When we got here it wasn't fit for rats. Your fine purchase. Yours. What was I to do. Eh? *Eh?*'

He dropped his hands. 'Ye could have come back to me.'

'Lemuel was ill. He was *ill.*' She heard her own voice shrieking into the evening. Exhausted, she sat down.

The Scotsman sat down beside her, resting his chin on his knees. Late-to-bed larks flittered upwards and then down into the grass of the meadow. 'I won my case,' he said.

What case, and did it matter? 'Will you tell the magistrate about me?'

'I'm a rising man in my profession. Sir Robert himself consults me.'

Punctilious little pricker, he was telling her he wouldn't condone her crime, even by keeping silent.

'I could support ye.'

If she'd been less anxious of betrayal, if she'd considered him more, she'd have recognized devotion when she heard it. It was a long time before she did. As it was, she was sick of being always disadvantaged in his presence. 'Thank you, I do not wish to live on charity.'

He sighed and whipped away the metaphorical cloak, which he had laid at her feet, like Sir Walter Ralegh under his queen's, before she could step on it. 'Ye prefer robbery under arms, is that it?'

All that was left of the sun was an aureole over the trees where a nightingale had begun its arpeggios.

He said: 'I must ask ye, madam, if that man . . . your accomplice last night, is he your lover? Why are you smiling?'

Because he'd overstepped the mark by showing prurient

118

interest. She had the advantage now. She stood up. 'I thank you for your concern, sir. I want neither your charity nor your questions. Do what you think best in this matter but, whatever it is, I bid you goodnight.'

He remained on the ground, looking up at her. 'At least give me your word ye'll not repeat last night's performance.'

'No.'

He scrambled to his feet, furious, surprising her again by being taller than she was. 'Lord, how I loathe a Tory. Ye think birth is everything, ye'd steal rather than do an honest day's work. Look about ye. This place is no' much now but with investment it could be a fine hostelry.' The Glaswegian Rs rolled in temper, the vowels shortened. 'There's such a matter as loans. Have ye heard of them? No. Lady Cecily'll not soil her hands with common innkeeping. She'll terrorize innocent folk and steal their living rather than earn her own.'

'Goodnight.' She was already walking away.

'Before I go, madam, I'll have back my timepiece and one pound four shilling and eightpence halfpenny.'

As she turned into the stableyard on her way to get them, his voice came after her: 'And I'll have the tuppence I gave ye for the letter ye never sent.'

Tinker Packer had set up rope and pulley to carry his tiles to the roof. It hung from a gargoyle over the balcony and so into the yard. When Cecily had collected the timepiece from the cupboard, counted out Cameron's money and added tuppence, she put it into a saddlebag, which she attached to the rope and lowered.

Cameron was waiting in the yard with his horse. He retrieved his goods in the silence with which she'd sent them down. Humiliated and angry, Cecily didn't regret breaking the laws of hospitality but, as his horse was about to go under the yard arch, her conscience gave a tweak. 'If you turn north, there's some sort of inn at Stevenage.' She was tempted to add, 'Beware of highwaymen,' but decided against it. She listened to his horse's hoofbeats diminish into the distance.

'Where's Archie?' asked Dolly, when Cecily returned to the taproom.

119

'Gone.'

'Gone? I just made a bed for him upstairs.'

'He won't be needing it.'

'Sent him away, din'cher? Din'cher? Gawd, what a noddle. Supposed to be a whashical, a scholar? I seen cleverer dead pigs.'

'What are you on about, woman?'

'He give us this place, that's what. Reckon it was one o' your fancy friends done it? I'm the Queen of Sheba. While they was all sitting scratching their ballocks, it was Archie Cameron got us out the dismals. *An'* bought this scran. All right, it ain't up to much but all he could afford, poor bastard, and a bloody sight more than any other bugger did.'

'Nonsense,' said Cecily, 'he wouldn't do that. He's a purse-proud, penny-pinching little Scot. I've seen him quibble over tuppence. He wouldn't do that.' Then she said: 'Would he?' Then she said: '*Why* would he?'

Dolly turned away. 'Lemuel was his client, wasn't he? Didn't want him homeless, did he? He's a good man.'

Intermittently, Dolly experienced jealousy of her sister-in-law's looks and accomplishments. Cecily, she felt, gave herself too many airs already. So what Dolly would not say at that moment, though she thought it, was: 'The poor bleeder loves you. Don't want to, can't help it.'

But she was right. The Scotsman, at that moment riding towards Stevenage at a pace dangerous to himself, his horse and anyone on the road, felt a resentment against Cecily as fierce as Dolly's own and shouted it to the night around him in language that would have shocked the elders of his kirk, not to mention the harsh, pious old grandmother who'd raised him in the even harsher poverty from which his excellent brain had released him.

Archibald Cameron had laid down his life's plan as meticulously as a gardener planting seeds with a slide rule. Advancement in his profession, mebbe to the Lord Chancellorship or, at least, to a bench in the High Court. A town house, a country manor or two, servants. A mild, pretty, attentive wee wife and healthy bairns. Thanks to keen political acumen and a memory that retained every word he read, he was on his way to achieve the first; the rest would follow.

In this neatly hoed row, unexpected, unwanted, Lady Cecily Fitzhenry had taken root and sprouted like a weed, infiltrating his mind as quickly as he worked to pluck her out of it.

Aye, well, he'd be free of the slut now. That's one slice of Adam's spare rib he'd help no more. Ravaging the roads like a harpy, Lord save us. And in breeks. Granted, it was not much of an inn – and the agent would hear of it – but he'd gone without to purchase the place. Even had he been prepared to see her roofless, he'd have still done as much for the poor, ancient sumph they'd wed her to.

'*Ha til mi tulidh.* Let the piper play.' In extreme moments, joy or anger, Archie Cameron sang. 'A bride to wash ma feet afore my age slips awa'.'

Obliterate memory of the hag, that's to do. Pluck out her bloody image from his bloody eyes. With her 'indeed-Mr-Camerons' as if she addressed a packman, and holes in her kirtle. Her arms about poor Sir Lemuel in the bridewell, hollering like a banshee at the warden. She had courage, he'd give her that. And well favoured. But no longer would she be beef nor brase of his.

Usually a considerate rider, Archibald Cameron applied his spurs to his lathering horse. 'Get on, will ye? A pudding could creep faster.'

'*Ha til mi tulidh.* Let the piper play. I return no more.'

What made him crosser yet was the knowledge that he would.

Cecily, too, retired in resentment. What was Hecuba to him or he to Hecuba that he should buy her the Belle? *If* he had. *Which* she doubted. But *if* he had . . .

For Lemuel, Dolly said. Lemuel had put work his way, so perhaps it was his due. But that still left Lady Cecily squirming in the debt of a pedantic, puritanical, pen-pushing North Briton in a fox-coloured wig. Lecturing her on morality.

She was satisfied on one point: he wasn't going to give her away. Nevertheless, she found it difficult to sleep.

The next coach she and Tyler stopped was on the Essex road, outside Stansted Abbots. Cecily was passing behind the row of passengers, collecting the filch. Tyler was holding the reins of her mare, his pistol trained on the line.

There was a shot. The mare screamed and bucked. Another shot. Cecily heard the whip of the bullet over her head before it hit the coach roof coping. Tyler was struggling to hold the mare, shouting, 'Epasky, epasky.' Escape.

As she pushed aside two passengers to get to her horse, one of them stuck his leg between the two of hers and brought her down. They rolled on the ground. Then a louder shot made his body jerk on top of her and go slack. She pushed him off and scrambled to her feet, clawing away a woman who clutched at her coat. She ran, bent double, to Tyler. Still holding a smoking pistol in his right hand, he hoisted her behind him with his left, and they were away. The mare, loose, cantered behind them.

Another shot spurted twigs up from the ground as they entered the trees.

When they stopped at last, they were panting into a forest silence that covered them like ointment. Cecily slid off, held on to a tree and vomited down its trunk. Tyler was swearing, patting her back and asking if she was hurt.

She wiped her mouth. 'What happened?'

'. . . prick-scouring, cunt-itching, crack-fishing, bun-buttering . . .'

'What *happened*?'

'Padders. They was down the road waiting for the jack, I reckon. The shots were angled. We must've been on their patch.'

'Bastards. They could have killed us.'

'Bloody near did. *And* I dropped one of me pistols.'

'The bleeder fighting me, they shot him. He could be dead.'

'That was me. I shot him.'

'For God's sake, why?'

'Some bugger had to do something and *you* weren't shooting him.'

'No.' It hadn't occurred to her. 'We aren't in the pad to kill people.'

'Ain't in it to *be* killed, neither.'

Tyler was soothing the mare. He walked into a patch of moonlight and regarded his hand, which was shining black. 'She's got a bullet in her shoulder. We'll have to walk her home.'

It was twelve miles through the forest avoiding Hertford. Steady walking took the shake from Cecily's legs. She felt an abject dreariness: it was possible that a man, who had been living, was dead. Because of her.

Tyler had done the only thing he could if she were not to have been killed by the bleeder himself, the rival padders, or the hangman.

But, she was forced to admit, the bleeder had been within his rights too. A fool, but within his rights. Not a big man, not one used to violence; he'd merely scrabbled at her. I'd have got away from him. My knee in his whats-its would have done it.

She'd felt his desperation when he'd clawed at her; could hear the sobbing scream in his breath as they'd struggled together on the ground.

For the first time she realized how awful it was to be robbed. Her victims weren't Walpoles after all, but ordinary men and women suffering indignity and loss. Perhaps the bleeder who'd attacked her couldn't afford to give up the filch she'd taken from him, perhaps it was his total savings, money to pay his rent and keep a roof over his children. And now he could be dead.

As Cecily walked through the forest, its trees assumed the bent shapes of widows evicted from their homes.

I was evicted from mine, she told them. Your man should have stood in line like he was told. But they answered in the voice of the Scotsman: 'Ye'll terrorize innocent folk and steal their living rather than earn your own.' Now, perhaps, she had killed.

Her high adventure was over, she knew. It had fallen sick. No more to be one of Diana's foresters, a gentleman of the shade, a minion of the moon. It turned out she never had been; it was just a killing game.

(When she learned two days later that the bleeder was recovering from a scalp wound, Cecily walked up to Datchworth church and knelt in it for a long time.)

The mare was anaesthetized by shock for the first few miles; after that it took all the two of them could do to persuade her forwards. The dawn had come up by the time they reached Woolmer Green and they had to wait among the trees for an opportunity to cross the road to the inn without being seen by the traffic.

As they waited, Cecily regarded her inn. The windows of the taproom were glazed now and blinked at her in the first rays of sun. She saw in them the wink of the Scottish lawyer to whom she would now have to send a grovelling letter and a request.

'Tyler,' she said, heavily, 'it's time we tried our hand at an honest trade.'

CHAPTER SEVEN

WHERE GOD, through His Son, said: Blessed are the Poor . . .

. . . and where the Middle Ages backed Him up: Blessed are the Poor and those who relieve their poverty . . .

. . . and where the Tudors said: True, the Poor are blessed but they shouldn't run all over the place, threatening the peace with their begging and rioting; it is Christian duty to make sure they don't starve and it is also politic that the parishes levy a Poor Rate to look after those who can't work and find employment for those that can. Oh, and whip the vagrants . . .

. . . and where the Stuarts didn't say anything . . .

. . . it was Sir Robert Walpole's Whigs who were the first to make the discovery that there *were* no Poor, just lazy, immoral men and women breeding on the Poor Rate – using the tax to get drunk, finding it more advantageous to accept parish charity than work for manufacturers, the creators of the country's wealth. Admittedly, manufacturers couldn't pay much but, if they offered what the Poor regarded as a living wage, it would cut down England's competitiveness with France in foreign markets.

The Whigs lived in the real world.

As Bernard Mandeville, a student of human nature, pointed out at this time in a tract on Charity Schools, there was no gain in educating the Poor. Every hour they spent at school was so much time lost to Society. If they were to endure a life of labour, the sooner they were put to it the more patiently they'd submit to it ever after.

Parish overseers did their best. Women about to give birth to a child likely to be a drain on the rate – and whose father wasn't a parishioner – were bundled across the parish boundary to be somebody else's concern.

In London orphaned and deserted babies were put into the charge of nurses under whose care three-quarters of them obligingly saved their cost of two shillings a week by dying.

Despite all this, the parish rates, like crime, continued to rise and the Poor insisted on remaining poor.

In the countryside, expanding landowners grew tired of thatched cottages littering their estates. They wanted to look out on parks and gardens designed by Kent or Bridgeman and on Palladio's temples. Intent on a literary and pictorial panorama, they moved hills, dammed streams, excavated lakes and grottoes and changed in a trice a landscape that had grown slowly over a thousand years under the care of woodsmen and farmers. Villages and hamlets were razed and their inhabitants dispossessed. The village of Edensor was moved to improve the view from Chatsworth, the village of Henderskelt levelled to make the south front of Castle Howard.

When Sir Robert Walpole began pulling down the Elizabethan home he'd inherited from his father and building instead a Palladian mansion such as had never before been seen in Norfolk, his Houghton villagers were commanded out of their homes and sent away, their furniture piled on wains and handcarts, their eyes looking back on the gimcrack cottages that had occupied the site as long as memory ran.

Where did they go? It didn't matter. Sir Robert and the rest had an uninterrupted view, that was the main thing. Peasants never could appreciate classical beauty.

Perhaps they went to join the indigenous families of the forests who made a living by taking such deer as wandered into their cottage purlieus, trapping wild coneys, fish, using wood they could reach by hook and by crook, digging turves.

The forest people called these activities ancient rights and privileges granted to their ancestors by the barons of the Middle Ages.

The new Whiggish landowners called them poaching.

This wasn't the first time the word 'poor' had been associated with the word 'criminal', though the two were now virtually synonymous. But it took the genius of the Prime Minister, Sir Robert Walpole, to add a subtler, equally panic-bearing, connotation – 'Jacobite'.

The inn at Woolmer Green opened for business smelling of new wood and the brick that had mended the outside walls, of the fresh lath and plaster that had constructed the inner, and very faintly of the cow dung which made tensile the new firebacks in the grates.

The chestnut tree that had shaded the inn's frontage was now a stump, allowing light into its windows and making it more visible from the road. Part of the tree had been made into a gibbet, which stood on the edge of the newly gravelled forecourt, carrying a large, chestnut board only a blind man could miss. The sign depicted a woman warrior, spear aloft. Underneath ran the legend: The Belle Sauvage.

Most had resisted the inn's title. The Packers said it was too foreign, Colonel Grandison, too frightening, Dolly and the local parson, too heathenish, but Cecily felt a superstitious obligation which she translated as: 'It's bad luck to change a name.'

Archibald Cameron, who'd raised the loan for the renovation – and hadn't been forgiven for being nice about it – grinned and said that if the name didn't fit the inn, it fitted the landlady.

The Packers had found thirty feet of oak linenfold, the hall screen of an old manor that was being rebuilt in Palladian style at Bramfield, 'going begging'. With it, Cecily divided off part of the taproom into a snug for her regulars, leaving a main area for passing trade.

From the rest of the panelling and an old door she made an office for herself in a corner that had a window on the Great North Road, and had another cut so that she could keep an eye on the yard.

On a fine July day in 1723, she sat at the escritoire Colonel Grandison had given her, doing the accounts. Flies, the smell of horses and hay came through the open window to the yard. Archibald Cameron looked over her shoulder, an irritating stance but one to which she could hardly object: as well as investing in the Belle, he'd become its lawyer.

'Are those Ned's accounts?'

'Yes,' she said. Ned was now the inn's ostler.

'Does he write Greek?'

'He hardly writes English.'

'He has the Greek flavour.' Cameron picked up Ned's slate that Cecily was copying into her ledger and read: '"To anos. 2s. To agitinonimom 6d."'

'For goodness' sake.' She snatched the slate back. 'It's clear enough. Squire Leggatt was too drunk to ride home last week and went back to the Colonel's to sleep it off. We stabled his horse for the night and Ned had to return it to Knebworth for him next morning. "To a horse. 2s. To a getting on him home. 6d." See?'

She turned back to the accounts and he continued to watch until the last entry had been sprinkled with sand and drops of sweat from her forehead. It was hot in the office. 'There. Thank God that's done.'

'Ye're no bad at it.' He took the ledger. 'It balances. But finely. Ye're making no profit after all's paid.'

Did he think she didn't know? 'I need the coach trade. We're popular with the locals, Colonel Grandison brings all his Tory friends to the snug. But the coach trade's where the profit is.'

'It'll no' be easy attracting it away from St Albans.'

He was a marvellous soul for pointing out the obvious. But she and Tyler had a plan to remedy the lack of coach trade which it would be impolitic to tell a legal man.

'Now,' she said, briskly, 'you're sure you can get Cole off?'

'Aye. I went to Hertford and looked at the charge. They've –'

The door opened. 'Cecily, my dear . . .' Colonel Grandison was petitely pretty in brocade but worried. 'How de do, Cameron, how de do? Just the man. Can you save our poor Cole Packer?'

'A good afternoon to ye, Colonel. I was about to tell Mrs Henry here. He's been indicted in the name of *Walter* Packer . . .'

'Lord in His mercy be praised.' The Colonel turned to Cecily. 'My dear, we can produce the parish register where, plain as a pikestaff, the man's given name is writ Waller.'

For all her relief she couldn't resist a hit at the Scotsman. 'How interesting that justice depends on technicalities.'

'It's no' ideal,' he said, shortly, 'but yon technicality will save the laddie's neck from the noose.'

'Indeed,' Cecily said. 'It's interesting, too, that smashing a fishpond, which had no right to be there in the first place, is become a capital offence. Don't you think so, Mr Cameron?'

Shutting her ledger with a slap, she led the way into the tap-room to give the two men ale.

Unfair perhaps, but she was unsettled, almost fearful; cross with Cole Packer, cross with the new owner of the forest and crossest of all with this, the only representative of the even newer law on whom she could vent her spleen.

These last two years had shown that Lady Cecily Potts possessed a capacity for hard work and attendance to detail that made her into a more than competent landlady. She was disgusted to find herself such – when she had time to consider it. It suggested a plebeian streak. She consoled her shame by telling herself it was her wifely duty – from which the bluest feminine blood was not exempt – to provide for Lemuel while he made his recovery, as indeed he was doing.

Yet, with Cole Packer's arrest had come the revelation that, busy as the two years were, they'd been as fulfilling as any she could remember. Insidiously, the people with whom she worked, Tyler, Ned, the Packers, Colonel Grandison, even Dolly, had become necessities she could not spare and, therefore, hostages to Providence.

Now the shadow that had chased her out of London had reassembled itself into something more general, more poisonous to the harmony of her landscape, everybody's landscape.

Walpole, of course. Always Walpole.

His increased taxation of Catholics had forced the ancestral owner of Bramfield forest, a forest of which Datchworth was a

128

part and which crossed the Great North Road to encompass her inn and purlieus, to sell it to the newly created Whig peer and friend of Walpole, Lord Letty.

With the appointment of Letty's verderer had come the introduction of a forest law that the people who lived in it neither understood nor recognized.

Suddenly, the trout stream that had run alongside Cole Packer's cottage for as long as anyone could remember ceased to run. Following the drying bed, Cole found it diverted into a large, stone-bound fish pond belonging to the new verderer. Not caring who saw him, he took a mallet to the pond-head and set the stream flowing back into its old course.

He was arrested immediately and taken to the Hertford bridewell. Cecily, expecting him to come up before the Hertford magistrates, went to the gaol armed with a lecture and money for his fine.

She was refused permission to see him. 'Sorry, mistress,' she was told, 'he's charged under the Black Act.'

'What's the Black Act?'

The gaoler scratched his head. 'Don't rightly know, mistress. Some new law they've come up with in Lunnon that's like to hang un.'

'*Hang* him?'

Colonel Grandison, when applied to, was as mystified as the gaoler. Act 9 George 1.c.22 had been passed so quickly – there'd been less than a month between its first reading in the House and the royal assent – that it had only now arrived on his desk. He read it while she waited, 'Fifty,' she heard him mutter. 'Fifty, do you think?'

'Fifty what, for goodness' sake?'

'Fifty capital offences.' He looked up at her. 'Oh, my dear. Fifty new hanging matters put on to the statute books at the stroke of a pen. A rabbit – you can now be hanged for poaching a deer, a sheep, a rabbit, or a hare or even a fish if you go armed or disguised while doing so. In the King's forests you can be hanged for it, disguised and armed or not. Cutting down a tree in any garden, orchard or plantation . . .'

Cecily supposed mildly that, retrospectively, she could be

taken to the gallows as accessory. Neither she nor the Packers regarded the occasional haunch of venison served up at the Belle as poached; she bought, and the Packers sold, in good faith.

Poaching. A poacher was Johnny Marsh who'd taken too many of her deer in the old days. Her keeper had caught Marsh, whipped him, shot his hunting dogs – as was the gamekeeper's summary right – and that had been an end of it. It hadn't occurred to Cecily or the keeper to go back two hundred years and hang the man.

For that matter, the Stevenage Hunt – the same hunt that boasted three JPs other than the Colonel among its members – frequently chased a deer into Bramfield forest without bothering its owner for licence. It was the give and take of country living, understood by all. Even the deer expected it.

She returned to the matter in hand. 'But Cole smashed a fish pond, that's all. Letty's man stole his stream.'

'Fifty,' Colonel Grandison was saying, rubbing his wig. 'I doubt if any other country possesses a criminal code with anything like so many capital provisions as in this single statute.'

He seemed to be absorbing some enormity which she hadn't grasped and wasn't interested in grasping. 'But what about Cole?'

'And passed *nem con*,' he went on. 'Not a word raised against it. Damn the Whigs – your pardon, my dear. They set more store by the life of a beast than a man.'

'Cole, Colonel,' Cecily said sharply.

'The death penalty for him, my dear,' the Colonel told her, tapping the Act copy. 'Breaking a pond-head carries the death penalty.'

'Nonsense.'

'I agree. Damn the Whigs – pardon again, my dear. What will they do next?' Now he was all activity, clapping on his feathered hat and calling out of the window for his horse, a miniature knight errant. 'I'm for Hertford.'

Entering the Belle later that night, he was tipsy. Fellow magistrates had been as confused by the Act as he was, though the

130

Whigs among them not quite so appalled. ' 'S only an emergency measure, my dear. 'S against Jacobite ruffians, Blacks in Windsor, naughty, naughty men. 'S the Black Act. Jury . . . jury'll never convict our Cole.'

'What do you mean a jury? Won't he be tried by magistrates?'

Grandison shook his head. 'He'll . . . to go to King's Bench.'

'That he won't.' Cole's wife, Marjorie, was as small as the Colonel, twenty times more ferocious and the only living thing her husband was afraid of. 'You get me that bugger back now, Colonel. He an't fixed my dairy roof. What for's that have-his-corp?'

'Habeas Corpus . . . ss-suspended, Marjorie, my dear, because of Japcop . . . Jacobite plots. Emergency.'

'Then you un-suspend it. I don't care what blacks and Jacobites do down south, they ain't hanging my Cole.'

Even she wasn't too disturbed. Cole had been a frequent guest of the Hertford bridewell in his early days: he'd always come out. And whatever the national emergency necessitating such ferocious legislation, news of it hadn't reached Hertfordshire and, therefore, it was considered neither national nor an emergency.

It was when an Enfield Chase labourer, twenty miles off in Middlesex, was hanged for stealing a sheep – unlike horse-theft, sheep-stealing had not previously been a capital offence – that Hertfordshire woke up to the fact that the Black Act meant business.

The emergency that occasioned the Black Act had arisen in Windsor Great Park, once Queen Anne's favourite hunting ground – even in her arthritic years she'd been sped through it behind her hounds in a little horse-drawn chariot. In those days her benignity had kept an equilibrium in the age-old running battle between keeper and poacher.

But the accession of King George and the Whigs had brought a new officialdom to the forest which damned such laxity and came down hard, not only on poaching but on the taking of fish, rabbits, turves and wood – perquisites that had kept many a forest cottager off the Poor Rate.

Windsor magistrates were slow to convict for crimes that had formerly been misdemeanours, and received letters of condemnation from the Prime Minister for being so.

An ancient battle escalated into war, with viciousness on both sides. A keeper was killed. The poachers, now a gang smearing soot on their faces to avoid recognition, thus earned the sobriquet 'Blacks', and were heard to shout: 'God damn King George.'

That – and as far as Colonel Grandison could discover, that alone – gave Prime Minister Walpole the opportunity to denounce a Jacobite plot that was overrunning the country's forests and leaving no property-owning Englishman safe in his bed.

'Hence the Black Act of a black bastard – begging your pardon, my dear.'

If Sir Robert had managed to bend the House of Commons to his will, he wasn't managing to subdue all protest from a country already restive at the number of Walpole relatives now appearing in high office. Even his third son, still at school, was receiving an official salary.

A certain amount of nepotism and corruption in ministers was to be expected but Walpole, it was felt, was overdoing it. As Colonel Grandison said, 'The French called Cardinal Richelieu the best relative there ever was. They hadn't met our Sir Robert.'

The Tory *True Briton* asked why a highway robber 'committed perhaps for a trifle or the mere relief of his necessities' should be executed 'whilst another, who has enriched himself at the expense of his country, shall not only escape with impunity, but, by a servile herd of flatterers and sycophants, have all his actions crowned with applause'.

The Belle Sauvage's taproom sang the song that was sweeping the nation: 'When all great offices, by dozens/Are filled by brothers, sons and cousins . . .'

Cecily's erstwhile friend Alexander Pope pitched into the fray when his brother-in-law, Charles Rackett, another Catholic, was accused of being a Berkshire 'Black':

Tell me, which knave is lawful game, which not?
Must great offenders, once escap'ed the crime,
Like royal harts, be never more run down?
Have you less pity for the needy cheat,
The poor and friendless villain than the great?

Cecily gleefully repeated it to Archibald Cameron, who winced.

However, it was thanks to the foxy-wigged Scottish lawyer that Cole Packer came out of Hertford bridewell. His wife gave him a clout on the ear for having got into it in the first place. Cecily lectured him, but served a round of free ale to a celebrating taproom that night.

She thought that Cameron, hero of the hour, could have accepted the company's cheers with more modesty. As she passed his tankard she hissed Shakespeare: ' "First thing we do, let's kill all the lawyers." It was the Law put Cole in jeopardy in the first place.'

'And it was the Law got him out.' He was in high fettle. 'Confess I did fine and ye're pleased to see the man back.'

'I am pleased at the return of a useful servant.' The Packers were the bedrock of the Belle: plumbers, builders, chuckers-out. At night they brought their friends, other foresters, to drink. Their wives, aunts and cousins served in taproom and kitchen.

But she was aware that her relief was more than that: at first she had commanded the brothers as she'd commanded her former servants, through an aloof courtesy with a whip in its boot. Without effect. If the Packers thought a job wasn't worth doing, they didn't do it; if they thought it was, they did it to their own satisfaction, not hers. They responded more amiably to Dolly, who amused them, until, as ever, she fell out with them one by one.

A conversation one day between Warty and Stabber, which Cecily was meant to overhear, used the word 'pad' six times.

'She do want that pump padded against frost, Wart.'

'Ain't worth it, Stab. That's like my Mary's dumplings, don't need padding.'

'Us'll pad on over to it, shall us? See if that needs a pad?'

And so on. They *knew*.

It wasn't that they disapproved of Cecily's highway activity, they were merely informing her that loftiness was unacceptable from a coach-robber. After thinking it over, she had to agree with them.

It was difficult for her to unbend to them as she did with Tyler: with their smocks, their hugeness and the slow oy-oy of their accent, each looked the archetypal bumpkin. She'd heard London crowds sharpen their wit on a hundred like them.

But the Packers had their own wit. When Cecily, remonstrating with Cole, who'd been working outside in a thunderstorm, for walking into her newly cleaned taproom, said: 'You're wet, man,' Cole stared at his smock in simulated amazement. 'Gor dear, if that in't rain all over. Does it every time.' And Cecily laughed.

To see Packer faces, like round, lugubriously humorous clocks, about the place became a reassurance that all was well. Tinker was the most troublesome, only because he couldn't resist women – nor they him – but fondness for all of them crept up on her. Packer chaff, she learned, was not *lèse majesté*, but liking. Somewhat uneasily, she learned to chaff back, wondering at lowering herself, more often marvelling at their subsequent willingness to please. When Cole looked likely to hang, she'd experienced not the remote concern of an employer but the panic of a soldier for a fallen comrade.

None of this would she admit to Archibald Cameron. He'd become as indispensable to her as the Packers and the two of them had been forced into a somewhat uncomfortable *modus vivendi* that they eased by exchanging insults, teasing on his part, sincere on hers.

Knowing how much she owed him, Cecily, who loathed owing anybody anything, kept a distance between them. His frequent visits to the Belle – he now had his own room – she suspected as emphasizing her debt, as well as a cheap method by which he could enjoy his favourite recreation of fishing the local rivers.

'I've a letter for ye,' he said, and produced a folded paper so rubbed that, in the flickering light of the crowded taproom, she could only just read the superscription: 'To Lady Cecily Potts, last heard of in London. Haste. Haste.'

I'll be back for you, Lady Cecily, Lady Cecily. The seven years of his transportation were up: she'd counted every day of them. He'd found her. Somehow, through the mercy of God, he'd found her.

She opened her eyes to find she was holding the letter to her cheek. The Scotsman was watching her with what she divined to be pity. She covered up with rudeness: 'The seal's broken. Have you read it?'

'I have not.' His thin lips thinned tighter. 'Yon's been lying on a shelf in the General Post Office for three months since no body kenned where ye were. I have been conducting a case for the laddie in charge at Lombard Street, who told me of it. I undertook to become your postboy. And here it is.' He looked around at the uproarious drinkers. 'Haste away now and read it.'

Haste, haste. She snatched up a candle from one of the tables and was unfolding the letter as she went upstairs, turning to the last leaf. Such a vile hand, bless him, oh, bless him. She stopped her rush on the landing to let the flame burn still so that she could decipher the signature.

It wasn't his.

It was Sophie's. 'Sophia C,' it ran.

She went into her bedroom, put the candle down on a table, blew it out and sat on the bed in darkness. It wasn't from him, Lady Cecily, Lady Cecily. It never would be. He was dead. Years gone, in chains, in the transport ship. Or dead in whatever colonial spew-hole they'd landed him at. Or dead under the slavery he'd endured there.

Had he been alive he'd have clawed his way back to her, as she would have clawed her way to him, had she been able.

But to what purpose? She tried to rationalize the unendurable. For one gaze at each other before she told him she was married?

But you were forced to it, Lady Cecily, Lady Cecily.

Indeed, my dear love, but you and I are not such as to indulge in adultery. We are not shabby, like common clay. We have honour.

One kiss before we part, Lady Cecily, Lady Cecily . . .

Goddam, but Sophie's letter was from France. In an escape, he would make for France: it was death for him if he came to Britain.

Nor would he endanger Lady C., Lady C., by sending her a letter from a rebel. He was writing through Sophie. Or Sophie had news of him. Bugger it, why'd she blown out the fucking candle? She groped for it, felt her way down to the kitchen to relight it, and came back.

'Deerest cosin Cecily never wood I have left you even to marry my deer earl had I nown the trubble that would come to you which belattedly I have news of that it has got wors.'

The misspellings brought Sophie into the room, breathless and unstoppable.

She'd written the letter in April this year at Paris. It was now August. She and her husband had been travelling Europe before settling in Bohemia where the young Earl had relatives . . . 'yet are now maiking homeward for an occasion that wood pleez deer Anne who was ever matternal. We were with that deer sole but yestereen.'

Skimming though she was, Cecily paused to smile. Sophie was pregnant. The baby was having a baby. And she'd found Anne. *Dear* Sophie.

'Wurd is you are without meens. Pleez deer cuz if it be of use take the small gift I offer whereof you wood have done as mutch for me and in any caze if you mislike it it bee too late for the layers are charged to it . . .'

Layers? Lawyers.

'. . . that you have the house ware we plaid when I was 12 for your own. Littel enuff, but a place wich my deer earl and I maike for to be ther by Mickelmas before we proceed on to my lying-in and have with us a purson you will be pleezed to see. Light the lantern for our cumming in. Ever your loveing Sophia C.'

He *had* found her, the purson she would be pleezed to see.

Sophie, dearest dear Sophie, care-less, youngest and certainly most illiterate friend of her past, the only one to charge to the rescue.

Wise Sophie now, careful not to name the proposed meeting

place – a necessary caution if she was bringing with her Guillaume Fraser. Guillaume had contacted Anne and, through her, Sophie.

And the house ware they had plaid when Sophie was 12 was Hempens. Sophie had bought Hempens, her fenland bolt-hole, and given it back to her. Cecily laid the letter down to sob. Oh, Sophie.

After a while, she dried her eyes. As a place to lodge an attainted traitor to the Crown, the island couldn't be bettered, hidden as it was deep into the fens yet available to the sea by the Windle river as long as the Lantern, its lighthouse, was lit to guide a boat through treacherous sandbanks. She had it back, she was once again a Fitzhenry of Hempens. And in September, at Michaelmas, she would go there. In joy.

She went to sleep with the letter in her hand.

And woke to screams.

Running from her room into the corridor, she encountered Archibald Cameron. He put out a hand to stop her heading for Dolly's room. 'Let it be.'

'It's Dolly.'

'Aye. Let her be.'

'Go to Lemuel. He'll be frightened.' She broke away and ran to where the screams were becoming rhythmic and rising in pitch. She threw open Dolly's door, shouting to scare off the attacker. 'Leave her alone. Leave her alone.'

There were two people struggling on Dolly's bed in the dark. The moonlight from the dormer window reflected itself in the rise and fall of something white. An arse. A man's arse. 'Get off her, you pig.'

As she reached the bed to haul off the rapist, she saw Dolly's face, blind, turned towards her, mouth open in a last, drawn-out, throbbing howl.

Cecily backed out and closed the door. Further away, Cameron was just leaving Lemuel's room: 'He's asleep.' He cocked an eye at her in interrogation, his mouth pursed. A man trying not to laugh.

She stalked past him to her room and closed its door behind her.

'How could you? How could you?' she demanded next morning.

Dolly's head was up: 'And why shouldn't I?'

'Why not? Because it's . . . disgusting. Tinker Packer.'

'A good lusty man, Tinker. Nothing wrong with Tinker.'

'He's married for one thing,' Cecily said. 'Not to mention –'

'Ain't, then. He's living in sin with. He's getting rid of her, anyways.' Dolly poked her forefinger into Cecily's sternum. 'An' just because you ain't getting any, Miss Don't-Touch-Me, it don't mean I got to do without my bit of loving.'

'Then do it somewhere else, not in my inn, you, you . . . screamer.'

Part of Cecily's anger was because she had looked ridiculous – again – in front of the Scotsman.

Dolly knelt, dragged her box from under her bed and began packing.

For the rest of her life Cecily was to ask herself whether she would have made up with her sister-in-law and stopped her going if she'd had time in which to consider; even at that moment she was aghast that Dolly was taking her at her word.

But there *was* no time in which to consider. Last night's letter – Haste. Haste – set the tempo of the following twenty-four hours; a day of events, each needing a period of reflection but which, instead, coming full pelt one after another, hurried far-reaching decisions.

She was called from Dolly's room by Marjorie Packer: 'You want to come down and see what's in the yard.'

Most of the staff was in it, so was Archibald Cameron, as well as some passers-by, encircling something Cecily couldn't see but which clanked. She forced her way through the crowd.

In its centre knelt a Negro, his wrists manacled to an iron collar round his neck. The clanking was caused by Ned, who'd propped a log under the locked flanges on one side of the collar, inserted a chisel upright between them and was slamming his farrier's hammer on it. The Negro's head was turned sideways towards Cecily, his eyes staring; they didn't blink at the blows of the hammer which, mis-hit, would crack open his skull.

She heard a whimper behind her. Lemuel was shaking. 'Take . . . take . . .'

She went to him and led him indoors. 'No, my dear, they're not going to take you back.' As his speech haltingly returned, he was able to enunciate his nightmares. His mind, like Cecily's, had been transported back to the Fleet and Bartholomew Fair. She sat him in a settle, drew him a tankard and returned to the yard. 'Where did it come from?'

'Fell off the back of a stage, we reckon,' Warty Packer told her. 'Half-seven from St Albans, could be. These lads,' he indicated two goggling carters, 'they come north and south and they in't seen un.'

'Could've flew,' said one of the carters. 'Evil powers.'

'They're monkeys, in't they?' asked someone, interestedly.

'Never. They're French.'

'Same thing.'

'No need to cuff it like that, though.'

'In my opinion,' Cameron said to Cecily, 'the laddie jumped.'

'Why?'

'Wouldn't you?'

Cecily looked at the stable clock. If the Negro *had* jumped from the St Albans coach, his loss might not be discovered until Buckhill, the next stage. 'Presumably somebody will be coming back to collect him.'

'That'll take a bit o' doing,' said Stabber.

True. Whether the slave had jumped, fallen or been pushed, his owner would be hard pressed to discover the particular landing point in the miles between Buckhill and St Albans.

A sharp crack announced that Ned had severed the collar's lock. Taking the thing off was difficult: the hinges gave little clearance for the neck, which was bleeding by the time it was freed. The trickling blood resembled strawberry liquor oozing from chocolate and brought a murmur of surprise from those who'd expected it to be as black as the skin. One or two of the men gallantly pushed their womenfolk behind them in case the Negro showed a tendency to ravage.

He crouched where he was, the top of his crinkled hair brushing the yard cobbles like a Mohammedan's on his prayer rug.

Ned handed the collar to Cameron. The lawyer turned it in his hands: 'Aye, punishment collar, right enough. Or maybe for whilst the man was travelling. So he couldnae escape.'

'Should have used leg irons.' Cecily became brisk. Time was being wasted, her time. 'Back to work all of you. Ned, give him a drink from the pump, clean him up and bring him to my office.'

Walking indoors with Cameron, she said: 'I had one once. Queen Anne gave him to me when I was five. He used to stand behind my chair.' She'd never forgotten the thrill inspired by the jewelled turban, emerald jacket and striped silk pantaloons. His collar had been silver. He'd marched to her orders, like an outsize piece of clockwork; she remembered being disappointed that his innards didn't play a tune when he moved.

'What happened to him?'

'I don't remember. You know how things disappear when you're moving from place to place.'

'Should've used leg irons,' said Cameron.

Cecily was irritated. Cameron had ordered Ned to remove the collar, for it was to him that Ned had handed it. He was taking a lot on himself. It wasn't *his* inn, even if he had bought it.

'Well, I suppose we must advertise so that the owner can claim him back. That's the law, isn't it?'

'I know of nae law that renders a man on British soil into a chattel.'

'Indeed? I wonder if I should keep him.' If she and Tyler brought off the coup they planned that very night, to bring coach trade to the Belle, the Negro could prove useful as long as he was house-trained and not dangerous. A talking point.

Most big houses boasted of one or more, but no inns that she could remember. They were usually very loyal if treated well. Which, presumably, this one hadn't been.

The black man was brought in, hair and face dripping. 'Scrubbed un,' said Ned. 'The colour don't come off.'

'Thank you, Ned. You may go.'

'Brushed him and all. That's velvet, that jacket.'

'Thank you, Ned. Now, my man, what's your name?'

140

'Them buckles is silver.' Astonishment had made Ned voluble.

'Ned. You may *go*.'

With the dust curried off him, the black man proved well dressed, as Ned had said. No turban, unfortunately. It was difficult to judge their ages, though a frosting of grey in the black sheepskin cap of hair suggested this one to be fiftyish. Well muscled, short-backed and a good, straight, brown eye. Slow, though . . . 'Your *name*, my man.' They were usually Sambo or something biblical.

'Bell.'

'No, *this* is the Belle. *Your* name.'

'Bell.'

Why did she have the impression he'd plucked it off her signboard? Well, it would do.

'Bell, *madam*,' she said. 'How do you come to be here, Bell?'

She and Cameron waited until it was obvious they wouldn't get an answer. There was silence, too, when Cecily asked who was his master.

Cameron said, at last: 'Can ye no tell us where you hail from?'

Another pause, as if the question were being examined for traps. 'Barbados, master.' The voice was resonant bass, comprehendable but with a placing of emphasis that was new to Cecily.

'And what skills have ye, always supposing Mistress Henry here wishes to employ ye?'

For the first time the black man showed animation, but the reply was still slow in coming. 'Command me, master, and I can do it.'

'For instance, can ye cook?'

Cecily gave Cameron one of her looks. He was always urging her to find a more adventurous cook than Dolly, saying the Belle would never achieve a good reputation merely on boiled mutton.

A black cook? The genus was unknown to her. However, she waited while the Negro thought the question over.

The reply was momentous. '*Viandes, poissons, les sauces, consommé, potages, légumes, tartes de fromage, de poires, pâté, pâtisserie, confiserie . . .*'

141

'French?' Cameron's voice went high, as if on the point of tears.

'An' Bajan, master.' A slow, gleaming smile stretched the thick lips. 'I make a rum punch'll make you think you just christened.'

'Stay here,' said Cecily, and led the whimpering Scotsman outside.

'Employ the man,' he was saying. 'I beg ye, employ the man.'

'This is my inn,' she reminded him. 'I'll employ whom I chose. Anyway, you've always condemned everything French as popish.'

'Except their provender. Employ the man. I'll even pay his wages.'

From one who guarded his purse as carefully as did Archibald Cameron, this concession surprised Cecily in more ways than one. She hadn't thought of paying the Negro wages at all: if he was a runaway, he'd be grateful for just his keep. 'Are you sure slavery doesn't apply in England?'

'It's a legal point yet to be tested.'

Cecily was harassed: there was a great deal to be done that day and she had already lost much time in which to do it. The weight of what she and Tyler would be venturing when dark fell pressed on her. She made up her mind. 'Very well. He can have a month's trial, though what Dolly will say to a black man in her kitchen . . .'

But when Cecily went to broach the subject with her sister-in-law, it was to find that Dolly had already left the inn to take up residence in the forest with Tinker Packer.

Whether the Negro's true name was Bell or not was irrelevant: by noon the intrigued staff of the Belle had given him another.

Cecily found Marjorie Packer, who'd inquired of the man with genuine interest if his colour came from eating liquorice, apparently frozen to her broom in the act of sweeping the floor as she awaited the reply. When, up in the bedrooms, she overheard another question concerning a part of his anatomy put to him by Cole and Warty Packer and the following pause, Cecily hurried downstairs to put an end to a conversation that promised to be indelicate and discovered the brothers slumped over the kitchen window-sill in the attitude of death.

142

Cecily snapped her key chain at their rumps. Cole turned glazed eyes on her. 'Quick, in't he?'

'Quick' was what the black man came to be called.

'Aye, well,' said Cameron, 'mebbe if you've been raised in slavery ye're gey careful wi' your words.'

Cecily was dismayed to find the Scotsman still in residence. 'I thought you were going back to London.'

'I was thinking I'd mebbe stay for dinner.'

'It will be crowded. Colonel Grandison's having an electoral meeting in the Green Room. You hate Tories *en masse*.'

'I'll put up wi' 'em. I want to sample our laddie's cooking.'

'Then you can damn well help him cook it,' she said bad-temperedly. 'We're short-handed without Dolly, blast her.'

Whatever Quick's shortcomings, or long-comings, as a con-versationalist, he was a deft cook. The smells wafting from the kitchen that afternoon suggested he was also living up to Cameron's expectations. Marjorie reported that the Scotsman had donned an apron and was assisting the Negro with the reverence of an altar boy.

'That's all furrin dishes he's doing, though,' she said. 'Tories'll puke. They're for beef and dumplings.'

'They'll get what they're given. Did you tell him to make extra?'

Marjorie nodded, helping Cecily to make up yet another bed. 'We expecting extra?'

'Some of the Tories might stay the night,' said Cecily vaguely.

Marjorie raised an eyebrow but said no more.

The dinner was a triumph of culinary art and Cecily received undeserved applause from Colonel Grandison and his fellow diners. Asked to produce the author of the feast, she refused: she didn't want word that her cook was black to spread too far too soon in case his owner heard it and came to reclaim him.

She stayed until sounds of Toryism rampant and incoherent came from the Green Room before slipping away.

To Cole she said: 'If anyone enquires for me, especially Master Archie, say I've gone to bed exhausted and mustn't be disturbed. Don't let Squire Leggatt try his sword-swallowing again and stop them dancing on the sideboard.'

'You leave it to me, mum.' She'd never managed to persuade the Packers to call her 'madam'. He patted her back as she went off towards the stables where Tyler was waiting for her.

She *was* tired: she wanted nothing better than to retire to bed. The thought of going on the pad again wearied and scared her so much that she greeted Tyler with: 'Let's not do this.'

'Suit yourself.'

She was unprepared for his acquiescence but continued with her reasons: 'The Belle's making do. We're paying back the loan, we manage the wages, we can making a living. Just about.'

'All right by me.'

'After all, why the coach trade? It'll be more work, more trouble than we need. So let's not do it.' His silence made her cross. 'Eh?'

He lifted up his lantern so that they could see each other's faces. 'Look, Duchess,' he said, 'you ain't no common woman. You didn't want for to be a landlady of no inn, but now you *are* a landlady you want for your inn to be a *great* un.'

'Are you implying I'm ambitious? For a damned inn?'

He shrugged, in no good temper himself. 'Some of it's for that revenge you wanted, some of it's because it's the way you are. Now, we going or ain't we?'

He knew her uncomfortably well, better than she knew herself. 'We're going.'

'Right, then.' Together they rode off by the meadow path.

Other than as the Belle Sauvage's sleeping partner, Tyler had proved a disappointment. Cecily had expected him to work with her at the inn like Ned, though at a higher level. He was, after all, an investor – part of their mutual robbery money had furnished the Belle.

He'd tried, becoming the inn's buyer of liquor, a subject on which his varied life had made him knowledgeable, but advising customers on their choice of wine, ale and spirits had not been his forte: he'd been ill-at-ease, almost sullen. Gradually, though he continued to choose the inn's liquor, he retired into the background until he'd disappeared from the public rooms.

Unlike Ned, he refused to live at the Belle. Cecily still didn't know where he did live – somewhere in the forest, she

144

supposed – nor with whom, though he made occasional references to a 'she'.

His explanation was that respectable company made him uncomfortable. 'One of 'em might recognize the voice that padded 'em, as the saying is.'

'You said you liked risk,' Cecily had protested.

'Not that sort.'

She'd come to think that the risk he did enjoy was flouting authority: unless he was riding along the high, thin ridge of illegality, life lost its savour for him. His spirits were already rising as they turned north along a track parallel with the Great North Road.

The spot where they would pull tonight's jack had been selected with extra care: it had to be far enough away from the Belle to dismiss suspicion, but near enough for the benighted passengers to reach it. They'd chosen the hill to the south of Stevenage.

As they waited for the north to south coach, under a huge pumpkin-coloured harvest moon, Cecily felt the familiar weakening of terror, redoubled this time by the intervening period of respectability since she'd experienced it last.

Yet she knew Tyler was right: neither she nor the inn could continue as they were. The Bell Sauvage deserved better than to be a wayside tavern and she deserved her revenge. Each time she woke up, sweating, from a Fleet nightmare, each time she looked at the wreck of her husband, when she thought of the gallows that had nearly claimed Cole Packer and was claiming men like him every day for even slighter crimes, she begged the Devil to whom she had sold her soul to keep his part of the bargain and help her punish the perpetrator.

Walpole had sent her down to hell with no more thought than he'd skim a pebble over the sea, and hadn't even watched to see if she'd bounce. She'd begun her rise out of the abyss, but there was a long way to the surface before she could reach for her enemy's throat.

The jack was coming up the hill: she felt the tremor. Her saddle creaked as she shifted, forcing herself to sit straight.

She whispered her battle-cry: 'Walpole.'

'Walpole,' muttered back Tyler. They put on their masks, took out their pistols and rode out into the middle of the road.

It was business as usual. The Walpoles lined up against the coach, protesting and afraid. What was different this time was that a female Walpole held a baby. 'Not the rattle,' she begged, as Cecily reached for it. 'Not her rattle. Her father gave it to her.'

Cecily snatched the toy from the child's fist. It was silver. 'He gave you the baby,' she hissed. 'You got enough.' The woman was younger than she was. Walpoles had children.

This time, another departure from the usual, she and Tyler backed their horses down the road instead of into the forest. Fifty yards, seventy-five ... a hip flask they'd taken became dislodged from the sack Tyler was holding and fell into the road, clanking against an exposed flint.

They turned and cantered south, other valuables falling at intervals behind them. Once they were out of sight and bullet-range they were able to place the articles where they wanted. 'Not too reg'lar,' Tyler said. 'There's supposed to be a hole in the sack, not a bloody hopper.' He watched while she laid the silver rattle carefully on the grass that grew between the road's wheel ruts.

Normally, this would have been dangerous work, in full view of passing traffic. Tyler and Cecily had chosen their night carefully: the north–south coach would have been the last to pass this way until morning, commoners were too tired from harvesting to venture abroad and most of the local gentry were bacchanaling at the Belle. The road was deserted, the stolen pieces showing up well under the bright moon.

They dropped the last, a snuff box, a little way into the mouth of the track to Knebworth House. A few yards further on, Tyler's gelding made its own contribution to the subterfuge. The two highwaymen regarded the steaming heap with admiration. 'Proper padder's horse.'

As they rode up the track and made the long circle back to the Belle, Tyler said: 'You're still young, Duchess. It's not too late.'

'I'm twenty-five.'

'Young enough.'

'Have you got children, Tyler?'

She was breaking their rule, but he was sorry for her. 'Boy's in the army. Girl's married. Haven't seen 'em in a bit.'

'I envy you.' She could say it to nobody but him. She shook her head. 'If those bleeders go back to Stevenage for the night, I'll shoot the bastards.'

At the Belle, the Green Room still resounded with uproarious Tories. Cole Packer lit her upstairs. 'Squire Leggatt fell off the roof, but he ain't hurt much. They been goodish, on the whole.'

'Where's the Scotsman?'

'Gone to bed.'

'There may be late guests arriving tonight, Cole.'

'Thought there might be.'

While she changed, she watched from her window. Where were they? A near-sighted ox with a limp could have followed the trail quicker. Well, if they'd gone north, to Stevenage, on their head be it: the White Lion was ghastly.

At last, the light of a coach lantern wavered on the yard's open gates, there was the sound of discussion and they came straggling in, two coachmen, eight passengers, most silent with exhaustion, one of them hysterical. Cecily met them, tidying her carefully disarranged hair. 'Of course, of course. How dreadful. What *is* the world coming to? Hanging's too good for them. Enter and welcome. We have company already, so we can find you some food. And beds, yes indeed. Oh, you poor dear . . . and a baby too. *Isn't* she bonny?' She took the little fist that held a silver rattle and shook it gently.

She especially fawned on the coachmen, refusing payment from 'such brave men or what is Christian hospitality about?'

'Better bub and grub here than the old Fighting Cocks, eh, Cokey?' one of them asked his companion, tucking in. 'It's dog stew at the Fighting Cocks.'

'You're kind to say so,' said Cecily. 'And is the hill up to St Albans as steep as they say?'

'Killer,' said Cokey. 'Company's lost more 'osses gettin' to the bloody Cocks than we've had hot dinners, ain't we, Rick?'

'An' highwaymen behind every bush on the Heath,' said Rick.

'Killers an' all,' Cokey said, 'not like the amateur bloody fumblers you got round this way.'

'We should stop here, Rick. Better vittles, better road. Only twelve mile from Albans . . .'

'I hadn't considered the coach trade,' said Cecily, brightly.

'Profitable, lady, very profitable. You should think on.'

'I will,' she said.

'I don't know what this is,' said Cokey, mopping new-baked bread in his *ragoût*, 'but it's tasty.'

'It ain't dog stew,' she told him.

Going to the kitchen, she met Archibald Cameron leaning on the door-frame. 'Fortunate ye had enough food in,' he said.

She avoided his eyes. 'Indeed.'

'And beds made up.'

'We were expecting Squire Leggatt and the others to stay over.'

He nodded towards the taproom. 'Attacked by two highwaymen, they tell me.'

She met his eyes. 'Fortunately, they got all their property back. Excuse me, I need more hot water for the brandy.'

As she pushed past him, he grinned and took the jug from her hand. 'I'll fetch it,' he said. 'Ye stay in there and win.'

Before they rose to go to their beds, the travellers drank to the Belle Sauvage and even to the ineptness of the highwaymen who'd led them to it.

'I can't understand it,' Cecily said in her reply. 'The Belle's a safe house. There's been no robbery here in years. Not like St Albans.'

As Rick helped Cokey to the stairs, Cecily reminded him: 'You'll commend the Belle to your company?'

He took the proffered sovereign with his free hand. 'Depend on it, lady.'

She didn't entirely. Following up the good report of the Belle the coach company would have received, she sent Archibald Cameron to negotiate with its owner, Mr Sherman, of Sherman and Sons, which operated from the Bull and Mouth at St Martins-le-Grand, asking to buy a share in their Great North

Road coaches and offering to provide the horses for the stage north and south of the Belle in return for a proportion of the profit. 'The Fighting Cocks takes a sixth, tell them I'm prepared to take a seventh,' she instructed the lawyer.

'That's no' much.'

'It's enough to begin with. By the time I'm finished I'll be running my own coaches.' If the company accepted her offer, she wouldn't have to accommodate their passengers until spring – coaches didn't run in the winter, the roads were too bad. 'And point out how, er, free we are from robbery most of the time. And how gentle our hills are ... They'll have good report of us from the coachmen.'

'Teach your grandmother to suck eggs, woman.'

She told him, then, that Hempens had been returned to her and at Michaelmas she would be joining her cousin Sophie there for a while. Cameron noticed the stiffness that had become habitual to her ebb from her face and body as she thought of the prospect. A salmon returning to its spawning ground, he thought. Who else will she meet there?

'Is she the slip that mocked me all the way from Edinburgh?'

Cecily shied away from the subject of Edinburgh. 'I'm hoping Dolly will come back to look after Lemuel while I'm away. Cole and Marjorie are capable of seeing to the local trade and Colonel Grandison will look in every day, yet I was wondering ...'

She disliked asking him a favour but she was relieved when he said he would come up from London as often as he was able.

'It's a long step. Ye're no going on your own, I trust?'

'I'm taking Tyler with me.'

He seemed less than comforted by the information.

CHAPTER EIGHT

IT WAS TYLER'S second visit to fenland. The first had been two days after Cecily received Sophie's letter when she'd sent him to Hempens to tell Edie that the island was in Fitzhenry hands again, to ready the place for Michaelmas visitors and light the Lantern to guide them in.

'Better give me a letter for her,' he'd said.

'Edie can't read.' Instead she entrusted him with her father's heavy gold ring devised with the outline of a bittern, the family crest, which served as her seal and which Dolly had saved from the creditors.

Despite minute instructions, he'd got lost. The unremitting flatness of the land, its lack of prominence to give him bearings, the all-enveloping carr of alder, willow and bulrush in which droves and streams insinuated like escapers wriggling through undergrowth, had unnerved him, as had the apparent absence of living souls though, he'd thought, watching the jack-o'-lanterns glimmer and shift in the marshes, there'd been plenty of dead ones. Not a religious man, he'd found himself praying to be delivered from evil that stalked by night. People benighted in the fens usually did.

'Might as well sent me to Africa,' he accused Cecily on his return – not the first to ascribe black foreignness to that unmapped area of England – 'an' when I did see a African, the bugger looked like a nine-foot heron stalking against the sunset.'

'They use stilts to cross the streams,' Cecily said.

'I know *now*,' Tyler said. 'Fair chilled me crackers then. Close to he still looked a bloody cannibal.' Reluctant, in case the cannibal murdered him for it, but desperate, Tyler had displayed Cecily's ring. Immediately he'd been escorted to spend the night in a hut, which he described as being made entirely of withy and reed, and from there, by boat, to Hempens. 'You're king-post thereabouts, Duchess. Didn't understand half they said but they was very respectful saying it.'

I am Cecily the Wake.

With it all, he'd been intrigued by the land and its people. The draining of the fens instituted by the big estate owners had not yet affected the stretches around Hempens where the inhabitants led their water-borne lives untrammelled by authority.

It wasn't that fenlanders were discreditable, more that they respected no law but their own; their rulers were not kings but weather and water-levels. They were up Tyler's alley.

So was their food – Edie'd fed him on lampreys. 'Tasted them, have you? Ugly-lookin' buggers, same as the people, but rich. Same as the people. Gawd, not a penny in their breeches but birds and fish beggin' to be taken, as the saying is.'

'I know,' Cecily pointed out.

Tyler was not to be stopped. He'd supped taxless brandy and smoked dutiless pipes. 'Smuggling? They invented it. Edie's boys cross to France for the stuff easy as I'd sail our dewpond.'

'I *know*.'

'So why din't you tell me? Think what they'd bring in for the Belle.'

Not all his news of Hempens was as happy. 'Edie don't live in the gatehouse no more,' he told her. 'He's gone and pulled it down.'

'Who pulled it down?'

'Bleeder from Peterborough. Your creditor. As took it after the Bubble. Told Edie he only wanted the place for its stone.'

There was no rock indigenous to the fens, just peat and silt. Blackbirds and thrushes congregated at Hempens in order to crack open snails on the only stone for miles.

Tyler shuffled. 'Duchess, he's pulled a *lot* of it down.'

She steeled herself. What had not been taken from her these past years?

Even so, as Edie's Edgar rowed them on to Windle Mere and the rank suffocation of the waterways gave way to a sniff of the sea that lay beyond the low hump of her island, Cecily gave a huff of shock as if someone had punched her in the stomach.

Against the sunset the shape that had been Hempens, always carried in her mind like an amulet, was a scarecrow, a plump old friend turned haggard by disease.

The medieval gatehouse was gone, so was the Jacobean gate, so was the curtain wall Hubert Fitzhenry had raised to guard the island from terrible Hugh Bigod in 1185. The deep-roofed grange was gone. The chapel built by Lady Priscilla Fitzhenry in the thirteenth century in penance for her husband's sins – she'd had the stone brought by sea from Caen – was gone, its

151

buttresses now arching against the sky, like skeleton ribs sticking up sideways in a desert. The cloisters where had walked the ghost of mad Great-great-aunt Matilda, she who had donned the habit of a nun after vowing to some eccentric god of her own – all were gone.

Denuded of their lovely corseting, the orieled gable ends of the house itself – its two flint wings raised at different Tudor ages – blinked at her with the embarrassment of one caught naked.

Whig, thought Cecily drearily, a Peterborough Whig. The price of stone more valuable than its grace. Not an ancient home to him: a mine to be plundered. Did the bastard take the tombstones as well? The Lantern . . .

She shook the boat leaning forward to pull at Edgar's knee. 'Did he pull down the Lantern?' Though he could not have or Tyler would have told her.

The fenman jerked his head to his right. There it was still, beyond the twirl of Elizabethan chimneys, on the island's far side: small for a lighthouse but significant enough in this vast flatness, a tower topped by an octagonal gallery of glass, like an upraised finger stuck into an eight-sided bolt.

Ah, well, she thought, comforted, we can rebuild the rest.

As long as memory ran, Cecily's family had maintained the Lantern on Hempens, partly from philanthropy to warn shipping against the Snappers, the shoals that lay offshore and – with a secondary beacon – to act as a transit guiding vessels upriver, and partly from self-interest, to collect resultant light dues through its agents in the East Anglian ports.

The stone lighthouse that had replaced previous simple wooden beacons never recovered its cost: Trinity House had built a bigger, better light further down the coast and, in any case, the great storm of 1682 had shifted the seabed and so silted up the Windle that only shallow-draught boats could now gain Hempens and the mere beyond.

But the Fitzhenrys had still maintained it as a symbol of power, and for another reason. Every so often the Lantern flickered again – to guide in smuggled booty from France and Holland.

It wasn't lit now.

Cecily jogged the boat again. 'Tyler told Edie to light –'

'They visitors come yesterday, bor.'

They were here. *He* was here. Guillaume's face came vividly before her, fitting to completion the imagined hero she had tried to conjure when she was a girl dreaming her dreams at the top of the Lantern. He'd been the one she'd awaited.

If she'd arrived a day earlier, if she could have been here, dressed in her best, to call to him from the Lantern, what perfection then, returning at last to this depleted but still most beloved of homes to regain adolescent magic . . .

. . . and she wouldn't have had to stump ashore travel-stained and with a smear on her skirt's arse from sitting in this scow.

She fumbled for the tiny looking-glass attached to the ribbon of her belt, surreptitiously trying for her reflection by the boat lamp. She saw only crows' feet at the corner of her eyes and a frown line deepening vertically between her brows. Twenty-three and withered. Adolescence was unreturnable.

It was presumption to think he'd want her. *I am married, dear one. We can be nothing to each other.*

Who asked you, Lady Cecily, Lady Cecily?

Oh, but he was here. She saw his cloaked figure, a darker patch against the shade of the house behind him, waving, reversing the roles of her dream.

'Pull harder, Edgar,' commanded Cecily the Wake. Haste, haste me to my home and my love.

The thump of oar in rowlock kept up the rhythm maintained since they had left the uplands, no faster, no slower, pulling her nearer to the figure on the jetty. An oddly smooth shape, too wide, too short.

It wasn't him.

It was a nun. Did the ghost of mad Matilda, maddened further by the loss of her cloister, beckon to her? In fenland twilight anything was possible. Nor did her great-great-niece care. *It isn't him.*

Then she did, because it was Anne Insh.

When Cecily let her go, Anne asked: 'Do you forgive me?'

'I never blamed you in the first place.' They had been two

women acting out of love. Nobody was to blame for love. 'I'm so sorry about your father, Anne.'

The moment his father was dead, the new Lord Insh, Anne's brother, had ingratiated himself with King George, condemning his late parent's involvement with the 1715 Jacobite rebellion in terms barely decent for a son to utter but which had, nevertheless, enabled him to win back the attainted Insh lands.

If there was fault, it was that Anne hadn't been in touch before; obviously she'd known of Cecily's descent into the depths, was even aware that she now kept an inn.

'Spender Dick,' explained Anne. 'He crosses the Channel regularly to bring news to us exiles. He travels the Great North Road frequently for the Cause and saw you outside the Belle one day as he passed in a coach. He made inquiries.'

Did he, indeed? The Jacobite network was more efficient than she'd thought. 'Why didn't you write to me? I've worried and worried about you.'

'Walpole's spies open all letters from France. It would have done you no good that you were in touch with an attainted traitor.'

Spender Dick could have brought a message, thought Cecily. She didn't say so: there was more to this. The old Anne would have hugged her with abandon but, even as they'd embraced, there'd been resistance, a drawing-away. *Don't leave me now we've found each other again.*

But something of Anne had already left: she was telling Cecily so by persisting in wearing a Catholic nun's habit when she was already risking arrest merely by landing on English soil. *Noli me tangere.* It was like that. As if renunciation of the flesh prohibited hugging a dear cousin. Not that she'd renounced all fleshly pleasures: Anne had become fat.

'Where's Sophie? Where's Fraser?' Cecily was already walking towards the house.

Anne stopped her. 'Before you go in . . .' While Tyler and Edgar carried baggage and supplies indoors, the two women sat on a bench in what had been the cloister before Peterborough plundered its flagstones.

'Sophie's upstairs in the Rupert room. She's in labour.'

154

'So soon? I thought she wasn't due yet.'

From a window at the front of the house came a remote and angry mooing that ended in a huffed 'aaahbuggerit'. Sophie, at least, even in the throes of a contraction, had not changed.

Cecily stood up. 'I must go to her.'

'No. Not yet. She has her woman with her. Cecily . . . the Earl . . . her husband is dead.'

'No. Oh, no.'

'He died of smallpox on the way from Paris,' Anne said. 'She brought his coffin to my convent and we buried it there.'

'Oh, Sophie.' Sophie's happiness in her marriage had been Cecily's only refreshment through the misery of her own.

'It was her wish to come on here, she was quite violent about it, that his son should be born in England. She was desperate to see you. I couldn't let her make the voyage alone but the crossing, perhaps her loss, affected her condition.'

'Why did it happen to her? Not Sophie.' There was a joyousness that should never be dulled. 'Why her?'

Anne answered dutifully: 'God willed it.'

'Why? Why we three? Look at us.' All of them bearing crosses and – the stillness of the woman at her side reminded her – perhaps Anne's the heaviest of all. Sophie would have her baby, she herself had her inn, both of them growing things, future things. Anne, the celibate, the cloistered, had only a present that would never change.

Cecily put her hand on her cousin's. 'Tell me. I wrote to your brother asking after you, twice. He didn't reply.'

'He wouldn't.'

'Tell me.'

'Lord Insh,' said Anne of her brother, 'saw fit to renounce me for helping to deprive George of Hanover of his prisoner. He also saw fit to negate my father's wish that I should receive a portion of money. I was alone and penniless in a foreign country.' Gently, she withdrew her hand from Cecily's. 'I was happy to enter the Order of St Agnes' Martyrdom and am happier still to have risen in it to the position of Prioress of the Order's daughter house in Dunkirk.'

She spoke like someone reciting a times table. Happy?

Obliged, more like. And making the best of it. Anne's only alternative would have been marriage but her fellow exiles were so equally poor that their unmarried sons were forced to look for wealthy brides among the French.

Someone had given the lawn a last scything before winter and the evening was scented with bruised grass, overlaying the pungency of vegetation from the fens. It had been a St Martin's summer and swifts, soon to be replaced by bats, turned and swooped in the air.

Princess Caroline's lost Maids of Honour stared ahead of them, untouching, as a last band of red in the sky caught the stippling of rushes in the blackening water of the mere. Edgar's boat tapped against the jetty, there was another snarl from Sophie's window.

Cecily forced herself to sit still. Anne's need seemed to take precedence. Of the three little girls who had played out their summers here, it had been Anne who carried a rag doll, Moppet, everywhere; Anne, always the instigator of their games, who insisted they scatter hempseed on St Martin's Eve to raise the wraith of their future husbands. With rakes over their shoulders, they'd circled the church twelve times as the clock struck midnight, frightened silly, excited.

> Hempseed I set, hempseed I sow,
> The man that is my true love,
> Come after me and mow.

If she could hear their voices now, a thin, off-key pipe among the ruins, how much more could Anne.

This was maudlin. She said: 'And now. Where is Fraser?' She had been concerned for others long enough.

'Who?'

They stared at each other.

No, thought Cecily, no, no. She used anger to withstand the sudden chill. 'Guillaume Fraser. Anne, you owe him your father's escape. Where is he? Sophie wrote . . . she was bringing him here.'

'There is no man here.'

'But she wrote. She was bringing someone I should be pleased to see, she said.'

'That was me.'

Of course, of course. Sophie had meant Anne. She'd used her own code to thwart Walpole's letter-openers. But the expectation had been so strong since the letter that Cecily couldn't rid herself of it. She stood up, poised to go to Sophie and ask her what she had done with Fraser.

From the reeds that freckled the mere, the heavy, dark shape of a bittern, legs trailing, flapped over the water giving its dusk-flight call, kwah, kwah. It was answered by a rasp from the upper window: 'Aaahbugga-a-ah.' Anne made no move.

Cecily went. He must be here. Let him he here. A little happiness, God. In the name of Christ, give me some recompense.

The smell of marsh had insinuated itself into the house during its long neglect, portraits that had lined the wall of the Jacobean staircase had been removed, leaving bleached squares and rectangles on the plaster.

Yet the great wrought-iron wheel of a candle-holder still hung from its long chain, warming the lovely brick of the floor below and the nymphs and gods painted on the high ceiling. Furniture remained – the massive oak pieces too old-fashioned for a Peterborough Whig. And in the passage that ran back from the foot of the staircase to the servants' quarters a partly opened door let out light and the smell of cooking and a voice talking above the rattle of pans.

Edie, the only constant in a childhood kaleidoscope of governesses, attendants, duennas, chaperones; Edie and Hempens. Hempens and Edie. For this much, God be thanked.

But she must go to Sophie first.

The scene in the Rupert room was a Rembrandt. Candle-flame against reflectors sent all light towards the bed, illuminating the sufferer on it and leaving the woman who sat beside it an inclined shape in the shadows. Sophie's red hair was dark with sweat, her small face brick-coloured. She radiated a furious energy. 'God's taken my earl, Cessy.' It was a shout.

'I know.' Cecily crossed to the bed and kissed Sophie's hand, holding it in both her own. 'I know, I know.'

'It's not fair, Cessy, it's not fair. I want him back.'

'I know, darling, I know.'

'But I'll have his son, I'll have a bit of him back in his son.' Sophie's eyelids drooped. 'A bit of him back, a bit of him back.' Then her eyes opened to stare. 'Here it comes again, sod it, oooh, buggerit, buggeraaah.'

The yell was reassuring. Anybody capable of issuing so uninhibited a sound still had strength.

When the contraction was over and Sophie dozed, Cecily looked across the bed. 'It's straightforward, isn't it, Matty?'

'I'm hoping so, Lady Cessy. But 'tis early and us Hatfields ain't strong with babbies. Her dear ma lost three before we had our ladyship.' Matty, having been Sophie's nurse and her mother's before that, regarded herself as family.

A pink-cheeked, solid West Country woman, neither her years of service nor, more recently, her travels around Europe with the honeymooning couple had weakened her manifest capability or her Somerset accent.

'I'm glad you're here, Matty.'

'And ah'm glad you are, Lady Cessy.'

'Matty, did nobody make the crossing with you?'

Matty took it as a criticism. 'Ah couldn' stop her. You know her ladyship, mule-headed like all Breffnys. Cecily, got to see Cecily, 'twas. French ship ut was, tew, tossing and rolling, typical Frenchy – she's coming back to fetch Miss Anne laader. Then lowering us into a liddle biddy boat to come up the Windle. Miss Anne showed un how to follow they lights or we'd have drowned surely. 'Tis no wonder that poor babby's coming afore its tahm.'

'Sophie didn't mention a Mr Guillaume Fraser?'

Matty shook her head and saw Cecily droop. 'You'm not too viddy, seemingly. I'll watch here. Ut won't be yet. Down ee go to your dinner, Lady Cessy, afore Lady Anne eats ut all.'

Wearily, Cecily made her way to the kitchen and stood in its doorway to rest her eyes on the thick-bodied old woman who stood against the glow of the fire, stirring a pot with a long spoon and talking through the window at Tyler, who'd been sent with a rushlight to pick wild celery from the reeds by the kitchen stream – all Edie's herbs had to be gathered with night dew on them.

After a while, Edie looked round. Without a change of expression, she put down the ladle, wiped her hands on her apron and lumbered over to a battered wicker chair. Then she held out her arms.

Anne had overseen the dinner, much to Edie's disgust. 'Gone to garlic, she has, bor,' she said, as if it were to the devil. 'And what good's it done her?'

At least it had animated her cousin. 'I've brought you a wine we grow in our own priory vineyards. Quite an acceptable white, I think. Try some, it will go well with the fish.'

They ate alone; Tyler, with Edgar and some of his brothers, was below stairs, tucking into Edie's lamb stew and 'floaters' – light, delicious, fen dumplings.

In the dining room, candlelight was reflected in the polish of the black oak board and sent gleams from the crystal. Through the open windows came moths, a lapping from the mere and short, sharp intervals of swearing.

They served themselves, or, rather, Anne did the serving, piling her own platter, raising her eyebrows at Cecily's lack of appetite and commenting on each course as if she gossiped of old friends. 'Nowhere produces lampreys like the fens, not even Normandy . . . I cooked the duck, I could not trust Edie to leave it pink . . . At the Priory my kitcheness stuffs it with *pâté* made from goose-liver with just a touch of thyme . . .'

Cecily had hoped her cousin might have found at least some solace in God, but to listen to Anne was to gain the impression that her priory bell rang less for prayer than for meals. From her end of the table she watched her cousin, trying to see in the face of the prioress, with its soft, clear skin bulging round the edges of the wimple, the ascetic, caring, daughterly girl. *Don't leave me.*

'I want you to tell me of England,' Anne said, using a carving knife. 'Now taste this lamb, I made Edie broil it in prunes . . .'

She's nervous, realized Cecily. She's making *me* nervous. We should be with Sophie. 'The politics? The countryside? Old friends?'

'Not old friends.' The knife sliced deep into the lamb.

'No. Well, I'm cut off too. Mary Astell has –'

'Tell me of the Cause. I rejoiced to hear you'd joined us.'

'Did you? But I've been so busy with –'

'I've seen him.' At last the chewing and chattering stopped. They had arrived at whatever it was: it was old, intense Anne looking at her. 'I went to Rome first, then he did me the honour only the other day of visiting my priory. It had to be in secret, of course, and by night.'

'The Pope?'

'*Cecily*.' For the first time Anne grinned. 'The King.' She rolled her eyes in pretended patience. 'The Chevalier St George. James Stuart. *The* King.'

'Ooh-er.'

'Ooh-er indeed. *Ecce homo*, Cessy. Our Deliverer, chaste, pious, brave, the man to return our country to harmony . . .'

Anne had found her god after all, but the altar before which she prostrated herself was to a living man, the Pretender, and the exultation of her chant was secular. Her devotion blazed down the length of the table, certain it was received with similar fervour.

Cecily's enthusiasm for the Cause had become thin through lack of nourishment. The fight for her own and Lemuel's and Dolly's survival since the bursting of the South Sea Bubble had left her no resources with which to aid anyone else's war. Had she really felt strongly enough to spy for the Cause? What a lass she'd been.

Anne was still exulting, demanding her attention. 'Cecily, Cecily, do you realize of what use *you* could be to him?'

'What?'

'The opportunity to serve? Now that you have Hempens back? The isolation, my dear, its proximity to the Continent. Cessy, Hempens is a postern into England. His emissaries could come and go . . .'

Anne's plump little fingers were steepled in prayer. Just so, though slimmer, they had besought Cecily's help once before. *My father is taken ill . . . I beg you to come with me*.

'He . . . he wants to . . . he asks me if you will receive one such emissary a week from now. Can I light the Lantern, then? Can I? Can I?'

Amazed, Cecily stared at her. *I beg you to come with me.* And she'd gone. To ruin. As this woman knew. Who was asking again.

She stood up. 'I'm going to Sophie,' she said. 'Are you coming?'

Anne put her hands over her face. 'No.'

Haring furiously upstairs, Cecily thought: How dare she? How *can* she? She's prepared to risk my life – and Sophie's – all over again. Is doing so merely by being here. But to allow a Jacobite spy into my house on his way to blow up Parliament or whatever the plan is . . .

By the turn at the top of the first flight, Cecily paused, indignation expending with the thought that Anne had only the Cause to give meaning to her life, doomed to childlessness as she was.

After all, the danger was fractional. Nobody but Edie's family, whose loyalty to Cecily and her friends was absolute, had seen Anne arrive or would see her go. Her cousin was right: in its difficulty of access, Hempens was as isolated as any house in England. Through the hidden waterways it *did* provide a secret back door into England . . .

Well, and it was engaging to have power again. To be begged for help by a king, even one who lacked a throne . . .

We'll see.

First of all there's a baby to deliver. Cecily went in to help Matty deliver it.

Sophie's baby came with the dawn, a girl already dead from the cord strangling her neck.

Cecily picked up the slippery, still warm, little body. She took it to another room and laid it on the bed. She ripped up a petticoat of Brussels lace and lined a drawer with it. She kissed its forehead and laid the baby in its improvised coffin.

I thought I knew grief. She'd never felt any like this.

Sophie contracted birth fever and for some days her unwillingness to fight it seemed likely to kill her as well. The other four, Anne as desperately as any of them, fought it for her.

The nearest doctor was at Ely, too far to be brought to Hempens in time for the crisis that was undoubtedly coming. In any case, Cecily doubted that any leech could better the experience of Matty and Edie, who used herbs gathered from Hempens' overgrown garden to make simples that brought some relief and sleep.

A marsh priest, a ragged old man, was fetched and agreed to perform the baby's obsequies though, as he pointed out, it had never lived and therefore could not properly qualify for the ritual of death.

'Do it,' hissed Cecily the Wake, so he did it.

The child was buried with Cecily's ancestors in Hempens' graveyard. Cecily and Anne stood by the tiny oblong of earth long after the others had gone back to the house.

It's not my child. Why do I feel this anguish? As she'd taken vicarious joy from Sophie's happiness in marriage, the advent of Sophie's baby had substituted for the one that Cecily, in all likelihood, would never have.

It was a fine day. The mere reflected a sky like blue enamel. Hidden in the reeds, a hundred species of wildfowl cheeped and dived. A late iridescent dragonfly hovered over the grave before flicking away. A thrush tapped a snail shell against the tomb of Sir Francis Fitzhenry.

Walking back to the house, Anne said: 'If I may, Cecily, I should like the Lantern lit tonight.'

It was badly timed. Cecily's thoughts, still with the baby, were too distressed to stop the rebuke that came into them. 'You're a stranger to me, Anne.'

After a pause: 'You think I have no feeling,' Anne said. 'Sometimes I think I have none either. But Sophie will marry again; there'll be other babies. And I'll tell you this much, cousin, I want for them that they grow up in an harmonious society, not one as dishonoured as England's is now.'

They went round to the rear entrance of the house where the Lantern key hung with others on hooks in the passage, then through the orchard and down to the tower, neat and erect against its foreground of slithering grey marsh. Sticking out

162

from one side of its base was its candle house, actually a round beehive of stone which, with its juxtaposition to the Lantern's column, had once caused Sophie to remark that the whole thing put her in mind of a single-testicled but *very* happy man.

Anne's snort, as she remembered too, was good to hear.

Cecily turned the key in the iron-bound tower door and they went in together, unlocked the low connecting door of the candle house and, bending, began dragging out the candles. Finest beeswax, these, and made for processions, each one four foot high and weighing over forty pounds. By the time they'd carried eight up three hundred steps to the Octagon and lifted them into the sconces, Anne was near collapse and Cecily glad to sit on the window-sill and consider the view to the sea.

The tide was out. Immediately below them, Hempens sheep grazed on reclaimed land, then came a sheen of silt dotted with wading birds and runnelled with shallow streams among which the deeper Windle was barely distinguishable. As far as the eye could see, the tallest object in the landscape was a foreshortened Edgar gathering samphire, with boards strapped to his feet, to make one of Edie's strengthening messes for Sophie.

She opened one of the Octagon's windows and called to him. They'd need his expertise to place the secondary beacon on the other side of the river, whose light, when brought in line with the Lantern's, gave a boat safe passage through the ever-changing silt of the estuary.

Unhurriedly, he tied his slithery harvest into a bundle and began his stump back across the marsh towards them.

Visitors found the flatness of the view depressing. To Cecily, it had always held expectation, a hand laid level to receive the unknown, some portent, a bolt of lightning, a lover, a miracle, the word of God. In mountainous country whatever-it-was had already happened; fenland was always waiting for it to happen.

It comforted her. Perhaps the baby will be born again. Perhaps one day the man in the boat will be Guillaume Fraser.

Anne caught something of it. She said: 'Souls are never wasted.'

They went down to give Edgar his instructions.

*

Nobody came up the Windle that night, nor the next, nor the one after. Mist came in with October and turned Hempens sombre.

With so few people, and those too busy, to care for it, dust dulled the surfaces of the Jacobean furniture and autumn leaves lay in the hall. Extra shadows gathered in corners and along the cloister walk. Jack-o'-lanterns glittered out in the marshes. In the suffused light of the Lantern, pelicans riding the mere became phantom flotillas.

The fever diminished but left Sophie so weak as to keep her hold on life still uncertain. Matty wove agrimony and vervain round her bed. 'To fend off evil,' she said. They all felt it. To Cecily it centred on the awaited emissary, who nightly assumed more and more sinister proportions in her dreams just as, by day, the half-glimpsed shape of a heron was a watching Walpole spy.

Tyler had chopped kindling from an old elder tree to start the fire they now lit every evening to counteract the damp. When Cecily saw it, she went out and sawed boughs from an overgrown rosemary bush instead. Elder had made Christ's cross; no need to release the death within it into a house already grieving.

A dark figure appeared out of the mist and took the basket from her. 'Why you keeping that light lit, Duchess?'

How much did he know? Or guess? 'I'm expecting another visitor from France.'

'There's enough of them here already.' Tyler hadn't taken to Anne. Her nun's habit made him nervous.

'It's none of your business.'

'It'll be my business when we all end up dancin' at Tyburn.'

'That didn't worry you when we were on the pad.'

'The pad's one thing. So's smuggling. Entertaining traitors another.'

'Go home, then,' she said, and was terrified he might. His grunt told her he wouldn't.

A wind came up that set the leaves in the hall leaping around it like tiny animals in agony trying to bite their own backs. It creaked the weathercock on the roof with nerve-scratching insistence, slammed doors and moaned through windows. Cecily lay awake listening to Hempens' history return to it in noises resembling mailed boots marching the passageways and shrieks from the crenel where a serving girl hanged herself in the days of lecherous Giles Fitzhenry.

Somewhere in the cacophony was a new disturbance. She got up and from her window saw cloaked men climbing on to the jetty in the moonlight. A figure in religious habit crossed the lawn to greet them.

Dammit, *dammit*. She dressed slowly, begrudging the effort of finding something pretty to wear.

Anne met her at the bottom of the stairs. There was light from the dining room where men had gathered round the table but the prioress led her past it to the door of the parlour. 'You know who is here, Cecily?'

'Yes.' From the window she'd seen Anne's deep curtsy.

As Anne opened the door to lead her in, Cecily stopped her. 'And I shall see him alone.'

Anne glared but Cecily's resentment was too high to collapse. It wasn't only that the Act of Attainder made anyone harbouring the Pretender liable to execution, it was the slight to her, that he had been invited as if she weren't to be trusted with the knowledge.

'This is my house,' she said.

And because this was *her* house, by God, she'd meet *her* guest on her terms, untrammelled by sycophants.

She went in alone to meet James Francis Edward Stuart, Chevalier of St George, Pretender to – or rightful heir to, depending on your point of view – the throne of England, Scotland, Wales and Ireland, son of King James II, direct descendant of a line of monarchs that had ruled Scotland for four centuries and the United Kingdom for one, and which was so unlucky and so obstinate as to have had two of its number exiled while six more had met violent deaths.

Anne had lit only two candles and the fire so that the parlour was in semi-darkness as befitting a man who must stay out of the light. Cecily saw that her best crystal decanter and glasses had been set out on a table beside one of the chairs. *Busy little Anne.*

165

A figure came forward with hands outstretched. 'Lady Cecily, Lady Cecily,' it said.

She had told herself she would not succumb: she was a working woman with no time to spare and an investment she was not prepared to lose. She told herself she *wasn't* succumbing but from that moment the old mystery took hold again. Cecily had come to Hempens to meet a lost lover and here, in his place, was a lost king; as once before, the two were inextricably combining.

He took her hands to raise her from her curtsy. 'I wish you to know that I am conscious of the sacrifice you made seven years ago in returning to me a dearly loved adherent. I am in your debt, Madame. I should have communicated my gratitude earlier had it not meant endangering you further.'

He was thirty-five years old, slender enough to look younger. He spoke English easily but with a French accent. As had someone else.

I didn't do it for you, she thought, struggling. But not for a long time had someone addressed her with courtesy like his, genuine courtesy; whatever else, the man was sincere to the bone. She was in the presence of the blood royal.

He handed her to a chair and sat himself in one across from her, on the opposite side of the fire. He had the Stuarts' long eyes and nose, the heavy lower lip. On the father they'd formed a sneer; they gave the son a mournful intensity. He's not Guillaume, she insisted to herself, he's not. Yet in the poor light and the presence of danger, James was his representative. Seven years had faded the exact features of the man with whom Cecily had fallen in love at Edinburgh. To remind herself, she had looked long and often at the profile on the medal she had been given during the Jacobite gathering at Battersea so that the memory of Guillaume Fraser had become that of James Stuart. And vice versa.

He was dressed like an ordinary traveller, clubbed wig, a mulberry coat with plain metal buttons and vertical pockets, buff breeches. The long lawn tie bound round his throat had its plain ends tucked into a plain waistcoat and was slightly grubby. His excellent boots had a white tidemark round the uppers from boat bilge.

Her parlour suited him. The dark linenfold behind him, the blazon of the chair he sat in, Grinling Gibbons' profuse mantel, the worn and beautiful Isfahan rug at his feet, these were dark varieties of shade forming a setting that matched him as if he, like all good things, was out of date. Not a Palladian man, this. No cleared, sterile landscape for this king: he belonged in the tangled, peopled, wooded tapestry of Toryism, as did she.

The decanter reminded her that she was the host. She got up and poured him a large brandy and herself a small one. She rarely drank nowadays. 'Have you eaten, Sire?'

He shook his head; it wasn't important. When she'd sat down he said: 'Lady Cecily, I have only trespassed on your home because I was persuaded that I have your allegiance. Am I wrong?'

Anne *had* been busy. 'Always your servant, Sire.' Polite, non-committal.

'I was further persuaded that the fens can provide a postern through which I may come and go in secrecy when I wish to see my friends. As long as I have your permission.'

Certainly this was one coast impossible to secure; once landed, he could travel unremarked through a country he'd been smuggled out of when a baby. She said: 'You take a hideous risk, Sire.' And so do I.

He nodded. 'It is a risk worthy of taking. Of necessity I must be in touch with those who will uphold my right when the time comes. You know they increase daily?'

She thought that English Jacobites were undoubtedly telling him so, citing every petty squire's and every yeoman's discontent with the Hanoverian millstone round their neck. They would say that Oxford openly toasted the king over the water, that Winchester's aristocratic pupils were so equally and deeply divided into Jacobites and Georgites that each party refused to take lessons with the other.

As Walpole's hold on government strengthened so did the desperation of an opposition with no chance to dislodge it. Even at the Belle, the local Tories pondered on whether another blood-less Glorious Revolution, such as had got rid of James II, should reinstate his son. Squire Leggatt and Colonel Grandison, incensed by the Black Acts, had worn white cockades in their hats for a week. But underneath the bawling and protest lay England's antipathy to papism.

Lodged in John Bull's mind, even if he were poor, in prison or about to step on to the gallows, was the belief that his was a better country than any other. It wasn't merely that his racial memory retained pictures of Protestant martyrs burning on Bloody Mary's bonfires, but that in his nostrils popery had acquired a foreign scent, a flavour used by overdressed, capering frog-eaters that went uneasily with good English roast beef.

Cecily knew it because, even while she was aware it was illogical, she felt it. Can *you* know it, she wondered, you, who smell of incense, who believe yourself an Englishman? Have your Jacobites in sending you so much information told you this? That, honourably as you compare to the fat, wenching German who occupies your throne, we English understand him through our shared Protestantism better than we do you?

You don't and they haven't. She should have realized he was here to plot his return to the kingship. Where did they get their energy, these seekers after power?

England had made it a condition of her peace with the French that they drive this man from their soil. Jamie the Rover. Walpole's assassins harassed his travels, so that he had to hop out of windows and adopt disguises to escape them. Other countries, equally unwilling to offend Walpole, had chivvied him from place to place until the Pope had taken pity on him and lent him and his Clementina a *palazzo* in Rome.

Why didn't he stay in it, peacefully enjoying his young wife and the son she'd given him?

Open an inn, lad, that'll keep your mind off politics.

But, of course, he couldn't. The voice of all his ancestors since Robert the Bruce tormented him, waking and sleeping. The vein at his temple throbbed from an invisible crown.

Oh, poor young man, she thought loftily. I know what it is to have a lineage so threaded through a country that it feels every pull of its land. Then she thought: Don't get involved.

But it seemed she was being asked to. James was requiring

her co-operation, something about the Post Office. Incredulously, she applied herself to what he was saying . . .

'. . . ideally placed to circumvent the spies whom Walpole has set to open letters in the sorting house in London.'

'What is?'

He was startled by her inattention. 'Your inn, Lady Cecily. With your co-operation and, I think, without endangering you too much, it could be my *poste restante*. Sister Ascension suggested that you might be persuaded to send and receive letters on my behalf through the mail.'

Sister who? Anne, of course. Such a name. Risk the Belle? Like fuck, I might.

In that moment, Cecily was vouchsafed another revelation.

A log dropped in the grate so that the glow of the fire's innards spilled over the man opposite her, lighting his wet, dark, elongated eyes, warming his sallow face and hands. All at once she was in the room not only with Guillaume/James but with an icon come to life. Her breath was taken as if a flat, painted Christ had acquired three dimensions, stepped from its frame and addressed her: Lady Cecily, Lady Cecily.

'Yes, my lord?' she answered.

'Lady Cecily, do I ask too much?'

'No, my lord.' All the atavism, all the mystery of kingship was here, with her, in Hempens' parlour. In the rosemary-scented woodsmoke, in the fumes of brandy from her glass, Cecily thought she caught a whiff of the anointing oils that awaited him.

What would await *her* if she helped him to his crown and he gained it?

In her temptation, all the kingdoms of the earth unrolled themselves before Cecily's feet: a duchy, her lands returned twenty-fold and, most glorious of all, a prone Walpole trussed for trampling.

'Your Majesty,' she said, 'I wonder if you remember one of your captains in the 'Fifteen, Guillaume Fraser.'

'Most certainly. A gallant soldier.' James's face was eager. 'Have you received word of him?'

'No. I hoped that you had.'

169

'We made efforts to trace the transportees. We know he was shipped to Barbados but could discover no further word of him. God send he is still alive and may the angels guard him.'

Cecily leaned forward so that she was almost on her knees to this most worthy king. 'Oh, Sire,' she said, 'if you would only become a Protestant all England would rise for you.'

He was kind about it. He took her hands and helped her back to her chair.

'I swore to my father on his deathbed that never would I put the Crown of England before my eternal salvation, nor will I. I cannot gain a kingdom by losing my soul. But, Lady Cecily, I have promised liberty of conscience. I have brought with me men on my staff, here at your own table, who are Protestant and they will tell you I have never interfered with their worship.'

His earliest proclamation to the British people had been an assurance that he would guard the Protestant faith as he guarded his own. 'I show tolerance for men of all religion and hope they will do as much for me.'

Cecily believed him; the rest of England would not. It had believed his father when he made the same promise at his coronation. She thought: But you are a more honourable man than he ever was.

Slicing through the brandy fumes and anointing oils that were making her head spin came a draught of air: I helped another honourable man once and was sent to hell for it.

Perhaps he felt it. He said: 'I ask much of you, Lady Cecily. It may be too much. Consider carefully, and when you are certain, send me word.'

He got up. 'May I command your waterman to row some of my fellows to the uplands? They have horses awaiting them and will command little attention. They are, after all, Englishmen. They merely carry certain messages from me to my supporters.'

'And you, Sire?'

'I shall return to my ship. I came only to see you.'

As they moved to the door, she noticed that his brandy glass was still full and hers was empty. But it wasn't the brandy that intoxicated her.

She wined and dined him and his retinue quickly so that they could scatter before dawn came up.

Anne, it appeared, was to go back to France in James's ship. The cousins parted on the jetty. Anne's small portmanteau was neatly packed; she had the air of business well completed. 'Say goodbye to Sophie for me.'

'Yes.'

'I knew he had to ask you himself. The postern, the Post Office business . . . you wouldn't do it just for me.'

Cecily thought about it. 'No,' she said, 'No, I wouldn't.'

The wind had dropped, allowing mist to return; Cecily stood and watched until the boat disappeared into it. James Stuart waved. Anne, facing him, talking to him, had her back to the shore and didn't.

Three days later, Cecily stood on the jetty again and for the last time thanked Sophie for her gift of Hempens, aware that Sophie, blaming the journey to the island for the loss of her child, wished she'd never made it.

Helpless, she'd watched Sophie hedge her pain behind a furious bitterness, seen herself reflected as hideous by association in Sophie's eyes. When Cecily had promised that the baby's grave would always be lovingly tended, Sophie became impatient. 'What does it matter? I seem to have scattered graves all over Europe.'

'Come to the Belle,' begged Cecily.

'I'll see she do,' Matty said.

But Cecily, watching the frail, swathed figure rowed away from her, refusing or, like Anne, forgetting to wave, knew she wouldn't.

Herself, she stood on the jetty long after the boat was out of sight, flapping her handkerchief back and forth, not so much in farewell as in an unconscious, pleading signal for the return of a childhood that was departing for ever.

CHAPTER NINE

THE ST MARTIN'S summer still held in Hertfordshire. Tyler and Cecily avoided the traffic of the Great North Road and approached Woolmer Green by the deep lanes of the east, their horses' sides brushed by blackberried branches from the hedgerows, by rose-hips, hemlock and wild parsley. Women gleaning with their petticoats pinned up wiped sweat from their eyes to wave as they went past.

At noon they breasted the hill that led steeply down to Watton-at-Stone. Tyler pointed to the next ridge where Datchworth church's tower with its spike showed above the trees.

The church's builders had known little more of ecclesiastical architecture than how to keep a pitch roof supported on a rectangular box for six hundred years. Twelfth-century Datchworthians had carted flints from the fields for its walls because they were too poor to afford stone.

What they did have was one of Hertfordshire's highest prospects and on it they'd sited a church that could be seen for miles from all directions.

The first time Cecily had passed through its Norman doorway, she'd been shocked by the starkness of the interior, plain windows, plaster walls, roof-beams like those of a barn put up by a local carpenter. Here were none of the stone scrolls, brasses and monuments with which benefactors endowed richer churches. Only a sword carved into a plain stone slab set in the south wall recorded the unknown Datchworth man who'd gone to the Crusades.

She'd yet to meet the rector, an absentee pluralist who cared for more important souls in London parishes and instead paid a weary curate five pounds a year to ride up the hill from Aston on his donkey once a month to administer communion and give a sermon which invariably irritated Colonel Grandison into interrupting it to give his own.

Despite outbursts of mirth among the congregation at abstruse doctrine – 'What's that transsubstation we're not supposed to believe in, then, Parson?' – with hens pecking the straw at her feet, the bats that hung like reversed gargoyles from the chancery roof, Cecily found periods of peace during prayers at Datchworth church that had escaped her fashionable attendance at St James's, Piccadilly.

There were moments when her fellow worshippers' soil-engrained fingers entwined so tightly they became bloodless and when the bubbling of larks came through the open doorway with the scent of grass and cow-pats and when house sparrows clattered among the roof beams, when the church became an extension of its surrounding countryside where forest edge ran along the rise of a field like a graceful eyebrow.

Not a spectacular landscape this, but its contours had a dignity reflected in its people. Archibald Cameron, an enthusiastic fisherman, had told her it had been the favourite county of his hero, Izaak Walton, and on reading *The Compleat Angler* she'd found an echo of her surroundings in its quiet rivers, its singing milkmaids and well-kept inns, such as the Belle was attempting to be.

She was amazed at how this glimpse of a poor church on its hill was a homecoming. Airy lightness after Hempens' darkness and grief.

Tyler had been silent for much of the journey. Whether he was aware that Cecily's visitor from France had been the Pretender, she didn't know. Judging from his unspoken dis-approval, she thought he probably did.

Now they were back on his native heath, she was his comrade again. He began to hark on the subject of smuggling and the ease with which Edgar and his brothers brought in the small amount of contraband for their own consumption.

'I told Edgar, I said he'd got to think larger as the saying is. There's the makings of a rare little business there. Be criminal not to exploit it.'

She laughed for the first time in days. 'Be criminal to do so.'

He grunted. 'Far as I can make out, you'd be the first Fitzhenry to think so.'

She didn't think so. Nobody thought so. Except the customs.

Where they could, all sane souls avoided paying duty on imported goods. Society hostesses invariably served their guests best leaf tea and, almost as invariably, it was smuggled, brought in by East India Company captains whose profit was thereby equivalent to a year's wage – the duty on legal tea, like tobacco and sugar, was as high as its cost of production.

A tap on the window of a respectable parsonage preceded an exchange of silver for brandy or silk handkerchiefs. Lady Holdernesse, a former acquaintance of Cecily's, found her position as wife of the Warden of the Cinque Ports handy for illegally importing French gowns. Robert Walpole thundered against smuggling at the House of Commons while using Admiralty barges to bring him in untaxed Flemish lace for his mistress. Everybody did it. What had galled Cecily, as landlady of the Belle, was that, through lack of knowing how, she hadn't. Cellarsful of dutiless gin, wine and brandy piled themselves up before her mind's eye.

'How do we go about it?' she asked.

'I thought we might go into the hemp trade.' Tyler had regained his element, risk. His plan was to use Hempens as the landing and storage place. It involved buying a bigger boat and another, a barge, ostensibly to bring the hemp, the cover for the real cargo, through the waterways of East Anglia to Cambridge where it could be loaded on to mules for the thirty-mile journey to the Belle.

Cecily considered. Edie's sons, she knew, had little trouble avoiding patrolling customs cutters. The danger of discovery would lie in the remainder of the route, especially at the inland port of Cambridge. 'Won't customs officers at Cambridge search the barge?'

'They might,' Tyler said, 'but they won't.' He scratched the palm of his left hand to show that they were bribable.

Cecily considered. The original outlay would be daunting – she'd have to borrow again – but worth it if they could bring in enough contraband. The profit in supplying the coach trade with liquor on which she'd paid no duty would be enormous.

'Very well.' Her conscience was untroubled: this wasn't like going on the pad, more a joining in with a general pastime, a happy avoidance of a tax that would otherwise go into Walpole's pocket.

Despite their preoccupation with the project, they became aware as they approached Woolmer Green that few people were about.

'Market day,' Tyler said. 'They'll all be gone to Hertford.'

But that didn't account for the emptiness of the Belle. The stableyard lacked people and most of the horseboxes were empty. Only Ned was in it, sweeping out – and crying as he did so.

Cecily's immediate thought was for Lemuel. She left Ned to Tyler and ran indoors.

Lemuel was seated in the taproom talking to a packman, his face intent with the effort of enunciation. The packman's polite, fixed smile was thinning and his eyes roamed the ceiling as if looking for sublime rescue.

She knelt down beside her husband. 'All you all right?'

The mobile side of his mouth turned up and his right hand kneaded hers in the pleasure of seeing her and to show her how its grip had improved. 'Well. Well. All. Well.'

'Good.' Whatever had happened here had left Lemuel un-touched; she must look to someone else for its explanation. There *was* no one else. The rest of the inn was deserted. She saw Tyler still talking to Ned out in the yard. On her way to join him she heard a movement from the open trap of the cellar and saw Marjorie and Cole's elder daughter coming up its steps with a bottle in her hand.

'What's happened here, Nancy?'

'They left me in charge, missus. Master Lemuel wanted the French brandy so –'

'Where have they all gone?' The girl was barely adolescent and distressed. You turn your back for a minute . . .

'Hertford, missus. To stop the hanging.'

'Whose hanging?'

'And Colonel Grandison, he's gone with 'em and Warty's gone to Lunnon to fetch Master Cameron . . .'

'Whose hanging, blast you?' As Cecily shook her, the child dropped the bottle, which rolled down the steps and smashed on the brick of the cellar floor.

The girl's face creased. 'Miss Dolly's, missus.'

'Oh . . . clear that up.' Crossly, Cecily continued into the yard to get some sense from Ned. He was holding two horses so that Tyler could saddle them.

'They all seem to have absconded to Hertford for some reason,' said Cecily.

Tyler tightened a girth, then took her arm and led her to the horse. 'Get up, my duck,' he said. The kindness in his voice localized an unformulated fear.

'Tyler,' she said, 'That child wittered something about Dolly.'

'Yes. Up you get, now.'

He mounted the other horse and led hers through the yard gates, across the road and back up the track they'd travelled down minutes before. 'Seven mile,' he said. 'Thank Gawd the fields are mown. We can gallop 'em. Be a short-cut.'

'Tyler,' she begged.

'I don't know, Duchess,' he said, 'Seems Dolly burned down a hayrick.'

'But they wouldn't . . .'

'Can't make sense of it. Warty went to London to fetch the Scotch lawyer. Maybe he's there already. He'll stop it if anybody can.'

'But . . .'

'Gallop now.'

Cornstalks flipped up in the air behind them as they went. Gleaners scattered. They jumped gates and hedges that threw afternoon shadows over dry, pale fields. They ducked under Tudor oak trees sheltering deer that raced before them.

Cecily became two persons, one who noticed these things, amused at the ludicrous haste. How could Dolly be hanged? She wasn't that sort of person. It was too nice a day. This wasn't Hempens where momentous things took place: it was Hertford-shire. The other Cecily rode blind, sobbing when Tyler insisted on walking the horses.

From the rise after Bramfield they saw the spires of Hertford where the town stood on the marshes of the three rivers' conflu-ence that Alfred the Great had drained to build it.

Market-day had coincided with the end of the Assizes. That

morning the judges had left in their gilded coaches for another part of the circuit, trailing trumpeters, leaving the words they'd pronounced to be translated into bleeding backs and the slamming of prison doors or to burgeon into fruit on the tree set up in the square.

The gallows were the attraction. They might have been a lodestone instead of two twelve-foot trestles supporting a long beam over a stage, as if Hertford's citizens, its market sellers and buyers from out of town were iron filings that had been jumped out of their houses, streets and stalls to be pressed in a struggling mass against it.

Tyler was looking over the crowd from his vantage of horseback. Cecily saw only the three nooses dangling from the beam like empty dog collars.

Tyler pointed: 'My Christ, there she is.'

Cecily dragged her eyes away from the gallows. A farm cart parked against the right-hand trestle had three figures in it, a man and two women, one of them Dolly whose mouth was open in an endless scream that couldn't be heard.

As if she'd been expecting her, Dolly saw her over the heads of the crowd and threw herself against the side of the cart. *'Cesseeee.'* The cry carried through the noise like the far-off yelp of a seagull.

'Get the Sheriff,' Cecily said. 'I must get the Sheriff. Get the Sheriff. That's what I must do.' To search for help so that she need not stay; she wanted it more than her existence. She couldn't. To turn away from that beseeching body: there could be no greater betrayal.

'I'll get him,' Tyler said. 'You go to her. Delay 'em somehow.'

She supposed she rode forward but it seemed an involuntary progress, as if the distance between her and Dolly shrivelled like scarred skin pulling them together.

The crowd was good-natured with expectation. It was prepared to suffer pain in the cause of pleasure, to burn itself on the charcoal-lit trays of the muffin-sellers, get its purse stolen, lose its children in the press, all in a good cause. It gave way to the woman lashing out with her whip and maddening her horse with her spurs, as long as she didn't obscure its view.

'Cessy.'

'I'm here, Dolly. I'll stop it.'

Dolly was in her shift, her arms were pinioned at the elbow. Her eyes were opened so wide that the iris showed as a complete blue circle in the white. Her mouth was a rictus.

Cecily edged her horse against the cart. 'I'm here, Dolly. I'll stop it. I'll go to find somebody . . .'

'No.' Dolly inhabited a dimension of minutes where the only imperative was not to be alone. She pushed her body further over the cart side. Her face knocked off Cecily's hat. Her teeth closed on a piece of Cecily's hair to keep Cecily with her, so that the two of them should be joined together. Behind her locked teeth, her breath huffed in and out of her throat; Cecily felt its heat come and go against her scalp.

The horse shifted and moved away, so that Cecily had to grab one of the cart's struts and was left clinging to it, like a bear to a tree. She pulled her head round, not to shift away from Dolly but to beg. 'Help us. Won't anyone help us?'

The only faces that weren't laughing were familiar – Colonel Grandison's, the Packers', Squire Leggatt's.

Cole pushed through to her and held her up. Colonel Grandison ducked under somebody's arm so that he stood below her, his face turned up, a white miniature.

'Stop it,' she told it.

'We've tried. My dear, we've tried.'

'Haven't you told them who she is? Tell them who she is.'

'I will. I will. Who is she?'

There was movement at the rear of the cart. The male prisoner and the other woman were being taken off it.

Colonel Grandison was quarrelling with a hooded man. Cecily screamed at them: 'This is Sir Lemuel Potts's sister. He's a friend of the Prime Minister. She's Sir Lemuel's sister. You can't hang her.'

The hooded man patted his leather jacket. He was telling her he had a legal paper and would hang Dolly, whoever she was. Cecily wasn't hearing properly through the hubbub in her ears from Dolly's panting. Someone was slicing her hair with a knife,

178

her head jerked free. They were dragging Dolly off the cart and on to the platform. The crowd's roar came in waves, like Dolly's breath.

'Come away, my dear,' Colonel Grandison said. 'You shouldn't see this.'

The hangman was putting one of the nooses around Dolly's neck. Dolly had passed from the human world into an animals' abattoir. The rictus stretched her mouth into a smile and she uttered eek-eek noises that made the crowd laugh, but her eyes never left Cecily's.

'I'm here, Dolly.' She whispered it. They were still joined; Cecily felt Dolly's disintegration in her own arms and legs; they were coming away from her trunk. Her eyes stared through Dolly's when the rope tightened and lifted her off her feet. She rose as the rope winched Dolly up, choked as Dolly began to choke.

Then Cole Packer did the kindest, bravest, most terrible thing Cecily had ever seen or ever would see. He hauled himself up on to the platform and lumbered forward so that his arms could wrap around Dolly's waist. He lifted his feet and swung. There was a snap. Dolly's eyes released Cecily's and closed for the last time.

Later that night Archibald Cameron entered Cecily's bedroom to find her sitting in front of her looking-glass with scissors in her hand.

'Did you get the body?'

'Aye. She's in the taproom, in her coffin. The Packers are guarding her.' He looked from Cecily's shorn head to the pile of fair curls that lay in her lap.

She picked them up. 'Put these in with her.'

'Ye shouldnae blame yourself.' He drew up a chair and sat beside her, so that they stared at each other's reflection in the mirror.

The candlelight made Cecily's short hair into an aureole. She thought with hatred that she looked like a *putto* on some Renaissance frieze. I should have shaved it. 'I wasn't here.' She added, with venom: 'Neither were you.'

'I came as quick as I could.'

'Did you discover the reason for it?'

'Reason,' he said. 'Reason, Lord save us.' He was slouched and unshaven, the dust still on his wig and coat from the ride. It was the first time she'd seen him dishevelled.

Cecily thought: He could save Cole Packer but not Dolly.

'The reason is Act 9 George 1.c.22, a Black Act well named.' Almost to himself, he chanted: '"If any person or persons shall set fire to any house, barn or out-house, or to any hovel, cock, mow, or stack of corn, straw, hay or wood, being lawfully convicted . . ."'

'Don't speak it, don't even speak it. What did you find out?'

Watching him in the looking-glass as he told the tale distanced her from it – and from him. In any case, his level, pedantic voice robbed the story of passion, though passion was what it was about.

During his absence, Cameron told her, Dolly had returned to the Belle to look after Lemuel, leaving Tinker Packer in his cottage to look after himself. 'A Lothario, that one,' Cameron said. 'Having rid himself of one woman for Mistress Dolly, he now rids himself of Mistress Dolly for another, a tinker female whose trampings through the countryside he has followed, the Lord knows where.'

When Dolly returned to the cottage to be told by a neighbour that Tinker had gone off with his new *inamorata*, she had smashed what items of his furniture could be broken by an axe. 'For which, mebbe, she wouldnae be blamed too much in a magistrate's court,' said the lawyer.

But Dolly had gone on to commit one of Parliament's new capital offences. In Tinker's yard – 'and ye'll remember that the laddie resides in the forest, making this a messuage under the Black Act . . .'

'For Christ's sake,' said Cecily.

. . . there'd been a hayrick which Dolly herself had helped to gather and build on Tinker's behalf. She set fire to it. One of Lord Letty's keepers had reported her.

Immediately she became subject to prosecution, not in the petty sessions of Colonel Grandison as she would have been only a year before, but by His Majesty's judges anxious to display to King George and the Prime Minister their zeal under the new Act.

'Even then a plea by such as mysel' could have had the sentence commuted,' Cameron said. 'At worst she'd have faced transportation. God forgive me for it, when Warty Packer came to fetch me I was away in Kent.'

And God forgive *me*. She had been at such pains to keep her identity secret that nobody'd known Dolly had once had powerful connections. Had her judge been made aware that in her day Dolly was entertained by the very Prime Minister who'd framed the Act that condemned her ... As it was, he'd seen in the dock before him a literally defenceless woman and an opportunity to make an example of her that would deter other forest-dwellers from attacks on property.

There had been no time such as had allowed the lawyer to get Cole Packer's similar offence struck from the list. It was Mistress Dolly's misfortune – Cameron used the word 'misfortune' – that the legal process had gone through quickly, that the Assize judges were at the very moment in Hertford, that death sentences were carried out two days after they were pronounced.

Dolly had been hanged alongside a man who'd robbed and killed a Tewin house owner and a woman who'd smothered her baby.

Cecily felt Cameron's hand take hers. 'No need to shear your head, my poor lass. It wasnae your fault, it wasnae mine.'

She snatched her hand away. 'Tinker Packer,' she said.

'Mebbe no' even his. She was a gey passionate woman.'

Perhaps, but Tinker Packer would never set foot in the Belle again.

Cecily knew whose fault it was. Before she'd cut her hair, she'd written a letter to a priory in Dunkirk saying that she was willing to co-operate in any activity to advance the cause of James III, thereby overthrowing the throne of George of Hanover and the Government of Sir Robert Walpole.

Tyler would deliver it on his first excursion as a smuggler.

She wasn't acting from principle; she couldn't honestly say that it was her answer to the cry of the oppressed people of

England, though perhaps they were part of it. Nor had she chosen treason as a source of revenge. She was doing it because there were some political crimes that had to be refuted.

Parliament and the judiciary had co-operated to lever the avalanche of their authority down on a creature whose only crime had been that she was human. Such power used against such helplessness necessitated reaction or the world would be too unbalanced for Cecily to walk on its surface.

Dolly had been part of her life. It didn't matter that sometimes she hadn't liked her. It *did* matter that, at the end, the two of them had been joined by their insignificance. She'd felt Dolly's breath on her head as she wrote the letter. In the looking-glass she saw Dolly's face staring at her over the lawyer's shoulder. She would hear Dolly calling to her for the rest of her life. And something had to be done about it.

'What shall I tell Lemuel?' It was a question to herself.

Archibald Cameron said: 'Will I do it for ye?'

'No.' Lawyers. Co-operators in murder. State bandits. Cecily stood up and looked down at him. 'I assume you'll be continuing with your present profession?'

'I will.' He rose as she turned away from him, taking her arm and turning her round to face him. 'Ye may not regard the law too highly at this instance, mistress . . .'

'Law? What law? Law made by murderers? Law that hangs Dolly? Law of greedy tradesmen who've no care for the land except to stop anyone else having it? What do these vulgarians know of England? My ancestors owned it and kept it safe. Peasant, aristocrat, they all co-operated. Each in his place respected the other and the soil they came from. People had rights that we gave them. Upstarts like George, like Walpole, they give nothing. They're bludgeoning England to death from a whim that gives them profit and calling it law.'

She was panting with the effort of putting into words what had until then existed in her blood. She pulled her arm out of his clutch. 'So get away from me.'

'I'll not. Ye'll understand if I die for it.' He grabbed her shoulders and shook her so that her head snapped back and her face was turned up to his.

'Law has form, procedure: there's nae point to it if it serves only the powerful. It must aye extend to others or else it's tyranny – and the powerful are fine aware of it. Sometimes it must work against them. Hear me when I tell ye the law is greater than a form of legitimizing property or class or ruler. Aye, it's conflict. It's not even justice, it wasnae justice today. But it's no' tyranny. Tyranny has no law.'

He shook her again. 'D'ye see? And I'll tell ye this, mistress, it's given commoners like mysel' a mercy we nae had under your aristocracy – Habeas Corpus, privacy, protection against the absolute rule of monarchs. King George is inhibited in his actions and those inhibitions were placed on him by law. By law.'

Credo countered credo. It was an intimacy of antagonism that reached into them both. His thin mouth made patterns that riveted her even while she refused to understand the words they made.

'So you'll go on serving Walpole.'

'I'm serving the law.' He shook her again. 'Take law away and what are we? Savages rending each other over a carcass. Aye, Walpole's bent it for his own ends and ye hate him for it, so do I. Shameless, shouts you. Unfair, shouts I. But ye know it's shameless and I know it's unfair because we possess an ideal of what law should be and that ideal has been given us by grand jurists and grand men. And I tell ye, mistress, I'll fight for that ideal while there's breath in this body.'

Another breath on her hair, heat from another body. She was being drawn so close to him she could see the candlelight on stubby eyelashes that were too white to be seen in daylight.

He spoke low, seeming suddenly disconcerted. 'It's important, d'ye see, Cecily? The law's important. I'm important.' The naked eyes were asking a question.

She said: 'Not to me.' And he let her go.

She told Lemuel that Dolly had died in an accident and trusted to the grace of her people not to disabuse him. Nor did they.

He cried, but it was as if the news was incidental to him and she thought that, as with someone very old, his fight to stay alive took all his concentration and left no energy with which to grieve for others.

That winter, just before Christmas, a beggar crawled into the Belle's stableyard. A not infrequent occurrence: London attempted to reduce its begging population by transporting offenders thirty miles off. Woolmer Green was on the line of its northerly thirty-mile limit.

The Belle had got used to them, gave them its scraps and sent them on in a cart to Stevenage. Stevenage people complained that the beggars put up their Poor Rate. But, as Cecily pointed out, Stevenage's was the nearest poor-house 'And they're not staying at my inn.'

It was evening and she was in her office, listlessly going through the ledgers. Regular coaches had stopped running for the winter, giving the Belle an intermission with only locals and passing trade to entertain.

Marjorie Packer reported the arrival: 'Another shabberoon at the gate.'

'Put it in one of the stalls for the night, then.'

'Done it. It's another nigger. And it's a she.' Marjorie was fidgety.

Cecily looked up. 'We're not a haven for Negroes, Marjorie. One's enough.'

'From the looks of it, her'll make it three. Any minute.'

'Damn.'

Cecily felt her slippers skid on the ice of the cobbles as she crossed the yard to the stables. Ned had hung a lantern from a manger to make a Nativity. Yellow light concentrated on the black-skinned, black-shawled figure who lay on the straw, glossing a horse's head as it looked over the partition, turning Ned, Stabber and Cole into helpless, watching shepherds.

The woman was dying, her eyes fixed with the stare of the moribund. She could have been between sixteen and forty; famine had aged her face and robbed it of individuality so that it was the mask seen everywhere on the streets of London that made the starving, black or white, appear members of the same family.

What little nourishment her body had received had been absorbed by the foetus in her distended belly. She was already advanced in labour.

'Will I carry her indoors?' Stabber asked.

Cecily glanced at Marjorie, who shook her head. 'She's better not moved. This'll do.' The straw was clean, the air heated by horses.

'Tell Quick to warm a flip, lots of eggs, milk, brandy.' Cecily was invigorated for the first time since Dolly's execution. She felt a fury directed at the stupid black female's indifference. The *carelessness* of these indigents. The woman had been granted the opportunity to give life and was throwing it away by dying. What wouldn't Sophie give for the chance? What wouldn't I?

She got down on her knees in the straw and snapped at the woman: 'You're going to have this baby, like it or not.'

Marjorie was Cecily's ally and adviser. The two of them became the unborn baby's champions pitted against a mutual enemy, the mother. They forced flip down her throat, they slapped her face when she lost consciousness, they bathed her, demanded her name, crooned to her, shouted at her. It was a race, literally, between life and death.

The men sat on bales of hay at the stall entrance, puffing pipes. 'Leave the poor soul die in peace, Marje,' Cole said.

'Go stick your head 'n a bucket,' said Marjorie.

Quick came to lounge against the stall post. 'Know her, Quick, do ee?' asked Stabber.

The black man shook his head.

'Thought you'd a known her,' Stabber said.

Cecily told the cook: 'Ask her who she is. Where she comes from.' Perhaps blackness was another language.

Quick said slowly: 'Who are. You? Where. Come from?'

Useless. The woman's head lolled, only her womb responding to the urge of the child trying to get out of it. 'Push, you bugger,' said Marjorie. It was like helping somebody escape from a collapsing building. '*An*' again. There's the head, I can feel un.'

'Push, damn you,' said Cecily. 'Damn you, *push*.'

The only sounds the woman made were involuntary huffs as air was expelled from her lungs by the last contractions.

The head was visible. Marjorie's hands cupped round it as if she would pull, but from a final heave the body came squirming out and plopped between its mother's thighs, a shining mole in its sac.

Cecily probed her little finger into its mouth, which issued a mew of sound. Thank you, God, thank you, thank you.

Sobbing, Marjorie cut the cord with a kitchen knife and tied it with baler twine. Cecily held the baby up before its mother's eyes. It was a girl. 'Look how clever you've been.'

But the woman had gone. The afterbirth would remain inside her. As Cole said, wiping his eyes, 'One in, one out. Same minute.'

They wrapped the child in a fleece to carry it into the inn and drink its health, showing it to Lemuel, exulting in it as in a trophy from a battlefield. Marjorie sent Stabber into the forest to fetch her cousin's husband's sister, Polly, who'd just lost her fifth and was well in milk.

'What we going to do with un?'

'Shame to put her to the poor-house.'

'Train un up to be useful. Grow your own help, like.'

They were all looking at Cecily. Good God, they want me to keep her. Delivering a living baby had been the triumph; she hadn't thought beyond that. 'We're too busy,' she protested. 'There's no . . .'

There's no room at the inn.

'Damn,' she said.

Perhaps, after all, Dolly's loss penetrated Lemuel's mind and tipped the balance of his battle against him. On a bitter morning in the following February, Cecily took him his breakfast and found him dead.

He was buried alongside Dolly in Datchworth churchyard. Cecily had a block taken out of the Belle's wall to make them both a gravestone and hired a mason from Stevenage to incise it with the inscription: 'There the wicked cease from troubling and there the weary be at rest.'

Job, she felt, was appropriate.

The funeral service was well attended and there were tears

186

from some of the Belle's staff, and even a few of its clients who had watched Lemuel's struggle to gain mobility and speech. 'A sweet gentleman,' Colonel Grandison called him in his oration. Cecily's eyes remained dry. Dolly's stared at her from behind the reredos, just as they looked at her from every corner of the Belle.

At the graveside she was joined by Archibald Cameron. There'd been no contact between them since the day of Dolly's hanging but it had seemed necessary that someone who remembered Lemuel in his great days should provide official sanction to his death.

'I gathered ye didn't wish me to inform Sir Robert.'

'No.'

Birdsong had been stilled by the cold. Some mast from the leafless beech tree over the mourners' heads was frozen into the ground. The sheep that usually grazed the churchyard had gone in the winter slaughter, like the cows, and only Colonel Grandison's red bull peered over the hedge, sending streams of steam from its nostrils. Beyond the moat the earth of the fields fell away, showing pinkish brown against a colourless sky.

Would Lemuel have been content with these bucolic obsequies or, in his long-imposed dumbness, had he still hoped for the muffled drums, the minute's silence in the House, a memorial service at St Stephen's? Oh, Lemuel, I had neither the time nor patience to find out.

'Dust to dust, ashes to ashes,' chanted the curate.

Cameron stooped and took up a clod of clay displaced from the grave and put it into her hand. She let it fall. It was common Hertfordshire clay and didn't sprinkle but landed with a thump on the coffin.

'Ye harboured him well,' Cameron said, as they walked away.

Why did the man persist with the idea that she needed comfort? There'd been no requirement to love a plebeian husband foisted on her, no requirement to love his sister.

But, oh, God, I want them back.

On the way out of the churchyard, Cameron paused by the grave of the black woman with its low headstone that had been cut from the same block as Dolly's and Lemuel's. The inscription was from Exodus, chosen by Marjorie and Quick: 'I was a stranger in a strange land.'

'Did ye ever find out who she was?'

The Packers had tried but admitted defeat. The beadle of Welwyn, the parish on Woolmer Green's south, had denied knowledge of her, as had Stevenage's, though Cole suspected one or the other of pushing her over his boundary so that she and her child wouldn't be a charge on his parish.

'She didn't exist at all,' Cecily said. 'She was invented.'

She felt Cameron's arm tuck under hers to lead her away. *He thinks I'm not sane.* She wondered if she was.

After Dolly's hanging, she had known she was not – or, rather, that she wandered by herself in an insane world, staring at familiar objects and faces that had become distorted, studying her own hand as if it belonged to somebody else. Greyness closed in. Waking to the days had become as dreadful as the nightly encircling dolmens, Sophie's baby, Dolly, the death of friendship; colourless but of a mass which sucked at her ability to breathe so that she woke up choking.

Then one night, quite recently, light had come into the circle with a child, white as it began weaving in and out of the standing stones, emerging black at the end of its dance, yet still luminous. It had become a recurring dream and not even Lemuel's death had extinguished it.

It brought back the ability to function. It seemed to Cecily that the black woman had been invented somewhere on the Great North Road specifically to restore symmetry, to limp into the Belle's yard and deliver the baby to it. Birth for death, spring for winter. She'd been a requirement, a vehicle, to balance the scale left empty by Sophie's child.

Cameron persisted anxiously in his comfort: 'Ye've still the Belle to see to,' he said, 'and the wee girl.' He'd taken to the black child.

Cecily's smile of agreement appeared to worry him the more. *And a government to overthrow.*

CHAPTER TEN

THE COACH LEANED horribly as it rounded the bottom of the hill before righting itself to go through the Belle Sauvage's great arch, flecking the pillars with mud and sweat.

A boy ran alongside to open the door and let down the step even as the stage juddered to a stop. Ostlers unbuckled the horses' traces, luggage was hauled from the bustle-like net on the coach's rear, the landlady spoke the welcome of all good inns: 'Please to alight.'

Archibald Cameron watched her face take on the guardedness it always assumed when she saw him. 'How nice, Mr Cameron. Here for the fishing again?'

She looked bonnier than she had at Sir Lemuel's funeral, not so wraith-like and mad. She's out of the long sands, he thought. It's the child. 'How's my Eleanor?'

The Belle was flourishing. He looked about him at the large, tidy yard, its stables and coach-house into which the stage was even now being manoeuvred to leave space for other arrivals. Above him ran an elegant and ivied gallery with geraniums peeping over the rail; before him the open door of the inn showed a passage of polished flags with a low, pargeted ceiling. He sniffed the scent of apple-log fires, wine and good cooking. Who'd have thought a body as chancy as Lady Cecily Fitzhenry would have made so excellent an innkeeper?

Cameron stretched and stamped to get stiffness from his bones. A broken trace had slowed a journey from London made longer by his companions, a wordy Yorkshireman and two other gentlemen, one large, one medium-sized, whom he'd seen once before at the Belle and summed up immediately as glorified cattle-stealers. Sharing a coach with the callants hadn't changed his opinion.

'A fine morning to ye, Ned.'

'Good to see you back, Master Archie.'

'Are ye well, Cole?'

'The better for having ee with us, Master Archie.'

A happy discipline pervaded the Belle: she kept a good staff; another facet to her character he wouldn't have gambled on had he been a gambling man.

Marjorie unpacked his case, the lad cleaned his boots and Cameron joined the common table. The two cattle-stealers, he noticed, took their meal in a private room to be served by the landlady herself. And long-faced she is at doing it, he thought, seeing Cecily going in with a tray.

'Rusty-wigged crop we came up with, my dear,' Sir Spender was saying. 'The sawney. Holy fella. Close as wax. Wouldn't bet with me. Name of Cameron. Been here before, ain't he?'

'That's my lawyer.'

'Is he now? Useful, very useful. The Cause finds him worthy of investigation. Got its eye on him, it seems. Becoming a big toad in the Whig puddle, they tell me.'

'Not that holy,' Maskelyne said. 'There's a woman in Kent.'

'I shall not spy on my own lawyer,' said Cecily, firmly. *What woman in Kent?*

'Nevertheless, no harm in keeping an ear stretched and an eye open,' Sir Spender told her. 'For the Cause.'

At the end of his meal, as he always did, Cameron sent for the cook. 'Ye still wield a saintly saucepan, Master Quick. It was a happy day Mrs Henry hired ye.' The chef's reputation had spread to the point where the rival White Horse at Stevenage had hired a black cook in hopeful emulation.

'Happy day for me, Master Archie, thanks to you.'

The Scot had a joyful reunion with Eleanor in the taproom, where she was taken to say goodnight to him and Colonel Grandison. He'd brought her a little wooden horse on wheels.

The Yorkshireman didn't like the attention paid to the child. On the journey down he'd entertained the coach with details of worsted manufacture – an enterprise through which he was acquiring a fortune though not, it seemed, the confidence to dispel his suspicion that servants would take advantage of him if he didn't shout.

He'd already expressed his disapproval on finding that a black man had cooked his dinner, though he'd eaten it and called for more. The south of England's growing Negro population he regarded as infestation. 'They'd not be let in Yorkshire, I tell thee.'

Now, the sight of the child Eleanor being made much of by the Belle's regulars further offended his *amour propre*.

'What's that? I'm asking thee, what's that? The chimney broosh or the entertainment? Doos it dance with a dog or what? Hey, missis?' Cecily had appeared at the door. 'Is this a clean inn? Or a breeding ground for niggers? What I say is . . .'

Cameron rose, Colonel Grandison's hand went to his sword-hilt and Warty Packer lumbered forward from his place by the barrels.

Cecily was quicker. She smiled at the Yorkshireman. 'If I may have a word with you outside, sir. It's to do with your port-manteau.'

Cameron followed them outside to the yard, on watch for trouble. He heard the Yorkshireman say: 'What's to do with my portmanteau? Mislaid it, have thee?'

'Yes,' said his hostess. 'It is already on its way to the White Horse up the road and if you will be so good as to mount this horse, Ned here will guide you in its wake. You'll find it more congenial there. The coach will stop for you in the morning. Get him up, Ned.'

That the Yorkshireman's rage was only bluster had to do with the fact that Stabber and Cole stood like Gog and Magog in the lengthening shadows of the yard. The Yorkshireman's shouts diminished into the birdsong of a summer evening as his horse was jog-trotted out of the yard on Ned's leading rein.

'Neatly done,' said Cameron, as Cecily came back indoors.

'Thank you. Are you staying long?'

'Aye. I thought I'd do a wee bit of angling.'

Cecily went back out to the yard. 'Keep an eye on Master Archie's room when he goes to bed,' she told Cole. 'I don't want him wandering tonight of all nights, not with Tyler coming.'

'He'd not give us away,' Cole said.

You don't know the half. The Packers were cognisant of – indeed, willing participants in – Cecily's smuggling activities. What else she had to do that night was between her and the

Jacobites alone. 'He's a lawyer. Angling, indeed. He's angling for something and it ain't fish.'

Cole shook his head as he watched her return to the inn. He wondered when she'd see it. Everybody else could.

'Tonight of all nights,' Cecily said to herself. 'Damn him.' Then she thought: *What* woman in Kent?

It had been dismaying that her conversation with James Stuart at Hempens had been so quickly followed up by his secret agents – even more that the agents were a couple of Jacobites from her past and that their visits were frequent.

Their arrival always induced tension, partly because of what it entailed, partly because they invariably got drunk – Sir Spender indiscreetly, Maskelyne with aggression to anyone who looked at him sideways.

Secret my arse, Cecily thought. She'd seen more reticent fairground barkers. As usual, she tried to persuade them not to go into the taproom after dinner. As usual, they did.

'No, no, my dear,' Sir Spender said. 'Skulking only attracts suspicion. What should seem more natural than drinking with one's fellow men? We must congregate in order to feel the country's pulse. No, once more we'll wet the sawdust with these *ascriptus glebae*, these ploughers and reapers. Damask the claret, dear lady.'

'And put it on the sconce,' Maskelyne said. They never paid.

In the taproom Cameron settled himself next to Colonel Grandison, who was still fulminating against the Yorkshireman: 'Upstart Whigs, all damn unmannerly boors, begging your pardon, Cameron.'

A Whig upstart granted his pardon and, for a while, sipped his glass of bishop, listening to the Colonel's conversation, enjoying the scent of wallflowers coming through the window and watching his other two coaching companions across the room get drunk.

'I'm away to bed, Colonel. It's the early bird catches the fish.'

Upstairs, Cecily snatched a moment to make sure Eleanor was asleep and to marvel at the perfect mattness of the child's skin against the sheet.

To begin with she'd left the baby's care to Polly, the wet nurse, but a busy summer had called Polly into service as starcher, needlewoman and cleaner so that the child was passed around, turning up on each woman's hip at one time or another, including Cecily's, strapped to Ned's back as he curried his horses, in a pannier when Quick went to market, in the wash basket, on Colonel Grandison's knee in the taproom.

Her status was established: a charity orphan destined as a servant of the Belle Sauvage.

At first she was a curiosity with the locals, then a favourite. A healthy child with an easily gained chuckle, her confidence in everybody's goodwill rendered her vulnerable. In any case, the Packers, male and female, were her champions and nobody was going to argue with them.

Her blackness flickered in the eye of the beholder; sometimes marked, as when she played with the Packers' fair-skinned children, only to blend out when she was among adults, no more noticeable to those who were used to her than the mole on Marjorie's cheek or the tick of the parlour's grandmother clock, only to become surprising again when new guests commented on it.

In Cecily's mind the conviction that the child was a replacement grew rather than diminished. She had battled for a baby's life at Hempens and lost. This time she'd won. Obviously, it was inferior compensation – it was only a black beggar's child – but it counted as a victory among a series of defeats, an erratic, minuscule evening-out of the unfairness of things.

As time went on, she had to blink the negroid features into focus because what she began to see when she looked at the child was Sophie. The good humour, the trust in being loved, the response to make an audience laugh, these attributes were Sophie's as surely as if Sophie were whispering instruction into the baby's ear. She was nagged by the heresy that Sophie's baby had found a home in the body of this strangely sent Christmas child.

She put off naming it and it was variously known as Sootykins, Africa, Molly (from molasses) and, behind Cecily's back, not unkindly, 'that little black bugger', until Archibald Cameron, on one of his visits, had told Cecily she was acting like a heathen and that if the child wasn't received by the Church of England through baptism forthwith he'd personally see to it that she became a Presbyterian.

Contrite, Cecily said: 'I don't know what to call her.'

'Grisel. A good Scottish name.'

'Indeed. We'll call her Eleanor. I meant, what surname?'

'The Lord's sake. Cameron, if you must.'

She was as surprised at the freedom with which he passed around his name as he was that she withheld hers. Fitzhenry? It couldn't be given to anybody, especially a black anybody, however miraculous. And she wouldn't inflict the child with Potts.

Eleanor Grisel Belle Cameron was baptized at the font of Datchworth church the following week, with Cecily and Marjorie Packer as godmothers, Cameron and Colonel Grandison the godfathers.

Then, one day, Cecily had entered the kitchen to talk to Quick. Eleanor, playing in the apple barrel, looked up, stretched out her arms and said, 'Mamma.'

Quick's reaction was curious. He squatted down by the barrel as if putting his body between the child and Cecily. 'She don't mean it, Miz Cec'ly. She hear the Packers call you "mum" and she just added a piece.' To Eleanor he said: 'You don't call mistress that, chil', you speak respec'ful. You speak humble an' respec'ful to eve'ybody.'

He thinks I shall berate her, thought Cecily. It came into her head that Sophie's child would not have been made to show humility.

She said sharply: 'Why should she be humble?'

Quick stood up, his shoulders bowed, eyes studying the ground. 'She a black girl, mistress. She got a long hard row to hoe.'

'I shall teach her manners, thank you, Quick.'

After that Cecily increasingly interfered in Eleanor's upbringing. She talked to her more so that the child might not acquire a Hertfordshire accent, she had her clothes made by her own seamstress, she refused to let Polly cut the woolly hair: 'She's not a boy.'

194

'You can't keep a cap on it else,' protested Polly. 'Looks like a scrap o' lace on a dandelion.'

'Then she'll go capless.' Cecily considered that the wide mop balanced on the child's tiny neck looked charming, like topiary.

Polly gave in her notice. She was expecting her sixth, anyway. 'It ain't I don't love that little darky,' she told Marjorie, 'but she mun know her place. Mum's storing up trouble with her.'

On the night of Polly's departure, Cecily heard crying from the nursery. When she opened the door, she saw a small white nightgown standing by Polly's empty bed.

She picked the baby up. 'This won't do, will it? You must get used to sleeping by yourself.' There was wet on her neck from the face against it, a tiny heaving ribcage against her own, small feet and hands scrabbling for a hold.

She carried the child to her own bed. 'We're not making a habit of this, mind.'

The next night Eleanor's cot was put in Cecily's room and had remained there.

In the taproom only the Jacobites sat late. Warty Packer was clearing the tables when Cecily entered. Sir Spender was calling for more liquor. 'Where's me aqua vitae? Why's me glass empty? Is this damn Hanoverian tavern or – or place for gentlemen?'

Warty glanced at Cecily: 'They drunk nine men dead already.'

She nodded. 'Go and get the cellar doors open for Tyler, then come back.'

She took the drink to the Jacobites' tables. Sir Spender regarded her blearily. 'Are you the lad who took me order 'n hour ago? My, you've changed. No, Masky, 's our delectable hostess. Drink with me, madam. Another round with Aphrodite.'

'You've had nine bottles already,' Cecily told him. 'No more tonight.'

'No alehouse keeper's going to tell him when he can drink and when he can't,' Maskelyne said.

'Have you work for me or haven't you?' Cecily took care not to show she was afraid of Maskelyne, though she was. When he was drunk his verbal attacks on her or any of the inn's

195

women were filthy. 'Or shall I call Cole Packer?' Maskelyne had made the mistake of insulting Marjorie in Cole's hearing and been thrown in the horse trough, since when he'd curbed his tongue slightly. None of the staff understood why he was still given house room. If it hadn't been that Sir Spender pleaded with Cecily on his companion's behalf, saying he needed the man for protection, he wouldn't have been, Cause or no Cause.

Sulking, Maskelyne rummaged in his pocket and produced a packet of letters. 'Put these in. And in the bag there'll be one addressed to Clonkilty in Edinburgh. Copy it.'

'Franked, nat'lly,' Sir Spender said. 'The Whig bastards rob us blind. B'God, as soon 've a Turk for a ruler as 's bloody German. Lady Cecily, join me in a toas' t' when our king enjoys 's own again.'

'You'll toast us to the damned gallows,' Cecily told him. In a Tory taproom where expressions of disloyalty to George I were frequent, Sir Spender went more or less unremarked. But one of these days . . .

Warty came back and helped her get the knight upstairs to his room, Maskelyne following like a cold-eyed nursemaid.

Are they sodomites? Yet she'd heard them boast more than once about their exploits in brothels, Dick with ridicule of the prostitutes they'd used, Maskelyne with something nearer hatred. She supposed they were not untypical Englishmen in their contempt for women but neither among the aristocracy nor here, at the lower end of the scale, had she encountered it in such ferocity.

'You want me to wait up for Wallie?' Warty asked.

'I'll see to Wallie. You go and help Tyler.'

Returning downstairs she felt a tremor in the floorboards, the sign that the barrels on Tyler's pack mules were being unloaded. They were wrapped in felt but nothing could stop them vibrating the Belle's timbers as they rolled down the chute into her cellar. The cellar itself ran the length of the inn, a brick wall dividing the half shown to guests who wanted to choose their own liquor from the half containing the contraband Tyler brought from Hempens four times a year.

The entrance to that section was a concealed trap on the Belle's south side hidden from the road by trees. The only likelihood of its discovery by the authorities lay in someone informing them of it and, since most of Woolmer Green's and Datchworth's population – including, of course, the local magistrate – profited from her smuggling, Cecily believed herself safe on that score.

She went into her office to wait for Wallie. She wished she didn't have to tackle this, her other illegal and much more dangerous enterprise, without the knowledge of Tyler and the Packers. Compared to those reliable men, allies like Dick and Maskelyne were unnerving.

What had surprised her was the efficiency with which the ramshackle Jacobite spy network they represented had involved her in the Pretender's scheme for making the Belle Sauvage his *poste restante*.

Walpole's formidable system of intelligence to counter the Jacobite threat included the state monopoly of the General Post Office, and saw treason in every mail-bag. One of the complaints against the Royal Mail, especially by Tories, was the delay caused by the 'secrets room' in the GPO basement in Cornhill where suspicious letters were carefully opened and scanned for seditious content before being sent on.

So well known was the tight watch on communication, that Cecily had at first disbelieved Sir Spender when he told her that 'for the Cause' the Belle was to become one of the receiving houses for the mail.

'The White Horse at Stevenage is the receiving house for this area,' she said. 'Always has been.'

Sir Spender tapped his nose. 'No more. We of the Cause have . . . what is the word? . . . infiltrated, that's it, infiltrated the inner sanctum of the Hanoverian's Post Office. One of our agents, a Master John Lefebure, has breached that armoury of mail, holed its defences, has, in fact, been given high place in its employment. I think, dear lady, that you will soon receive official notification of some interest.'

Not for the first time Cecily winced at Sir Spender's lack of caution. The name of a man of utmost value to the Cause, who, if caught, could be disembowelled, ought to be kept secret even from his fellow Jacobites. *Does the old fool bandy mine about like that?*

However it was, Lefebure worked the oracle. Cecily received a letter from the Postmaster General informing her that from henceforth a postboy would deposit and pick up letters for and from the district at the Belle Sauvage, the White Horse's licence as a receiving house having been withdrawn.

Stevenage's inhabitants were displeased. They now had to travel five miles further in order to use the post than they'd done before. Totty Stokes, the White Lion's landlord, was furious at the loss of a lucrative trade. But, since Totty Stokes's mother had handled that part of his business, and since she was also the local laundress and the mail had acquired a dampness on wash days which made the ink of the addresses run, rendering them illegible, everyone else was delighted.

So was the postboy who carried the London mail on its stage from Potters Bar; the end of his ride came earlier and Cecily's food and ale were better and more plentiful than Totty's.

She heard his horse enter the yard and went out to meet him. 'Well met by moonlight, Wallie.'

'Bloody moonlight. Give us a hand, mum, me stamps is stiff.' He had to make two attempts to dismount before his legs obeyed him.

'There's mutton stew on the fire in the kitchen,' she told him. 'And a blackjack on the table.'

'Gawd bless you for a Christian.'

She took his horse to the stable for him, relieved it of its saddlebag and rubbed it down, leaving it munching from a manger.

'I'll lock up the mail as usual, shall I, Wallie?'

He looked up from his meal. 'Aye. Got to guard the mail.'

She took the saddlebag upstairs to her bedroom. By law, it shouldn't have left Wallie's sight. By law, Wallie should have blown his post horn as he entered the Belle's yard where a fresh horse should have been awaiting him on which he should even now be galloping north towards the next stage instead of getting ready to bed down on a palliasse by the kitchen fire until morning.

But, as Cecily always said to herself, if the Postmaster General wanted his postboys to obey the law, he should pay them better.

Wallie, like so many postboys, was an elderly and pensionless veteran of Queen Anne's wars. In winter he could be frozen to death – the 'boy' he'd replaced actually had been in the winter of '16, his horse ambling into Stevenage with his corpse still on it. The spring rains created mud Wallie could drown in if his horse tipped him off. Trying to keep to time in summer over ruts a foot deep, he encountered flocks of geese and sheep which wouldn't be hurried; in autumn he faced wide-wheeled slow-moving harvest wains, fallen trees that nobody bothered to clear and rotted bridges. All for 7s. 6d. a week.

Even if she hadn't had an ulterior motive, Cecily would have given the man bed and food. Who was to notice the delay? The Post Office's national delivery was all delay.

In London an excellent Penny Post ensured a speedy and frequent delivery that was the envy of the world, but if you lived more than ten miles outside the City, you got your letters and parcels when you got them.

The trouble was that the system hadn't changed since the days of Charles II. The post roads went north and south only so that a letter sent by Royal Mail from Newcastle, in the east, addressed to, say, Carlisle, 57 miles away in the west, had to travel to London and then out again – a round trip of 574 miles.

Again, while some receiving houses were coaching inns with horses available, like the Belle, some were mere homesteads where postboys had to wait while their horse for the next fifteen-mile stage was unharnessed from a plough.

With all this, the roads were so awful that it wasn't unknown for a letter sent to the Americas by the Falmouth packet to arrive quicker than one posted at the same time in London to a destination beyond the Home Counties.

So nobody at the next stage after the Belle was going to raise an eyebrow if the mail was late. It was always late.

In her bedroom, Cecily undid the saddlebag's buckles, slipped in the letters Maskelyne had given her and searched for the one it already contained to Clonkilty of Edinburgh.

If it was franked it meant it was likely to be from somebody important, a member of either the House of Lords or the

Commons who was therefore exempt from having to pay postage. There it was. 'William Clonkilty on the third stage of Mac-Lannan's tenement in Puckle Alley, Edinb'gh. Haste. Haste.'

Damn ... The letter was bulky. It'd be hours copying the bugger. Even opening it would take time. The wax had to be softened enough for her to ease it from the paper without breaking it but not so much that the seal's impression became distorted.

She had to wait until her hands stopped shaking. Suppose I break the seal and Clonkilty informs Walpole that somewhere along the Great North Road someone is tampering with the Royal Mail ...

The night-time sounds of her inn forced themselves on to her awareness as if, in the creak of its timbers shrinking after the heat of the day, in the tiny agitation from the cellar, in the breathing of the child, in the scutter of mice in its thatch, the Belle was reproaching her: *Will you risk all this?*

As always, when she faltered, she was confronted by the image that enforced her co-operation with shabby men like Spender Dick and Arthur Maskelyne. It wasn't Guillaume Fraser's nor that of King James but the face of a woman hanged in Hertford for burning down a hayrick.

I'm here, Dolly.

Her hands stopped trembling. She levered up the softened seal, opened the letter, dipped her quill into the inkpot and began to copy.

The letter was from Josiah Staples, a Whig MP, sending a report to his friend in Edinburgh that would warm Mr Clonkilty's presumably Whiggish heart as it chilled Cecily's. 'The Great Man do strengthen his hold with every Day that passeth,' wrote Staples of his prime minister.

The discovered Jacobite plot to assassinate George I and take over the Bank and the Royal Exchange had proved useful to Walpole, enabling him to quell even reasonable opposition as Jacobite manoeuvring. Because of it, the Commons was to vote money for the raising of four thousand extra troops. 'The Tories are in Disarray,' Staples wrote, 'for Whatever they do may be Suspect as for James Stuart.'

Britain's Catholics were still having difficulty in paying the fine of ten thousand pounds imposed on them by Walpole as punishment for their support (tacit or open or non-existent) of the Jacobites. 'It do serve them right,' wrote Staples, 'for are they not all traitors in their hearts?'

Bolingbroke had been allowed back into the country – ('A Mistake for a Viper be ever a Viper') – but was kept under close scrutiny and not permitted to sit in the House of Lords. Landowners' taxes were to be lowered ('a good Thing') and workers' wages were being cut ('the better for their employment').

Walpole, it appeared, was not only stifling Tories but any threat to his leadership from his own side. 'Our Great Man,' wrote Staples, 'has ousted troublesome Carteret and 'tis rumoured Macclesfield, Cadogan and Roxburgh will follow.'

Interesting if depressing stuff and pages of it. Dawn was gilding Datchworth church's weathervane by the time Cecily re-warmed Josiah Staples's seal and stuck it down.

Folding her copy, she took it to Sir Spender and Maskelyne's door and slipped it underneath before returning Wallie's saddlebag. Dutifully, she waited while he removed the letters for the district and handed them to her. She took those addressed to the Belle and put the rest on the hall table to be collected by their addressees.

She got Eleanor up and took her down to the kitchen. Outside Ned was harnessing horses to the coach, ready for its departure. The contraband delivery had gone well and Tyler had already left with the mules for wherever it was in the forest he kept them.

Usually Cecily was in the yard to wave the coaches off but she was too tired today. She watched from her window as two hung-over Jacobites were helped aboard.

She sat on in the window, enjoying the relief that they'd gone and the view of the road with its morning traffic. The sight of Colonel Grandison on his bay, trotting down the hill from Datchworth to pick up his mail, reminded her it was the Brewster Sessions tomorrow. She'd have the annual chore of reapplying for the Belle's licence.

Another horse, bearing Archibald Cameron and various

fishing paraphernalia, emerged out of the gate below her and stopped while its rider chatted to the Colonel, then turned right in the direction of Welwyn and the river Mimram.

What woman in Kent?

Marjorie put her head round the door. 'More trouble . . .'

Cecily ran into the taproom and fell on her knees by the small, crumpled figure in its big chair. 'Can they do this?'

'They've done it.' One of the Colonel's hands dabbed a handkerchief to his averted eyes, the other held out a letter. Beneath the Lord Chancellor's seal a curt paragraph told Colonel Fairley Peter Grandison that his commission as Justice of the Peace *quorum aliquem vestrum* was being withdrawn immediately.

Walpole. 'They must give you a reason.'

'The reason, my dear, is that I'm a Tory and Walpole will have every official in the country a Whig, down to the night-soil men. At our last meeting the Lord Lieutenant reproached me that I didn't administer the Test Act to Jack Ferris.'

'For God's sake.' Sir Jack Ferris was a dear old man; well known and well liked, nobody had questioned his position as a local Overseer of the Poor even though it was generally known that he was a Catholic. Insistence that he take the Oath of Supremacy and Allegiance, as all holders of public office were supposed to do to prove they were practising members of the Church of England, would have meant his refusal and therefore the loss of a dutiful and compassionate Overseer, so Grandison had refrained from doing it.

'This isn't London, Cecily, it's the country. We meld here, we tolerate. I told the Lord Lieutenant so. Do you know what he said? He said . . .' Grandison turned to look at her. Tears spurted out of his screwed-up eyes, like a baby's. 'He said I must therefore be suspect of Jacobite sympathies. *Me.*' He clambered out of his chair and drew his sword. It looked too big for him as he danced on his small feet, slashing at invisible enemies. 'I opposed James II in the Glorious Revolution. I fought against young James when he was in Louis' army at Oudenarde. And they call me a *Jacobite*?'

Confused, Cecily said: 'But I've seen you drink to the toast of the King Over the Water.'

He was indignant. 'That doesn't mean I'm a Jacobite.'

Such a contradictory little man. Magistrate and receiver of stolen goods. Yet no more corrupt than the Lord Chancellor who'd just dismissed him. The signature on the bottom of the letter had read 'Macclesfield', the earl at this moment under investigation for misuse of Chancery funds. And, thought Cecily, for a minister of Walpole's to attract inquiry into his peculation, said peculation must be enormous and undeniable. She sent Cole for some best contraband brandy and poured the Colonel a bumper.

Hypocrites, she accused the Government as she watched him cry. Grandy cares more for his little bit of England than you do for the whole nation. As magistrate, he'd been the chief organ of local government in the area, dispensing justice, seeing to the upkeep of gaols, fixing wages, licensing trades, reporting on the state of religion and any unrest in his division, setting levies for parish needs and suppressing nuisances. He was entitled, without trial, to send people to the stocks for swearing or being drunk and order a vagrant whipped.

Like all JPs he'd had the power of a despot. Yet nobody had ever appealed against his decisions. His people grumbled against 'that interfering little goblin' when he'd scolded and punished errant members of his flock, yet because he was interested, because he drank with them, helped them, tumbled some of their willing women, knew their children's names and shed his ever-ready tears when they died, they had accepted him as a generally beneficent part of their lives, like the weather.

May God send as good a man in his place.

But, as she found out next morning at Stevenage's Brewster Sessions, God and the Lord Chancellor had instead sent a Whig, Sir Samuel Pink. Hearing his name for the first time outside the court, she'd expected something small and fluffy, like the Colonel, but he was large and red, wore a full-bottomed wig as if he were a judge, and appeared possessed of permanent fury.

He refused her licence.

Standing in the dark well of the court with other inn proprietors, she wondered if she'd heard him correctly. 'I beg your pardon, your worship?' The Colonel had always passed her application on the nod.

'Renewal refused,' repeated Pink.

Walpole, she thought. He's found me and instructed this gargoyle to take the Belle away from me as he's taken everything else.

She stared upwards at the high bench and heard Pink mutter to his clerk: 'A hotbed of Jacobites.'

'If you're referring to the Belle Sauvage,' she said clearly, 'it is a hotbed of Toryism. I was not aware that to be Tory is yet against the law, though I suspect it soon will be.'

At the back of the court, Cole Packer began to move forward.

'Do you address me, madam?' asked Pink.

'I do, sir. May I ask for what reason you are refusing me?' As Cole jogged her arm, she added: 'Your worship?'

'You are refused, madam, because you are a single woman . . .'

'I am a widow.'

'. . . a sole woman, also the sister of a convicted felon . . .'

'Sister-in-law. Am I accused of a crime?'

'You are refused a licence, madam, because no respectable woman may or should run an inn on her own.'

'I have done so these five years.'

Pink leaned forward over his bench, smiling, as pleased with her fury as with his own. 'Then *your* respectability comes into question, madam. Now, leave this court before I sentence you for contempt of it.'

Cole's hand clamped over Cecily's opening mouth and he dragged her outside and bodily lifted her into the carriage. 'Lord's sake, missus, you courting gaol?'

'You stinking, Whiggish, fat-bellied bastard,' Cecily was shouting as Cole whipped up the horse. 'You Walpole-lover, you dare do this to me . . .' Her fury lasted as far as the Great North Road to be replaced by despair. She couldn't see the road, nor the sun. She was on a raft in a featureless sea. 'I can't lose the Belle, Cole.'

'You just lost it, missus. That's a matter of how to get un back.'

Without the Belle she would be unmade, thrown back to the

foot of the chasm she had been climbing out of ever since the Bubble burst.

Smell of ale and tobacco giving way to freshness from opened windows, beeswax on furniture, horsetail on pewter; sounds of the broom as Betty Bygrave swept out, tunelessly humming, Ned hupping horses in the yard, Marjorie's sharp speech coming from the kitchen and the slow boom that was Quick's reply, chopped herbs, whiffs of ironed, breeze-blown linen as Pru, the laundry-maid, made up beds. Looking at her timepiece in the evening and taking up position to wait for the distant two notes on the horn that told her the London coach had breasted Mardley Hill, reverberation through the soles of her shoes, the scrape of brake against wheel before it took the bend, the change of galloping hoofs to a trot as it swept into the yard, stink of sweating horse and leather, satisfaction in pleasing tired, hungry people, being too busy to think, the knowledge that the Packers were around if a drunk became violent, that Eleanor was safe asleep ... Eleanor, oh, God, Eleanor. 'What am I going to do, Cole?' she said, into the void.

'We're going to find Master Archie.'

Of course. Cameron would make it all right again. He always did.

The sunlight of a warm spring day reasserted itself through the crown of her wide straw hat and she stopped shivering.

Cole drove the carriage off the main road and they bumped over a grassy track running alongside the river Mimram which crossed the Great North Road outside Welwyn and meandered through fields and the Bramfield forest towards Hertford. On this side there was ragged meadow, yellow with marsh marigolds; on the other, alders leaned over water that ran olive-green under their shade.

'He's gen'ly along here somewheres,' Cole said.

It was as soothing to see the neat figure standing alone on the bank as it was to smell the weedy dankness of the river and hear the kurruk of moorhen. Cecily couldn't wait for the carriage to negotiate the track that ran in a loop towards him but clambered from it and ran through the meadow, scattering cows and yellow wagtails, falling, scrambling up again. 'Master Cameron, Master Cameron.'

He glanced up and doffed his hat, carefully lodging his fishing rod in the cleft of a stick. As she gabbled he spread his coat against the bank for her to sit and lean back on, produced an immaculate handkerchief, wiped her tears and made her blow her nose.

'It's Walpole,' she told him. 'He's hounded me since Edinburgh. Talk to him, make him give me back my licence.'

He squatted opposite her, surprised. 'It's no' him,' he said. 'To my knowledge Sir Robert has forgotten your existence. Was it Pink? A doughty fighter for the Lord, he'd say. He regards all women as transgressors since his wife ran off.'

'Talk to him,' she begged.

Cameron raised his ginger eyebrows. 'I doubt he'd listen. I acted for a neighbour of his in a land dispute and won the case. He's no' too fond of me is Samuel Pink.'

'Appeal, then. We can appeal.'

He shook his head. 'The magistrate's decision is final.'

'What can I do, then? Cameron, what can I do?'

He said to Cole: 'Draw off a way, Master Packer, if you will.'

Cecily saw Cole grin, heard the meadow suck against his boots as he tramped back to the carriage. She couldn't see the meaning of it; the lawyer's mind had always been a mystery to her. What course of action was he to propose that could be too illegal or too personal for Cole Packer to hear it? Then she knew. A second before he said it, she knew.

'You can wed me,' he said.

She waited for her reactions, as someone who's stubbed their toe has a second's grace before the pain starts. When they came they were so many and so various that, astonishingly, they formed a laugh. It began at her feet, surged up her thighs into her belly, swirled around her ribcage, stopped at her throat and came out as a squeak: 'Eh?'

Here we are again. Another low-born Whig. That's why then . . . you angler for a fine fish. Lady Cecily Fitzhenry and a ginger Scotsman. The effrontery. Marry you? Like fuck I will. But it's *funny*. Why is it *so* funny? *What* woman in Kent?

206

He was walking about as if the meadow were a courtroom and she a hostile witness. 'I put it to you ye're in need of a husband. Yes or no?'

Her jaw was still dropped. He leaned forward and put a finger under her chin to close it. 'Yes or no?'

'Certainly not.'

'Ah-ha.' He wasn't put out. 'But ye'll soon be seeing the strength of it.' He perambulated some more. 'Sir Samuel'd have no grounds to refuse a licence to your husband. So if ye're to keep the Belle, ye'll have to wed. Yes or no?'

He ignored her silence. 'As for me, I'm in need of a wife, being now in a position to support one in grand style and looked at askance for the lack. Ye'll admit, I think, that neither of us grows any younger.'

'Oh, thank you.'

'Granted,' he went on, 'ye'd be required to pass six month of any year in London wi' me, but I'd make no objection to ye devoting the rest of the time to the Belle. Excuse me a wee minute.'

He turned to his fishing rod. Its tip was bent over, the line tight into a dimple in the water. He called over his shoulder between pulls and puffs: 'Consider, will ye . . . while I land yon chavender . . . ?'

The absurdity of it was extraordinarily relaxing. She sat with amusement chasing round her innards and watched a kingfisher hunch on a branch across the river before it dived into the water and rose up again, a tiny flash of sapphire, green and chestnut, with a flapping sliver in its beak. It flew off along the bank.

So long since she'd had time to absorb the loveliness of England, *her* England, Tory, Plantagenet England. The England that this little man's employers were intent on degrading.

The landlady of the Belle Sauvage intervened, calculating profit and loss.

An upstart, said Lady Cecily Fitzhenry.

You could keep the Belle, said the Belle.

Another voice, elusive and faint, entered the conversation: *I'll return for you, Lady Cecily, Lady Cecily.*

And I'll be waiting.

And waiting, and waiting, and waiting, said the landlady of the Belle, childless, innless, sexless.

Cameron's coat was warm against her cheek, smelling faintly of clover, good worsted and fish. Tucked in its sleeve's cuff was a waxed paper packet. She pulled it out, undid it and began to munch on the bread and cheese Quick had cut for him, considering the muscles of his back under his shirt as he tugged and relaxed to land his fish. The sun, the river, induced a languor she hadn't experienced in years. His wig was the same colour as the kingfisher's breast.

The fish came flapping from the water in a spray. Cameron unhooked it and dropped it in a net in the river to squirm with the rest of his catch.

He came back to her and squatted at her feet. 'What's it to be?'

'My dear man,' she said, all Lady Cecily, 'I was coerced into marriage before, as you know. It's not likely I would consent again.'

'A good point,' he said, encouragingly, 'but I put it to ye that your price has gone down, your politics are misguided and ye've a criminal bent in a crisis.'

She laughed outright. 'Where's the gain in marrying me?'

He grinned back at her. He had white, uneven teeth, not unattractive. 'Unlimited free accommodation at the Belle and a half share in young Eleanor. The slip needs a father as well as a mother.'

She stopped laughing. 'The child is the orphan of a beggar woman. She is a Negro. I took her in for charity. I do not consider her my daughter.' He was presuming too much. This banter was enjoyable as long as it remained banter. She said: 'I presume we are discussing what is at base a business arrangement?'

His head jerked back in surprise. 'You presume wrong. No, oh, no, no, no. It's a true marriage we're discussing. Bless us, woman, what for d'you think I've put up with your havers these last years? It's not for what ye paid me, I'll tell ye that.'

'What, then?' She led him on, not with the idea of accepting him but because she was curious. It was as if she'd been looking at a cloud formation which had refocused itself into the shape of a lion.

They stared at each other, and if she was expecting his heart to appear on his shirtsleeve she was disappointed, yet relieved, that it didn't. In both of them, it seemed, was an area of dragon country to which the other would not be admitted. He shrugged. 'Ye're no' ill-favoured. Anyway, I've a charitable bent mysel'.'

She spluttered. 'And that's your courtship, is it, Master Cameron?'

'No, no. That's the argument. *This* is courtship.' And he kissed her.

Her night-time love put up a protest. 'Lady Cecily, Lady *Cecily*,' but it was day-time by a sinuous river, the air heavy with sun and mating butterflies. The cheep of brooding birds and the whirr of dragonflies drowned the bat's squeak from the dark. His lips were thin and hard and the tongue that ran along her teeth promised fecundity.

She was taken aback by her body's sudden liquidity. 'Well,' she said at last – they were both panting, 'well, so it's coercion, Master Cameron. Marry you or lose the Belle, is that it?'

'That it is.' He'd snuggled down by her side. He picked a kingcup and tickled her jaw with it. The hairs along his forearm were golden.

She said: 'Another forced marriage, then.'

'But this time it's no' with an old man.' The fish had splashed his shirt so that it stuck to his chest, rising and falling with his breathing. 'This time you get me.'

He was in command as a lover; to be this sexually confident he'd had success with women. *What* woman in Kent? She stabbed back. 'You should know that I love another.'

He winced, more at the triteness of the phrase than anything else. 'Ye love a memory.' He brought his head down to hers so that their noses rubbed. 'It's a cold bed to marry a memory.'

Too confident, too commanding: this was the enemy. The Whiggish maleness of the world had swamped her before and here it was once more pressing her down in a changed and more dangerous form. She was being *seduced*. And in a field, like a bloody milkmaid. He was kissing her again. The river in her body was dammed somewhere around the lips of her vagina, begging for release. She was beginning to squirm.

With his lips against hers, he said: 'Do we marry?'

'Yes.'

He sat up, suddenly vulnerable. 'D'ye mean it?'

'It appears I have no alternative.'

He was still arched over her, studying her face. She waited for him to kiss her again. Instead he pulled away, nodding. 'Well done.' He shook her hand warmly. 'Ye'll not regret it.' He was on his feet, gathering his fishing tackle together. Tidying up. A respectable little man again, doing things properly. And singing. Hideously. '*Ha til mi tulidh.* Let the piper play. A bride to wash ma feet afore my age slips awa'.'

And she was lying here, feeling squelchy. 'I suppose you realize I could with as much advantage marry one of the Packers,' she said.

Over his shoulder he said: 'They're no' as handsome as me. Anyway, a lawyer'd have to draw up the marriage contract. By wedding me, d'ye see, ye can save the legal fees.'

'Oh, good.' She sat up – yes, definitely squelchy. Had Cole seen?

She glanced downriver to where Cole lay, his arm plunged in the water, studiously tickling for trout. She picked grass from her hair, grumbling: 'First thing we do, let's kill all the lawyers.'

'Dick the Butcher,' he said.

'Jack Cade,' she argued, 'I know my Shakespeare.'

On the way home, with his coat and hat on, he was entirely the legal man, talking of widow's rights, free bench, inheritance, all of it designed to give her some independence and all of it suffocating her.

He seemed to expect the marriage to be soon and to produce children. She was to be introduced back into Society.

She was overcome by a remembered nausea. Whig Society on the arm of a Whiggish commoner, the old shame re-created.

What have I done? Why have I done it? To keep the Belle, yes. It's as much a forced marriage as the last. He hasn't asked me if I wish it; only stating that I shall lose the Belle if I don't.

He pursues his own social and sexual gratification. He wants a wife.

But as her mind argued, her body retained a temperature it had forgotten it could reach. In the wet, flower-studded meadow it had burgeoned a momentary cornucopia. Reject him, it told her, and we wither into fruitlessness. An old maid. Who else has offered? Where is your Edinburgh Romeo who promised to return?

Cecily came from a breed that, tormented by indecision, tossed for it. Her ancestors had gained and lost fortunes on the turn of a guinea. Let the gods decide.

Back at the Belle, she hurried up to her room and took down her copy of *Henry the Sixth, Part Two* that she'd found in Hertford market. Jack Cade had led the rebellion; for certain it was Jack Cade determined to kill the lawyers.

She leafed through the fourth act and found the place.

Bugger.

She became Mrs Archibald Cameron two weeks later at the door of Datchworth church with Eleanor and the Packer children throwing rose petals. If she'd had her way, it would have been a quiet wedding, her demeanour making it clear that it was not of her choosing, but Lady Mary Wortley Montagu – recently home from abroad – and half Hertfordshire celebrated a match which, Marjorie Packer told her, had been expected.

'*I* didn't expect it,' Cecily said, coldly.

'Best thing could happen,' said Marjorie.

Bucolic custom required the wedding party to carry bride and groom to their bed. Cecily could barely see it for the ribbons, love-knots, straw fertility symbols and flowers that hung about it. Cameron was flung in beside her.

When the final indecency had been pronounced, they were left alone. 'Let the piper play,' Cameron hummed, lighting a candle. 'A bride to wash ma feet before my age slips away.'

'Oh, *please*,' she said, sharply. The jokes of the Packers and Squire Leggatt, which even Lady Mary had joined in, had caused her to panic. At least Lemuel'd had the decency to attack her in darkness. And at once, so that the business could be over quickly.

He'd declined to wear a night-cap. He looked younger without his wig; his hair was the same colour. Beneath his robe, his skin was a freckled milk-white. 'Aye, well,' he said, 'we'd better get down to it.'

She drew the sheet closely round her neck. But he got out of bed and went to the door that joined their room to Eleanor's and looked in. 'In the arms of Morpheus, bless her.' He padded over to the aumbry in the wall and opened it. 'It's a thing I've noticed,' he said, 'that the only people who're denied the feast at these affairs are the bride and groom. So I asked Quick to set us a wee collation.'

He came back with a basket and knelt on the bed with it, raising the cloth. 'Oh, ho, his green chicken sallet, lamb patties. Taffety tart? There's joy. But first . . .' He broke the lead seal of one of the basket's two bottles. 'Margaux 'seventeen. I brought it from my own cellar.' He poured the wine into long-stemmed glasses and made her take one. 'Your health, Lady Cecily.'

It was difficult to be churlish. 'Your health, sir.'

He popped chicken and lettuce into her mouth. 'Ye're a gey comely woman, but ye need fattening. Could you no emulate Mistress Bygrave more?' Betty Bygrave had the build of a turn-pike cottage.

He made her eat – she was hungry – and drink. When the basket was empty he wiped her mouth with his fingers and kissed it.

'Put out the candle,' she begged him.

'I'll not.'

Their bodies crumbled an overlooked piece of Quick's soft white bread and rolled a glass containing the last of the Margaux to the bottom of the bed and crushed the grasses of the fertility tokens, so that the daytime element of his wooing in the meadow remained, as if they were drunken gypsies copulating over a stolen meal in a haystack.

In the morning she was ashamed at herself. At the time she was too astonished by his passion and her own, by her first climax which came before his and at the second clamping and gaping ride down a waterfall that forced a deep huff of abandonment out of her throat.

Lust, she decided, most deadly of the seven deadly sins. A thing for peasants and prostitutes. Guillaume, Guillaume, with you would have been enchantment and romance. Not an earthy, sweating, uncontrolled thing.

She wouldn't look at her husband. Anyway, he went fishing. That night when he stretched his arms in a wide yawn and said it was time for bed, it seemed to her that everybody in the taproom looked at her face and saw the flush that suffused and mortified her.

But behind the curtains of the bed, she swam in the common stream again and was sent down the rush of its fall.

Oh, God, she thought as she went over, I'm a screamer. Like Dolly.

CHAPTER ELEVEN

London roared with noise and stink. Accustomed to country air, Lady Cecily Cameron's nose flinched from the stench of concentrated sewage mingling with that coming from the establishments of butchers, tallow chandlers, pewterers, braziers, apothecaries, tanners and soap-makers.

Pedestrians too frail or polite to shoulder their way through shouting, running footmen, pie-men, carriages and drays were felled like infantry under a cavalry charge. Everything had intensified: more and poorer beggars, gaudier shops and customers.

'Was it always like this?' she asked her husband, as they drove to their new home.

'Like what?'

He'd bought a house in Arundel Street, one of a stately block running down to the Thames, close to the Middle Temple where he now had extensive chambers. A respectable enough area, but not fashionable. The *beau monde* had moved west to build its houses around Grosvenor Square and Cecily didn't blame it: the further away from the river the better. Sluggish with muck, already a neighbour to be reckoned with, she dreaded what it would be like in summer.

She wasn't any more pleased with the house's interior. Cameron had hired an architect of the Palladian school to design it. She'd approved the idea; she was, after all, a modern woman. Fashion talked of Andrea Palladio's symmetry, simplicity and restraint, the relation of elevation to interior, classical canons from the harmony of nature. Cecily looked forward to a slim and elegant contrast to the multi-levelled, shambling Belle.

She was disappointed. The rules of Palladianism hadn't been employed: the rooms were too high for their length, the windows too few, an over-large staircase dominated too small a hallway. The choice of pastel colours picked out in white might have suited Italy but a London winter would make the walls look as if they'd caught cold.

Typically Whiggish, Cecily decided, an undermining of warm old Tory homes by dour regularity. The architect, it appeared, was a friend, had come cheap and fulfilled Cameron's only other requirement: that his house be 'tidy'.

However, if No. 10, Arundel Street did not conform to Fashion's strictures, it seemed that – judging from the calling cards and invitations piling the mantelshelf – her husband did.

'Princess Caroline? Good gracious.'

'Aye, ye're reinstated.' He looked smug.

The Prince and Princess of Wales now lived in Leicester Fields, a quarrel with the King having forced them out of the palace. Although there had recently been a public, somewhat frosty, reconciliation, Cecily noticed that Caroline's invitation was for a garden party in June – the month when George was due to make a visit to Hanover. The Princess of Wales obviously wasn't risking another quarrel with her father-in-law by a reunion with an offending former Maid of Honour while he was still in the country.

Not completely reinstated, then. Still, it would be nice to see Caroline again.

She picked up another invitation. 'I shall *not* attend this one.'

'There's no need. I've already made our excuses to Sir Robert.'

214

So in this marriage she wouldn't be required to hobnob with the enemy. I suppose if I were a good spy, I would: the Jacobites would want me to. But to dine with the man who'd hanged Dolly without clawing at his eyes was beyond her capability.

As a *quid pro quo* she turned down an invitation from Bolingbroke. If her husband could be generous, so could she. Again, the Jacobites would be displeased: the viscount's manor in Dalton, now headquarters for every anti-Whig malcontent in England, provided an easy meeting place which, since he was her godfather, Cecily had a legitimate excuse to attend.

The request for their society that Mr Archibald and Lady Cecily Cameron disagreed on came from Alexander Pope. 'Your absence made a long winter,' he wrote. 'If your charity would take up a small bird that is half dead of the frost and set it a-chirping for half an hour, I will jump into my cage and put myself into your hands tomorrow at any hour you send.'

'No,' said Cecily.

'The man's a grand poet,' her husband protested, 'and there's a pathos in his wish to be friends again.'

'He can be as pathetic as he likes,' Cecily said, 'but mine was a colder bloody winter than his, and where was *he*?'

Her loyalty was for those like Mary Astell and Lady Mary Wortley Montagu, who'd made a point of visiting the Belle, Mrs Astell despite the return of her cancer.

'Very well. But I'd point out ye're back in Society now, not Billingsgate.' He hated her swearing.

'In any case, we can't be friends with Lady Mary *and* Pope.' The two had quarrelled, dividing Society as bitterly as the Capulets and other Montagues had Verona's, and were involved in literary warfare.

'I laughed at him,' Lady Mary said, when applied to for the cause of the rift between her and what had been a faithful admirer. 'Too horrid of me, I know. But my dear, he suddenly *launched* himself at me declaring a passion. So unexpected. So ludicrous. Like a frog jumping on an ostrich.'

Cecily ran up her Montagu colours next day by going shopping with Lady Mary to amend the provincialism of her wardrobe. Cousin's for undergarments and stays. Jacquemin's to

215

drink chocolate while gowns were paraded before her. Percy's for hats.

Her hair had been done that morning by Madame Racinet: 'Ah, *non*, Lady Cecily, we do not dress close *maintenant*, a lock hang over ze shoulder, like zis. Wiz your curl, we do not need ze irons.' Very fetching.

Rococo was holding its own: heads were still tiny, skirts enormous, but there had been one improvement. Hoops, though wider, had evolved into two articulated frames, like fireguards tied round the waist, which enabled one to fold them forward in order to get through a door. There were longer sleeves, tiny ruffs for the throat and what Jacquemin's called the *robe à la française* and Lady Mary 'the sack'. The high Louis heel at first tottered a landlady who'd worn only mules for nearly six years, but Cecily persisted. She was back – in Fashion.

By afternoon she was parading her finery in Hyde Park, nervousness raising her chin so high she could barely see whether its languid and beautiful fellow-strollers bowed to her or not.

Out of the side of her mouth she hissed: 'Are they cutting me?'

'Good *day*, Lady Mansfield. My dear, they daren't. How de do, Sir James? You are too lovely and your husband too important. Who knows but they might need his services in time to come. He is the best lawyer in London. A fine day indeed, Mr Carteret. And *so* attractive . . .'

'*Is* he?'

'You must know he is. The timbre of his voice, that mouth . . . my *dear* Countess . . . like an amused tiger's. He plays the plain North Briton but more than one judge swoons at his speeches. Small wonder he wins his cases.'

'*Does* he?'

London life with Lemuel had so humiliated Cecily that she was quick to be embarrassed by her second Whig husband. Cameron's ignorance of the arts – apart from music, to which he was addicted – went as deep as Dolly's. His accent, his tendency to call her 'my dearie', his awful Scottish songs, his frugality, these things revived echoes of shame in public, while his uninhibited love-making abashed her in private – afterwards.

However profound her own fall from grace, she was of the *ton* as he could never be.

She was taken back by most of her old set with comparative ease. Her Edinburgh exploit seemed forgotten, though there were sly references to the Belle out of which Lady Mary – a good friend but an inveterate gossip – had made a fine story. 'When is a badly run hostelry like a musical instrument?' Lord Hervey teased her.

'When it's a vile-inn,' she said wearily. 'I've heard it before.' Treachery, it appeared, was less culpable than stepping out of one's class. Nevertheless, her peers were prepared to overlook her lapse as a form of eccentricity, perhaps because so many of the once-grand eccentrics were being subdued by time. Mary Lepel was worn down by child-bearing. Mrs Howard had lost the Prince of Wales's attention through going deaf.

'And Sophie?' She'd heard no word since Hempens.

'Worst of all, poor thing,' said Lady Mary. 'Married again and gone to *Ireland*.'

On the whole, though, it was nice to be back, and gratifying that the aristocracy found her new husband worthier of acceptance than it had Lemuel.

But it became apparent, as the social season progressed, that it now accepted anybody as long as he had money or influence. At her own and other people's dinner tables the *ton* mingled on equal terms with wealthy shopkeepers, stock-jobbers and commission agents.

'Wendover's marrying his son to a button-moulder's daughter,' she complained to Lady Mary.

'A *successful* button moulder,' Lady Mary pointed out. 'My dear, blood has always married trade if trade were rich enough.'

But in her exile Cecily had idealized the years before the Bubble and couldn't be persuaded that Walpole Whiggery hadn't vulgarized Eden. She despised these new sharp-eyed men and women whose only concern was to outdo their neighbour yet who looked askance at Lady Mary, whose unorthodox dress and uninhibited speech they equated with moral laxity.

The dirt Pope was flinging at Lady Mary was beginning to stick.

Furthermore, while in Constantinople she had made the discovery that the one disease Turks did not suffer from – 'they have *everything* else' – was smallpox. 'They insert the disease into their child's arm as we would graft a bud on to a tree and the child is ever after immune, having suffered the least, mildest attack.' Bravely, in Cecily's view, Lady Mary had successfully carried out the operation on her own son and daughter and was now urgently spreading the good news that there was a remedy for the greatest scourge of the age. Instead of receiving praise, she was being reviled by a medical profession that resented an amateur blithely stepping in where it had not trod – not to mention thereby depriving it of income. She was openly denounced as a woman who would risk the lives of her children, while the Church thundered from its pulpits that she was flying in the face of God.

Cecily, having declared herself Lady Mary's friend, found herself called on time and again to defend her against a shocked bourgeoisie.

Travelling home with Cameron in their closed carriage from one particularly trying dinner, Cecily fumed: 'That cotton-miller's wife had the impudence to ask if I didn't think Lady Montagu – Lady *Montagu*, I ask you, they've no idea of titles – was a scandal and an impiety.'

'And what did you say?'

'I said Lady *Mary*'s true friends knew her for a virtuous woman, and that if her smallpox plan were generally adopted there would be fewer deaths and fewer plain women – which was a hit against Mrs Cotton-Miller who's as pocked as a prune. Lord, in this Walpolian age everyone must conform, people as well as architecture. Why Mary supports the Whigs I cannot understand.'

Her husband leaned across to kiss her. 'Born to trouble as the sparks fly upward, the both of ye. I like Lady Mary. And so, I'd point out, does Walpole.' He began to pay attention to the gilded strings of her bodice.

'Stop it.' Cecily was punishing all Whigs that night. 'What would Mrs Cotton-Miller say to you wanting to do that in a carriage?'

'I don't doubt she'd deem it impossible. Can we do nothing against yon hoops?'

'No.' Resent it though she did, the darkness and his hands were loosening more than her bodice. When they arrived home, her hoops were discarded on the landing and they barely made it to the bed.

Afterwards, in post-coital repulsion at her own abandonment – *Lady Cecily, Lady Cecily* – she returned to her complaint. 'And do you know what else the hag said? She said one shouldn't encourage beggars by giving them the scraps of dinner. And that Reverend Thingy agreed with her. Too busy enriching himself, like the rest of the Church. I ask you. We *always* gave the poor what was left over when the servants had finished. Your friends leave it on the midden to be fought over.'

Almost more than anything, Cecily had been shocked by the unkindness of the self-made rich to what it regarded as the self-made poor. Uncharitableness had become enshrined in law. The recent Mortmain Act said that 'charitable endowments are rather an act of injustice towards the heir-at-law than an act of charity in the donor'.

'Nowadays St Martin wouldn't be *allowed* to share his cloak with the beggar,' she grumbled.

Cameron said: 'Yet there's little virtue in individual giving. We need a national system of hospitals, kinder employment and more of it. A beatitudinous country. Now, will ye please sleep.'

In his own way, Cecily discovered, he was trying to bring about a beatitudinous country – another unsuspected side of his character. A careful man, he threw no purses or cloaks but formed committees with like-minded people in order to lobby MPs to bring in bills on behalf of ill-used apprentices, for the better regulation of parish poor children, the protection of chimney-climbing boys, of foundlings, debtors, Negroes – the list of his concerns seemed endless.

Not one of the bills had been brought into the House of Commons, let alone made law, but not through lack of trying by Archibald Cameron.

Cecily could almost have wished his philanthropy less: it brought to Arundel Street people to whom she wouldn't have given house room in former times: Enthusiasts, essayists, Grub Street scribblers, dissenters, *Quakers*, colonials and a truly appalling young man named Wesley, whom her husband told her was bringing method to Christianity.

'I wasn't aware Christianity needed method,' she said.

'Aye, everything needs method.'

Beggars she could have understood – and helped – but not conclaves of thick-booted men scuffing her carpets and drinking all her tea, not Wesleys preaching virtue to her in her own parlour.

She accused her husband of running with the hare and hunting with the hounds. 'You won that land case for Townsend, yet you want to change laws his ministry protects.'

'Aye,' he said, 'but if the hounds didn't pay my fees the hares would have a harder time of it.'

There were the petitioners who inevitably came at bedtime, slamming the door-knocker and shouting for 'Master Archie' to come because 'they've taken my Tommy/Alfred/Jane/Harry'.

'At this time of night?' she'd ask, as he pulled on his boots.

'Ye see, my dearie, Harry's a black runaway, a decent man. I'm reminded of Quick.' Or: 'Ye see, my dearie, Alfred's a debtor. I'm reminded of Castell and poor Lemuel.' And: 'Ye see, my dearie, Jane's a fallen woman through no fault of her own.'

'And who does she remind you of?'

He grinned at her and was gone.

And don't call me 'my dearie'. *What* woman in Kent? She was too proud to ask.

Her own contribution to the betterment of things came through Lady Mary, though not without misgivings.

'Cecily, I wish you to help me spread the word.'

'What word?'

'Inoculation. If I can but make Society see what a boon it is. But people incline to think me an oddity. The more friends who will have their children inoculated the better. Think of the advantage to them. Eyelashes, every one.' Lady Mary fluttered her lashless lids.

That's why the establishment won't take you seriously, thought Cecily, you make a joke of it. Yet you're in earnest.

And attempting something more useful than any man who's discovered why apples don't fall upwards or similar rubbish.

She failed to see how she could help. She herself had no need of inoculation: she'd been born with pockmarks on her stomach that showed she'd contracted and survived while in the womb the smallpox that had killed her mother soon after her birth. Cameron, too, had taken the disease lightly as a youth.

'What about Eleanor?' asked Lady Mary.

Cecily stiffened. 'It's unlikely Society can be persuaded by an experiment on an infant it would regard as expendable.'

'Bring her to London and let the world see how expendable she is to you.' She tutted at Cecily's affront. 'My dear, you *dote* on the moppet, I saw as much at the wedding. Were it not for her colour, one might believe you and Cameron her parents so highly do you extol her every lisp.'

'Nonsense.'

Cameron, when they discussed it that evening, reflected her own misgivings. Inoculation was sensible if it worked. Lady Mary was convinced or she wouldn't have endangered her children. On the other hand, to introduce venom into a child's veins . . . On the *other* hand, smallpox was scourging the East End at that moment.

The image of Eleanor's face had been with them ever since they'd left it, shedding tears, at the Belle Sauvage. Alongside it, they summoned up the unrecognizable features of those who'd died from smallpox, nostrils and throat closed by its malodorous pustules.

'I'll have a word with Edward Wortley,' Cameron said. 'He's a canny head on his shoulders. The physician who went with them on the embassy, Maitland, I'll consult him too.'

It occurred to Cecily that Cameron was prepared to trust Lady Mary's husband and physician, but not Lady Mary. Treacherously, she thought: And so am I.

'It'd be grand to have the lass around the place,' Cameron said. 'I've missed her sorely.'

'Indeed?'

Her husband shook his head. 'Why d'ye not admit you love her?'

Cecily was taken aback. He was overstepping a boundary she thought they had both drawn and respected.

By day they met as good acquaintances, often bantering, occasionally arguing, but never intruding on each other's reserves. By night they rarely talked at all, being too busy with energetic, physical exploration of each other's bodies.

So strong was the demarcation between the two states that the marriage seemed to consist of four people, the raging couple by candlelight having nothing to do with the sober pair that presented themselves neatly dressed in the breakfast room next morning.

Cecily had almost come to believe that the vulpine creature she encountered in bed was not Cameron at all but something subject to lycanthropy, which infected her with a similar metamorphosis. Whatever it was, it was not to be talked about.

The situation suited her. She was not called upon to rationalize either experience and had come to depend on the daytime husband not to embarrass her by referring to any variety of the deeper emotions.

Viewing her years at the Belle from the drawing rooms of London had emphasized what a distorted life she'd led in it. Now that desperation had dissipated, she wondered at the ease with which she'd consorted with highwaymen, blacks and bucolics, promoting to importance episodes that were best forgotten. It had been both a shock and a relief to resume conversation with people to whom idleness was an art and emotion a vulgarity. One could not, of course, expect a person born in the back alleys of Glasgow to understand that.

Oh, he was going to *harp*. Cecily took up her needlework, composing herself. Her hands and nails, she was pleased to see as she smoothed the silks, were responding to the ministrations of her maid.

'D'you see, Cecily, we were both loveless bairns, never mind your riches and my poverty. Orphans, the two of us, habituated to lovelessness. The difference is you're afeared of love and I'm not.'

He'd begun striding the room, hands behind his back. Counsel for the prosecution of sentimentality. And more Scottish by the minute.

'The peacock blue, do you think? Or the green?'

'Aye, I know it's a sore point but we must have it out. You told me once ye loved another. Aye, I ken well ye meant Fraser. I put it to you that love was mebbe disastrous, all the cruel happenings in your life deriving from it. I put it to you that ye blame yourself. That mebbe ye wouldn't have participated in the Castle escape if passion for Fraser hadn't overcome your better judgement. Yes or no?'

'The green, I think.'

'Let it go, Cecily, my dearie.' He was on his knees beside her. 'Fraser's mebbe dead, Edinburgh forgotten. Ye've come through the rough water to calm. And bravely. Ye can afford to love again.'

'Or perhaps the blue.'

'Aye, the bairn's black and I'm a commoner but better a dinner of herbs where love is . . . Admit it, woman.'

Carefully, she poked the needle through the canvas and pulled it out again. 'Mr Cameron, I do not wish to discuss these matters.'

He pushed the sewing frame on to the floor. 'Why? What sin to joy in loving? What's that which happens in our bed? How in hell d'ye regard that? The coupling of brute beasts?'

'Yes,' she shouted at him. 'If you must know, *yes*.'

'Ye're a fool, mistress.'

'Indeed. Unfortunately, I'm a fool who's carrying your child.'

She left him still kneeling by the overturned sewing frame.

The next day he was kind, congratulating her and himself on conception, but he'd retreated. Cecily found it less easy to forgive him for trying to probe into her soul. She felt dissected, the secret places of her dragons laid bare. The pregnancy also made her feel sick.

Ten days later, in the Arundel Street nursery, she held one of Eleanor's arms, Lady Mary Wortley Montagu the other, while Cameron played the fool to distract the child's attention from Mr Maitland and his lancet.

'Mamma, Mamma.'

'Be brave, Eleanor. Soon over.'

'Look, Nellie.' Cameron had taken off his wig and was holding its queue across his top lip. 'Chinee.'

'Be brave. Soon over.' To Maitland she said: 'Hurry, can't you?'

'It must be done with care, Lady Cecily.'

Did it need that much pus ladled into the cuts? She could feel the arm's slight bones quiver. What are we doing to you, my dear, my dear? You were safe at the Belle.

Over the other side of the cot, Lady Mary's face was bright and interested. Cecily wanted to spit at it.

Cameron's wig was ridiculously on the top of his marmalade curls. 'Look, Nellie. Hindoo.'

'There,' Maitland said. 'Very nice.'

'Now, my lamb. Drink this nice physic.'

'Fizz, Nellie,' said Cameron.

'Fill people?'

'Aye, but ye're not ill, my dearie. Ye're a brave, brave lassie. Mamma will stay while you sleep.' He staggered as he left the room and Maitland had to hold him up.

Hard-eyed, Cecily watched him go. That was the weakling to whom she was bearing a child. A man of breeding would have shown more self-control. She stayed by the cot until Eleanor's mouth relaxed into a full cupid's bow and air went back and forth easily in the wide, perfect little nostrils. You mustn't call me Mamma. Not here, my dear. They won't understand. God save you, I wish I did.

The resultant fever vindicated Lady Mary by being comparatively slight. Cameron wanted Eleanor to stay in London under his eye. 'Other children live healthfully here. We'll hire a Town nursemaid as well.'

Cecily was tempted but doubtful. 'She'll be lonely away from the Belle. Other people won't want their children to play with her.'

'They accept me, they can accept her.'

He is so odd, Cecily thought. From the first he'd been besotted by the child, yet he hadn't been involved in that strange, Christ-

224

mas birth which had marked out her nativity to the Packers and to herself. He would have scoffed at her own secret conviction that the baby was Sophie's reborn. He just seemed to equate himself with the child, feeling them both to be outsiders.

On the other hand, he liked to think of himself as a 'canny' man and had shown shrewdness in climbing the establishment's ladder. Could he not see it was the reverse of canniness to inflict on society a most unsuitable child?

She wondered if, for all his orderliness, he had a weakness for the *outré*. Perhaps that's why he married me. But I am re-established. Eleanor must always be an outsider.

Milkmaids garlanded their pails, there were lapwings' eggs at the poulterers, bluebells under the trees of the parks, scarlet beans on the sticks of the kitchen gardens.

Eleanor suited the sun; in her best white muslin, a miniature of Cecily's own, her skin glowed fittingly where other children were shaded with hats or went pink. She danced in the May procession to Westminster until the Hon. Carthew, who was five, pushed her so she fell. None of the watching adults picked her up.

Dogs were sheared and their hair used in the replastering of tenement ceilings. Children were taken to the afternoon parks to watch acrobats or the novel sight of lords taking off their coats to play cricket with artisans.

Cecily stopped taking Eleanor after the Countess of Crakan-thorpe offered her a blacker child in exchange: 'You've been away, my dear, and forgotten. The whole *point* of a pet slave is the contrast with the whiteness of one's own complexion. Your mite is still coffee. Now I *know* they get darker as they get older, but then you don't want them too close. I have just the thing, a truly *inky* little darling. No trouble, I assure you.'

'And she meant it kindly,' Cecily told her husband that night.

'I'll kill the hag. Should we not persist?'

'You can. I won't. I found the child rubbing her face with pumice. She said it was because she was dirty.'

Cameron sank back in his chair. 'I'll adopt her legally.'

'It won't make any difference.'

The parlour's grandmother clock ticked away Eleanor's inno-
cence of black footmen who might marry her, the bourgeois
who wouldn't, the aristocrats who'd take her to bed, the women
of all classes who'd despise her – black and white with different
perspectives but the same conclusion: she didn't know her place.

Nor do I know what it is, thought Cecily, I betray her every
day.

Some of the three-year-old joy had gone for ever, replaced by
puzzled caution. Anyone was free to lecture her. 'Don't call
this lady "mamma",' Lady Manley said sharply and, turning to
Cecily: 'I know they like to when they're little, but it sets an
unfortunate precedent.'

And Cecily had said nothing. She was confused by her repulsion for both attackers and the attacked. There were times when,
the hounds in full cry, she could barely look at the child, only
to be overcome by a panic to rush to the foxcub and gather it
up.

'She must return to the Belle,' she said to Cameron.

'Ach, not yet, not yet,' he said. 'When the term's over we'll
all go. Together.'

They didn't take Eleanor to Princess Caroline's garden party
at Richmond where aristocratic children paraded in petite imita-
tion of their pastel-clad parents. Violent scarlets, oranges and
greens were reserved for the livery of black servants who, to
Cecily's attuned eye, seemed everywhere, bobbing their powdered heads as they handed their owners from carriages, playing
trumpet in the bands, grinning, strutting to the music, sun winking on their silver collars, apparently as happy as the birds
singing in latticed cages hanging from the trees.

Damn them, Cecily thought.

There was an effervescence not due solely to champagne:
the King's departure for Hanover two days before had lifted
restrictions on the Prince and Princess of Wales. Furthermore,
the death of the Prince's mother in November had revived the
prophecy that his father would die within a year of it and was
causing happy speculation among the Wales's set that they
would soon be the courtiers of George II.

There had been no official announcement, no mourning for

the woman who might have been Queen of England but instead lived out the last thirty-three years of her life in confinement for her adultery, kept from contact with her children.

'Poor lady,' Cameron said. 'And poor king too. If the prophecy proves true, nobody present here this day will mourn.'

'Except Walpole,' said Cecily, pleasantly. 'He'll be out.'

'I'd not wager on it. Who else is there? Princess Caroline'll push for him and she'll not be wrong to do so. For all his faults our mannie keeps us out of war.'

'Huh.' She was displeased with Cameron: he who usually dressed soberly had today, nervously conscious that he would be in fancy company, put on an unwise waistcoat of *nouveau riche* beaded brocade which, she thought, lessened his dignity and reminded her of Lemuel's sartorial excesses. It irked her. She had punished him for his weakness by letting it pass unremarked when she saw it.

The shadow of 'our mannie', twenty stone of him, blocked their path. 'May I present my son?' boomed Sir Robert. 'Horace, that clever fellow Mr Archibald Cameron and his beautiful wife, Lady Cecily. What do you think of them, eh?'

Cameron's hand clamped on his wife's but Cecily stood like a stone. An old pair of eyes in a sickly triangle of a face regarded her from the level of Walpole's thigh. 'She is much prettier than the King's mistresses, Papa.'

'Good God, boy, so am I.' Stamping with amusement, Walpole put his arm round Cameron's shoulders and led him off to talk business. The boy followed, looking back.

'Mark the child,' said Lord Hervey's voice behind her.

'I shall not. Nothing of Walpole's interests me.'

They proceeded together, four foot apart to make room for Lord Hervey's grandiloquent cane and Cecily's hoops. The sun was unkind to Hervey, showing up the powder and paint on his face; the once beautiful young man had aged and become skeletal on the latest fad, the vegetarian Dr Cheyne's diet of seeds, green stuff and milk.

'Our prime minister is more good-natured than you credit him, dear Cecily. As I said, mark the child.' Hervey bent like a hairpin to put his mouth to Cecily's ear, overwhelming her with scent. 'Note the resemblance between the boy and my poor dear brother Carr. Recall the *amitié* that once existed between Carr and Lady Walpole and draw your own conclusion.'

Cecily glanced towards little Horace Walpole, who still looked back at her. There was no doubt . . . a Hervey in every line of his frail body. 'Indeed.'

Lord Hervey nodded. 'Sir Robert is too astute to have missed the likeness yet he loves the boy as his own and has requested an audience with the King for him. Such tolerance, such a *big* man. I beg you, forget how he harmed you as he has forgotten. Harden not your heart. He would be friends, he has told me so.' Hervey's ringed eyes were soulful, he seemed sincere – or as sincere as Hervey ever was.

Cecily was unsure whether he wanted to gain her sympathy for Walpole or inform her that his brother had slept with Walpole's wife. If the first, he wasted his time: the day she befriended that monster would be when pigs flew. If the second – and this surprised her – somewhere along the years she'd lost her taste for gossip.

The fountain of it spouted as they strolled . . . The Prince and Princess of Wales just *loathed* their eldest son, Frederick, who was being raised in Hanover . . . The Prince was *so* parsimonious he would not only *not* support his mistress, Mrs Howard, now she'd gone deaf, but, so that he might save on firing and candles, he never invited *anybody* to stay at Leicester House.

'Only dear, clever Caroline could persuade him to give a party of these proportions. *What* this country owes to that extraordinary woman. When the King dies she and dear Sir Robert will rule it between them.'

'Indeed?' Cecily was alarmed. 'I thought Walpole would be out if the King died.'

'Of course, the *Prince* does not like him – Walpole has refused to let him be regent in his father's absence – but dear, clever Caroline . . . Ah, there she is.'

A large woman stood under the trees surrounded by pretty young men and women, a bedecked carthorse amid colts.

Cecily hung back. Hervey regarded her, eyes glittering with divination. 'Is this . . . ? Surely not. Is it? Have you not encountered her since, er, since you left her service all those years ago?'

'No.'

He was thrilled, ushering her forward. 'Rest easy, my dear. She discounts politics where her friendships are concerned. Has she not engaged Dr Freind as physician for her children? And was he not most *deeply* involved in the recent Jacobite plot? She will be kind.'

He was right. The carthorse saw her and came forward, walking awkwardly, as if in pain. Gold ornaments chinked on the bronze silk of her gown. She was smiling. 'Zezily.'

As Caroline raised her from her curtsy and hugged her, Cecily thought what a nice woman she was. The Princess's continuous pregnancies had made her almost as fat as Queen Anne and, as with Anne, were beginning to affect her health. But she shared the late Queen's kindness and the engraved patience that came from enduring interminable, male capriciousness in order to get her own way.

She was the Jacobites' greatest enemy in the sense that, without her, the Hanoverians might already have been ousted for the virtuous James III. The natural goodness she emanated made her the only one of the royal family the English respected and liked. All this, while showing a tolerance for Jacobites that drove her friend, Walpole, to distraction.

Cecily found she was crying. Caroline cried with her: 'It vass your heart, *liebchen*. Always so much heart. It vass pardonable. We speak no more of it.' She dried her eyes. 'Now, I vant your advice.'

She reached across her hoops and took Cecily's hand as they walked. 'Lady Mary presses me to inoculate the *kinder*. She says you haf had it done on one you love. Is it varrantable?'

'It has certainly done her no harm, Your Royal Highness.'

'*Mais une petite nègre*,' said Caroline doubtfully. Experimenting on a little black girl was one thing: on royal children another.

Cecily found herself saying: 'I swear to Your Royal Highness I shall have it done to the child I'm carrying.'

'Zo-o.' That was better. Cecily's belly was patted and listened to, she was introduced to Princesses Amelia and Caroline, all the time wondering whether she'd heard a cock crow.

229

'Ve vill have it done while the King is still avay. He vouldn't approve.' Caroline smiled. 'I vonder what present he brings me back this time. Last it vas a vild boy captured in Hamelin running on all fours and scaling trees *à l'écureuil*. We have put him in fine suit vith red stockings but darkness still inhabit his head.'

She had a happy thought. 'Bring your little *nègre* to Leicester House and they shall play together.'

Cecily curtsied to the sound of a second cock crow.

Lord Hervey stayed with Caroline. Cecily, hot and queasy, sought shade in the pavilions. The smell of well-liquored wine cup and tables mounded with the confectioners' art made her queasier still and she wandered towards the trees, halted here and there by a burst of gossip. *Miss* So-and-So was with child. The Hon. This had been caught in bed with a maid, Lady That on the knee of a flunkey.

A Falstaffian figure at length under one of the oaks waved a glass at her: 'Well met by noonday, lady.'

'Oh, my God.'

Sir Spender Dick got up, brushing twigs off his breeches. 'Were you not aware, dear madam, that I am a regular visitor to Anspach? I bring greetings to Her Royal Highness from her old friend, the wife of the Margrave's *Geheimsekretär*.'

'Oh, God.' Sir Spender might well be a visitor to Caroline's birthplace but he visited Bolingbroke at Battersea a damn sight oftener.

'Be not dismayed, dear madam, Walpole's watchers may spy but what can they prove? Nothing.'

'Oh, *God*.' Cecily was poised for flight, away from a known Jacobite, a *tipsy* known Jacobite.

He moved with her. She led him away from the pavilions towards another, more remote tree.

'Forgive me for not having called at Arundel Street yet,' he said, 'but, as I indicated, I've been a-travelling.'

'Don't you dare come to Arundel Street. What do you want? Where's Maskelyne?' She looked round. 'He's not here too, is he?'

'Our good friend was not invited. Madam, we must have discourse.'

She'd chosen too small a tree: Sir Spender's bulk rivalled Sir Robert's and stuck out on either side of the rowan's slim trunk like a pear behind a toothpick. Cecily, half attending, shifted from foot to foot, hoping passers-by would think her trapped by a bore. Her fright wasn't decreased by the man's refusal to lower his voice.

'. . . this time we shall be ready, if you will instruct your servants at Hempens accordingly. What appellation did you give to His Majesty when he visited you?'

'Mr Robinson. Hush, will you.'

'What?'

'Mr Robinson. I told them he was a Mr Robinson. Sir Spender, we must discuss this another time.'

'Calm yourself, dear madam.' Sir Spender was at ease. 'What better place to plan the coming of the rightful King than in the bosom of the usurpers?'

Cecily could think of plenty. '*What* coming?'

'The next one.' Sir Spender's eyes disappeared into folds of fat as he beamed at her, wagging his finger. 'The next instant in which England shows ready to discard its German gaolers, its Hanoverian halter, its Georgian gyves, its –'

'Oh, *God*, will you be quiet?' She was in a panic. Princess Caroline was leading a procession of courtiers in their direction.

'To you the glory of lighting the Lantern, dear lady. As Shakespeare says, "We shall that day light such a candle in England as shall never be put out."'

'Latimer,' she said automatically. She curtsied and grinned weakly in Caroline's direction. Sir Spender curlicued his hand in a deep bow to which the Princess bent her head, smiling, in reply.

A Maid of Honour danced up to Sir Spender. 'We're going to play in Merlin's Cave.'

'Lead on, my Vivien, lead on.' His plump hand smoothed Cecily's sleeve as he went, leaving moisture on its silk. His look changed for a second and she saw he wasn't as drunk as all that. 'Be ready,' he said.

The band had taken the Princess's departure as a respite, leaving the air to the singing of caged and free birds. There was no sign of Cameron or Walpole.

Cecily made for the house and found a large, empty reception room on the south side in which to sit down. Betasselled curtains had been drawn against the sun. She rested on a couch, incalculably tired; two perspiring, ill-intentioned fat men in one hot afternoon had been too many, the one inspiring intense dislike, the other foreboding. And the cock of betrayal crowed on.

Suddenly she longed for the health of life at the Belle, for lack of complication, for country kindness.

She tried to compose herself and recall exactly what it was that Spender Dick had been saying. Hempens to be used as a springboard for a Jacobite rising . . . *Oh, God. I'm afraid. So afraid.*

Yet she saw the logic. Poor communication between James and his supporters in Britain had resulted in him arriving late for the 'Fifteen, and not at all for the previous invasion attempt in 1708. At the time of the South Sea Bubble when, Jacobites liked to think, he could have walked to the throne unopposed, he had been in Italy and too far away to do more than pull on his boots before Walpole had calmed the country down.

But if he were kept in constant readiness on the opposite coast for the moment when British Jacobites next saw their chance, he could be at Hempens with the tide, ready to travel to wherever-it-was that he decided to raise his standard.

She calmed herself down. *It won't ever happen.* The Jacobites planned invasions like children played 'when-I-grow-up' games. In the torpor of heat and her own pregnancy, among these exquisite, self-satisfied aristocrats, it was impossible to believe there would ever be sufficient energy of disaffection in the country to warrant another invasion.

The attrition of time had accustomed England to Whig rule. The fact that she hadn't clawed out Walpole's eyes this afternoon showed that even her anger was becoming worn down.

She was cooler now. 'What if the Pretender does come?' she asked aloud.

He wouldn't. 'Yet what if it does?'

He will fail and you, my dear, will end up in exile or under the executioner's axe. She had too much invested in property and people to play deadly Jacobite games.

But if he *didn't* fail? She remembered the kingdoms of the earth that had spread before her at Hempens when the Pretender, that wholesome prince, had sat in its shabby parlour and she had seen the promise of health and harmony restored to her nation.

Around her, in the great, shaded room, William Kent had incorporated his favourite motif, the sphinx. It spread its wings along the tops of mirrors, looked down from cornices, perched in the gilded foliage of consoles, the collar heavy round its slender neck, young breasts resting on claws, cruel and placid eyes.

She thought: Through apathy I've allowed myself to become part of this, which sneers at those it oppresses, which sees a black child as interchangeable with another.

And why have I? Why am I here? Because of a marriage that now divided her life into two pieces. Because of a Whig among Whigs.

He came looking for her. 'There y'are.' He stood in front of her. 'I'm glad to find ye alone. I saw ye talking with yon Spender Dick, him who's stayed at the Belle a time or two. I've to warn ye, Cecily, he's under suspicion for Jacobite activities. Walpole's in a fury that Her Royal Highness invited the callant. It does us no good to appear friendly with such and, for your own sake, I'd be grateful for ye to shun the man in future.'

He'd chosen the worst possible moment. In any case, she always bridled at his lectures – a rebuff from him could discountenance her for the rest of the day. That his reproof appeared to be parroting an order from Walpole struck memories of Lemuel's sycophancy. And then there was the waistcoat and the nausea and the heat and the continually crowing cock . . .

'You lick-spittle,' she said. 'You pompous, grovelling, bum-kissing little spaniel. You come running from that scabby-necked tyrant to tell me, *me*, who to talk to and who not? In a waistcoat like that?'

'*Cecily.*' He was taken aback by the savagery of her anger. He blinked. 'What's wrong with the waistcoat?'

'I *like* Spender Dick, do you hear me? He's the finest man here. And if he offends that fat prick-pig I like him the more.

He doesn't peddle scandal or nose up Walpole's arse. Yes, Sir Robert, no, Sir Robert, I'll go and tell her, Sir Robert. And he didn't sit around scratching his ballocks while Sir Robert *killed Dolly*.'

'So that's it,' he said quietly.

'Yes, that's it. And *that's* it . . .' she pointed at the appalling waistcoat '. . . and *that*'s it.' Her hand stretched out to a table on which rested a little brass sphinx, symbol of a society that reflected its own delicate brutality, grabbed the ornament and threw it, shattering the glass bowl of a lamp.

When footmen came running, Cameron said that his wife had been overcome by the heat, and took her home.

The next day came the news that King George had collapsed in Holland. Insisting that the journey to Hanover be continued – 'To Osnabrück, to Osnabrück' – he was jolted in his carriage for a night and a day before he reached it and died.

His son received the news without grief. His first act as George II was to have two portraits of his mother hung in the royal apartments. His second was to destroy his father's will. His third dismissed Sir Robert Walpole and appointed in his stead an amiable old man, Sir Spencer Compton, who was immediately out of his depth.

Everybody noted how well Walpole took it. Courteously, he waited on Sir Spencer Compton in more ways than one, obeying his orders, helping him take on the responsibilities, watching him flounder. To his worried friends he merely said: 'I have the right sow by the ear.'

The sow, now Queen of England, was equally circumspect. Without letting her husband think she was persuading him, Sir Spencer's incompetence was shown up and the advantages of keeping the former prime minister made obvious. Only a master of the parliamentary system could, as Walpole promised to do, increase the new King and Queen's private income beyond any previously enjoyed by an English sovereign and his consort.

Within weeks George II's opinion of the man he'd called a rogue underwent a sea change.

*

On the day Walpole resumed power, Cecily miscarried. It was her husband who wept. Once she'd recovered, she said: 'Eleanor and I will go back to the Belle now. There's no need for you to come.'

CHAPTER TWELVE

THE BELLE HAD maintained its general standard under Cole and Marjorie Packer, despite one or two plebeian habits having crept in.

Cecily reinstated lavender bags in every bed and the regular polishing of the silver, had the yard manure-heap removed from under the bedroom windows to the field and stopped the custom of free ale to the taproom which marked the arrival of any new Packer into the world. That apart, she commended her staff.

They showed their pleasure at having her back by truculence and, after a glance, forbore to ask when Master Archie would be arriving.

Eleanor said: 'I didn't like London, Marjorie. Quick, I didn't like London. Didn't like London, Cole.' Which pleased them even more.

There had been other hangings under the Black Acts. A simpleton, a distant cousin of Marjorie's, had experimentally fired a cock of wheat. A Codicote man had trapped two illegal rabbits while wearing a handkerchief across the bottom half of his face – thereby qualifying for capital punishment under the Black Acts for going disguised. And young Hawkins at Bramfield had broken down a gate put up by Lord Letty's men across a path to his cottage – he'd buttoned the collar of his great coat across his chin, that too constituting a disguise.

In London Cecily hadn't heard a word raised against the Black Acts; even her friends had shown surprise at her agitation. Were the laws not framed against Jacobites? When Cecily pointed out that they were being used against people who had no more involvement with Jacobitism than with metaphysics, there were shrugs: Walpole kept uncovering Jacobite plots, did he not? You couldn't make an omelette without breaking eggs, etc.

Under this indifference other legislation was creeping in without any pretence of being aimed at revolutionaries, making Walpole's government the most bloodthirsty in Europe. You could now be hanged for wilfully breaking any tools used in the manufacture of wool or, if you were a bankrupt, for failing to present yourself for examination within forty-two days, or for opposing Customs officers in the execution of their duty – which even the Lord Chief Justice, Lord Hardwicke, thought went too far.

The Tyburn tree had to be extended to take as many as twenty hangings at a time. Frequently, not one of the executed was a murderer.

In the forest the new Lord Letty showed equal impatience with the traditions of its kindling-gatherers, sawyers and hurdlers, spoke-choppers and faggoters, lath-renders and ladder-makers, men and women who rarely handled money but killed their own meat, and who were now denied use-rights which had been theirs for centuries. He made open land into paddocks, built deer pens, sold timber wholesale to the navy, granted turf to his rich neighbours and set man-traps.

But the foresters knew every covert, every hollow oak. They avoided the man-traps and continued occupations by night that had previously been done by day. Theirs was no venture for the luxury of putting an extra pheasant in the pot, it was for survival; encounters between the two sides were pitiless.

Stabber, once the handsomest of the Packers, had lost the tip of his nose to a keeper's bullet, giving him the appearance of a time-worn gargoyle. The loss of his looks and the subsequent teasing made him bad-tempered. He refused to talk to Cecily.

She was upset that he should be involved in the forest battles at all. 'I pay him enough,' she complained to Cole. 'He doesn't need to steal.'

'First place ut wadden stealing,' Cole said. 'Second place you don't pay our old gran. Her cow grazed Stapleford Lea 's long 's I remember till Letty enclosed un. Her teeth's gone, see. Her do need the milk. Stabber were tearing down the bugger's fences.'

'Well, I didn't put them up.'

Cole shuffled. 'Seemingly you been mingling with un at them grand balls and such. Us thought you'd maybe forgotten 'twas Letty got Miss Dolly hanged.'

Cecily shook her head. 'I never saw him.' But she'd mingled with Walpole, who cradled Letty and others like him, giving himself and them legal power to rob and kill. She'd known the claws that rested under that jovial breast and countenanced them. As for her husband . . . 'He keeps us out of war,' Cameron had said.

But what virtue lay in a peace that maimed and ravaged? Stability could have its own terror.

She appealed to Tyler, who had moved into the Belle during her absence: 'Can't you stop my people risking their necks?' When he didn't answer, she realized. 'God damn it, you're with them.'

'Letty's men burned my place down,' he told her. 'Reprisal.'

'Reprisal for what?'

'For us burning down one o' theirs.'

I am a non-combatant in the middle of the lines, she thought. And then she thought: No, I'm a combatant. She had chosen her side in the gilded, sphinx-riddled drawing room at Richmond.

Cecily's contact with the Cause was now through Mr Phineas, a traveller in buttons and a man of such underpowered character it was a wonder he sold any, leaving the nation's coats to be done up by string.

'Mole,' he'd said, on first stepping into the Belle.

'Welcome, Mr Mole. If you would follow the other guests . . .'

'No. Mole. It's the password.'

'Oh.' She gave him dinner in the private room and fell asleep over the capon. But the opposition literature he passed to her to be put in Wallie's postbag was enlivening. There were songs from Gay's *The Beggar's Opera* in which Walpole was pilloried as Peachum, an organizer of cutpurses who augmented his profits by betraying his people for reward, while the hero,

237

Macheath, was a highwayman and by implication, a country gentleman ruined by Walpole's 'Robinocracy'.

Among overtly Jacobite publications like *Fog's Weekly Journal*, whose publishers risked arrest by unceasingly warning the country that it was 'being enervated with Luxury, involved in an excessive national Debt and in Danger of being enslaved by Corruption if it does not restore Virtue', i.e. James Stuart, there was the wittier and more vituperative *The Craftsman* in which Cecily detected the fine hand of her godfather. It had fun describing Walpole as 'the monster now on exhibition at Westminster'. *The body of this creature covered at least an acre of ground . . . seemed to be swelled and bloated as though full of corruption.*

Squibs, ballads, cartoons, all attacked Walpole's government, all making the point that there was nothing to choose between its ministers and common criminals . . . 'according to the Definition of those Gentlemen – *Keep what you get, and get what you can.'*

Sending these to Scotland for copying was more to Cecily's taste than invasion, but she had to ration them so that Wallie's postbag did not seem heavier than it had before he set it down at the Belle.

Some were on public sale anyway and the taproom Tories chuckled over them and sang with Macheath:

> 'Since laws were made for ev'ry degree,
> To curb vice in others, as well as me,
> I wonder we han't better company,
> Upon Tyburn tree!'

They needed cheering up: the recent election had gone badly, the Whigs having managed to bribe more voters than they had.

Nothing, however, managed to invigorate Colonel Grandison, bereft of his magistracy.

Ironically, his stock had risen in his old division as it now compared him with Sir Samuel Pink, who'd earned the sobriquet 'Inquisition Pink' by proving himself a tireless upholder of the law's every tenet; who'd sent Harriet Bygrave to the house of correction for refusing to name the father of her illegitimate child; who'd had an eleven-year-old vagrant whipped; and had convicted Tewin's blacksmith, a former trooper, 'for profane cursing and swearing', and fined him a shilling an oath.

'Us diddun know when we was well off,' the taproom said, lovingly, shaking its head at the sad little figure sitting unkempt by the fire, refusing to respond even to Marjorie's sympathetic flirtation, as if loss of consequence on the bench had taken away all joy in life.

Cecily treated him gently until a flash storm carried away the culvert that directed the hill stream from Datchworth under the Great North Road to replenish the Belle's pond and into the fields behind. The resultant flood invaded the dining room. Then she lost her temper.

'I want that culvert mended, Colonel. Look at my damned floor.' The culvert was just within Datchworth's boundary and all parishes were responsible for the maintenance of the section of roads that passed through them. Colonel Grandison, for these purposes, was Datchworth.

It failed to rouse him. 'Those who profit from the road should mend it,' he said listlessly.

Cecily could have taken Datchworth and its squire to court for its neglect but she didn't want to kick Grandison when he was down. Few parishes did their duty by their roads; it would be unfair to prosecute Datchworth when Knebworth a little further north was equally culpable for the dilapidation of its section.

She had the culvert mended at her own expense: if her stretch of road collapsed to the extent that traffic was forced to bypass it, the Belle was finished. Nevertheless, for all that she could do, the road was deteriorating as not only her trade but the country's increased . . .

'A turnpike,' she said. 'We must have a turnpike. They've got one up at Stony Stratford.'

'They got it because of the brick trade,' said Colonel Grandison. 'No brick trade here.'

'But the bloody brick wagons tear up my bloody road to get to London,' she pointed out. 'Why can't they pay to have it repaired?'

'Need an Act of Parliament to put up a tollgate. And we'd

need to set up a trust.' All at once it was 'we'. For the first time since Cecily had returned to the Belle, Grandison showed interest: road tolls were the coming, profitable thing.

'Then we'll get one.'

There was no lack of parties willing to join a trust and no lack of opposition either. Totty Stokes was against it because Cecily was for it. Farmers to the north of the proposed site of the turnpike objected to the prospect of paying a toll when they sent their corn to London, among them Squire Leggatt, though he was eventually persuaded that a shilling toll was cheaper than losing his corn through a wagon overturning in the ruts – as had happened the previous year.

Unexpected and ferocious opposition came from Dr Baines at Knebworth who, it appeared, had gained a deal of business from broken bones caused by spills on the carriageway.

What was needed was someone who could persuade everybody that Woolmer Green turnpike would be a Good Thing, someone to guide the Act for it through Parliament.

'We need Archibald Cameron,' Colonel Grandison said. 'When does your husband come back?'

It was Cecily's turn to show listlessness. 'He's devising a scheme to provide a hospital for foundlings.' *I don't want him back.*

She told herself Cameron was to be blamed for, tainted by, the revulsion she had experienced in London society: he was part of it, had tried to re-establish her in it.

She left the turnpike meeting, which had been at Datchworth Manor, to ride home alone through a summer evening scented with grass and the acid sweetness of limes.

Shepherd's rose and honeysuckle were in the hedges, sheep nibbled the common, rooks scattered around the elms against a clear, textureless sky.

It was the first time since her return to Hertfordshire that she'd had time for reflection; she was reluctant to begin it, to face the misery that had followed her from London and which, no matter how she occupied herself, gnawed her – a knowledge that on the most basic and primeval of levels she had failed.

With perception, Cameron had said: 'There'll be other babies,

240

my dearie. Women o...

Had he known it, he ...
leave her when the pain ...
in the sheet from the maid ...
gentleness, to its disposal. W...

The sort of man who seeme...
humiliation of her life and had ...
mate abasement – that Lady Ceci...
the most feckless hedge-trollop cou...

She began to sob. Afraid somebody ...
turned off the lane at Mardleybury pon...
the horse could drink. She sat, hidden in ... ...loves
on the pond edge, and gave herself up to ... ... her dead
baby.

It was as if she'd unknowingly carried grief for it around
with her until now, here, fittingly, in the fecundity of a country
summer, it forced her acknowledgement. *It would have been such
a nice baby.* She rocked back and forth, apologizing to it. *My
fault, my fault, my grievous fault.*

The straits she'd been in when she offered her soul to the
Devil seemed less terrible now and her declaration a capricious
thing. But she'd stood among the ruins of the Belle and made
it. *I shall follow you all my days, if you will help me prosper so that
I can take revenge on him who has brought me to this.*

How ridiculous and how fatal. Dolly had known. 'You don't
cheat the Devil,' she'd said. She'd said he'd collect his dues.
And he had.

And that man, that *good* man, her husband, had been present
to watch the dues collected.

Damn him. Him and his woman in Kent.

Cecily sniffed and wiped her nose. Through the bars of the
foxgloves, the sky had darkened and acquired a fingernail of a
moon. Across the fields, between the trees, she could see the
lights of the Belle.

I'll stay here. I'm in control here. It's the one bloody place I
am in control.

She mounted her horse and went home.

*

...at bent crops, made coaches late
... that Cecily's work for the Cause fre-
...done in the early hours of the morning,
...bad-tempered as the weather – and as careless.
...usband caught her, ink-handed, copying a letter from
...Lord Steward, Lord Chesterfield, to a fellow peer in Scotland
giving details of the proposed secret treaty with Austria. With
rain like a waterfall washing the windows, she didn't hear his
arrival until he flung open the unlocked bedroom door.
The chest in which she kept the Jacobite literature was open
and on the floor were journals to infiltrate into the postbag that
night.

He was wet and jubilant, a battered bunch of roses in his
hand. '*Ha til mi tulidh.* Let the piper play. I thought ye'd be
asleep. I planned to leap on ye like a leopard. I've missed ye.'
As she stared, frozen, he said: 'It's your husband, woman, here
for his marital rights.'

And then he saw the letters, Chesterfield's monogrammed,
side by side with her copy. 'What's this?' She watched the stages:
bewilderment, realization, refusal of belief, appalled acceptance.

Now you know, she thought. And, illogically: *Serve you right.*

His hand passed over the embossed insignia of the postbag
lying open on the floor; one by one he picked up the rolled
copies of squibs, *Craftsman*, leaflets, running his fingers across
the invective as if touch confirmed what his eyes failed to
believe. 'Ye's a Jack,' he said to himself and turned on her: 'Ye're
a damned *Jacobite.*'

'Yes,' she said. She was jubilant with defiance. *Now I can hurt
you.*

'Ye're their agent. Walpole said the Jacks were using the
mail.'

'Yes.'

He shook his head. 'How long?'

'How long have I been an agent for His Majesty King James?'
she said deliberately. 'Years. Since the Bubble.'

You don't know me. It was like stabbing him, Walpole, shoving
a knife into all Whigdom. She stood at the stake, Joan of Arc,
Guy Fawkes; at this moment she wished she'd blown up Parlia-

ment. No doubts now. 'Everything I've learned that would help my Cause and harm yours I have passed on.'

His eyes narrowed, peering at her. 'My God,' he said. 'Ye're a fool.' His voice went high with a revelation more terrible than that she was a traitor. Through his eyes she saw herself sprout asses' ears, like Bottom. 'Ye're a *fool*.'

She became angry. 'Why? Because I oppose a system that has turned my country into a shop? Where cheats and sycophants prosper? Where only the vulgar and venal become rich? Where quality's despised? Where power's become cruelty?'

He kicked the mailbag so that it skidded across the room. 'Where it can change, woman, don't ye see that? There'd be no change under James Stuart, it'd be taken back a hundred year. Will ye no understand?' Now he was pleading with her. 'We alter from the inside, not by war and revolution. Ye'll kill people.'

'You kill people now, you bastard.' She lurched at him and hammered at his chest. 'You hanged Dolly.'

He caught her hands. 'And this is your revenge?'

She screamed, 'Why shouldn't it be? I was sold. Stripped in the market-place and sold. Walpole called it marriage. I called it rape. Everything I was, everything I had. Sold.'

'No.' He forced her to sit on the bed and stood over her, still holding her hands. 'They didn't sell the soul of you. I never told ye, and I should have. You were the bravest thing I ever saw and I loved ye for it. And now . . .' he pointed to the litter on the floor '. . . now I don't know ye.'

'No, you don't.' By Christ, did he think he could mop up everything with a compliment? 'You never did.'

He let go of her hands. 'So it seems.' Tiredly he took off his wig and ran his fingers through his curls. 'So it seems.'

He walked over to her table and tore up the copy of Chester-field's letter, refolding the original. 'How d'ye reseal the thing?' He put the fragments into her powder bowl, picked up the candle and set them on fire. A smell of burning paper and scorched, scented talcum filled the room. 'Is this the extent of it?'

'What?'

'Is this all they use ye for? Tampering with the mail? Ye're involved in no more of their plotting? I don't ask who gives your instructions, but I must know ye're free of other guilt. Is this all of it?'

He saw her as a tool. She had no credit for having chosen to support the Cause from conviction. The fact that she'd had her own doubts about its validity made her feel more foolish and therefore more defiant. At that moment the only man she could think of who'd treated her as a reasoning intelligence was James Stuart.

He repeated: 'Is this all of it?'

She lied, 'Yes.'

Neatly, infuriatingly, he began picking up the scattered rolls of paper. She watched the flames flicker tawny reflections on his hair. 'What woman in Kent?'

'Eh?'

She said: 'I'm informed that you keep a woman in Kent.'

'What's that to do with anything?' He turned to look at her. 'Aye, there was a woman. A good woman and dead four year since.' He cocked his head. 'Did ye think I was celibate while I waited for ye?'

She shrugged. 'It is of no concern. Except to demonstrate that we both had our secrets.'

'I hardly think poor Lucy constitutes a secret of equal weight with treachery.' He was dismissing it, a light matter. He said tiredly: 'Cecily. You must know I cannot countenance this Jacobite foolery. It's against everything I hold in faith. I want your word you'll abandon it. Come back with me to London.'

'To London? After the way it treated Eleanor? I'll never set foot in London again.' Society's bunting lay in the gutter, tawdry and limp, and had done from the moment it offered to swap Eleanor for a child that would more nearly complement her complexion. 'I'm surprised you tolerate it, you and your supposed philanthropy.'

'Because *there*'s the battleground.' He came forward to her, holding out his freckled hands. 'Ah, Cecily. Come back with me and change it. I need your help.' His lips twitched. 'Thee and me together. Lord, with the two of us they'll need a new form of governance.'

She dodged and stood up so that he didn't touch her. 'No.'

'Ye're breaking our contract,' he said.

He was only a lawyer after all. She said: 'Sue me.'

And the marriage was over.

She never found out how her husband did it without putting suspicion on her, but she received a neutral letter from the Postmaster General informing her that the Belle's licence as a receiving house for the Royal Mail had been withdrawn.

If, in many ways, it was a relief, it was also a reproof from all-powerful male Whiggery which Archibald Cameron had come to represent in Cecily's eyes almost as surely as Walpole – an injustice she did not try to analyse. He was male, he was Whig, he was righteous, he'd forced another marriage on her, he'd had another woman. It was enough.

Now he'd abandoned her, a high-minded desertion that resurrected the ache of Cecily's childhood at the irreproachable abandonment of her parents in dying before she could know them. *Everybody leaves me. I am alone.*

When, half waking in the mornings, her body expectant, she found herself rolling towards Cameron's side of the bed, she berated herself for carnality – his fault again – and weakness.

She'd invigorate herself from self-pity with two words: *Poor Lucy.* Always effective. Poor Lucy developed the persona of a rival; plump, adoring and unforgiven. Poor Lucy, who'd died these four years since and, it was to be hoped, painfully.

Cameron didn't abandon Eleanor or the Belle. He wrote to tell Cecily on which day he was coming to see the child and, when she could, Cecily arranged to be absent. In return, she wrote for his advice on legal matters, seeing no reason to surrender his services as a lawyer.

He co-operated in the turnpike, persuading much of the opposition that it was a Good Thing, became a trustee and guided the Act for it through Parliament. Within two years a squat little keeper's house with gates stretching across the road was built on the flat stretch between Knebworth and Woolmer Green along which Tyler and Cecily had once strewn stolen articles to tempt the passengers of a waylaid coach to the Belle Sauvage.

That section of the Great North Road, on its new foundation of broken flint and gravel, became straight, speedy and safe for the first time since the Roman legions marched along it. To Cecily it was an achievement; her contribution to the roading of Britain.

She built herself into the wider community, not only a member of the Trust but its committee for appointing and overseeing the turnpike's toll collector. She became acting churchwarden at Datchworth and joined the local Society of Coaching Inn Proprietors at Hertford. As a woman, her position was irregular but accepted by the provincials of Datchworth and Woolmer Green who lacked the niceties of convention.

The Coaching Inn Proprietors, however, had put up opposition. True, they said, one or two local women ran inns but they had the sensitivity to be represented at meetings by their sons.

Cecily was past sensitivity: if she didn't have a finger in the pie it wouldn't be cooked to her taste. She pointed out her sonless state and that there was nothing in the rules to bar female members. The implacable Totty Stokes said that was only because the Society had never expected a woman to be so insolent as to want to join.

'It didn't expect bloody fools to join either, Totty Stokes,' Cecily said, 'but it got you.'

This passed for wit among Coaching Inn Proprietors, gained her applause and membership. She understood now why women who ventured into the male world became outrageous: in order to succeed they must abandon the luxury of self-consciousness. Men, it seemed, would tolerate competition from a woman as long as she was eccentric. Oh, well, if that was what was needed . . .

So it was during this time that Cecily became a 'character', her passport out of the constraints of femininity. It was a matter of freeing an aspect of her personality that she possessed anyway and perhaps would have emerged in any case. Imperiousness became aggression with an acquired Hertfordshire accent, salted by the language of the Fleet.

She dressed for comfort and neatness rather than beauty – it didn't do to look handsomer than the handsomest guest – her shoes were kind to her feet, even if she wouldn't have been seen dead in them in the old days. A turban added another five to her years by hiding her curls. The monster of a reticule that accompanied her rather than a lady's dainty pocket was rumoured to contain a disembowelling knife.

Whether the inn shaped her, or she shaped her inn, the two became synonymous. Obscure Mrs Henry who'd arrived at Woolmer Green was now 'good old Belle' to some, and 'Mistress Savage' to those who didn't dare. Belle Savage became her signature on documents, the formidable name of a formidable woman.

There were times when she would have dropped the charade – *Who is Belle Savage? Rescue me from her* – but others forced it on her, giving her leeway as a harpy she would not have been allowed as a conforming woman.

Luckily, Tyler and the straight-talking Packers kept her from tyranny.

The small pool of her life contained its compensations: the control and interest of a squire in its fluctuations, Eleanor swimming, happily, in the shoal of its little fish.

And the answer to Eleanor's future was here. *I shall leave her the Belle.* The girl would have the independence that was survival for a woman, black or white. In time, one of the better local boys – a Packer, perhaps, she might do worse – could offer for her and wouldn't lose by it; Eleanor was accepted in her own community. As for strangers, in the impermanence of traffic where ordinary and oddity met then parted, on a great road with newness round every bend, she would be deemed no more unusual than any other passing feature. Look, the Yorkshire dales. Look, a black landlady.

Cecily left Hertfordshire only once in this period – to go to Mary Astell's funeral. The Chelsea church was poorly attended; Cecily had hoped to see Sophie but she wasn't there. Since Hempens there had been one letter from Ireland, where she'd remarried, giving details of her new children and making no mention of the one lost.

There were two men in a congregation of seventeen. Cecily decided that practically all England's well-educated women

247

were gathered in the church that day. *Oh, Mary, what happened to your Utopia of free, reasoned women?* In its lifetime the small voice that proposed feminine education had been either derided or ignored. Stilled, it had been forgotten. There was less agitation for female literacy now than at any time since the Restoration.

The preacher praised only Mrs Astell's piety and meekness under suffering. 'She embodied all the feminine virtues but those of marriage and motherhood, which were denied her.'

Cecily waited for the coffin lid to rise and Mary Astell's head to pop out, shrieking: 'I didn't want 'em. Marriage is a trap.' But the casket stayed still under its weight of flowers and platitudes.

As they went outside into the winter churchyard to watch the small coffin lowered into its hole, Cecily blamed the bones inside it. *Look at us. What good did you do us? Why did you give us knowledge if it was only to help us despair more?* The women gathered round the grave were middle-aged, dressed not for Fashion but, like Lady Mary Wortley Montagu in her eastern cloak and turban, for fancy, or for comfort, like Lady Catherine Jones and Cecily herself. *All of us oddities, all of us swimmers against the tide.* She looked around at the faces. *All of us lonely.*

Walking back from the graveside, she was made lonelier yet.

'I'm going abroad,' Lady Mary Wortley Montagu said. 'This time I shall not come back.'

'No.' It was involuntary. Abandonment again; without Lady Mary she would be consigned to provincialism for ever. Nor could she bear that such a spirit should admit defeat – and defeat was what it was. The clamour set on by Pope, whose slanders now included 'whore', had reached even the Belle so that the woman's name had become synonymous with feminine disgrace and, by extension, Edward Wortley's with that of cuckold.

Out of decency, pretending she didn't know, Cecily asked: 'Why must you go?'

Lady Mary covered a yawn with her fan. 'People are grown so stupid I can no longer support their company.' When Cecily stopped and turned to look at her, she shrugged. 'My children are a disappointment, my marriage no longer a marriage.'

They walked on. Pope's name wasn't mentioned. 'I have done

248

my best to be a good wife and mother, apparently without success. I was not cut out for it. However, the dearest concern I have in this world is to spare Edward. He has always spared me. If I go into exile, the calumnies on him will cease.'

'Oh, my dear.'

Lady Mary smiled. 'Nothing in life became her like the leaving of . . . her husband.'

At the lych gate, they turned to look at the grave of their friend. Two men with shovels lurked behind the yew tree, waiting to fill it in.

'What was it she always wanted for us?' asked Lady Mary. 'The freedom to decide for ourselves what is important? Such a dangerous woman she was.'

Land tax was lowered in order to keep estate owners happy. A salt tax was raised instead. Walpole told the House that a tax on salt was more equable than one which hurt only the landed gentry – presumably because it could then hurt everybody.

Opposing speeches pointed out that the poor were already hurting. 'I hope every man that hears me will allow his pity and compassion for the poor and the wretched.' This was William Pulteney, once an ally of Walpole's who'd been got rid of, as all potential dissidents to the Great Man's policies were sooner or later; Walpole's government now consisted of Walpole and yes-men.

The salt tax was carried by 225 votes to 187.

'Nothing can stop him, can it?' asked Cecily, as she and Colonel Grandison stood at the door of his manor and handed out packets of salt to a queue of Datchworthians. 'He can do what he likes. Look at them, they don't *mind*.'

As each packet was placed into each extended hand, its owner nodded slightly. There were no thanks – these were Hertfordshire men and women – but it seemed to Cecily that, had they been right-thinking, they should even now be tearing bricks out of the walls of a manor house which paid proportionally less tax than they did.

Colonel Grandison knew his people. 'They mind,' he said. 'They just don't mind enough. Yet.'

'When's *yet* going to be?'

It was glimmering, like an unrisen sun, over the horizon; a beam in the mind of a Prime Minister who believed he'd placated those who mattered and that the patience of the rest could be stretched indefinitely. An excise tax.

The first whisper reached the Belle in an article in *The Craftsman* which Mr Phineas, button traveller, still delivered to Cecily along with Jacobite literature, even though she was no longer its distributor.

She read the article. It accused Walpole of planning to bring in a 'general excise' which, it said, would be used to create a larger standing army which in turn would be used against its own people when they protested at the suppression of all liberty.

Mr Phineas was showing more animation than Cecily had ever seen in him. 'Word is to stand by,' he whispered. 'This'll do for Walpole *and* Hanover.'

She raised her eyebrows. Excise meant that goods shipped into British ports would be stored in bonded warehouses, untaxed until they emerged for sale. The system did away with customs duty, which smugglers evaded, and instead put the onus of tax directly on the customer. But where was the cause of Phineas's excitement? Would a people dormant under a salt tax wake up at this one? She couldn't see them flocking to the Pretender's banner merely because it read: 'Down with the excise!'

Showing the article to Tyler, she got her first inkling that she was wrong.

'Gawd,' he said. 'The old bugger's gone too far this time.'

'Why? *Why* has he? I don't understand.'

'He's losing too much revenue through smuggling, Duchess. But he'll do for hisself with this.'

'Why will he?' She could only think of it as it applied to her own smuggling: the tea and the brandy that came into her hidden cellar from the fens. 'Surely we can avoid excise like we avoid customs.'

Tyler looked pityingly at her. 'Ain't met many excisemen, have you, Duchess? They got powers customs men only dream about. They'll tear down the Belle in a search if they want to. An' they want to. Bastards, the lot of 'em. An Englishman's home'll be the exciseman's castle. People won't stand for it.'

Frightened for her smuggled profit, Cecily wrote to Cameron to see if he knew what were Walpole's exact intentions.

His reply was measured. Sir Robert's proposed legislation was logical since smuggling was getting out of hand . . .

And Sir Robert should know, thought Cecily. He's done enough of it.

. . . the excise was to be on wine and tobacco; 'general' only in the sense that it would be paid by everybody using those commodities. 'He has been advised against it,' Cameron wrote. 'The British perceive excise as foreign to their nature. Yet he swears he will take the Bill to the House and in this I believe he misjudges the public mood.'

For once, it appeared that he had. The Great Man, beaming good will and common sense, explained the logic and benefits of the scheme. Excise would affect only wine and tobacco but it would give its officials new power to search out smugglers who were a disgrace to the nation and a drain on its income.

It was no good. Smuggling was a national institution: excise was foreign. Nor did the British believe that it would stop at wine and tobacco; the term 'general excise' would eventually mean what it said, a tax on food, clothes, everything.

At the beginning of January '33, there was a muttering that, by the end of the month, had become a roar, egged on by an opposition which saw its chance. Pamphlets, ballad writers, cartoonists followed *The Craftsman* into battle and poured their response on to the streets. Excise was something France imposed on its people, the Catholic James II had used it, therefore it was allied to popery. There'd be an excise on boots next, and free Englishmen would have to start wearing clogs like downtrodden bloody Frogs.

Walpole could reason as much as he liked that excisemen would only search private premises with a magistrate's warrant; what protection was that? Whig JPs would give warrants at the drop of a hat.

'No Excise, No Slavery, No Wooden Shoes' became the slogan of the streets as an image became established in the public mind of vicious, corrupt excisemen breaking into homes, tipping the

251

baby on to the floor and ravishing its mother in the search for an illegal bottle and pipe.

When Walpole rose to lay his proposal before Parliament, magistrates, constables and Horse and Foot Guards had to control the crowd that hammered on its doors. He remained cool in the face of what he regarded as an organized demonstration by 'sturdy beggars', a phrase that did him no good because, for once, the 'sturdy beggars' included respectable City men.

Though Walpole wisely left the Commons by a back door, he was sure of his majority within it. He would bring the Bill in though the sky fell. The King was with him. He'd link the Bill to a shilling off the land tax, which would surely carry the country gentry onto his side.

At St James's Palace, George II called his prime minister 'a brave man', and fingered the sword he'd worn at Oudenarde. But the sword was double-edged: support from a king likely to profit most from the excise didn't raise Walpole's stock with a people who still regarded that king as a foreigner.

The sky looked shaky. Even the army, fonder of its smoke than most, threatened mutiny. Nor was agitation confined to London: Lord Hervey warned Walpole, 'The whole nation is in flames.'

At February's meeting in Hertford, the Coach Inn Proprietors put up a banner showing a coach drawn by the dragon Excise farting a stream of gold into Walpole's lap. They sang:

> 'Grant the tax, and the glutton
> Will roar out for mutton
> Your beef, bread and bacon to boot.
> Your goose, pig and pullet
> He'll thrust down his gullet,
> Whilst the labourer munches a root.'

Cecily, happily singing with them, thought: This isn't just reaction to the excise. That was only the last straw. They've been ashamed of their country too long. They've had enough.

Because even normally quiet Hertford was in riot, she had brought Tyler with her to drive her home but, in organizing an anti-excise petition and deciding on the delegation to take it to

252

Westminster, the meeting went on so long that they spent what remained of the night in rooms at the Golden Lion, listening to shouts of 'No Slavery, No Wooden Shoes' and the sound of smashing shop fronts.

The next morning Tyler had to lead the carriage horse around broken glass and window frames. A scorched rag, all that remained of an effigy of Walpole, hung from a lamp in Fore Street. He shook his head at it: 'Iffen the Stuart had walked in last night they'd a carried him to St James's.'

Cecily wondered how much he knew or guessed of her Jacobite activities and whether she should tell him. That she hadn't done so already had been to protect him. If the would-be use of Hempens as a landing place for the Pretender transpired and proved disastrous, at least her good friend would be free of involvement.

When they reached the track that led to Bramfield, she asked: 'If the Pretender *had* marched in last night, would you have helped carry him to St James's?'

Tyler was silent, thinking. The bare branches of trees, outlined with frost, arched over their heads, casting complex, geometric shadows in the low February sun.

'If Walpole falls,' Cecily went on, 'the Hanoverians could go with him. I've never seen people as angry as this. Worse than the Bubble. Even Totty Stokes was damning King George. Would they have James Stuart back, do you think? Would *you*?'

The carriage lurched as the horse picked its way over the rock-hard ruts of the track. Tyler guided it so that the wheels fitted into the grooves made by wagons. A dead branch fell off a tree in the forest, scattering rooks into the sky. It mattered that he should say yes. Whatever he was in the eyes of the law, to her Tyler was the measure of the reasoning common man. He was England.

'Don't know, Duchess,' he said. 'I don't know we want an outsider in this fight. I reckon we can manage it ourselves.'

Oh, God, she despaired, is that England's verdict? *But I'm committed.* Stand by, they'd said. The country's tumult would attract the Pretender like a lion scenting blood; even now he

253

could be heading for Hempens and invasion. The country's Jacobites would at last be lifting their sorry heads and scurrying.

All I wanted to do was bring Walpole down. Must I bring down Hanover too?

Panicking, she couldn't bear to sit still and told Tyler to stop the carriage so that she could get out and guide the horse. Her boots broke through the crust of ice on puddles as she walked but the exercise calmed her.

Walpole was merely the apotheosis of a society that had lost its way under an uncaring monarchy. The entire system needed reform and a kindly king, a James Stuart, was the man to do it. *Yes, yes, I was right. The Pretender's the man. Tyler's isn't the only voice of England.*

The sun sent out no warmth; if anything the frost was deepening. The track would be iced all the way home. 'At this rate,' she said, 'we won't get back in time to see the York coach off.' She liked to be in her forecourt to say goodbye so that she could deal with the complaints and receive the praise.

'Cole'll do it,' Tyler said.

'No. He was going to Stevenage this morning to see about another billiard table.' The Belle was becoming *sportif*: as well as billiards, it now offered a cockpit, a small golf course, a cricket pitch and a skittles alley.

They were so delayed by ice that, emerging into the Great North Road, they met Cole coming back from Stevenage. The York coach had long gone on its way to London.

All the Belle's staff was milling in the yard. Wrong, all wrong. She began to shake. For an instant, she thought: *They're going to hang Dolly.*

She sat still in the carriage while faces below her mouthed desperate things. There'd been a man, a man. On the York coach. Passed by the kitchen this morning, saw Quick. 'He had a pistol. He said Quick was a runaway, *his* runaway. He took him. In the coach.'

'I'll get him back,' Cecily said. 'The York stops at Potters Bar. I'll get him there.'

Her lips were stiff. There was something else. It was Marjorie who broke it to her. 'My dearie,' she said, rubbing Cecily's hand against her cheek. 'The man. He said Eleanor must be Quick's littl'un and so his property. My poor lamb, he took her an' all.'

CHAPTER THIRTEEN

IN HIS MIDDLE TEMPLE chambers, Cameron took off his wife's boots, levered open her mouth and spooned brandy into it, asking questions, listening to Tyler's replies.

'Could ye not find news of him at Potters Bar?'

The coach had stopped at the Bar for the night. Was probably still there, the coachman having pronounced the road too dangerous to proceed. 'But the bastard hired two horses and came on. He'd got Nellie in front of him under his cloak.' Tyler paused. 'Seems he snatched her without a coat.'

Cameron nodded. 'And Quick?'

'In manacles. On a leading rein.'

Cecily began to stand up. Cameron put his hand on her head and forced her down. 'Stay.' She stayed. He turned back to Tyler. 'Did ye find out his name?'

'The coach manifest's got him as Christopher Da Silva.'

'Unusual enough, thanks be to God. Mrs Tothill?'

'Yes, Master Archie?' The old woman had been wringing her hands by the door.

'Be good enough to step round to Mr Blurt and fetch him back here, if he'd oblige me. Quick as ye can.'

Tyler said: 'He'd talked to one of the passengers. Said he was from the West Indies over here on business for his masters, a couple of sugar-growers.'

'The passengers didn't try to prevent the abduction?'

'He was forceful, like. An' he had a pistol. Said Quick was his slave as had jumped off a coach last time he was over. Now he'd found him again he'd take him back to the Windies. Said he had the authority.'

'And Eleanor?'

'Said she was his property too. Said she must be Quick's.'

'A not unreasonable assumption.'

Why is he talking? Why are we sitting? She was in a glass bowl; figures moved outside it in blurred distortions, their words coming to her as if spoken through water. 'Injunction.' 'Habeas Corpus.' She was beating on the glass and they didn't hear her.

Her husband's face came close, grey and wavering. 'We'll find her, Cecily. We'll find her.'

His went away and another, seedy, squinting, took its place by the bowl, speaking slow: 'I'm Mr Blurt, Lady Cecily. I know 'em all. I know their places. And I know every ship.'

It turned away, still speaking: 'A course it might be the ship's at Bristol. Thought o' that, Master Archie, have you?'

Ships? *Ships. He was taking Eleanor across seas.*

'Now then, Lady Cecily,' said the squint, 'no need for that. You hold on to me. I'm Mr Blurt and I know.'

Her hands reached through the glass to clutch a coat. It smelt of mice. Her lips managed to move. 'It's important. She'll be very cold.'

'I know, I know. You stay here now and rest.'

Stay here now. Christ, they were going. Leaving her in the bowl. Her feet found her unlaced boots and she stumbled to the door.

Tyler's voice. 'Better take her with us. She won't rest else.'

Out into a white garden, metallic with frost. Into streets. Slush. Faces wrapped around and blue-nosed with a cold she couldn't feel. Blockades of wagons. Bonfires in the roads and people capering round them, toasted yellow on one side from the reflection. Shouting.

Good God, they're still rioting. Can't you see it's not important? My child has been snatched from me.

The freedom to know what's important. Mary Astell's voice had chanted all the way down the Great North Road as time expanded and contracted like rubber. A horse had slipped and broken its leg. Tyler'd shot it and they'd continued a-pillion, the moon beaming on them like an idiot. The only importance: reach Cameron, find Eleanor.

The analgesia of panic and cold was wearing off, allowing

256

her to become sensible of London's vastness. What if he'd taken her to Bristol?

'Blurt's sending a man to Bristol,' Cameron told her. 'We're using Habeas Corpus.'

'Use crowbars,' she said. 'Kill him.' He ran on all fours with Eleanor in his mouth.

A magistrate's house, tall, narrow, with stone steps. Argument, explanation, time stretching out again until it twanged her bones. Habeas Corpus. Have her body. She'd be so cold. So frightened.

Blurt: 'I'll take the docks. You take the nigger quarters, Master Archie. They know you. And one of 'em'll know Da Silva from somewhere – news runs round them neighbourhoods like the rats.'

At the end of the first day's hunt Cecily collapsed and Tyler had to take her back to the chambers while Cameron stayed on in Mile End, a lantern and his life in his hand as he climbed staircases that wobbled to doors showering woodwormed dust as he hammered on them, shedding light on faces that turned away from it, asking questions of people to whom secrecy was survival.

As Tyler helped her upstairs and Mrs Tothill stoked the bedroom fire, Cecily said: 'We're not going to find her, Tyler.'

'Get on with you, Duchess. Course we are.' He didn't believe they would either.

It wasn't sleep, more a parade of images: Eleanor growing up and thinning down, her hair like a black teazle atop the skinny body. Eleanor and Billy Packer in trouble with Colonel Grandison for tying the tails of two of his heifers together and swinging on the resultant rope, Eleanor climbing too high up the horse-chestnut for conkers, Eleanor whacking young Martin Bygraves with the tric-trac board because he'd called her a dingy slut when he lost. Eleanor refusing to apologize for a pert answer to those who commented on her colour.

God help her keep that courage.

Herself, afraid for her, paddling the child's backside with a slipper too often, too often, for transgressions arising from a refusal to be cowed, and Eleanor, tear-stained, subsequently coming into her bed for a cuddle, never holding a grudge but never admitting defeat either.

'Mamma?'

'Yes?'

'I expect you're sorry now.'

I always was. I am.

Somebody was knocking on the front door downstairs. Cecily rolled out of bed, her body obeying the summons almost before her brain had caught up with its urgency. *News.*

As she reached for her night-robe, she heard Tyler stumping along the hall to open the door. He met her on the staircase. 'It's them bloody Jacks.'

Over his shoulder she saw the bulk of Sir Spender Dick filling the doorway, Maskelyne behind him.

'Have they heard anything?' She squeezed past Tyler and rushed down to the hall and opened the parlour door, ushering them in. 'Have you news for me?'

'Indeed we have, madam. Shut the door, Masky.'

'What? What?' She watched Maskelyne shut the door in Tyler's face and stand with his back to it. 'Do you know where she is?'

'Where's who?'

Everything in her world had so narrowed to one point that she could not believe visitors who arrived at this hour of night had come about anything else. 'My . . . the child. Eleanor. She's been abducted.'

Sir Spender said: 'Little Nellie? The piccaninny at the Belle?' He was genuinely taken aback.

'I thought . . .' Weakness brought on by disappointment forced Cecily to sit down. Drearily, she asked what they wanted.

Sir Spender pulled a chair near hers so that he could take her hand. 'I commiserate with your troubles, dear lady . . .'

'We got our own,' said Maskelyne from the door.

'. . . but as our friend here rightly says, we ourselves are in difficulties. Walpole's dogs have picked up our scent and we are hunted men . . .'

'You can't stay here.' Cecily panicked. She could bear no complication, no diversion, that would delay the search for Eleanor.

Two hunted Jacobites under her roof could mean her arrest and exposure, not important in themselves at that moment except as another barrier between her and the lost child.

'We have no such intention,' Spender said reluctantly – it had occurred to him. 'Nor must you fear, madam. Things are ever darkest before the dawn and our Dawn is almost upon us, *advenit ille dies*, our day is about to break – your lamp shall but send forth its beam and our sun arises.'

'What?' snapped Cecily. Why was he burbling if it had nothing to do with Eleanor?

'Did you send to Hempens like you were told?' Maskelyne was as abrupt as she. 'Did you tell them to be ready to light the bloody lamp?'

Lamp? Had she? With difficulty she forced her mind back to Princess Caroline's garden party. 'Yes. I think so. Yes, I did.'

'Splendid.' Sir Spender patted her hand. 'Then all is ready with our Grand Design. We but await our King. In a month or so, perhaps less, you shall have the honour of guiding him through the darkness to his kingdom on the Stuart tide. Hark and you shall hear it flowing . . .' He got up and went to the window, raising its sash so that the sound of rioting in the Strand came into the room like the remote roar of the sea.

Sir Spender cupped his ear. 'What music.' He turned back. 'Dear lady, like all hunted creatures, Masky and I have been forced to flee our coverts. We find ourselves somewhat financially embarrassed . . .'

She gave them all the cash she had and took them to the door. They peered up and down the street before they stepped out into it. As she shut the door after them, Tyler stepped into the hall, his face set as she'd never seen it before. 'I knew you was playing with fire but I never thought even you'd go and set light to yesself.'

'You were listening at the keyhole.'

'Bloody right I was. I never liked them two. Your brain gone unfurnished or something? What's all this about lamps and tides? Bringin' in the King? We got a king. He ain't much but it ain't worth starting a war to unseat the bugger. I'm ashamed of you, Duchess.'

She stared at him. She thought, I'm ashamed of me and I don't know why. There'd been good reason for aiding the Jacobites, very good reason; just at the moment she couldn't find her way through the jumble in her mind to discover what it was. To anyone else she would have shown defiance, to Tyler she admitted helplessness: 'It's got away from me, Tyler.'

'It bloody has.' He hadn't finished berating her. She'd never seen him so angry. 'You're starting a war, that's what you're doing. A war. You been in a war, Duchess? I have. And I ain't prepared to fight another in me own backyard. I warn you, I'll stop it.'

'Then stop it,' she screamed at him. 'Stop it, stop it. Stop everything. I don't mind what happens. I just want Eleanor back.'

He spat. Then he sighed. 'All right, all right.' He put an arm round her shoulders and guided her back into the parlour and sat her down. 'Let's be hearing it all, then. What you been and gone and done?'

She told him.

He seemed relieved. 'One thing, we got time. The Pretender ain't going to be ready to sail for a month or more, so the fatty said, and if I'm a judge he never will. Most Jacks couldn't find their arse with both hands, let alone plan an invasion. As for them two, if they're on the run already, it's next stop Tyburn for them, sure as the Devil's in Ireland. They'll be in Newgate before they get round to lighting anything more than a bloody pipe. We got time. First thing we do is find young Nellie.'

The next morning Mrs Tothill forced breakfast down her. Tyler said: 'You going to be help or jelly?'

'Help.'

He nodded. 'We need it. Never knew the country'd got this many darkies. Where'd they all come from?'

From Sierra Leone, from the Niger Delta, from Barbados, Trinidad, Jamaica, with tribal markings and without, tall, short, speaking jargon English, good English, no English at all, albino black, milky black, coffee black, blue-black, coal-black, black-black, the fashion accessories of masters who'd abandoned them, or died, or whom they had abandoned; a process going on so long that Good Queen Bess's edict in 1596, to protect English jobs, that all blackamoors in the country should be shipped out of it, was ignored; they were too entrenched. Anyway, Elizabeth herself had imported a few into her court and set a tradition followed by every monarch after, so that there were black families who could lay over a century's longer claim to English citizenship than their German king.

Into this nucleus came the runaways and cast-offs of the prospering slave trade, finding precarious asylum in communities that were homogeneous only in colour and poverty: Mile End, Limehouse, Wapping, copses of deeper darkness in the forest of London's poor.

Fifteen thousand people, perhaps more. It was like looking for two particular fir cones in a pinewood.

Cecily hated them. She didn't want Eleanor a bridge between herself and these cellars and attics that stank of excrement from the vault under the staircase, where families of eight slept in shifts on the only bed, where there was no room to wield a whitewash brush or dustpan among the articles of trade that took up the rest of the space. She didn't want Eleanor the connection between herself and people who slumped like sacks at the sight of her white face and were too stupid to answer her questions.

'They're frightened,' Cameron said. 'What happened to Quick could happen to them.'

Did it matter? Quick was worthy; these were human dross.

As word spread that it was Master Archie who was inquiring for a nine-year-old girl and an old man, the same Master Archie who'd saved Harry Stockings from the slavers and given Chocolate Smith money to get her man out of the Fleet, who'd won the case for Sunday Pratt when he'd been left a portion by his master that the son said he wasn't entitled to, then intelligence came back. No, they didn't know a Da Silva but they was mighty sorry Master Archie was troubled and they'd do what they could.

With the thaw in attitude came distress. Hands clutched Cecily's sleeve. 'Missy, missy, you find your li'l girl back you ask for mine. Slavers dragged her t'rough dat window, dat one, and I ain't seen her since.'

Meeting Cameron at the end of the lane – they'd taken a side each – Cecily said: 'That woman says she was manumitted but they took her daughter just the same. This is England. Can they do that?'

Cameron shrugged. 'They do it. They'll have got a good price for her and others in the West Indies.' He saw her face. 'No, no. Blurt says there's no ship come in from the West Indies nor gone out this week past. She's still here. We'll find her. We'll find them both.'

Two men were waiting at the chambers when the hunters returned that night. Both had come to offer their service. One of them was an evil-looking little black man with a Cockney accent to whom Cameron said: 'How was Newgate, Solly? I'm pleased to see ye out.'

The other was Tinker Packer.

The chambers were becoming overcrowded; Cecily, with Tyler, was to move back to Arundel Street to sleep while Cameron kept the hunt's headquarters in the Middle Temple. Before she left, Cameron pleaded with her: 'Will ye no speak to Tinker? He's been keeping to the forest and Cole told him we needed his aid. He'll no admit it but he's gey sorry about Dolly.'

'You don't understand.' Cameron didn't speak Packer-ese. Sullen, slouching, Tinker hadn't said a word to her, nor she to him; it hadn't been necessary. They both knew that forgiveness for the desertion of Dolly that had led to her hanging had been asked for and granted in the fact that Tinker had come and Cecily hadn't sent him away.

The third day of the hunt began at dawn, sidestepping the surge of blacks heading into the City. Negro bandsmen in fierce cocked hats on their way to work were already playing their trumpets and clash-pans. Ruffled, satined, epauletted footmen, who'd had the night off, their powdered wigs and silver, pad-locked collars whitened by the frost, strutted to it; mulatto prostitutes swayed in thin dresses and high heels, ready for morning trade in the churchyards; cheap clerks wound their pocket watches to the music's time; acrobats on their way to Smithfield

Fair teetered to it, juggling, crossing-sweepers, night-soil cleaners, men pushing barrows of stockings, nightcaps and garden netting that had been knitted the night before swayed them from side to side through the dodging cut-purses, sneak-thieves and tricksters who went with them to begin the business of the day.

Then Cecily knew that Eleanor had inherited more than black-ness from a people who, despite an infliction more usually put upon animals, refused to surrender humanity.

She bridled, nearly smiling, at Cameron's look. 'She hasn't got their musical sense, anyway.' Eleanor had been begged to leave the church choir.

Today it was Limehouse, where the broken roofs of the houses gave little more protection from the cold than the spars of the docked ships that showed above them. Scarred, tarry men just out of bed came yawning to the door at Cecily's knock or puffed their answers to her questions in pipesmoke as they sat on the Basin's bollards, waiting for ships. Somehow she'd never associated Negroes with the navy; now she saw how a high proportion of its sailors was black.

'But where are the women?' There'd been few enough in Mile End, she realized; here there were virtually none.

Tyler was keeping her company in this section, with a pistol inside his coat. He said: 'Reckon the market's always demanded more black boys than girls. Imbalance of the sexes, as the saying is.'

The same indelicate question occurred to them both. It was answered by a gaunt white woman who came to the door of a shack with three mulatto toddlers clinging to her skirts. Further down, behind another door, white girls peered over the shoulder of a massive black woman: 'Da Silva? He a whitey?'

'Yes.'

'He don' patronize Ebony Bet's, then.' She winked. 'But I always got work for a fine set-up gal like yo'self.'

Cecily told Cameron: 'White women. How *can* they?'

He said: 'Aren't we planning for Eleanor to marry a white man?'

'Of course.'

263

He was irritable with fatigue. 'Then why so terrible the other way round?'

He's consorted with these people too long. He's lost touch with decency. And to what end? For all his liberality, we're not finding Eleanor.

The encounter at Ebony Bet's induced dreams that night in which Eleanor, taken for her body not her slave price, screamed for her in the padded room of a brothel.

Cecily woke sobbing. 'I can't find you, darling. I'm trying.'

She thought that the faint glow through her bedroom window was the dawn and welcomed it for the day's activity that would subsume some of her dread. But it came from bonfires still burning in the Strand. She spent the rest of the night half awake to shouts of 'No Slavery, No Wooden Shoes' mingling with the cries of her child.

Cameron was at the door with early news. 'Solly says there's a Mr Da Silva has lodging in Holborn.'

It wasn't far. They all went, Tyler, Tinker, Solly, sometimes breaking into a run, dodging through riot detritus. The house was on a busy corner but pumiced steps led to a door with a gleaming fanlight – white and respectable, like the landlady, though she was built on a scale reminiscent of Ebony Bet's. But Ebony Bet never pursed her lips this tight.

Yes, Mr Christopher Da Silva was a regular tenant: always stayed here when he was in England. She was sure she gave satisfaction. No, he'd gone away. No, she didn't know where. 'I don't inquire into other people's business.' Like some, said the closing door.

Cecily held it open. 'Did he bring a little girl and an old man here? They were black.'

'Certainly not. This is a decent house.' Slam.

The hunters went into a huddle at the bottom of the steps while the decent curtains twitched above them.

'We don't know if he's coming back, what he looks like, anything.'

'We will.' The assurance was Solly's, nodding his cunning head at the crossing sweeper at that moment brushing a path through horse-droppings so that a gentleman could traverse the road. The sweeper was black. 'That old bat got Mingo on her doorstep, she got a maid I can see in the basement windy this minute and she got tradesmen. Know 'im? We'll know the colour of his bloody stockings. Leave it to Solly.'

So they did.

'What does Solly *do*?'

'He's a pickpocket.'

Limehouse again, then on to Wapping, as if they were rats burrowing deeper into the riverside's grey silt. The feeling of being underwater encroached on Cecily with growing fatigue and desperation. Sometimes she couldn't hear what people said; things became vivid, others swam out of focus; she couldn't remember how she came to places that had no connection other than the smell of tar and sewage and river. Inn-signs: 'Ship and Whale', 'Hope and Anchor', 'Queen's Landing', 'Prospect of Whitby'. Iced corpses in chains at Execution Dock. A chandler's-cum-ironmonger's stacked with nets, blocks, oars, tins of biscuits – and boxes of iron half-circles set with a flat, inward-pointing plate. Tinker, picking one up: 'What's this bugger for?'

It was a muzzle, the chandler said. Big export of 'em to the sugar plantations. 'Called "sulkies" they are. Use 'em on sulky niggers, see, to stop 'em gnawing the sugar cane or eating dirt.'

A christening at a church where baby, parents, godparents were black. Somebody, Cameron, saying: 'Poor things, they think being Christian will guarantee them the status of freedom.'

Another voice: 'Don't it?'

'No.'

A muscled barber on a quayside pulling out a young Negress's teeth to make dentures for the toothless of St James's.

A black face sneering: 'Why for you want this piccaninny back, missy? Plenty more slaves in the sea.'

The final admission: 'I love her.'

If the hunters accreted help, they gained a hinderer, a tall white man with the tippets of a parson on his black surcoat, trumpeting Enthusiasm: 'Why do you search among the people of Ham, you English? They are as mischievous as monkeys, a stain and contamination on the beauty of our Christian land. Seek for your servants among the white race, good people, for these of the Morisco tint will but grow refractory and expect wages according to their own opinion of their slender merits.'

He attracted a black and grumbling crowd to which he seemed oblivious. A deep voice came out of it, articulating like an actor. 'Remember Aesop's fable, preacher. There are many statues of men slaying lions, but if lions were sculptors there would be a difference in the statues.'

The Enthusiast was delighted: 'Ha, a learned Negro. Admired for being like a parrot who speaks a few words plainly.'

A dispute. The crowd was hemming them in. *We don't have time for this.* Before Cameron could stop her, Cecily had walked up to the preacher and kicked him on the shin. 'Piss off,' she said.

That night Solly knocked on her door, a new light in his narrow eyes. She'd won respect. 'Thought I'd tell you first, miss. Da Silva's tall, dark and skin yellow as a guinea, wiv a smacking great turquoise on his finger. An', miss, *his luggage 's still in his room.*'

She took Solly's horrible head between her hands and kissed it. Then she wished she hadn't; not because it was filthy – though it was – but because assurance that Da Silva hadn't left the country didn't mean that Quick and Eleanor had not.

She had three hours' rest before Cameron ran into the room and told her to get dressed. 'Gravesend,' he said.

It was dark in the coach, and crowded with all the searchers except Tinker, who was on the driver's seat. She could smell Solly and hear a chastened Mr Blurt: 'I should have thought of Gravesend, Mr Archie, indeed I should. We've been looking in the wrong place.'

'Ye've done well, Mr Blurt.' She felt her husband's hand take hers. '*The Swan*. Out of Barbados carrying sugar. Came into Gravesend thirty-six hours ago.'

'Thirty-six. She could have gone again.'

'Now, now, Lady Cecily.' Blurt's voice. 'None of that. You trust me. She's got to unload, recommission and let her sailors get drunk.' She saw the little man's shoulders outlined against the coach window as he leaned out to peer at his timepiece by the light of a street flambeau. 'The tide's against her, too, won't turn for another six hours. Still, she'll not be idle. Time's money in the Triangle.'

And Gravesend was twenty-four miles downriver, at least five hours away in this weather. And they'd have to change horses.

'Triangle?' asked Tyler.

'Goods from England to the Guinea Coast. Slaves from the Guinea Coast to Barbados. Sugar from Barbados to England. Triangle. Always a cargo. They'll not put your man or the young lady in the slave hold, Master Archie. They'll be wanting to keep 'em healthy. They'll fetch more in Barbados than the niggers fresh from the barracoons who can't speak the King's English . . .' She was defenceless against the flow of information.

Cameron's voice rose above it: 'They'll be in Gravesend, Cecily, be sure of it. He'd lodged them there, that's why he left Holborn – to put them aboard. We'll find them there. Be sure of it. Be sure.'

The repetition told her he was as frightened as she was, and possibly tireder.

Once across the river, Tinker drove like Jehu, rattling them through the sleeping streets, mercifully stamped free of ice by the rioters who had retired only an hour or two before. The same moon that had seen her into London that terrible night – how long ago? A week? A year? – saw Cecily and her allies out of it.

At Dartford they had trouble rousing the landlord of the Golden Fleece and getting fresh horses. By then they were driving against the dawn and wagons carrying coal and logs for London's fires. At Northfleet they were stopped by pickets who suspected their coach of coming from St James's – Cecily's arms were gilded on the door – and its passengers, therefore, of being for the excise. It took Tyler's pistol to convince them that they weren't.

It started to snow.

Out in the river, yachts and skiffs slowly swung their prows eastward and it was possible to see a swirl of water around the buoys. The tide was beginning to turn.

It was no longer 'when' we board Swan, it was 'if' we board

her, then it was 'if' we miss her we can catch up with her in the estuary, and Cecily knew her child was sailing further and further away from her.

Suddenly, Cameron shouted: 'By Christ, I'll have my wean off that ship if I have to pursue her a thousand mile.'

Cecily buried her head in his shoulder. *We've lost her.*

All roads in Gravesend led to the river; Tinker took them down the hill at a gallop to a wharf. Pedestrians jumped out of the coach's path and Tyler had his head out of the coach window, screaming at them: '*The Swan*. Which one's the fucking *Swan*?'

They trampled on each other to get out. *Oh, my God.* The river was full of ships, big, little, squat, graceful; you could nearly reach the opposite bank jumping from one deck to another.

An old man was fishing with rod and line from a jetty. Blurt had him by his coat, shaking him. He came running back, still towing his informant. 'That one. That one. The schooner. See her?'

Cecily couldn't. He was pointing through the ships at the quay to the middle of the river where there were three, each with two masts. Which one was a schooner?

'Thanks be to God, she's not set sail yet.'

'In't goin' to,' said Blurt's prisoner, amiably. 'Not till her's past Tilbury. She's goin' down under sweeps. Look.'

They were seeing something through the snow and confusion of hulls and rigging that Cecily couldn't. They milled around. Cameron shouted from a slipway and they ran towards him, Cecily following; he was trying to right an upturned skiff. Tyler helped him while the others cast about for oars. Blurt, Cameron, Tyler and Solly were in the boat, Tinker up to his thighs in water, launching it with a shove that carried it clear of the causeway. Cecily began wading after it. Tinker pulled her back. 'Ain't room for us. We'd just weigh her down.'

The two of them stood, their feet in water, watching the skiff veer while the men in it tried to synchronize their stroke.

'They'll not catch her,' said the old angler behind them. It seemed to give him satisfaction. 'She's got the sweeps on. She'll be off in a minute.'

The skiff was lost to sight among hulls and hawsers. Cecily and Tinker ran along the wharf to a jetty for a clearer view. A small group of men stood at the jetty's end, watching the traffic of the river. No need to ask which was *The Swan*: from behind the hull of another ship at anchor it was just possible to see the prow of a ship with lines leading to rowing boats, crabs harnessed to a giant turtle.

A captious wind flurried snow into the watchers' eyes as if curtains were being closed and drawn back but each time Cecily blinked the flakes from her eyes more of *The Swan*'s prow was visible. She was moving. There was a cheer from the men on the jetty. 'She's off.'

Cecily stood still in the winter landscape, Demeter watching Persephone taken down to Hades.

She made a last clutch at hope. *Perhaps she's not on board. It's another ship.* Then, as the man standing beside her waved his hat to the ship and shouted, 'God speed,' she knew it wasn't.

'She's small for a slaver,' somebody said.

'Oh, we cram 'em in,' said the man, replacing his hat and tapping it so that the turquoise ring on his finger showed like a tiny blue exotic bird. 'We cram 'em in.'

'Do you?' asked Cecily, mildly. 'Do you really?' She held her arms out in front of her as if she were sleepwalking, turned and pushed Da Silva into the river.

Some of the men restrained a struggling Tinker while others took the madwoman to the harbourmaster's office. Da Silva was brought in shivering, wet, to be wrapped in a tarpaulin. There was a lot of shouting and questions that Cecily ignored, didn't hear.

The focus of it changed. They were all outside again in the black and white world of the wharf. Men pointing. Tinker howling triumph. Snow closed in and cleared again. Through it came a skiff, dangerously low in the water with new weight – an elderly black man and a bundle that Cameron had wrapped in his coat, which he held to his chest like the treasure of the Indies.

269

CHAPTER FOURTEEN

By April England was still rioting. Public houses shook with curses against the King. Justices threatened to read the Riot Act and the mobs responded: 'Damn your laws.'

Walpole, certain that lowering the land tax would give him the support of the powerful, and equally certain of his hold on the House of Commons, put his case time and again: the excise was logical; the honourable members must not be led astray by an orchestrated howl.

What the honourable members knew was that an election was in the offing – and fifty-four constituencies had already instructed their MP to oppose the tax. Even courtiers began to desert the Great Man, partly bowing to public opinion, partly from a late attack of social conscience. Tax on necessities was already higher in Britain than in Holland or even France; much of the poor's taxes went towards paying the interest to government fund-holders.

The Jacobites were excited and on the move.

In all this furore, few had attention to spare for a case concerning a thirty-pound piece of property to be heard at the Court of Common Pleas that Easter term . . .

'Reasonable?' asked Cecily, furiously. 'You're calling Da Silva "reasonable"?'

'Not unreasonable,' Cameron said. 'He's admitted his mistake in taking Eleanor and is deeply apologetic . . .'

'*Mistake?*'

'. . . and merely demands Quick back.'

'He's not bloody having him.'

They stood at the chambers' window watching Eleanor take her exercise by walking round and round the courtyard flower-bed. Tyler was with her, pistol in pocket, but they became nervous if she wasn't under their eye. The little girl walked quietly, her hand in Tyler's. *She used to skip.*

She asked: 'I want revenge. Why aren't we suing the bastard for kidnapping or assault or whatever?'

'Because he would counter with your assault on him at the jetty. I am anxious to avoid your appearance in court.'

'That wouldn't matter.'

'I think it would, my dear.'

My dear, not my dearie. *I'm the Jacobite again. We've had time to collect ourselves.*

'Also a writ of Habeas Corpus would mean the King's Bench where Lord Juniper is sitting. I'm no favourite of his. No, let Da Silva sue for restitution of property in Common Pleas. It's what the case will be about, pure and simple: is Quick, is any man, a chattel or is he not?'

He said it without emphasis but it was like standing too close to a firework: she could hear the fuse fizzing. 'Don't go on crusade,' she said. 'Don't make legal history. Just get my cook back.'

She wanted it over: Quick, free, chopping his herbs in the Belle's kitchen, Eleanor helping her stem daffodils for the parlour table. Everything as it was, if it could be. Which it couldn't, of course: Eleanor had been introduced to fear and would never throw it off. *And I shan't ever be easy if she's out of my sight.*

The child's nightmares told her what the child wouldn't: dark, cold days in a cellar, Da Silva's matter-of-factness, shelving in the hold of *The Swan* on which slaves would be packed like library books when she reached Africa. Only Eleanor's devotion to Quick showed that she'd had a protection for which Cecily would be ever grateful.

Worse was Eleanor's confusion as to who she was. Future references to her colour would, necessarily, be translated to slavery in her mind; once assured of being part of a loving household, she would henceforth see herself a misfit in two races.

New truths for Cecily too. On the wharf she had rocked the child and told her how much she loved her, to see that Eleanor had known it all along. And how important Cameron was to the girl: even in Cecily's arms she'd not let go of his hand. 'I knew you and Mamma would get me back.' The thin little face crumbling: 'But I didn't know when.'

Slavers dragged her t'rough dat window, dat one. Watching her

271

daughter, Cecily remembered the woman who wouldn't see hers again. I don't have to fight her war, she thought. It's not the same. She was too common to feel agony like mine.

But the woman had. And the bloody Scottish little Don Quixote by Cecily's side knew she had and was going into battle for her.

She sighed. 'Will we win?'

He went through the procedure so far: Declaration, Plea; the Replication, Rejoinder, Surrejoinder, Rebutter, Surrebutter. 'Da Silva won't issue a writ of *ca. sa.*, that is *capias ad satisfaciendum*, though he might go for *fi. fa.*, *fieras facias*, to seize his goods – in this case Quick . . .' He was deliberately boring her.

She grinned at him. 'First thing we do, let's kill all the lawyers.'

He didn't smile back. 'By the way, my dear. There's a warrant out for the arrest of a certain Sir Spender Dick. Sedition. An acquaintance of yours, I believe.'

Through the law which dictates that the worst must happen, and through a winter that had broken one judge's leg and given another pneumonia, it was Lord Juniper who sat on the bench – actually a great Jacobean chair – to hear the case of Da Silva v. Cameron.

He was a fleshy man who peered out from his wig like a pug that had grown spaniels' ears. As he smiled on Prosecuting Counsel Jennings it was a not unattractive pug. 'Ah, Sir Peter, how nice.' But his greeting, 'We meet again, Mr Cameron,' had the rasp of a sword drawn from its scabbard. Lord Juniper didn't like Scotsmen, particularly this one.

He didn't like blacks either. He glanced at the public gallery, where Cecily's was one white face in a row of black: 'I see the court has gathered soot today.' He had a mistress – the legal profession retained the monastic tradition of university colleges and rarely married – four illegitimate children and a large staff that included one Negro.

Unlearned – the legal profession accepted the semi-literate – but intelligent, he made his position clear from the beginning: 'Gentlemen of the jury, Mr Cameron is the defendant in this case and is choosing, most unusually, to conduct his own defence. He is precluded from giving evidence. He is going to try and waste our time with a lot of fol-de-rol about the Rights of Man but I would urge on you that what we have here is a property matter, pure and simple. Mr Da Silva, the claimant, will tell you that his cook, a certain Sambo Vickery otherwise known as . . .' the judge looked at his papers, '. . . Quick Bell, was unlawfully taken from him by Mr Cameron here. Whether he was or was not – and *only* whether he was or was not – is for you to decide.'

The jury, stacked like chessmen in the lidless box that was their gallery high on the court wall, nodded in unison and awe. *Grocers*, Cecily decided.

'I should tell you,' continued Lord Juniper, 'that when the request for a writ was brought before me, I advised the defendant to purchase the disputed cook from the plaintiff and save everybody's time.' He sighed. 'However, let's to it and see if we can all be home for tea.'

Cameron had put this solution to Quick, for whom Da Silva had insisted he stand surety before he could take him home to Arundel Street. 'I can buy ye back, Quick. It would ensure your freedom for I'd give ye manumission at once.' He stopped there but they could all hear the qualification hanging in the air while Quick considered. Cameron wanted to fight a case that wouldn't just get Quick back but which would add a principle to Law itself: that no man, whatever his colour, could be somebody else's property.

Mentally, Cecily urged Quick to agree to his purchase. *Say yes. Yes. Save yourself. Don't worry about the rest. The case may be lost. Say yes. It's a save-yourself world. Let's go home to the Belle.* Quick had become more than the inn's masterly cook: he was its paterfamilias. His pronouncements could bore her to tears but she asked for his opinion. Standing in his kitchen, among his apprentice cooks, he was nearer the Belle's heart than Cecily herself, a respected, self-respecting old man.

She remembered the figure that had crouched on the cobbles of her stableyard, wrists manacled to its neck, eyes unblinking as Ned hammered off the collar. *Damned if you're going back to that.*

Quick asked: 'Can we win, Master Archie?'

Cameron grimaced. 'I'll be straight with ye, Quick. It's no' certain. I'll try, but it's no' certain.'

'What you think, Miz Cec'ly?'

She was touched. 'You have to decide. I just want you home.'

'See,' he said, 'Ah want to stay with you, Miz Cec'ly. Ah'm too old to be treated bad.'

Good. Let's go.

'But see,' said Quick, 'Massa Da Silva, he took our Eleanor. He shouldn't ought to have done dat. He shouldn't ought to take anybody.'

Damn . . .

Quick's slow eyes went back to Cameron. 'How much he askin' for me, Master Archie?'

'Thirty pounds.' It was his original price: Da Silva had been fair.

The beginning of a tired smile. 'Ah'm worth more'n dat.'

So the case went ahead. *What can you do?* In the face of courage like that, what could anybody do?

Cole came up to London so that he could give evidence of Quick's upright character and hard work. Tyler went back to take his place at the Belle. Tinker and the nurse remained with Eleanor at Arundel Street.

As Cameron prepared the defence he'd become convinced that Da Silva wasn't pursuing his claim merely in order to recoup thirty pounds. 'There's money and purpose behind this case. It couldnae have been brought so quickly else. The plant-ocracy want to . . .'

'The what?'

'West Indies planters. Terrified for themselves. England must allow slavery on her soil or what of the colonies that are built on that very system? No, no, they see the chance of settling the matter for good and aye. They're bringing this case to confirm Yorke-Talbot.'

She didn't ask what Yorke-Talbot was. She was sure she'd find out.

There were two long benches in the high public gallery. Cecily had arrived late, seconds after the judge himself, to catch his eye. She'd dressed gorgeously: it must be seen that not all the great and beautiful were on the plantocracy side.

And planters there were. On the gallery's front bench sat three white men with overlarge hats and diamonded fingers, whose skin had suffered under a foreign sun and their figures, by the look of it, from too much rum.

She'd scandalized the usher in choosing the row behind, where all the spectators were black. She made a business of settling herself in its centre, only to wonder what impression it made to be sitting between a convicted pickpocket, Solly, and a notorious madam, Ebony Bet.

Da Silva was dignified in the witness box. Yes, he was Christopher Fernandez Simon Da Silva, resident of St George's Parish, Barbados, agent for the owners of the Vickery sugar plantation in the same parish.

Yes, he had a bill of sale dated 1683 – he produced it, much worn – which showed that the fourteen-year-old male slave, subsequently known as Samboth or Sambo Vickery (' "Vickery" being the name of the estate which purchased him'), had been bought in the market at Bridgetown. When the estate had passed to its present owners, so had the ownership of its slaves, including Sambo. When he, Mr Da Silva, had come to England on the estate's business some nine years ago, its owners had kindly made him a gift of Sambo, who had accompanied him as a manservant. Yes, he had the deed of gift – here it is. And one of his employers was in court who would testify to it if need be.

Sir Peter Jennings: 'It was a valuable gift, was it not?'

Da Silva: 'Yes, sir, it was. Sambo's a skilled cook.'

Lord Juniper, who'd been dozing, woke up: 'Good cook, is he?'

'Yes, m'lud. But on arriving in England the boy . . .'

'Boy?'

'Beg your pardon, m'lud. In Barbados a nigger's a boy until he's decrepit. Anyway, Sambo became uppity –'

' "Uppity", Mr Da Silva?'

'Lazy, my lord, an' disobedient. Other niggers told him he

was as good a man as the King of England, he didn't have to serve a master no more, but must rise up.'

'Rise up?'

Clever phrase, that, to a Whig judge in a court where the sound of riot made a faint background. And, thought Cecily, to a jury of grocers who'd more than likely had their windows broken.

Da Silva explained how, after two attempts at escape on a journey north, Sambo'd had to be manacled but had still contrived to jump, unseen, from the coach and disappear, only to be found years later 'staying at an inn, like a lord, on the Great North Road'.

Another nice touch: a cartoon Negro, fat and lazy.

'So I took him, m'lud, determining to send him back to Barbados so he shouldn't be no more nuisance. He was my responsibility. Wasn't fair he should go on the Poor Rate or keep an Englishman out of a job.'

Somebody's tutored the bastard. Da Silva had played the three-note chord – rebellion, poor relief, employment – that stood up every hair on a ratepaying head. He was the middle class's saviour; Quick, its nightmare. *We're doomed.*

There was a blast of garlic in Cecily's ear. 'Dat one noble nigger-beater,' said Ebony Bet.

'Shush,' begged Cecily. The judge had glanced up in annoyance, disturbed by a black whisper. He hadn't minded the 'hear, hears' of the planters every time Da Silva scored a hit.

The court heard how Quick had been taken off *The Swan* as she went downriver. Sir Peter Jennings posed the questions so that the replies drew a picture of a boarding by pirates waving cutlasses rather than men carrying a writ of Habeas Corpus.

Cross-examination was made a farce. Cameron attempted to tarnish Da Silva's uprightness by inducing him to say he'd threatened Quick with a gun, had kidnapped Eleanor. But at the first question . . .

Lord Juniper: 'Are you charging Mr Da Silva with assault?'

Cameron: 'Not at this stage, m'lud.'

'Then it is of no concern. I will try only this indictment.'

One of the planters in front of Cecily said: 'Home and dry, I think, gentlemen.'

Quick wasn't expected: dignified, softly spoken, not fat. But he irritated the court by the slowness of his replies: obviously a ruse to concoct lies.

Yes, he was the Sambo Vickery of this case.

Lord Juniper: 'But you adopt an alias, do you not? Hurry up, man. We haven't got all day.'

'Quick's what dey call me at de Belle, master. Dat's affection. Among my people, the Ashanti, my name was Opoku Ware.'

Lord Juniper: 'Poky what?' (Laughter in court.) 'And what cooking did you do at this inn? Hens you'd sacrificed? That sort of thing?' (More laughter.)

Here we go. Cecily smiled inwardly and watched Juniper's face change at the chanted menus. Quick was *en route* to the judge's heart.

Lord Juniper: 'Oregano? Really?'

Quick: 'Judge, it ain't proper *côtelette de veau* lessen you marinate her in garlic, equal parts oil an' vinegar an' oregano – an' it got to be fresh oregano. I don' consider dried. You come to de Belle one day, judge, an' I make her for you.'

Juniper recalled himself, sat back. 'We'll see, my man. We'll see.'

Cameron tried to call Cole to give evidence of Quick's good character and hard work. However . . .

'The cook's character is not in question, Mr Cameron. We shall not hear your witness.'

The court adjourned for half an hour while the judge went to his retiring room to drink or pee or kick the usher; whatever judges did.

In the marble corridor outside, Cole put his arm around Cecily's shoulders. 'Not so good?'

She shook her head and rested it on his coat; it smelt of Hertfordshire and the Belle. 'We're going to lose him, Cole.'

At one end of the corridor the planters and Da Silva were drinking from celebratory hip flasks. At the other, Cameron talked to his clerk. He'd taken off his grubby court wig and was combing his hair with his fingers as he did when he was worried.

He's won every case but this one. And this is the most important to him. She realized: *To everybody.*

Cole, not having to testify, was able to sit next to her in the public gallery. Ebony Bet kept squeezing his knee: Cole was her size of man. He didn't seem to mind.

Judge: 'Very well, Mr Cameron. But keep it short. This is merely a property case, remember.'

'Aye, m'lud. It is.'

Her husband stood up. Against the prosecution's tall and elegant Sir Peter Jennings, he was a diminished figure, the Glasgow accent an intrusion into a well-spoken court, another outlander who'd arrived to take employment from good Englishmen. The grocers in the jury box looked on him with disfavour: they liked their law distinguished.

'Gentlemen of the jury, ye have heard the learned judge in this case address the subject of it as "man".'

Lord Juniper sighed audibly and slumped in his chair.

'So the alleged property, ye see, is not a purse, nor a timepiece, nor a kerchief, but a man. Can a man be stolen against his will? Aye, every day. The records of our own Royal African Company and their competitors will show ye that two hundred and fifty thousand . . .'

'No matter, Mr Cameron, no matter.'

. . . men. Women. Children. A quarter of a million unwilling souls have been shipped from the coasts of Africa since 1640 to the English West Indies and sold as slaves.'

Good God, thought Cecily, *I love him.*

The judge was shouting: 'No matter, no matter, no matter.'

But there it was. It had been knocking on the door all day, a persistent tap beneath the crashings of the riot. Now it was in and rampant: the guilt stirred into tea and cakes, sold in little white hills in the jury's shops, the unacknowledged, unwritten, unfaced, unspoken, uneasy, unclean debit on the balance sheet. One ton of sugar: one slave dead. Every year England ingested fifty thousand tons of it. The taint was on every breath. It clung to the clothes of the West Indies grandees sitting in front of her, ran in beads down the back of their necks.

You've done it now. An industry supporting a quarter of all British shipping, half Lancashire, every port.

Walpole invested in it, George and Caroline wore jewels from it. It paid for the ermine on the blood-red robe of Lord Juniper. *Too big a windmill, my love.*

'But England, gentlemen? What for did this man become restive when he arrived in England? I'll tell ye. For the first time since he was fourteen years old his nostrils scented freedom. He'd been told so. Word had spread even to Africa of a people that had won a great charter, a Magna Carta, from a tyrant king . . .'

He'd told her once. After Dolly's death. 'Law has form, procedure; there's nae point to it if it serves only the powerful. It must aye extend to others or it's tyranny – and the powerful are fine aware of it. Sometimes it must work against them . . .' He was out to make it work against them.

Did I love you then? I suppose I did. You didn't save Dolly but you saved me. Time and again. Always. But I was looking down, not up. She was looking upward now – at one of the human race's necessities: pedantic, stubborn, deciding what was right and refusing to let go; the irritant that stung fellow men into progress. He'd made good law, him and his kind, and bored those who'd use it for their own ends by reminding them that it applied to everybody, even a black cook. A pain in the world's backside – *and my lover.*

She was entranced, not by romance, not with the cheap champagne she'd drunk for Guillaume of Edinburgh; here was a vintage wine for the sustenance of maturity. Even so, her toes wiggled like a little girl waking to a free day and a summer's dawn. *Let's go to bed.* If he lost this case, she'd run to him and tell him he was her pride. Snatch Quick and Eleanor and escape Walpole's England to live happy ever after with her man.

Through the haze of her enchantment came the words: 'Yorke-Talbot.' *Ah, good old Yorke-Talbot.* Now she'd find out.

'You are raising a point of law, Mr Cameron. Must I remind you of Yorke-Talbot?' Lord Juniper turned to the jury. 'Only four years ago, Attorney-General Philip Yorke and Solicitor-General Charles Talbot were asked for their opinion on this question and gave it that a slave coming from the West Indies to Great Britain does *not* become free and *is* his master's property.'

'Thank you, m'lud,' Cameron said. He faced the jury in his turn. 'But, as the learned judge has stated, Yorke-Talbot was an opinion asked for and given. It was not pronounced in court nor in response to a specific case.'

Lord Juniper: 'Valid, nevertheless, Mr Cameron.'

Cameron: 'Yes, m'lud. I'd argue that even more valid is the judgment in the case of Smith v. Gould in 1706, heard before Lord Chief Justice Holt, which said that common law takes no notice of Negroes being different from other men. By common law no man can have property in another . . . There is no such thing as a slave by the laws of England.'

He stood up straight. 'Gentlemen, I'll quote ye another case, from the days of Queen Elizabeth the First. In 1569 a slave was brought from Russia, much as Quick Bell was brought from Barbados. The court freed him. I'll give ye the beautiful words of the ruling: "That England was too pure an air for slaves to breathe in." '

The court was quiet, letting the sentence reverberate as if all subsequent and venal monarchs had never existed, as if the fabled old virgin still ruled and had spoken.

Then Cecily knew that Quick was free.

The judge lobbed a few more case laws at Cameron. Cameron lobbed back Holland and Scotland, despised nations, which refused slavery on their soul.

No need, my dear. You've won.

Lord Juniper attempted to limit the damage in his summing-up. He didn't want to be the man who brought down the entire slave trade: he'd got money in it.

'Gentlemen of the jury, I reiterate that this case is particular and not general. I fear financial disaster to proprietors, that untold business would be lost to them and this kingdom if the question be widened. Those whose passions are fired at the name of slavery have no cause here. Some right of compulsion there must always be by master over servant. All you are asked to decide is whether Mr Da Silva has right of property in this one Negro, Sambo Vincent. If he has, then Mr Cameron took the said Negro unlawfully. If he has not, and you decide that the laws of England give him no such right, then Mr Cameron did not purloin him and must be acquitted.'

Cecily watched the jury file back in. Not grocers now: twelve apostles of good news.

The clerk of the court stood below the jury box and held up a stick with pincers on the end of it. The foreman put a slip of paper into the pincers. The clerk took the stick and raised it to the judge who took the paper, read it without expression and laid it down.

'Gentlemen of the jury, what is your verdict?'

'We find the gentleman Mr Da Silva had no right of property to the man Vincent, my lord. We find Mr Cameron not guilty.'

The howl that went up from the public gallery's rear bench was not for the nervous. Every black soul was on its feet, stamping, clapping. Cole was in the arms of Ebony Bet, Cecily in Solly's. Judge, clerk, sergeants were calling for order.

Through the uproar a man on the bench in front of Cecily directed his voice at her: 'Don't fuck that nigger yet, lady. Nothing's changed.'

She disengaged herself from Solly and restored her hat from over her eyes to see who'd spoken, but the three planters were already shouldering their way out.

In the well of the court, barristers' clerks were chatting, Sir Peter Jennings was gathering up his papers with a win-some-lose-some insouciance. Her husband sat by himself, his head in his hands.

Cecily began struggling through the press to tell him she loved him. Downstairs, the door to the court was impassable with white-wigged lawyers trying to get out past jubilant blacks chanting Quick's name and trying to get in. She'd have to wait.

In any case, there was another matter.

Blurt was on the edge of the crowd. 'Mr Blurt, Mr Blurt.'

'Congratulations, Lady Cecily. Your husband did well.'

'Yes.' She pulled him into a doorway. 'Mr Blurt, would you do something for me?'

She watched him trot along the corridor to where the three planters were talking to Da Silva, saw his exchange with the largest: largest everything, hat, diamonds, jowl, heaviest belly.

Blurt trotted back. 'Known as William, m'lady. But answers to Guillaume.'

'Yes,' she said, quietly. 'Yes, I thought he might.'

'Transportee, wasn't he? I remember helping Master Archie try to find out what happened to him after the 'Fifteen.'

'Yes.'

'Should imagine he's paid Sir Robert to be allowed back in the country. Purged his treachery, like. Surprising how many of 'em do well out in the colonies once they've served their seven years. And they don't stay Jacobite long, not after they've made their pile. Looks like Master Archie and me needn't have bothered.'

'Nor any of us,' she said. 'Thank you, Mr Blurt.'

She was caught up in the crowd as it made for the entrance hall, allowing it to push her along; Cameron would find her. Here, too, among the columns, were noisy, capering people. Did the whole world rejoice at Quick's freedom? Lawyers, barristers, ushers were throwing their wigs in the air, others slapping them on a colleague's shoulder and causing a dust. A few, less pleased, were involved in elbow-raising argument that billowed their gowns. Cecily approached an usher who seemed soberer than most. 'What is happening?'

He stared at her, trying to concentrate. 'Excise, madam. Walpole's withdrawn it.' His gravity was a bedazzled disbelief. He looked up at the hall's vaulted ceiling as if expecting it to crack open. 'Old Brazen-face's backed down. He's lost. The old bugger's backed down.' He recollected himself, frowned, and hurried off to remonstrate with a group of young clerks minuetting to a chant of: 'No Slavery, No Wooden Shoes.'

'He's lost.' She kept repeating it until it made sense to her. Then: 'We've won.'

In the crowd somebody said: 'He'll resign now. Have to.'

We've won. Oh, Dolly, he's gone. She glimpsed her husband's wigless red head swaying high above the crowd on the other side of the hall as he was carried in triumph on black shoulders towards the steps to the street. *We've won. We've won, my dear love. We've won everything.* He didn't see her.

282

Cole shouldered through to her. 'Can't get Master Archie away from them singing niggers. Quick's with 'em.'

'We'll go back to Arundel Street and wait for them there.'

Sconces were lit in the street. It had been a long day's trial. News of Walpole's defeat had streamed from Westminster to the Law Courts on the last rays of the sun. All England would know it soon. Already, windows were being raised, the light from them blocked by leaning figures listening to the message shouted up from below. Wigs, chalk-white in the dusk, bobbed eerily among a morass of hats.

Arundel Street was quiet. Cole turned off to the mews to ready the coach for their return to the Belle the next morning. Tinker was waiting up for her. She told him the news and gave him the rest of the night off before she went upstairs to see Eleanor. The nurse met her on the landing, finger to lips: the child was asleep.

Cecily tiptoed in and stood at the bedside for a long time, watching her daughter. We won, Eleanor. You won.

Don't fuck that nigger yet, lady. Nothing's changed. It came like the hiss of a snake lying in wait somewhere in the room. Cecily found herself reaching out, as if she would snatch the sleeper away from a flickering, reptilian tongue.

Her euphoria ebbed. No, nothing had changed, not hatred, not the dominion of one race over another. Cameron's triumph in court merely added one more case to the see-saw of law which, another time, for another black man, might be weighted the opposite way. He'd told her himself: 'There's only an Act by Parliament can abolish slavery.' With so much of the country's profit arising from the trade, small hope of that.

But we made it more difficult for them, Eleanor. Today the slavers had stumbled because a good man shamed a jury. One day possibly, perhaps when this black child was an old, old woman, enough people would have become ashamed. One day freedom might beat economic interest. Miracles happened. One had happened today.

Gently, Cecily went out and closed the door. In her bedroom she began to pack. Tomorrow the Belle, thank God. Her husband could go fishing again. He looked so tired. She'd go with him,

283

back to the meadow and the Mimram. Cole said one of the kitchen flues needed relining. She'd have to see to it. Totty Stokes was raising opposition to the turnpike among the carters. I'll reline you too, you bugger.

The noise of rejoicing crowds in the Strand reverberated gently against the window, emphasizing the quiet of her house.

Again Guillaume's snake's hiss. *Nothing's changed.*

But it has, she thought. You beyond all recognition. And me too.

She could almost mourn for the Guillaume Fraser that had been – before he'd been brutalized into a brutalizer. *Don't fuck that nigger yet.* There'd been an underlay in the venom, as of fresh grass relinquishing to sewage. Somewhere beneath the Barbadan accent had been the recognized timbre of the voice that had said: *I'll return for you, Lady Cecily, Lady Cecily.*

She could accuse him on behalf of Quick and a quarter of a million slaves but not on her own account. God only knew what suffering and striving had wrought the young Jacobite in an Edinburgh prison cell into the caricature of self-made man she'd encountered in court today.

It was herself she had to condemn for wasting years of her own time and Archibald Cameron's with a fallacy. She writhed in self-contempt at being such a nitwit.

It wasn't Guillaume's fault he'd enamoured her into contriving the escape from Edinburgh Castle that had destroyed Lady Cecily Fitzhenry. Clambering from the ruins had widened the world for her; she could not regret the process which had created Cecily Cameron.

It wasn't Guillaume Fraser's fault that she'd confused the image of love for its substance, not his fault she'd worshipped at the altar of an idol she herself had created.

How long did you tend *my* flame? I wonder. Not long probably; it would have become a pale thing in the hard glare of West Indian sun.

She could even forgive the man for growing physically and mentally gross.

What she couldn't forgive him for – and at this point Cecily's hands travelled in dubious exploration over her face and down

284

to her waist – was that he hadn't recognized her. *You bastard.*

With that, Guillaume Fraser was consigned to history.

There was a knock on the door. *Cameron.* Cecily ran downstairs to open the door ahead of the footman, ready to embrace her husband.

It was Sir Spender Dick.

Almost mute with disappointment and irritation, she began to say he couldn't come in when he pushed past her and lurched into the parlour. He was alone and he'd been running. His dishevelment, his breathing, were reminders of wild things – her pastel parlour had a quarry in it.

Not now, she thought, I can't do with this now. Then she thought: It was always going to end like this.

'See if they've followed me,' he said. He pulled her to the window and arranged the curtains behind her so that light shouldn't shine into the street. She raised the sash, smelling London, bonfire, river. Arundel Street was empty, all activity concentrated at its top and the Strand where celebration at Walpole's defeat was necessitating the same fires and noise as the rioting it had replaced.

Her one idea was to get rid of the man but from pity she poured him a brandy. He downed it and poured himself another without asking.

She began to make excuses. 'I am pressed, Sir Spender. We're bound for the Belle first thing tomorrow.'

He ignored her. 'They found us. We . . . had to separate. The hounds were on us. Masky . . .' He sat down and rubbed his forehead. 'Poor Masky. Fought like a tiger. Killed one of them.'

'Killed? Maskelyne *killed* somebody'

Sir Spender interpreted it as concern for his friend. 'He got away, madam, never fear. They can't down our Masky, oh, no. With luck and a fair wind he'll meet us at Hempens.'

'Hempens? What do you talk about? I'm not going to Hempens.'

'You are, dear lady. Nor must we be long about it.' Shelter and brandy had calmed the man. He stood up and moved to the centre of the room to strike a deliberate pose. 'The Lantern must be lit. *Dies irae, dies illa.* Our day has dawned.'

Cecily sat down heavily on the chair Sir Spender had vacated. He looked down at her kindly. 'Exactly. Tomorrow King James the Third sails for England. The armies of the godly gather for him in the corners of the country, awaiting his coming. You and I, dear lady – and Arthur Maskelyne, we hope – will light him in.'

She tried to gather her wits. Hadn't it always been a game? She remembered another parlour in which a magical, uncrowned king had asked to make Hempens a postern to his country, much as he might have requested the use of a spare bedroom. *Surely we're not all still playing?* It appeared they were. Horribly.

Reasonably, she said: 'It's too late, Sir Spender. He should have come before. The country has settled itself, it'll not rise for him now. And anyway . . .' she got up '. . . my husband will be home any minute . . .'

'And is not friendly to the Cause,' he said, nodding.

'No,' she said. 'He isn't. So . . .'

Sir Spender Dick smiled, ruefully. Only a few times in his and Cecily's acquaintance had he shown himself more than a *poseur*; he showed it now. 'But you see, dear lady, if you do not come with me as part of my disguise I shall be caught. If I am caught, who knows what hideous stratagems Walpole's interrogators will use to find out the list of my helpmates. Naturally, I should be reluctant to give it yet we are but flesh and spirit and when those can stand no more . . .'

'You'd give me away,' Cecily said.

He let the sentence ride the air for a minute before he said: 'And I do not think Sir Robert, old-fashioned as he is, would believe that Mr Cameron's wife had been acting without Mr Cameron's complicity. Do you?'

She swallowed. 'No.'

'And you would not wish that on your husband.'

'No.'

He was in control now. He said skittishly: 'And you *did* promise to aid His Majesty. I saw the letter.'

Sent to Anne. Long ago. After Dolly's death. Before she'd come to know that Cameron mattered more to her than anything else.

'Very well,' she said briskly, and got up. The imperative now was to get out of the house before Cameron came back.

Sir Spender's need of a disguise was met by dressing him in a coat and breeches of Cole's – 'Madam, how delightfully plebeian' – the only clothes that would fit him.

For all that the man had recovered his poise, desperation oozed out of him like sweat. She saw him transfer a pistol to the pocket of Cole's coat.

Cole returned while they were still rummaging through his cupboard. 'What's *he* doing here?'

'Go back to the mews, Cole,' she said, 'and hitch up the chaise. Sir Spender and I –'

'But I just got the coach ready.'

'So now hitch up the chaise,' said Cecily.

'We're going on to the Belle before you,' Sir Spender interjected, with a hand to his pocket.

'You're wha'?'

'Quickly, Cole.' Cecily began to push him towards the door. 'And, Cole, when Tyler comes in, tell him I'm going home.'

'Tyler? Tyler's –'

Before he could say in his confusion that Tyler was at the Belle, Cecily said: 'When he comes in, tell him I've gone home early. He's to fetch my lace from Brodin's. I was to do it myself in the morning.'

Cole wasn't as bovine as he looked. He nodded.

'And, Cole,' she said, 'take care of Eleanor.'

When the man had gone, Sir Spender said: 'Should we encounter any other acquaintances, dear lady, a simple "goodbye" will be sufficient. We don't wish to arouse curiosity.'

There was only time for her to cram some necessities into a travelling bag before the chaise was at the door. Cole held the horse's bridle while Sir Spender, humbly lowering his head, helped Cecily in, got in beside her and took the reins, the perfect manservant.

It was nakedness to be outside. Every bollard, the very window boxes, seemed capable of challenging them: Stop, traitor. What would she say if Cameron emerged from the crowd at the top of the street that minute? Just 'goodbye' it seemed.

Suppose he protested, attracting attention, or making Sir Spender shoot him?

But he won't. He'll see his wife riding off with the wanted Jacobite he's warned her against. He'll feel disgust. He'll just let me go.

Damn you, she thought, I'm doing this for you. And you'll never know it.

Church bells rang out, 'No Slavery, No Wooden Shoes'. As if it were lava escaping a volcano, news of the people's victory ran through the streets and set them alight with bonfires and torches and blazing fat dummies. By the time the carriage reached Highgate Hill, Cecily, looking back, saw London twinkling in the darkness below her like a new constellation.

CHAPTER FIFTEEN

They avoided inns and stayed overnight at the homes of Jacobite sympathizers: a bakery in Potters Bar, a farm outside Cambridge, a run-down manor at Downham Market.

Nobody stopped them. The hunt was on for two male Jacobite agents, one a killer: if huntsmen saw the sedate and monogrammed chaise, their eyes – human nature being what it is – went to the elegant lady in it and not the stolid, dun-coated servant who drove her.

Cecily was aware that, whatever the outcome, she was likely to die at the end of the journey. The zest with which the country was coming into spring, flickering lambs' tails, hawthorn emitting pale scent, newly minted leaves on beeches, accentuated the knowledge that she had finally gained all the happiness life had to offer – and was now about to lose it.

She tried reminding herself she was going north over ground she had last travelled southwards on the night that Da Silva had abducted Quick and Eleanor. *Compare your condition now to the woman who begged God to accept her life for Eleanor's – and be grateful.*

She was: He'd blown so cold on her that night the wind could never be so chill again. It was merely her personal tragedy that He was calling in the debt when bluebells carpeted the woods at the sides of the road and when the slide of rivers under the bridges she crossed reminded her of the Mimram and the man who'd fished it.

But, as she travelled, she saw the larger tragedy about to be enacted against this English spring. Her Jacobite hosts were resurgent, like men and women waking from sleep – not to the life burgeoning around them, but to expectation of war. Once they were sure that the Pretender had landed, Sir Spender said, his English troops were to make their way to Oxford ready for the unfurling of the Stuart standard at the end of the month. Muskets and pikes that had last seen the light in the cause of his father were being brought down from attics to be oiled and refurbished for use against the enemies of James the Third.

It's too late, she wanted to shout. You'll be killed. You'll kill your countrymen. And it's too late.

And *she* was too late in understanding. Watching the Potters Bar baker whet the edge of his pike she saw the wound it would inflict equated with her informing and letter-writing. With the fretful desire for revenge on a government that had done her wrong she, Cecily Fitzhenry, had helped to activate the muscle that would plunge that weapon into somebody's bone. Icons, princes, loyalties, in the end they translated into carnage as terrible as, and more wholesale than, Dolly's death. An escalation of wrongs. Too late to see it now. Perhaps.

The Potters Bar baker waved them off from his gate, shouting: 'To the twenty-ninth of April, Sir Spender.' Cecily wondered why he didn't employ the town crier. And Sir Spender shouted back: 'To the twenty-ninth, Master Tippet,' as though they planned a village outing and weren't laying a trail of gunpowder that would explode the world – if it didn't blow them up first.

'How many men has James got with him?' she asked.

'Only a few.' The French had refused to participate in the plan – Sir Spender always called it the Grand Design and damned them. A certain Mr Robinson, silver merchant, was to slip ashore at Hempens unseen. From there he'd proceed to Oxford where the might of Jacobitism would be waiting. As soon as he'd landed, the West Country and Scotland would propel their forces east and south respectively in a pincer movement. A smaller force in London would simultaneously capture the Tower, the Exchange, the Hanovers, etc., etc.

'Walpole's prepared for a Rising,' Sir Spender said. 'He's increased the watch on those coasts likely to expedite James's passage ashore. But not East Anglia. Sir Robert's own birthplace? He'll not expect our audacious king there.'

It had also been the birthplace of arch king-killer Cromwell. Hempens was, perhaps, the only unsuspected Jacobite house in anti-Jacobite territory providing easy access inland. But *because* it was in anti-Jacobite territory, James Stuart must land only there: he dare not go wading about in hostile fenland. Hempens and its Lantern were vital; Cecily, lord of Hempens, was vital, to the Grand Design.

She wanted Tyler. Whichever way the cat jumped, she wished Tyler could be with her when it did. In a time of crisis, she'd be happier with her old comrade-in-arms beside her. Her attempt to get a message to him via Cole had been clumsy but as good as she could manage. 'Tell him I'm going home.'

When she didn't arrive at the Belle, Tyler might wonder which other home she'd meant and follow her to Hempens. It was a long shot – they didn't come longer. Considered now, it felt uselessly short.

It was hard to pass the Belle.

As they crested Mardley Hill, the stubby tower of Datchworth church welcomed her home from its vantage point across the valley. There, below, glimpsed through the trees, were the inn's roofs and chimneys. She hung over the side of the chaise as it swept round the bend at the bottom of the hill so that she could be a few inches nearer.

The Grantham coach was in. During the seconds it took to pass the open gates she etched the scene on to her memory for ever: the passengers alighting, Marjorie bobbing a curtsy, Ned unharnessing the horses, the Roman trough, the stable where Eleanor had been born . . .

A little further along, they had to draw up to pay at her tollgate. 'Evening, missus. Hear you got our Nellie back safe.'

She managed to nod. 'Evening, Tom.'

Flicking the horse to a trot, Sir Spender said: 'I feel for your tears, dear lady. These toll prices are outrageous. Sheer Whiggery.'

The fen where Edgar lived turned green then silver as breeze flipped the willow leaves down-side up and back again. The weathercock on Edgar's thatch was pointing east.

'Where's your boatman?' demanded Sir Spender. The cottage, usually full, contained only a small girl plucking a duck who said her father hatta goo moolin' and the booys was buds'-nesenin'.

'Mole-catching,' translated Cecily. 'The rest are bird-nesting. They'll not be back until night.'

Sir Spender was alarmed. 'We can't wait till then. He comes tonight.'

If there was no boatman, there was a boat, rocking lightly in the breeze with oars lying in its bottom. 'Can you row?' asked Cecily, who could but didn't intend to.

He said with dignity that he was an Oxford man. Cecily sat in the stern and watched him lose sweat and weight from a skill he hadn't practised since university days.

The carr closed in almost over their heads, occasional catkins brushed the oarsman's cap, the river divided itself to pass islands of reed and kingcups, meandered through meadows grazing small black cattle and again became the tunnel floor of a green arcade.

'Damn wasteland, this,' puffed Sir Spender. 'Empty.'

Not wasteland, not empty. No country teems with life like the fens. In the waterweed below us are eels and fish to heap the tables of England, in the banks water-rats and otters, coot and moorhens, in the reed pochard, shoveler, wigeon, grebe, teal and mallard. A million eyes are watching us, Sir Spender, some of them human. *And I command them all.*

She'd done one good thing and done it early, immediately after the Pretender's visit. 'I may come back and light the Lantern to guide that gentleman to Hempens again,' she'd told Edie. 'But if I do, nobody, *nobody* – do you hear me, Edie? – is to help.

Not Edgar to ferry, not you to be here. Shut up the house and go back to the fens.'

It was an older allegiance than the one to princes, the oldest duty she had – to protect her people. If the Rising failed, they could not be accused of aiding it. If it succeeded, they could not be impressed into its service. If it turned bloody, they would stay alive. Most free of all the English, they should remain free.

One other thing she'd done: she'd taken the key to the Lantern. It was in her travelling bag. She was Cecily the Wake and she would say who came and who didn't. She clutched the bag to her lap like a piece of armour.

Cecily the Very Frightened. All very well to be high-minded when there was no danger but now she wanted to scream out for Edgar and his brothers and to hell with what happened to them. She wanted Tyler. She was afraid of Maskelyne.

The sun was beginning to slant as a clatter of disturbed uprising birds and a scent of salt told them they'd come to Windle Mere. Sir Spender flopped over his oars, cursing, then bent to them again.

There stood her poor house and there the phallic Lantern. What fool had seen it as a symbol of romance? Now she thought of rape.

By her own orders, there was no friend on her island, only Maskelyne roaming it like the rogue animal he was. *He's my end.* He was nemesis. The Devil to whom she'd sold her soul had smudged her life with the man as a warning of hell to come.

Perhaps he drowned getting here, she thought.

By the shadows gathering in the carr behind her, by the heightened instinct indigenous to her fens, she knew he had not – even before she saw his miniature standing on the jetty, swelling with every pull of the oars. *He'll be the one who kills me.*

Sir Spender missed a stroke as he turned to look. His voice skipped across the mere, sending up more ducks. 'Well met by water, good Masky. How was the going?'

The rope Maskelyne threw came with a force that rocked the boat. He was muddy and murderous: the going had been rough. 'Not a bastard to row me. But I found one, I found one. Hid in the fucking rushes then leaped in the fucker's boat.' His voice was high, the accent pure Cockney. 'Even then the cunt wouldn't row me, not till I swore I'd shoot 'im. Orders, he said. *Her* orders.' Maskelyne's foot kicked towards where Cecily scrambled on to the jetty. 'Nobody does nothing round here lessen Madam Prick-scourer tells 'em.'

'An obstinate Anglian,' said Sir Spender, soothingly. 'Yet it's to be hoped you didn't –'

'He dived in the lake like a fucking fish,' Maskelyne said. 'I shot at him but I missed the bastard.' He'd been gabbling. Now he stopped. He preened his neck to adjust his collar, getting himself under control; the fear brought on by isolation relieved. The mask of withdrawn dislike was tighter for having slipped. He drawled: 'Supposed this to be a gentleman's place. No servants, no welcome, everything locked. No food. I thought you told her to be ready.'

Sir Spender said: 'Come, Masky, we can hardly blame Lady Cecily under these precipitate circumstances.'

'I brought bread from Downham Market,' Cecily said, eagerly, 'and there'll be hams in the smokehouse. I'll go –'

'No, no.' Sir Spender caught her sleeve. 'First, the light. It'll be dark soon. Where *is* the famous Lantern?'

'Beyond the house,' Maskelyne told him. 'Locked, like every other bloody door.'

'Where's the key, dear lady?'

'Hanging in the kitchen passage. I'll get it.' Cecily picked up her travelling bag and went ahead of them, across the incline of grass towards the front of the house. Trying to assume the gait of a hostess, the weakness in her legs gave her a sensation of waddling.

There was no need to unlock the house: Maskelyne had taken the axe from the woodpile to chop a hole in the front door.

She went into a hall streaked with auburn light from the setting sun. It smelt of damp and memories.

Now. It must be quick. It must be *now.* How far behind her were they? Still ambling across the lawn, talking. Cecily unbuckled the travelling bag and fished out the Lantern key, a massive thing which alone would slow her down. Drop the bag.

She gathered up the front of her skirt with her free hand and ran. Past the staircase, down the passage, past the silent, cold kitchen. As she fumbled with the bolts of the back door the Lantern key dropped on the stones with a clang audible to Ely. She let it lie, tackled the bolts, opened the door, picked up the key.

The men were in the hall, alerted by the noise and sudden draught. Maskelyne's voice came echoing: 'Where's the bitch gone?'

She was out, dodging the backyard pump. The wind caught her hoops and slowed her down as she made for the wide, wide stretch of unkempt grass between her and the Lantern. *Run.* Oh, God, it would take an age. They were out and chasing, shouting. He'll kill me. Another age to manhandle the key in the door. Don't be rusted, don't be rusted. He'll shoot.

The Lantern reared up, closer, the thick base with its side lump of candle house filled her field of vision. The great door was arched, like a church's. Sanctuary. Don't dare trip. Not now. As she ran, she held the key in front of her like a cavalryman's sabre, aiming it at the ornate steel lock, missed first go and scraped it into the hole. Turn, you bastard. Both hands, every muscle.

They were closing on her. And the door opened outwards. She leaned back in her effort to pull on the great ring that was its handle. Like a reluctant bull, it resisted. Her back was a spasm expecting a bullet. She could hear the men's feet pounding the grass. There was a gap. She twisted round the jamb of the door to get herself inside and bent back, almost horizontal, pulling it to.

Immediately she was in semi-darkness.

As fingers scrabbled for the ring on the other side, Cecily shot the first bolt home, felt for the next and rammed it into place, then the one at the bottom – and collapsed on the floor with her head between her knees. Gone to ground.

Through the keyhole came air and Sir Spender's wheedling. 'Dear lady . . .'

She heard Maskelyne's voice: 'I'll fetch the bloody axe.'

Without raising her head she felt for the keyhole guard and snapped it down. Fetch a bloody regiment, she thought. The door was nine-inch Kentish oak reinforced with iron, too thick to break, built to withstand storm, flood and siege. When Dutch pirates had ravaged the East Anglian coast, seventeenth-century Fitzhenrys with their servants and valuables had taken to the Lantern to sleep, just in case – uncomfortable but secure.

Even so, she shook with every vibration of the door as the axe swung against it. There was a judder, then nothing. Still sitting, Cecily raised the keyhole guard and heard swearing (Maskelyne) and sympathy (Sir Spender). The axe had glissaded off one of the door's closely packed iron bosses and wounded its wielder.

They might try to stave in the roof of the candle house, though even there the stones were so curved and cemented as to leave little purchase for prising up. For precaution she stretched forward and bolted the tiny door, almost as strong as the Lantern's, which led to it.

They were going away. Back to the house for bandaging and restoration. They'd break into the cellar, of course. Maskelyne in drink came nastily to her mind's eyes.

Still, she'd won the castle. Now to see if she could hold it.

As she got up to climb the stairs, she was held back by her skirt hem which had got caught by the door. She tried to cut away the restraining part with scissors from her hussif but her hands were too enfeebled with trembling. Eventually she wrenched herself free, tearing a section of silk to the hoop.

She dragged herself up the steps, resting on each landing. Where did I find the energy to do this? How did I dare? She heaved up the trapdoor to the Octagon and climbed in.

The room was beautiful in itself. From outside, the eight glass walls winked like crystal but from inside their thickness allowed in a light tinged leek-green, wavering and subtly darkening the view of the surrounding landscape into a painting laminated with age. Candles, readied by Edgar, clustered like a grove of slender, creamy in the massive holders bolted to tiles in the floor. A window-seat ran round the Octagon, its top a series of lids which gave access to cupboards holding lighthouse paraphernalia: tinder fungus, flint, buckets of water and sand, cloths, candle-snuffers, wick-trimmers . . .

Everything but food. Cecily was at once ravenous. If the

Pretender didn't come tonight she might have to keep the Lantern until tomorrow night. Or the next.

There was a view like the frontier of the world to feast on: to landward an entire county laid out, to seaward the Wash looking like pink champagne in the windy sunset.

I can eat the candles. There was no other use for them. It was why she'd come: to keep them unlit.

As if the men could see her, she kept her eyes away from the secondary beacon on the other side of the Windle's mouth which, together with the Lantern, made the transit for incoming boats. Uplanders that the two men were, they might think it just a pile of peat and firewood awaiting collection.

It was hot here, like a greenhouse. She moved to one of the eastern windows, unbolted it and pushed it on its horizontal cantilever and had to hold it from slamming back. What had been a breeze was freshening into a lively wind. She shut the window and walked round to open one facing the house. The graveyard where Sophie's baby lay was a neat, still square among bending bushes. Somebody had mown its grass. Hempens' roofs and chimneys blocked a view of the jetty but, in any case, the mere was empty of anything but darkening reed and waterfowl settling for the night.

Nobody will come. Why should they? Her fen people would keep clear as she'd instructed: there was no reason for them to believe her endangered. And well for them: Maskelyne had already killed one man and tried to shoot another.

She sat herself down to wait. They'd try persuasion first.

A shepherd's warning of a sunset, one of the reddest she could remember, streaked the west. A shower slanted in from the east in a block of speckles out of lowering purple that promised worse to come.

The alarm call of a thrush nesting in the kitchen-garden hedge alerted her to the portly shape coming from the house. One of Sir Spender's hands held his hat from blowing off, the other swung awkwardly away from his pocket flap, a flag of truce: he was showing her he had no weapon.

'Dear lady.' He had to shout against the wind. From her angle and in the twilight his upturned face was a small pale moon.

'It's time, dear lady. *Dies irae, dies illa.* Your king approaches. Light him in. To you the honour.'

Dear, dear, she thought, does he think I'm sulking? This is *my* house: *I'll* light the lamp?

'The Cause, Lady Cecily. Think of the Cause.'

To keep silent seemed a breach of etiquette and she had to fight the atavistic desire of a hostess to explain why she disappointed him. Nothing personal, Sir Spender. Do take advantage of my cellar. But the longer she kept them in suspense, the later it would be before they began the assault.

His voice came up to her, wet with dear ladies and madams through the raindrops: he was crying.

Cecily watched his hunched figure walk back to the house and was sorry. Despite his threat to give her away if he was captured, she didn't dislike him. After all, it might be true that no man could stand questioning by Walpole's men without revealing everything.

Harnessed to Maskelyne as he was, it had been impossible for her to plumb the man's depths over the years. Undoubtedly he had some. His loyalty to James Stuart had a different quality from his friend's: the travelling, the acquaintance with Princess Caroline, all the risks he'd taken with apparent nonchalance, when, she suspected, he had more to lose, argued a devotion to the Cause inspired by conviction for it rather than, as with Maskelyne, a hatred against everything else. What that conviction was – religion, belief in the inalienability of kingship, personal loyalty to the House of Stuart, hope of reward – she still didn't know and now, probably, never would.

Raindrops began to hit the windows with a patter like thrown gravel. He was coming back. Towing Maskelyne. Wind, rain and shouting up a hundred-foot drop hampered his usual prolixity but he tried: 'Lady Cecily. If any misunderstanding. Desperate times. Masky here. Rough diamond. But stout heart. Wish to apologize.'

Good God, they *did* think she was sulking.

Maskelyne was nudged forward. A white triangle looked up at her, teeth bared. 'Apologies, Lady Cecily. All friends now, eh?'

What appalling token had she represented to him, she wondered, that he had never been able to hide his hatred of her or any woman? Had his mother not smacked him enough? Or too much? Had she found him doing naughty things in bed? Or vice versa? Perhaps he was one of those to whom any infliction by person or country caused irredeemable spite. A spoiler, she decided. If it were a Stuart on the throne at this minute, he'd be supporting Hanover.

It was a subject with insufficient interest to pursue. She must make herself comfortable for the night – she retired from the window to divest herself of her hoops. The Octagon was cooling down. She investigated the cupboards, found a tarpaulin and arranged it on the window-seat for a bed.

When she returned, the men were going back to the house, Sir Spender chasing his hat.

There was no moon yet, an almost total darkness outside. A glimmer showed suddenly in one of the attics of her house. The men were using their highest vantage point to keep a watch on the sea while they wondered what to do.

Cecily began a circular walk, keeping her own watch on the full round. The windows rattled against the iron tracery that held them.

Maskelyne was running in her direction, pushing a handcart, while Sir Spender loped beside him with a torch in his hand, its flame flattening out behind them. The cart was used for carrying logs from the woodpile. A battering ram? *Christ, they're going to burn me out.*

She threw open the trapdoor, ran to the window-seat and lifted out the bucket of sand, lowered it through the trap, climbed through herself and lugged the bucket down the steps, lopsided with its weight, one hand clutching the staircase rail. At the bottom, she poured a draught-excluder of piled sand along the lower edge of the door and hammered the keyhole guard closely into place. The upper edge and sides she stuffed with silk torn from her poor skirt, stopping any crack that would suck in flame.

Up the stairs to fetch the water bucket. Down again. She stood it by her feet, ready; she needed her hands to clutch the area below her left breast where her heart was breaking loose.

She listened to a bonfire being built against the door. Far above, rain hammered on glass. *It won't light in this. Don't let it light in this.*

Smoke was coming through the sides of the keyhole. She pressed her hand flat against the guard.

After a long period of smokelessness, she realized the wind was wrong for them. It blew towards them, not her. And it would take ferocious concentration of flame to burn down a door as seasoned as the Lantern's. She risked going upstairs and, cautiously, peered over the sill of the open, landward window. One head, Sir Spender's, was just in view and turned towards the door hidden from her by the overhang. His flare hissed in the rain; from his demeanour and fitful billows of smoke she gathered that the fire wasn't catching.

It took a while for Maskelyne to give up. He came into view, snatched the torch from Sir Spender and hurled it upwards. In the arc of light she saw his face – and ducked. There was a tinkle of glass and a neat hole radiating cracks in the window by which she'd been standing.

Shooting? I'll give him shooting. Crouching, Cecily crossed to the candles and tugged one out of its holder, went down on her knees, crawled back with it and rolled it through the gap between the cantilevered window and the sill. *Teach you, you bastard.* A forty-pound object falling one hundred feet carried respect.

The noise of the rain covered any impact but, when she next dared to look, there was no sound and no light below. They'd gone.

Anger ebbed out of her as the last warmth left the Octagon. She pulled up one of her petticoats for a wrap, feeling cold, frightened and unfitted. I'm the wrong age for this. A maiden withstanding this crazy siege might be the stuff of storybooks but a mature innkeeper dropping candles on the heads of her besiegers touched on the ludicrous.

In any case, hers was the negative of romance. Minstrels could only sing of the woman lighting a hero home; one who kept the house dark against him would have them stamping on their lutes.

In any case, Cameron would never hear of it. Nor rescue her. Unromantic Scot ... First thing we do, let's kill all the ... In any case ...

Discomfort woke her up. She jog-trotted round the light to get her blood flowing and see what was to be seen. At the house, figures moved against the light in the attic. The moon was up, wind blowing ragged cloud across it so strongly she wondered it stayed in place. Pity poor Pretenders on a night like this.

At first she barely registered the speck of light that flickered to seaward. She leaned her head against the glass and screwed up her eyes to focus through the residue of raindrops. Again. A ship. Signalling. Not signalling – rolling. A blinking, tiny star from here; out there in the black sea a ship's lantern rearing to the sky and then dropping as if the Pegasus it rode had folded his wings in mid-air.

Dear Christ, he's come. Until that moment she might have been enacting a melodrama composed by amateurs, a reluctant player in a private performance that had just now acquired an audience. Out there, probably vomiting his heart out, was Britain's real king, the most admirable scion of a most ancient house. Wanting, beseeching, to enter his kingdom.

You can't come in. Oh, my dear lord, I can't let you in.

Raindrops rolled down the outside of the window; inside Cecily's tears rolled with them.

She ordered the thinking that had brought them both to this, trying to project it to him in airborne apology.

It isn't only the people who'll be killed, the women with no men, children with no fathers, the transported of either side. It's that you don't matter any more. Even your usurper doesn't matter.

I'm sorry. I'm so sorry.

She'd thought as he did: put another king on the throne and all would be well. But the battle had moved on – to a frowsty, overcrowded chamber in Westminster, to men who, corrupt as they were, still pretended to democracy and, because they pretended, occasionally had to bow to it.

Betterment couldn't come from above any more; perhaps it never had. Its hope was in small, decent voices joining other small and decent voices so that, gradually, very gradually, they raised a shout that even Walpoles had to listen to.

Would James understand? He wouldn't. He would tell her, as he'd once told her: 'I have promised liberty of conscience, Lady Cecily.' As if that were the be-all and end-all and he could deliver it, like Jehovah showering manna.

Liberty of conscience. A battle cry. Britain couldn't afford the battle; it was out of date; it would delay the welfare that could only be gained by ordinary people nibbling away at rottenness.

She was flooded with a loving anguish. I'm married to one of those nibblers, Sire. I watched him wake a jury's conscience. A little case, concerning thirty pounds and a man's freedom, but he made twelve other men think, Yes, this is unfair. Eventually, he and his kind will bring the entire country to say, Yes, this is unfair, that's unfair, we shan't put up with it.

Whether a Stuart was king, or a Hanover, made no difference. So, you see, we might as well keep the one we have and save commotion. The battle's moved elsewhere. It's the people's fight now against a different authority. All you will do is get in their way.

If only she'd told him this face to face. But she hadn't known it then. She saw again her parlour fire glow on the sallow face and hands of the icon seated in its chair, sniffed the scented rosemary logs and the mystery of kingship. And rejected it.

She said aloud: 'I'm sorry, my lord, but you must go home. Kings have become irrelevant.'

The sight of the small light jumping up and down was unbearable and therefore annoying. She scolded it. *You shouldn't have left your arrangements to the likes of Sir Spender and Maskelyne.*

But what else could he have done? Planning an invasion by remote control had always entailed leaving its organization to others – who had invariably shown themselves incompetent. At his first attempt, in 1708, he and his expedition had bobbed up and down off the Scottish coast waiting for an arranged signal, which had not been given. He'd had to go back to France without landing then.

And you must do it again.

But the little light was still pitiful to see and she walked away from the window to notice, almost without interest, that the men in the house had caught sight of it. They were running across the grass. Sir Spender tripped and stayed on his knees, arms stretched out to her in prayer.

Maskelyne came on, his limbs jerking in an ape's dance. The tight cord that had always vibrated in the man had given way: unreasoning malice was loose – this time with reason. She saw the glint of teeth as he mouthed at her. His pistol must have refused to fire because he threw it at the glass, then stooped to send clods of earth after it. She heard the thump as they hit the tower below her.

All at once he stood still, summoning energy for something. It came in a shout loud enough to pierce the wind: 'Light the Lantern.'

The moon was between clouds and clear behind her. She could see her own shadow elongated at the man's feet. She shook her head.

'Then I'll light one.' It was sober, even as a shout.

And she knew. As he turned away, she knew.

I beg you.

Sound came from her mouth. Yes, yes, I'll light the bloody candles. She thought later that she'd yelled the words but if she did he ignored them. Rock against the pain. He won't. He wouldn't.

A new and fiercer light sprang up in the attic.

She turned away so as not to see her house burn.

It isn't mine. Behind her, a thousand ghosts put up soundless protest at the intruder with the match. *Theirs, mine, history's.* Not just a house, a chain that linked her back in time. Shambling, rose-bricked, multi-roofed, twisted-chimneyed, ivy-covered, willow-clustered, the date over its door read 1497. Alain Fitzhenry had built it on the site of the keep raised in the reign of Richard Lionheart by Geoffrey Fitzhenry who had uncovered the sword of Hereward in its footings.

In its interior of mazed corridors and creaking, elm-floored rooms, Cecily, Anne and Sophie had played hide-and-seek like thirteen generations of children before them. With the diamond ring given to her by Queen Anne on her tenth birthday, Cecily had cut their initials into one of the leaded panes of her bedroom window. Anne Boleyn, in 1534, had done the same with her own and Henry VIII's to a pane in the oriel of the hall.

Tiny yellow columns writhed and twisted in the mirror which night made out of the glass in front of her. Flames were licking up the curtains of her house and running along the floorboards.

He's opened every door. The wind will make it a stove.

She stood with her back to it, watching miniaturized orange tongues waggle from every aperture of the house behind her. *Te morturis*, said her ancestors. We who are about to die salute you.

She couldn't face them. They had heaped a bounty of estates upon her, the last of their line. She had lost every acre. Now this, their navel, their bolt-hole, the first and last of their refuges, she had delivered to destruction. Their valediction hissed at her through the useless rain.

No good to shut her eyes; no shutting a memory where fire chased through every passage, curling paint on her parents' portraits, rendering the tester of the bed on which she'd been born a canopy of flame, the staircase a roaring chimney.

There was a *whoomph* that changed the house-shaped image in the mirror into a head whose Gorgon hair streamed back across the mere. Lost somewhere in it was the bobbing light at sea.

And still he can't come. Even this oriflamme wouldn't draw him. Without the plebeian beacon across the river, Maskelyne's bonfire of her lineage was useless. The Pretender's captain, with an onshore wind behind him, dare not attempt to come nearer. Nor, with an English fleet on patrol in daylight, could he stay where he was much longer.

In that sense, she had won. England had won. She found little joy in it; she couldn't even say, as Pyrrhus had said: 'One more such victory and I am undone.' She *was* undone.

Cecily stood at the window until rain extinguished the glowing heap behind her and her eyes were too tired to see whether a ship's light replaced it in the glass or not. Exhausted, she sank down and went to sleep because staying awake was intolerable and she couldn't do it any more.

Seagulls' yelping woke her up as a squadron of them flew inland with the dawn. The seaward windows above her were letting in pink-tinged light. No mirrors now. No house either. *I don't want to see it.*

On the other hand, there was a pressing reason for not staying where she was. Flinching from stiffness and cold, Cecily made a coward's crawl to the trapdoor and went downstairs to avail herself of the empty sand bucket. She washed in the water pail, listening. There seemed no human activity outside, only the call of a cuckoo and the *kleep* of oystercatchers coming through the keyhole on fresh, slightly seaweeded air as if it were any spring morning in the tidal fens.

It hadn't happened. Her brain had been disordered and was now right again. God had restored her and her house. Warily, she lifted the keyhole guard and blinked through it. She shut it again, gently. *Ah, well.*

Upstairs once more, she kept her head determinedly to the north and opened the seaward window, letting in the slight breeze that kept away from the Lantern the stink of ash from the pile of checkered grey spars that lay behind it.

She hadn't slept long. The moon was still up, a wafer in a laundered sky that turned primrose-yellow to the east. The tide had filled all the inlets and was now going out, leaving a pearl's sheen of silt on which dunlin were already feeding. It was going to be a beautiful day.

She breathed it in and felt mended – heavily patched and darned, but mended. She'd lost a house, not her life. Nobody had died or, with luck, was going to. Houses could be rebuilt.

She was at once bereft and weightless, as if an ancestral responsibility had been lifted; sad, yet not without a curious exhilaration. The ghosts had burned with the house and were no more. While Hempens existed, even in the hands of a Peterborough builder, the golden chain of the Fitzhenrys had hung round her neck. With its removal, she stood unadorned; only her individuality as a resource. Not a bad resource, either. Lady Cecily Fitzhenry might have died with her home but the creature that replaced her was Belle Savage, a woman to be reckoned with on her own account, whose business acumen had created a renowned inn and whose heart had adopted a splendid daughter.

Neither inn nor daughter would appear on the Fitzhenry escutcheon. *By God, they'll be etched on Belle Savage's* – symbols of the new, common adventurers' world to which she had succeeded by right of saving it.

For there was no ship. The horizon of the Wash stretched without interruption in a ruled line across her view. The Pretender had gone home.

About time too. Last night's sympathy was over. Caused enough trouble. Coming here. Burning people's houses down.

Spender Dick and Maskelyne were discounted; mere grotesque *dei ex machina* in the drama of which Cecily and James Stuart had been the protagonists.

But where the hell were they? Unless she was sure they'd gone, she dare not leave sanctuary – though she was getting damn sick of it.

Where the hell was *anybody*? Had the burning of the only mansion for miles escaped notice? Did she have to save England *totally* alone? She must face the view to the south and see what was to be seen: the moment couldn't be put off any longer.

An object moved at the edge of her vision. She looked left and downwards to see the two Jacobites rowing Edgar's boat down the Windle towards the estuary.

Going fishing, the bastards. Hadn't spared time to eat before they burned down her kitchen. And not *dei ex machina* now, but *dei ex navicula* – or whatever the Latin was. Not gods either. Clowns.

The terrible Maskelyne had diminished into an indifferent oarsman. As she watched, he caught a crab and fell back with his head in his companion's crotch and his legs in the air.

There was enough water to carry them over the sandbanks but, if they went much further, the tide, stronger than its opposing breeze, would take them out to . . .

By God, by God, by God. *That's where they're going.*

It was Belle Savage who shoved the window open further

and whooped a triumphant goodbye. 'Drown, you buggers.'

Quite probably they would. They could have no hope of over-hauling the Pretender's ship. Risk-takers ever, they had calculated a crossing of the North Sea as a better gamble than staying to be hunted through England. But in a rowing boat?

'Personally,' she admonished them, pleasantly, 'I'd have gone along the coast and begged a passage on something more substantial.'

Yet they were undoubtedly heading out to sea as fast as they could, Sir Spender rowing like a man in a race . . .

She whirled round to see what it was the Jacobites were fleeing from. Beyond the skeletal heap that had been the house of Hempens, small boats were coming across the mere, lots of them, heading towards the island like a flotilla of determined ducks – one, with two figures aboard, ahead of all the rest.

Tyler, she thought. *Edgar*. And was down at the bottom of the tower on the instant, tugging back the bolts of the door. Which wouldn't move. With all her weight on her arms and her head down, it wouldn't shift. Maskelyne hadn't spared the logs he'd piled against it.

God dammit, if she had to go up these bloody steps one more time . . . but if she didn't, they'd start picking over the ruins in a search for her corpse.

Irritable, hungry and all at once nauseous with reaction, she stamped up the stairs, clambered into the Octagon and slammed open a southern window. 'I'm here.'

One lone chimney still hid the jetty but the breeze carried the cry over it. Two men, hatless and running, appeared round the side of the ruins. One was Tyler. The other wasn't Edgar.

A great peace settled over Cecily Cameron. She leaned over the window-seat on folded arms and waited to be rescued.

This, then, was the latter-day hero: of medium height, ginger-headed, neat, even while breathless and having lost his hat, a man of concern, not romance; one who, if she was any judge, felt himself considerably put out, yet one who, anticipating an army of invaders – Tyler would have told him – had brought no army of his own to face them. There'd been only fenmen in the boats behind him. Had he thought to save England and his wife by argument? Yes, he probably had. Well, but he suited her.

Tyler saw her, grinned back, and disappeared from view to tackle the blockage at the door.

Archibald Cameron saw her, took off his wig and wiped his sleeve across his forehead. He jerked his head towards the pile of rubble behind him. 'Rot ye, woman, I thought you to be in yon ashes.'

'No,' she called down, brightly. 'I was up here. Preventing another Rising.'

Running his fingers wearily through his hair, he nodded. 'Tyler said ye'd try. It seems he knows ye better than I do.'

'We share a criminal bent. But you came after me just the same.'

'It's over, then?'

'This time.'

He glanced back to the ruins. 'And that?'

'The price.'

'I'm sorry.' He was suddenly full of his own grievance. He, too, was suffering reaction: 'But could ye no' have left word? There was Eleanor to be carried to the Belle and Cole not knowing where ye were off to with your Jacobite friend that Tyler, when applied to, said was planning invasion . . .'

'Yet you came after me just the same,' she reiterated. One had to be patient.

He looked up. 'You want me to say it? I'll say it. If the hosts of hell were swarming ashore, I'd still have plucked ye from the arms of the Devil himself.'

'So I should hope.'

He sat down on the grass, leaned back and propped himself on his elbows. They rested their eyes on each other for a while in mutual assessment.

He was humming in the Gaelic, bless him, something about a wife before his age slipped away.

But he had to know. She could only be rescued on her own terms: 'I shan't come back to London. I'm an innkeeper. And there's Eleanor. I'm finished with Society.'

'Society'll be relieved to hear it,' he said, and got to his feet.

'I'm not sure but what, following Quick's verdict, Society hasnae finished wi' me. There was a deal of havering in chambers after. But I'm needed in London and I'll not leave it. Bad for business.' He put on his wig and called querulously: 'Can we no' have this argument somewhere more private?'

Her fen people were standing in a discreet but interested semi-circle around the Lantern. Tyler was signalling that the door was free.

'Do you think we can resolve it?' she asked.

He smiled back at her.

So, for the last time she descended the steps of her tower and went through the open door into the sunlight, to try.

AUTHOR'S NOTES

DESPITE HIS DEFEAT over the excise in 1734 – a massive victory for the popular will – Sir Robert Walpole remained in power until 1742, dying in 1745, having held the office of prime minister for twenty-two years.

In order to fit them into the frame of the book I have telescoped somewhat the years from 1716 to 1733, but have kept their events in the order in which they occurred.

To sort out fact from fiction . . .

Mary Astell was a real person and has been described as the first English feminist. While I think that title more properly belongs in the previous century, with Aphra Behn, there's no doubt Mrs Astell was an amazingly free thinker for her time.

The escapes described at the end of Chapter Two, by Old Borlum and the Earls of Wintoun and Nithsdale, as well as the transportees, actually took place.

The architect, John Castell, died in Corbett's sponging house after pleading not to be sent to it. His friend James Oglethorpe told his story to the House of Commons, which agreed to appoint a Commission of Inquiry into debtors' prisons. It learned that Bambridge, Warden of the Fleet, was making a regular annual income of five thousand pounds a year from bribes and torturing prisoners who wouldn't pay them. Hogarth painted a scene showing a prisoner on his knees demonstrating Bambridge's method of fastening a man's hands and neck. Bambridge was acquitted of Castell's murder and all other charges. He lived a free man for another twenty years before slitting his throat. Little change was made in the laws of insolvency until 1808, when an Act of Parliament improved the debtors' lot by allowing anyone who had been in prison for a year for a debt of less than twenty pounds to be freed as having suffered enough.

Lest anyone think I made it up in Chapter Three, the account of Dolly's loss of bladder control in the House of Commons is based on a real incident.

I have set the Belle Sauvage into a section of what is now the B197 between Welwyn and Knebworth, but there was no such inn there. The village of Datchworth had no responsibility for the road and the men and women I've peopled it with never existed as far as I know, though they are based on real eighteenth-century characters.

James Stuart, whom we meet in Chapter Eight, was, of course, the Old Pretender, a much nicer man than his more famous son, Bonnie Prince Charlie. He made more than one attempt to invade England. However, the account of his landing at Hempens comes from my imagination.

Perhaps because she was an amateur and, worse, a woman, Lady Mary Wortley Montagu's battle to introduce inoculation against smallpox into Britain was castigated by many doctors and churchmen and has been treated frivolously by more than one of her biographers. Princess Caroline was wiser and allowed the royal children to be inoculated by her. She deserves the inscription on the monument in Lichfield Cathedral: 'Sacred to the Memory of the Right Honourable Lady Mary Wortley Montagu who happily introduced from Turkey into this country the salutary art of inoculating the Small-pox . . .'

The court case depicted in Chapter Fourteen is, of course, fictional but could have taken place. The conflicting judgments in what were mainly property suits involving black men and women, as the question of their legal position increasingly cropped up, had begun as far back as 1569 and were sometimes in their favour, sometimes not. In essence, the situation could only be resolved by an Act of Parliament, which didn't transpire until 1807, with final emancipation coming in 1833.

READ MORE IN PENGUIN

In every corner of the world, on every subject under the sun, Penguin represents quality and variety – the very best in publishing today.

For complete information about books available from Penguin – including Puffins, Penguin Classics and Arkana – and how to order them, write to us at the appropriate address below. Please note that for copyright reasons the selection of books varies from country to country.

In the United Kingdom: Please write to *Dept. EP, Penguin Books Ltd, Bath Road, Harmondsworth, West Drayton, Middlesex UB7 ODA*

In the United States: Please write to *Consumer Sales, Penguin Putnam Inc., P.O. Box 12289 Dept. B, Newark, New Jersey 07101-5289.* VISA and MasterCard holders call 1-800-788-6262 to order Penguin titles

In Canada: Please write to *Penguin Books Canada Ltd, 10 Alcorn Avenue, Suite 300, Toronto, Ontario M4V 3B2*

In Australia: Please write to *Penguin Books Australia Ltd, P.O. Box 257, Ringwood, Victoria 3134*

In New Zealand: Please write to *Penguin Books (NZ) Ltd, Private Bag 102902, North Shore Mail Centre, Auckland 10*

In India: Please write to *Penguin Books India Pvt Ltd, 11 Community Centre, Panchsheel Park, New Delhi 110017*

In the Netherlands: Please write to *Penguin Books Netherlands bv, Postbus 3507, NL-1001 AH Amsterdam*

In Germany: Please write to *Penguin Books Deutschland GmbH, Metzlerstrasse 26, 60594 Frankfurt am Main*

In Spain: Please write to *Penguin Books S. A., Bravo Murillo 19, 1° B, 28015 Madrid*

In Italy: Please write to *Penguin Italia s.r.l., Via Benedetto Croce 2, 20094 Corsico, Milano*

In France: Please write to *Penguin France, Le Carré Wilson, 62 rue Benjamin Baillaud, 31500 Toulouse*

In Japan: Please write to *Penguin Books Japan Ltd, Kaneko Building, 2-3-25 Koraku, Bunkyo-Ku, Tokyo 112*

In South Africa: Please write to *Penguin Books South Africa (Pty) Ltd, Private Bag X14, Parkview, 2122 Johannesburg*